The FOG MACHINE

Praise for THE FOG MACHINE

"Thank you for remembering my brother. Great book! Great job!"
　　　　　—**BEN CHANEY**, James Earl Chaney Foundation founder

"A literal page turner. Poetic and prophetic, woven from the spectrum of cultural collisions our society offers. *The Fog Machine* should be read, heard, and shared."
　　　　　—**JACKIE ROBERTS**, Seattle's The BookClub

"Captures essential, often overlooked elements of the Freedom Schools: teachers encouraged to improvise in response to their students and African Americans courageously offering hospitality to young whites from the North. Bravo!"
　　　　　—**STAUGHTON LYND**, Freedom School Coordinator,
　　　　　Mississippi Freedom Summer

"Insightful and highly readable. Written with sensitivity and insight about the nature of prejudice. *The Fog Machine* will resonate with teens and older readers alike."
　　　　　—**JOHN DITTMER**, *Local People: The Struggle for Civil Rights in Mississippi*

"Susan Follett beautifully weaves the story of main character C.J. Evans's struggles: protecting herself and those she loves while following rules she increasingly suspects can change. Never patronizing, *The Fog Machine* paints an honest picture of the Civil Rights Movement. Follett understands that those we love shape our worlds."
　　　　　—**SARA L. WICHT**, Senior Manager, Teaching and Learning,
　　　　　Teaching Tolerance

"Immensely enjoyable, with characters you want to know what happens to after the book ends. Offers young adult readers a way to understand the world and history through relationships—the way they learn best."
　　　　　—**VICKIE MALONE**, McComb High social studies teacher,
　　　　　whose Local Culture class informed Mississippi's K-12 public
　　　　　school mandated civil rights education curriculum

"Engaging and impeccably researched. Sure to spark discussion of social change in the 1960s as perceived by people of different racial and socioeconomic groups and locales."
　　　　　—**DEBBIE Z. HARWELL**, *Wednesdays in Mississippi:*
　　　　　Proper Ladies Working for Radical Change

"This beautifully crafted story of young people grappling with the deep wound of systemic racism invites us to remember history and 're-member' relationships. It reaches beyond the silences of our history toward the connection to which faith calls. Recommended for anyone compelled by the ways in which race still divides us."
　　　　　—**MARY E. HESS**, Professor, Educational Leadership,
　　　　　Luther Seminary, St. Paul, MN

"Eloquently captures your heart and mind from first page to last. A powerful book for use in schools. A must read for anyone interested in truth and justice."
　　　　　—**MICKI DICKOFF**, Filmmaker, "Neshoba: The Price of Freedom"

"Wonderfully truthful on the issue of race. A treasure trove for teachers and students."

—**FAYE INGE**, 1964 Freedom School student and career educator

"A thought-provoking story of the fragile relationships between black and white—as well as Christians and Jews—during a troubled time in America. *The Fog Machine* is especially valuable for young people who, if they know this period at all, know it only through history lessons and old newsreel footage."

—**CURTIS WILKIE**, *Dixie: A Personal Odyssey Through Events That Shaped The Modern South*

"Follett's ear has perfect pitch in capturing the ingrained attitudes, nuanced feelings, and voices of hope at the 1964 Meridian Freedom School. Children naturally play together; it's the grownups who teach them to hate and fear. The more we reveal how that happens, the more we can be hopeful about changing it."

—**MARK LEVY**, Coordinator, 1964 Meridian Freedom School

"A beautifully written and deeply moving, well-executed historical novel that examines a difficult time for us all. Factually accurate and socially and psychologically realistic in its representation of the Deep South in the 1960s."

—**JAMES P. MARSHALL**, *Student Activism and Civil Rights in Mississippi: Protest Politics and the Struggle for Racial Justice, 1960-1965*

"Follett's depiction of prejudice and its dissolution via relationships is a marvel—like seeing electrons move! *The Fog Machine* is something different and quite special, with so much to offer YA readers."

—**SHEA PEEPLES**, Teen Librarian, Wescott Library, Eagan, MN

"A portrait of the complexity surrounding race in America, then and now. At once overwhelming—revealing so much more than we often want to consider or accept—and imperative."

—**ANNA STEPHENSON**, Meridian Freedom Project: a college pathway program in the spirit of Freedom Summer 1964

"Beautifully written and impeccably researched, *The Fog Machine* engages as it explores the dynamics of relationship."

—**JACQUELINE BYRD MARTIN**, McComb, MS Civil Rights/ Labor History Curriculum Development Project

"In depicting problems and solutions from our past, Follett shines a light on the present. Civil rights-era segregation in Chicago Public Schools parallels today's shuttered neighborhood schools and teachers forced to teach scripted curriculum. Critical and participatory education was at the heart of the 1964 freedom schools and is equally essential in the ongoing struggle for social justice."

—**BYRON SIGCHO**, educator and activist, Chicago Teachers for Social Justice

"Follett's voice gave me goose bumps of recognition."

—**JANIE FORSYTH MCKINNEY**, former Anniston, AL, resident who became part of local civil rights lore by aiding victims of the 1961 Freedom Riders bus burning

Mississippi's McComb High and Washington's The Overlake School Adopt THE FOG MACHINE In innovative pilot program For civil rights education

As author Barbara Kingsolver said in a 2012 NPR interview for her novel *Flight Behavior*, fiction has the power to create "empathy for the theoretical stranger." Students at Mississippi's McComb High and Washington's The Overlake School put this theory to the test by reading *The Fog Machine*.

Their teachers, Vickie Malone and David Bennett, set out to explore the value of historical fiction in teaching history to young people. More essentially, they sought a shared language to allow the students to talk about civil rights history and race when Overlake visited McComb in April 2014.

Indeed, the two schools are worlds apart.

Bob Moses came to McComb in 1961 to begin the work of the Student Non-violent Coordinating Committee (SNCC) in helping secure voting rights for Mississippi's black citizens. Herbert Lee, a black farmer, was murdered for his role in the campaign, as was witness Lewis Allen. In 1964, SNCC arrived in force as part of Freedom Summer. Violence escalated, earning McComb the name "the bombing capital of the world." Today, the McComb school district is predominantly black, and the median household income (2011) is $28,000.

In contrast, The Overlake School is a private college prep day school with an enviably low student-teacher ratio in the affluent suburb of Redmond, Washington. Overlake's Service Learning Program, part of Project Week, emphasizes experiential learning. The 2014 group of twelve students and two teachers was the second to visit McComb and other sites of significance in the civil rights movement.

Read about the pilot at http://www.susanfollett.com/academic.html.

With its report "Teaching the Movement: The State of Civil Rights Education in the United States 2011," the Southern Poverty Law Center hoped to "spark a national conversation about the importance of teaching America's students about the modern civil rights movement." Mississippi, one of only 12 states to receive a grade of C or higher and the first to mandate civil rights education in public schools K-12, rolled out its curriculum in 2011. McComb High and Vickie Malone's Local Culture class served as a model for the Mississippi curriculum.

As Henry Louis Gates Jr. said in *The Root*, August 12, 2013: "Want a meaningful 'conversation about race'? That conversation, to be effective and to last, to become part of the fabric of the national American narrative, *must* start in elementary school, and continue all the way through graduation from high school."

As Bob Moses said to SNCC workers gathered in McComb in 1964, singing "I'm on My Way to the Freedom Land" shortly after the Freedom House was bombed: "If you can't go, let your children go."

Let the national conversation begin.

Susan Follett

The FOG MACHINE
A novel

Susan Follett grew up in the epicenter of the civil rights movement: Mississippi in the sixties. When the first African American stepped into the Highland Park pool on the same day Neil Armstrong stepped onto the moon, she was attending summer journalism camp at the University of Mississippi. Her graduating class at Meridian/Harris High School was the first under federally mandated desegregation.

Armed with a masters' degree in computer science from Mississippi State University, she left Mississippi. Her career in corporate technology management, coming at the height of the women's movement, took her to the Twin Cities of Minnesota, the Bay Area of California, and Portland, Oregon.

A television documentary Ms. Follett saw as a young adult, about the March from Selma to Montgomery, haunted her, raising questions about the time and place in which she grew up. She returned to Mississippi time and again for the stories, turning an adult eye on her childhood under Jim Crow, wondering what she would have done had she been older when James Chaney, Andrew Goodman, and Mickey Schwerner were murdered in the summer of 1964.

She now lives in Minnesota with her husband and two children.

The Fog Machine is the story of what if. It captures history lest we forget or never even know it. Ms. Follett relates the title to the mission statement of the William Winter Institute for Racial Reconciliation, which describes prejudice as "systemic and institutionalized."

The FOG MACHINE

A NOVEL

Susan Follett

LUCKY SKY
PRESS

LUCKY SKY
P R E S S

This book is a work of fiction. All characters, with the exception of some well-known public and historical figures, are products of the author's imagination. However, historical events and their context have been rendered in a manner as true to life as possible.

Grateful acknowledgment is made for the following:

Gratis use of the partial line of lyric . . . *police'll catch and you're workhouse bound* . . . from "Prettiest Train" (New words and arrangement by Benny Will Richardson. Collected and adapted by Alan Lomax.) Global Jukebox Publishing (BMI). Courtesy of The Association for Cultural Equity.

Permission from the family of James Earl Chaney to incorporate young Ben Chaney as an active character in certain scenes of THE FOG MACHINE, with descriptions, behaviors, and dialogue.

FIRST EDITION

Book Design: AuthorSupport.com

Cover Imagery: Shutterstock/Maryna Kulchytska/Laurie Barr
Young Negrito girl, Mariveles: Philippine Photographs Digital Archive, Special Collections Library, University of Michigan
Author Photo: Dani Follett-Dion

CATALOGING-IN-PUBLICATION DATA

Follett, Susan.
The fog machine : a novel / Susan Follett. -- First
edition.
pages cm
ISBN 978-1-941038-50-5
ISBN 978-1-941038-51-2
ISBN 978-1-941038-52-9

1. African Americans--Civil rights--Fiction.
2. African Americans--Mississippi--Fiction. 3. Mississippi
Freedom Project--Fiction. 4. Civil rights movements--
United States--History--20th century--Fiction.
5. United States--Race relations--Fiction. 6. Historical
fiction. I. Title.

PS3606.O455F64 2013   813'.6
                QBI13-600204

www.LuckySkyPress.com

For Gary, my bashert, whose support has never wavered

For Roberta, who first nurtured me as a writer

Fog machines are a relic from my childhood in the sixties—a memory as unrelenting as the heat and humidity of summer in Mississippi. Around supper time, as the sun began to slide down the horizon like a riff, aging pickup trucks would emerge like mosquitoes. Soon, the aerosol generators bolted to their beds began to burn oil, forty to eighty gallons an hour, and belch insecticide fog. The cloud was thick and white, like the cumulus formations that skidded across the sky during the day under our watchful eyes from our positions flat on our backs on the grass. But the cloud from the fog machine was within our grasp. We had only to chase it to find ourselves inside. And so, children were excused from the table, released into the approaching night. We ran then, down the street behind the machine, as if it carried our very dreams and hopes. Unaware of the danger.

Contents

MISSISSIPPI BEGINNINGS

CHICAGO

FREEDOM SUMMER

In tribute to the James Earl Chaney family

Until the killing of black men, black mothers' sons, becomes as important to the rest of the country as the killing of a white mother's son, we who believe in freedom cannot rest until this happens.

—ELLA BAKER

Historic Timeline

11/26/45	Saxophonist Charlie Parker records "Now's the Time" with Dizzy Gillespie, Miles Davis
4/18/46	Jackie Robinson signs with Brooklyn Dodgers, beginning demise of Negro Leagues
1877 – mid-60s	Jim Crow laws in effect
1916-1970	Great Migration brings more than 500,000 African Americans from South to urban North
1950s – 1980s	Thermal fogging trucks used extensively to control mosquitoes
8/28/55	Emmett Till murdered
12/01/55	Rosa Parks arrested for refusing to give up her bus seat
12/05/55	Montgomery Bus Boycott begins
1956	Alternative newspaper *Chicago Defender* becomes a daily
11/13/56	US Supreme Court rules segregation on buses unconstitutional (Browder v. Gayle, 352 US 903)
2/14/57	Ella Baker starts Southern Christian Leadership Conference with Dr. King in Atlanta
9/15/57	Little Rock 9 successfully enter Little Rock Central High School
May 1958	Clennon King committed to Whitfield Mental Hospital after attempting to enroll at Ole Miss
2/01/60	Woolworth sit-ins begin in Greensboro, North Carolina
1/20/61	President John F. Kennedy inaugurated
1/25/61	President Kennedy holds 1st presidential press conference
3/04/61	F2 tornado devastates Chicago's South Side
10/01/62	James Meredith's enrollment at Ole Miss sparks riots
January 1963	Chicago Area Friends of SNCC (Student Nonviolent Coordinating Committee) founded
5/28/63	Woolworth's sit-in in Jackson, MS, most violently attacked of 1960s
6/12/63	Medgar Evers assassinated
July 1963	CCCO (NAACP, Friends of SNCC, CORE, Woodlawn Org.) calls for Chicago "Freedom Movement"
8/28/63	March on Washington
9/15/63	Birmingham's 16th Street Baptist Church bombed
10/22/63	Mass boycott of Chicago public schools, known as "Anti-Willis Freedom Day"
11/22/63	President Kennedy assassinated
1964	College students recruited to join Mississippi Summer Project
6/21/64	2nd session of orientation for Mississippi Summer Project volunteers begins in Oxford, Ohio
6/21/64	Civil rights workers James Chaney, Andrew Goodman, and Mickey Schwerner reported missing
7/02/64	President Lyndon B. Johnson signs Civil Rights Act
7/21-23/64	Wednesdays in Mississippi Washington/Maryland Team visits Jackson and Meridian
8/04/64	Bodies of slain civil rights workers James Chaney, Andrew Goodman, and Mickey Schwerner found
8/04/64	Pete Seeger performs at Meridian's Mt. Olive Baptist Church
8/07/64	James Chaney's funeral held at First Union Baptist Church
8/08/64	Statewide Mississippi Freedom School Convention held
8/08/64	Neshoba County Fair opens in Philadelphia, MS
8/24-27/64	National Democratic Convention held in Atlantic City
8/25/64	Mississippi Freedom Democratic Party attempts to be seated
6/14/65	Lawyers' Committee for Civil Rights Under Law opens Jackson, MS, office with full-time staff
8/06/65	President Lyndon B. Johnson signs Voting Rights Act
5/28/68	Reform Temple Beth Israel in Meridian, MS, bombed
7/20/69	Neil Armstrong is 1st person to walk on moon
7/20/69	Highland Park pool integrated in Meridian, MS
9/05/69	US Supreme Court orders statewide desegregation of Mississippi schools (Alexander v. Holmes)

Author's Note

Because it is grounded in history I lived through, *The Fog Machine* has been with me my entire life. Yet, history is marked by watershed moments. As Freedom Summer forever changed America, so did a documentary I saw in 1984, about the March from Selma to Montgomery, forever change me. It was unfamiliar history, and I wanted to know why. After all, it took place scarcely more than 100 miles from where I grew up in Meridian, Mississippi. Though my focus remained on my career for years after seeing the documentary, I never let go of these questions: *Why hadn't I known about it? And what might be different if I had?*

I did my first interview in 2000. Meridian civil rights attorney Bill Ready Sr. painted a picture of the time and place in which I grew up. Meridian had one TV station and one newspaper, each owned by the same man. Parents, white and black, were intent on protecting their children from the harsh realities of Jim Crow life. How, I wondered, did life and attitudes elsewhere in the U.S. compare? In 2007, I began interviewing in earnest, across the movements: civil rights, anti-Vietnam War, and women's rights. With each interview of aging history makers, I became more determined to explore what enables and disables change in human beings and to capture and present the past as authentic historical fiction. Through sharing my manuscript—with those I'd interviewed, educators, and book groups—I realized that Freedom Summer was the pivotal element of my story. I had been drawn back home to Meridian, and a journey of discovery was giving birth to a novel.

Not only was Freedom Summer a watershed moment in the civil rights movement, but it took place in my hometown and home state. Once it became the pivotal element of my story, I faced a plethora of difficult decisions about what to omit. What aspects of the history would be focused on? What misinterpretations might arise from my choices?

And, at the core of these decisions, whose story would *The Fog Machine* be? One of the many brave black activists whose stories have been told in non-fiction and memoir? Hate-filled white racist? Freedom summer volunteer on the front lines, doing voter registration?

C.J. Evans, Joan Barnes, and Zach Bernstein emerged. And with them came dangers of misinterpretation. While C.J.'s pastor feeds her drive to stay safe with his waiting-on-heaven ministerial posture, there was a range of support for the movement among black ministers in Mississippi during the period of this story. Although Zach's path to volunteering for Freedom Summer is influenced by his visits to fictional Mevakshei Tzedek in Chicago and there were a disproportionate number of Jewish volunteers, support for the movement was not at all a universal position in the Jewish community. Neither were the Freedom Summer volunteers all white or all teachers at freedom schools. While voter registration and the Mississippi Freedom Democratic Party are included, Freedom Summer in *The Fog Machine* is set primarily at the Meridian Freedom School, as a way of bringing all the characters together.

In the end, the story belongs to C.J., Joan, and Zach and to as many and varied supporting characters as they can reasonably interact with. C.J., rather than one of the many black activists, because she represents someone I thought I knew and wanted to better understand. By virtue of navigating Jim Crow life without compromising her character, she is, for me, an everyday hero. Joan, rather than a hate-filled white racist, because her circumstances position her to experience the Freedom School and consider the many questions her unique experience presents. Zach, rather than a volunteer facing the danger of attempting to register voters, because in being asked to teach, he receives the opportunity to learn, as his beliefs and desires come face to face with the influences that have shaped C.J.

MISSISSIPPI BEGINNINGS

He prided himself on being a man without prejudice,
and this itself is a very great prejudice.

—**ANATOLE FRANCE**

CHAPTER 1

April 1959
Unexpected Directions

The black wrought iron table called out to her as if it held a sign: *Reserved for Joan Olivia Barnes*. It was the best table in King's Drugs, the one that let you see everyone. As she skipped across the linoleum, her petticoat billowed out the skirt of her white eyelet dress like a cloud.

"May I, Mademoiselle?" said her dad.

She giggled as he held one of the heart-back chairs out for her, just as he had for her mom, scooted her up to the table, and wandered off to chat with the druggist. She swung her legs, careful not to scuff her new patent leather Mary Janes. Her mom peeled off her gloves, one finger at a time, and set them on her purse. Studiously, Joan did the same.

Now what?

"We'll go out after Mass to celebrate," her mom had said after both grandmothers sent cards with money for Joan's First Communion. "Anyplace you want."

"Just the three of us?"

Her mom agreed. C.J. was called to take care of Joan's little brother. She was at their house right now, missing her Sunday services, but Joan's mom said that was okay for Baptists.

Well, here they were. Right where Joan asked to be. But where were the other kids? No one else was in the store—unless you counted Howdy

Doody on the Colgate display, waving just like he did on the show, the Negro sweeping the floor nearby, and, of course, Mr. King.

Joan slid lower in her chair. She poked her little finger through one hole, then another in her skirt. Her mom chatted about the morning at St. Stephen's—whose communion dress she liked the best and how proud and tall Joan had stood, waiting her turn to receive the host. But Joan was thinking about Carol Gleason. Carol was so lucky, celebrating at this very minute with more relatives than any one person ought to have. She almost hated Carol, even though Carol was her best friend. And what about every other first-grader at St. Stephen's Academy? Celebrating with dozens of cousins, aunts and uncles, grandmas and grandpas, no doubt. Grandma Olivia lived in Wisconsin and Grandma Joan in Illinois, too far away to come for Joan's big day. Good thing, too. If her friends heard her grandmothers talk, they'd be thinking Joan was a Yankee for sure.

The bell over the side door jingled. In came a wave of late morning April heat and a girl about Joan's age. The girl's skin was dark, like C.J.'s. She kept her head down and slid soundlessly on worn-out shoes over to the man sweeping the floor. Joan sat up. Now things were getting interesting. Maybe the girl's dress was from St. Vincent DePaul. Joan's Brownie troop helped organize donations, but she only knew one other person who wore clothes from there. She peered at the girl, studying her. She hadn't seen many Negroes this close—just the men who rode on the back of the garbage truck, women coming and going from neighbors' houses, and C.J.

"Must be Sam's youngest. Addie, I think," Joan's dad said, sitting down.

With their heads bent toward each other, the Negroes whispered, like they had secrets. How did her dad know them? Negroes didn't get sick much. She'd never seen a single one in the waiting room at her dad's office, and C.J. had certainly never missed a day of work on account of feeling bad.

The Negro man pulled a coin from his pocket. His daughter stretched to kiss his cheek, then hurried over to the red case with "Coca Cola" in big white letters. Joan liked the way the girl's hair crinkled away from her forehead and gathered at her neck, all wrapped up in a braid. Addie—she liked the girl's name, too.

Addie fumbled with the bottle opener, finally got the cap off, and disappeared back outside. Through the window, Joan could see her sitting in the sliver of shade cast by the drugstore's wall, nursing the stubby green glass bottle.

Even inside under the giant ceiling fan, sweat ringed Joan's face like beads on a tiny rosary.

"Why doesn't Addie stay inside where it's cooler?" she asked.

"The Negroes don't get as hot as we do," her mom said. "Now what would you like?"

"Cherry Coke, please. At the counter."

When her dad nodded, Joan ran over to the stools. She was certain she could get up all by herself if she grew just an inch or two more.

"Here, Joani." He hoisted her up.

"Spin me, Daddy."

After sending her around in several circles, he warned, "Now don't do that by yourself," and went back to the table.

Joan patted the gleaming Formica countertop and watched Mr. King work. Dark brown liquid shot out of a spout, followed by cherry flavor and the fizzies. In the mirror behind him, she saw a man and woman come in with two children.

"Another fine sermon this morning, Mr. King," called out the woman. "Such a shame your business keeps you from joining us at First Baptist."

Mr. King handed Joan a tall frost-glazed glass and a straw in a white wrapper just as the boy and girl hopped onto stools.

"My sister and I'll have us some banana splits," said the boy.

Joan ran a fingernail up and down her glass, making patterns on the frost, watching Mr. King peel bananas and slice them lengthwise into long glass dishes. He doled out perfectly round scoops of vanilla, chocolate, and strawberry ice cream, drowned it all in chocolate syrup and whipped cream, and added a cherry with a stem.

"Your parents letting y'all sit here, too?" Joan asked.

"'Course," said the boy.

"What you wearing such a fancy dress for?" asked the girl, her spoon poised over her dish. "Easter's done come and gone."

"Today was my First Communion." Joan touched her hair where her veil had been.

"Huh?"

"At St. Stephen's."

"Must be one of them Catholics," the boy said.

"Oh." His sister was busy making a muddy river of syrup and ice cream.

"No. Cath-*licks*. Get it? Like this." The boy leaned over his dish, stuck out his tongue, and slurped up a gob of whipped cream. The girl laughed.

What a dumb joke; they were dumb. Joan wouldn't let them ruin the day for her. She shifted to keep from seeing them and concentrated on peeling paper from her straw. The Coke tickled her tongue. She sucked on the straw, absently twisting her stool ever so slightly. The arc grew wider and wider until, glass in hand, she spun full around. Suddenly, the glass slipped from her grasp. It crashed to the floor, sloshing cherry Coke all over her dress.

Joan came down immediately behind the glass, grabbing the seat to break her fall. She clung to it guiltily.

"Joan Olivia, what did I tell you?" Her dad was at her side, plucking her from the stool and standing her away from the broken glass. "You could have been hurt. And look at this mess."

Sam hurried over. "I'll clean that up, Doc Barnes."

"Oh, thank you, Sam. Joan, wait outside until your mom and I are finished." Before her dad headed back to the table, he gave her that look that said how disappointed he was.

She stared at the stain creeping across the front of her beautiful dress. The snickering of the awful boy and his sister seemed to roar in her ears.

Someone jabbed her shoulder. She looked into the boy's nasty face, crowded with freckles and a smear of whipped cream still on his cheek.

"You deaf?" he hissed. "Your daddy said get on outside now. Niggers—" He was shaking his head.

Joan's eyes shot clear across the store to her parents. She'd gotten in big trouble for repeating that word one day after school. Her mom and dad said it was disrespectful and they wouldn't have it. She peeked at Sam. His head was down, as if the figure-eights of his rag mop needed to be perfectly drawn.

"—and Cath-*licks*," the boy went on.

Enough with the dumb joke. Joan planted her feet and got ready to say so.

"Shouldn't niggers or Catholics be in here." He glared at her.

Her mouth flopped open. As tears stung her eyes, she rushed through the side door into the bright sunlight and tripped over something. She looked down and realized it was only the Negro girl. *Excuse me* died on her lips.

"What'd you do wrong to have to sit out here?" Addie asked.

"Got born wrong is all I can figure." Joan slid down against the wall.

Addie nodded knowingly. "Me, too."

❊   ❊   ❊

The last few weeks of school rushed by. Suddenly, the first day of Joan's first summer vacation stretched before her, wider than the big picture window. Raindrop gems from an early morning thunderstorm decorated the grass and her mom's prized tea roses. And there came C.J. from the bus stop, skirting puddles as she wound her way up their long driveway.

Joan dashed to the door. Standing on tiptoe, she wrapped her arms around C.J.'s waist.

"Hey there, little friend." C.J. hugged back. "Can you talk with me while I iron, tell me what all you got planned for summer?"

Joan beamed as she followed her into the dining room. C.J. called her "little friend" but treated her like she was a teenager, too.

A mountain of fresh laundry waited by the ironing board. She dropped onto the floor at C.J.'s feet. "I'm having company!"

C.J. donned a calico apron over her sleeveless work dress. The pink cotton was faded nearly white but, just like her other dresses, this one had a tiny touch of embroidery. She said it was her momma's mark. She picked a bed sheet from the basket, spread it across the board, and sprinkled a section with water. "Who's coming?"

"Girls in the neighborhood. We're gonna play Barbies."

"You sure are lucky to have you one of those new dolls." C.J. moved the iron back and forth.

"I got new outfits just in time to play with Cindy and Sally Ann."

"They're important, then? These girls?"

Joan nodded, impressed by how C.J. understood things she hadn't even explained. "We've been friends, but now we go to different schools. I'm hoping that won't matter."

"I reckon they'd be pretty lucky to be your friends."

She tilted her head at C.J., picturing the mean boy and girl in the drugstore. "They're *Protestants*, you know."

"Well—"

The doorbell rang. Joan didn't move.

C.J. started to smile but put her hand to her mouth. "Well, you'd best go see do these Protestant girls want to come in."

The bell rang a second time. Joan hurried to the door.

"Hey, y'all." Cindy and Sally Ann stood on the porch, loaded down with shoeboxes. Joan gestured toward the living room. "We can play in there. Mom said she'll get us a snack when my brother wakes up."

The coffee table had been moved aside. Joan squatted by the upright trunk that held her Barbie things—clothes on tiny hangers, accessories in drawers.

"Wow! Where'd you get that?" Sally Ann said, peering over her shoulder.

"It was my mom's."

"Look what all Joan's got," Sally Ann said, pointing.

Cindy glanced over, humphed.

"What are these stretchy pants?" Sally Ann asked.

"They go with 'Winter Holiday.' It's for snow skiing. My mom's done it—"

"Well, I'd shove that to the back, 'cause we don't do that here." Cindy nudged Joan's trunk out of the way and spread her doll's dresses out. "Let's put on these."

She watched Cindy slip the apple-print sheath over her doll's head, then reached for her trunk. The best outfit was the "Commuter Set." Her Barbie looked so sophisticated.

"How're we gonna tell our dolls apart when they're all named Barbie?" Joan wondered, fixing a sleeve on the tiny plastic arm.

"Easy," Cindy said. "Yours is different."

"No, it's not."

"The *hair*, Joan. Your Barbie's hair is dark."

"Yeah," Sally Ann said. "Our Barbies have blond."

Joan jammed her long brown hair behind her ears. She added a Chanel-style jacket over the checked blouse and navy skirt.

"Tada!" Sally Ann said, waltzing her Barbie forward in a blue-and-white sundress. Cindy and Joan pushed their Barbies forward, too.

"What you so dressed up for, Joan?" Cindy frowned. "We got beauty shop appointments."

"I'm going to the office."

"My mom says girls who work turn into old maids," Cindy said.

"That's not true! I'm getting married." Joan pointed to her trunk. "See, my Barbie already has her dress."

Cindy snatched up the white satin gown. "Let's have us a wedding. *My* Barbie will be the bride."

Sally Ann let out a small sigh. Joan quickly dug in the jumble of their shoeboxes and pulled out two pink "Plantation Belle" dresses. "Sally Ann, these can be our bridesmaids' dresses. Help me find the picture hats."

"Y'all get dressed," Cindy said. "You have to help the bride."

But Sally Ann hopped up and began walking across the living room, bringing her feet together after each step. "I'm gonna be a beautiful bride. I'll have a dress just like that when I get married."

"Me, too," Joan said.

"I'll be walking down the aisle at First Baptist—"

Joan joined her, humming "Here Comes the Bride."

"Pitiful," Cindy said. "Y'all make pitiful attendants." Her hands were on her hips. "Let's play garden club."

Sally Ann dropped to the floor, reached for a dress. "Oh, no!" she said, seeing Joan's. "We can't both wear the same thing. My mom said she near about died when two ladies walked into church last Wednesday in the exact same dress."

"Here, Joan, put this on." Cindy handed her the chef's apron from the "Barbie-Q" outfit. "We need us a maid anyways."

"I'm not doing it. You do it."

"Well, never mind, then. I'm thirsty. Get your girl to fetch us something."

Joan's stomach did a little flip as she followed Cindy's finger to the dining room. It wasn't so much Cindy's words as the way she said them. Joan could almost hear the nasty boy in the drugstore saying "niggers." So she hedged. "C.J.'s awful busy."

Cindy's hands were back on her hips. "Won't she do what you tell her? Mine does. Maybe *yours* is one of them uppity niggers."

Joan thought she heard the phone ringing, then realized the noise was coming from inside her head. Maybe C.J. hadn't heard that. Her eyes darted to the hall. If her mom would hurry up, she could fix the drinks. Or maybe Joan could, then pretend C.J. did it. One thing that probably wouldn't satisfy Cindy was asking politely.

"C'mon, Sally Ann. We can get something at my house."

Cindy was stuffing outfits back into her shoebox. Joan counted pieces of clothing and accessories, suddenly seeing each one as a day she would be playing alone this summer.

"Y'all stay, please." Joan hated the whine in her voice. "She'll mind me. I'll be right back."

Stepping into the dining room, Joan said loudly enough for her friends to hear, "C.J., we'll have us some lemonade outside on the porch."

C.J.'s green eyes flashed a disappointment that was worse than her dad's when she'd spilled the Cherry Coke. Without a word, C.J. turned for the kitchen.

"I'm sure it'll just be a minute." Joan tried to look confident as she led her friends to the porch. She nodded and smiled while Cindy and Sally Ann talked and giggled, but she really had no idea what they were saying.

"Here, Miz Joan."

Joan's head jerked up at the strange sound of C.J.'s words. C.J. stood so stiffly she seemed to have grown a few inches beyond her six feet. She carried a tray with a pitcher and glasses.

"Thank you," Joan mumbled as C.J. poured each girl a glass, left the pitcher and tray on the round wicker table, and disappeared.

"Delicious," Cindy said, sounding like she was playing garden club. She and Sally Ann swung their flip-flopped feet and clinked their glasses. Joan's first sip was as hard to swallow as pickle juice.

Soon her friends had set down their glasses and gathered their shoeboxes. As they waved goodbye, Joan slumped on the porch steps, watching steam rise from the puddles like upside-down rain. If only it would rain again and she were still waiting for everyone to come. Finally, she crept inside, hoping to make it to her room.

"Joan," C.J. called softly.

Joan stopped but did not turn. She could feel C.J. watching her from the dining room. "I think I had too much lemonade. I'm feeling kind of sick."

"Well, I'd like to tell you a story. That is, if you can stay a mite longer."

C.J.'s voice was low and gentle like always. If she was mad, why didn't she just say so? Joan backed up against the door jamb. She wanted to put her hands over her ears. She crossed her arms over her chest instead.

"I was born in the Wilsons' house, north of town."

The story C.J. had been telling since Joan was three years old started just like that. Joan nodded helplessly, carried away again to the farm where C.J.'s parents worked. To the tiny cabin the Evans family called home until C.J. was nine. With its tin roof rusted red and walls that let in the winter dampness, the three-room cabin sat way back on the property, well hidden from the big white house where C.J.'s mom cleaned and tended the Wilson kids while C.J.'s dad worked the fields.

Joan could feel C.J. waiting for her to play her role. "Why weren't you born in a hospital?" she said dully. "My daddy came to see me through the window where all the new babies stay."

"That cost too much money. Momma's friends all helped each other when a baby was being born."

Joan wriggled against the door jamb, trying to get at an itch that was hard to reach.

"Momma was getting the house ready for the Wilsons' big party when she got a pain and asked for someone to fetch Nellie from down the road. It took a while 'cause Momma's friend couldn't just leave work right off. By the time they showed up, I was lying right there on the bed beside Momma."

"Just like a magic trick," Joan snapped.

"That's right. Momma said, 'Y'all meet Crystal Janelle. This girl wasn't waiting for me to finish making Miz Wilson's crystal and silver all shiny. She got ready to come on, and here she is. She's gonna be strong, with a mind of her own.'"

C.J. was silent then. Her eyes walked all over Joan's face, like she had misplaced something there.

Finally, C.J. spoke. "My little friend, *that's* what I want you to always remember."

❊   ❊   ❊

After yesterday, being alone with C.J. just didn't feel right. Joan pushed her supper around her plate while Andy, one chubby fist wrapped around a fish stick, chomped happily. At this rate, she'd still be at the table when her parents got back from the movies. Why did they have to go out anyway, leaving C.J. to babysit?

"Isn't your food the way your momma makes it?" C.J. asked.

"It's fine, thank you."

C.J.'s sad look made Joan dip her head. She forced down a few more bites before asking, "Can I go outside 'til dark?"

"All right. Let's take Andy for a walk."

Outside, C.J. held Andy's hand and encouraged him down the driveway.

Gauging the dwindling light, Joan chafed at their pace. What if she just ran ahead by herself? C.J. hadn't told Joan's mom about the lemonade. Maybe she wouldn't tell no matter what. Without a word, Joan scooted past her mom's two-tone station wagon, picking up speed when C.J. didn't object. She cut across well-tended yards until she'd arrived in Sally Ann's driveway.

"Hey, Joan!" Sally Ann said. "I got a new jump rope. Now there's three of us, we can play."

"And since it's Sally Ann's," Cindy said, "I guess she gets to jump first."

Joan and Cindy swung the rope low, back and forth, while they chanted, "I like coffee. I like tea. I like the boys, and the boys like me." When Sally Ann ran in, they began looping the rope and repeating, "Yes. No. Maybe so . . ." They finally tripped Sally Ann up on a yes.

"Ooh, my fortune is good. The boys like me." Sally Ann clapped her hands.

"My turn," Cindy said. The rope circled just three times before Cindy stumbled on a yes. "Me, too. I knew it," she congratulated herself, hopping up and down and twirling in circles. When she stopped, she was facing C.J. standing in the street with Andy. "What's the matter, Joan? Can't go outside without your girl tagging along?"

Joan felt what little she'd eaten of supper beginning to rise and she swallowed hard. As she handed her end of the rope to Cindy, she said, "You know how *they* are."

Cindy laughed. While her friends turned the rope, Joan jumped and jumped, not noticing the fog that crept up the street, overpowering the sweetness of the azaleas in Sally Ann's yard. Only when Cindy suddenly stopped looping the rope did Joan hear the old truck clanking down the street on its mosquito-control mission. She turned to see the lumbering white pickup with the machine bolted to its bed. The nozzle burned red-hot and belched thick clouds of insecticide.

"It's the fog machine, y'all. C'mon!" Cindy yelled.

Like mice after a piper, the girls threw down the rope to trail the billowy stream. They chased it, fading in and out of view whenever a slight breeze took the fog in unexpected directions.

Joan ran with them, as if she were riding one of the thick white clouds that skidded across the sky, delighting in the feel of being inside.

But then C.J. had to ruin it all. "We're losing the light, Joan," she called. "It's best we head on back now."

Joan turned to go, but one of the girls bumped into her. What if it was Cindy? She couldn't just run on back, not after Cindy had already made her feel like a baby because C.J. had tagged along. So she ran on with her friends, until the truck rounded the corner and left their street. Only then did she emerge from the cloud, walking backward toward home.

"Goodbye," Sally Ann called to Joan. "It sure was fun using my new jump rope!"

Joan waved, and as she finally followed C.J. and Andy, she was glad for the falling darkness that hid the slight flush on her cheeks. Embarrassment was all it was, she told herself, though she knew it was more. Satisfaction suffused with shame, over learning what to do to fit in with her friends. And as much as C.J. knew, that was something she would never understand.

CHAPTER 2

April 1954
For Charlie

Yesterday, Crystal Janelle Evans had been, more or less, a carefree twelve-year-old. Today, right after school, she would become one more Negro woman cleaning houses for white folks in Poplar Springs, Mississippi.

While she sat on a city bus headed for one of the fine homes off Langley Road, her brother Charlie would be walking home alone. She wouldn't be able to hold his hand, the way she had on his first day of first grade. Or follow twenty paces behind, the way she had for the past week, watching to make sure he looked both ways before he crossed the road. This morning, though—with Daddy out in Mr. Wilson's field since dawn doing the spring planting, Momma up at the big house, and their sister Metairie walking the three and a half miles to the colored high school—C.J. could take care of her little brother same as always.

"Brush your teeth and go to the bathroom fast as you can," she yelled. Her hands moved from memory, scouring the cast iron skillet with salt, rinsing, and seasoning. When Charlie came back, she threw the dish towel over her shoulder and grabbed his arm.

"Ah, C.J." Charlie twisted to get away while she buttoned a button he'd missed and spit on a corner of the towel to wipe away a speck of egg caked on his cheek.

"Okay, we got to go. Here's your—what on earth? Has Momma put a rock in here with your sandwich?"

Charlie lunged for his pail, but C.J. had already lifted the lid. She held out a baseball. Not just any baseball, but the one their daddy brought home from the Army in 1938. Its red lacing, sewn as neatly as if by their momma's hands, was still tight. The smudges here and there were Louisiana dirt and grass. Until now, the ball had sat in the curio cabinet, turned just right so they could admire the signature—John L. Bissant of the New Orleans Black Pelicans. "Daddy would take a stick to your behind if he saw this."

Charlie had his hands on his hips and his face scrunched up in a frown, but he didn't meet C.J.'s eyes. "I'll put it back."

"What you'll do is explain what's come over you."

"I wanted to have a catch with William is all."

"With Daddy's special ball?" Her voice grew louder. "Have we *ever* played with this?"

Charlie stared at his feet.

"What do we play with?"

"The one Daddy made us with the rags."

She put on one of their momma's stern faces. "This sure isn't any way to be starting your very first day being a big boy."

"You gonna tell?" he asked in a voice so small she nearly relented.

"Don't you remember what all we talked about?"

Her bright and eager little brother, the child she loved almost as her own, looked up at her now. "Watch out for cars and go straight to Momma at the Wilsons'?"

C.J. sighed. She wanted him to remember and do so much more. But what she really wanted was to be there with him. She looked around the living room and kitchen as if memorizing a place she would not see again for a long time. Then she took his hand and led him outside.

❖   ❖   ❖

The bus stop outside the Mill Road School was busy in the afternoons, with so many colored girls headed across town for work.

C.J. watched Charlie until he was out of sight, then stepped to the edge of the crowd. She could tell who'd done this before from the way they stood—some like they owned their little patch of dirt, others like they were already dead on their feet. C.J. would be starting once a week for a family her momma's boss had referred her to, but if all went well she'd soon pick up families for other days too.

"Bet the house I work at is finer than yours," said a big eighth-grader named Essie.

"Don't want no fine house," said a scrappy girl named Mae. C.J. and Mae Willis had been best friends since they sat next to each other in Miz Clayton's room for first- and second-graders. "Fine don't get you more than twenty cents an hour. Just means more work."

When the number ten bus pulled up, Mae gave C.J. an encouraging hug and climbed onboard, the doors closing behind her.

"Your first time, too?" C.J. asked a scrawny sixth grader who was suddenly standing much too close.

"Yeah." Lucy started rocking faster from one foot to the other. "Ain't never rode the bus before. All's I know is I got to catch the number seven."

"Well, I'm waiting on number seven my own self. Just do what I do."

The sight of their bus caused Lucy to shake hard enough to get ticks off a dog. As the other girls pushed past them, C.J. pried the nickel from Lucy's fist. She pulled her up the steps and dropped both their nickels into the glass cage. But it was too late; every seat behind the "Colored" sign was occupied. By the time she realized the white section was totally empty, the driver had moved the sign forward a couple of rows, allowing her and Lucy to be seated.

The bus meandered through narrow dirt roads without stopping, but once it crawled up onto smooth paved streets, the white section began to fill up. At the stop across from Poplar Springs High, three white girls with long ponytails got on. They squeezed together in one of the last available rows.

"If too many more get on, we'll lose our seats," C.J. whispered, all the while watching the white girls and listening.

Their ponytails swished to the beat of their laughter. "The new *Photoplay* should be out," said the one in the middle. "Reckon Bobby will be there today?" asked the one on the right. "Maybe he'll get a cherry Coke and two straws!" said the one on the left, nudging the one in the middle and starting the giggling again.

C.J. wondered how Metairie didn't stay mad all the time. Boarding the bus at Booker T. High, stopping at the white high school to pick up girls free to do as they pleased, then going on to work. She felt anger grip her and realized Lucy had a firm hold on her arm.

"My Lord a mighty! They gonna do that to us?"

She followed Lucy's finger to the Negro men scattered along Langley Road, chained at the ankles and sweating under the menacing stares of a couple of white men. "No." She peeled Lucy's hand from her arm and patted it reassuringly. "It's men from jail keeping up the roads. Look at the trees instead."

The magnolias were coming into bloom, their saucer-shaped white blossoms unfolding like so many sheets to be ironed. Through the trees, they could see enormous houses with beautiful yards. Here and there, children were playing. "Wonder how many families live in those places?" Lucy asked.

"Oh, all that's for just one white family." C.J. spoke with authority, though she could scarcely believe it herself. A block or so down the road, she spotted the large white church her mother had told her to watch for and reached up to pull the cord. Before she stood to go, she squeezed Lucy's hand. "You're gonna be fine. Just give your fear to Jesus."

Up the hill, C.J. took the fourth left, then the third right. Two ladies chatting across a box hedge and children riding bikes seemed to look straight through her. Brick houses pressed toward her, though they were set far back from the street. In the Harwells' front yard, two boys about C.J.'s age were having a catch. The boy facing her was tall and big-boned, with hair almost as white as milk. When he glanced her way, he threw high.

The ball rolled to C.J.'s feet. As if she were playing with her daddy and Charlie, she scooped it up, feeling the smooth leather but seeing the horsehide-covered ball Charlie had wanted to use. She rifled the ball back to the pale-haired boy, throwing for Charlie. Her aim was true, her arm strong, and the ball thwacked against the boy's glove.

"Wow, what an arm!" he said. C.J. put a hand to her mouth to cover her smile.

"That's nothing," said the other boy. "That's just my momma's new girl."

Still, the look on his friend's face somehow said respect. C.J. nodded ever so slightly, walked to the doorstep, and rang the bell. To the unsmiling woman who answered the door, she said, "Ma'am, I'm Crystal Janelle, Sadie's daughter, here for the work."

❉   ❉   ❉

C.J. trailed Agnes Harwell through the parlor and into the hallway, where French doors opened to the dining and living rooms. She gaped at the furniture, heavy yet graceful, the paintings on the walls colored soft peach. Vases and glass eggs waited to be dusted, threatening to crack under her touch. Up the stairs and down again, in and out of rooms, she counted toilets, sinks, and tubs to scrub, floors to wash, carpets to vacuum, and beds to change. Suddenly the three and a half hours she had to be in this house seemed impossibly short.

When Miz Harwell finally led her into the dining room, she had to stop herself from reaching out to caress the top of the buffet. Her daddy built fine, sturdy furniture from pine and oak. This furniture had curves like the delicate necks of birds and wood like the petals of a pressed rose— dark, almost black, with a memory of red. She dared not begin her dusting in this room, for fear she would linger too long.

In the living room, Miz Harwell stroked the piano. "This was Mother's," she said, her eyes remembering. "She used to play it so beautifully." C.J. wished Miz Harwell's mother would play it now. As fine as it looked, this piano must surely sound a hundred times better than the scarred upright with the broken key that C.J. listened to Sundays at Hope Baptist.

Just inside the kitchen doorway, Miz Harwell stopped. "I can't have you in here until my cake comes out. It's got to be just right for the Johnsons. They've had their first child."

"Yes'm. I'll start upstairs then."

She swished the feather duster so carefully at first, afraid she might break something or move things and not get them back exactly where they belonged. But growing up with a momma who couldn't abide dirt, she had learned early on how to clean thoroughly and quickly. Her hands grew a little steadier and her pace quickened as she imagined she was cleaning her own house. In the second bathroom, she knelt on the cold, hard tile and leaned into the tub, sprinkling Comet and scrubbing in small circles, feeling as she rinsed to be sure the grit was gone. She sat back on her heels and rubbed the small of her back, smiling at the way the tub sparkled.

"Crystal," Miz Harwell called. "Come to my bedroom."

Could she have done something wrong already? She dried her hands on her skirt and hurried. Miz Harwell stood by the four-poster bed holding fresh sheets.

"Let me show you how I like the bed made." C.J. watched patiently while Miz Harwell made the bed exactly as she would have, but in twice the time.

When C.J. had finished the other beds, she went downstairs and peered into the kitchen. An angel food cake pan cooled on the counter, perched upside down on a Coca Cola bottle. She took a moment to breathe in the cake's sweetness before opening the Pine Sol. She had almost finished the floor when she heard, "Crystal, come in the living room."

Miz Harwell was kneeling on the floor, squinting at a yardstick. Her daughter stood on a chair with her arms crossed, tapping the toe of one low-heeled pump. Her skirt was lined unevenly with pins.

"I'm having the hardest time getting this straight. Hold the hem just this way so I can get a better look."

C.J. folded and flattened the fabric, closing her eyes and sinking into its smoothness, so unlike the sackcloth and muslin of clothes that had to stand up to life against the washboard. As Miz Harwell came to a dip or a rise, she rearranged pins.

"Ouch! I'm not a pin cushion, Mother," Lacey whined. "Can't you hurry up? I need to call Janine."

"All right, Lacey, go take that off. Crystal, you can get to the dusting. I've got pie crusts to roll out."

"But . . . I was almost finished with the kitchen floor . . . ma'am."

"You can do that later. I'll likely spill flour on it anyway."

C.J.'s shoulders sagged. It was almost certain she'd miss her bus home now. She rushed through the rest of the downstairs, then slapped at the linoleum. "Miz Harwell!" she called, running from room to room until she found her, upstairs hemming the dress. "I believe everything's done, ma'am. I'll need to hurry to make my bus."

Miz Harwell took her time, finally handed over two quarters and two dimes, and showed C.J. to the door. As C.J. flew down the hill, she could see people boarding. She pumped her arms and legs harder, but the bus pulled away, leaving only lingering exhaust fumes.

Her family would all be home by now, Momma fixing dinner while Metairie sat nearby doing homework, Daddy working in the lean-to off one side of the chicken coop—crafting a toy or piece of furniture, something to barter with neighbors. Before that, her parents would have finished another in an endless stream of days laboring for the Wilsons, and Metairie would have cleaned someone else's house. This was C.J.'s life now. Only sweet Charlie was still free, his days not yet stolen, the course of his life not yet set.

She stared at the church before her. Up and up, into the clouds, its steeple climbed. She dared not go in. "Be strong and of a good courage." It was Brother James's soothing voice she heard, as if from the pulpit of her little church. "Fear not, nor be afraid of them: for the Lord thy God, he it is that doth go with thee; he will not fail thee, nor forsake thee."

She turned to face the hill and willed herself to put one foot in front of the other, back the way she came. She would call their nearest neighbor and ask them to fetch her Uncle Eugene. He could come get her in his wagon.

Arriving for the second time on the Harwells' front step, she looked at the doorbell as if it were made of fire, but forced herself to push it. When the door finally opened, there stood Lacey. "*Mother!*" she yelled. "Your girl is back."

Miz Harwell came to stand behind her daughter. She was wiping her hands on her apron. "My word, Crystal, what are you doing still here?"

"I missed the bus."

"I'm right in the middle of fixing dinner." Miz Harwell sighed.

"If I could please use the phone . . ."

Miz Harwell led her to a little table in the hall. C.J. picked up the phone and dialed three numbers before her hand froze.

"You don't know your own number?" Lacey said.

C.J. directed her response to Miz Harwell. "Our neighbors. We don't—"

"You don't have a phone?" Lacey crowed.

"Anyways, they can go find my uncle. He'll come in the—" C.J. stopped herself.

"Probably don't even have a car," Lacey went on, despite the look her mother gave her. "Wow! No phone. No car. How *do* you get on?"

"We'll call the operator," Miz Harwell said, just as the kitchen door opened.

"What's holding up supper?" Mr. Harwell's voice was harsh, grating. He pointed to the table that had yet to be set.

"Crystal has gone and missed her bus." Miz Harwell made it sound like it was all C.J.'s doing. "We were fixing to call her uncle."

"We could be waiting on him 'til who knows when." Sweat trickled from C.J.'s underarms as Mr. Harwell watched her. Arms crossed, his expression like those of the white men who lolled while the Negro chain gang labored on Langley Road. What if he told his wife they ought to find themselves a girl who wasn't so much trouble?

"I'll carry her on home," he said finally.

Miz Harwell was taking silverware from the drawer and beckoning to Lacey. Lacey rolled her eyes at C.J.

As she reached for her purse, C.J. noticed her reflection in the French doors. With effort, she pulled back her shoulders and held her head high. She was a grownup now, and that meant more than just working to survive.

CHAPTER 3

August 1955
No Second Chances

Nearly a year and a half of working for the Harwells made the time C.J. spent home with her family all the more precious. She swiped her brow with her sleeve and shooed the squawking birds into the corner of the coop. Slow, shallow breaths, she reminded herself. On a Mississippi August afternoon, the smell of chicken manure could overpower a strong man.

"Where's that boy gone off to now?" C.J turned toward the garden, where her momma was bent low, plucking snap beans for supper, dropping them into the pockets of her bright yellow apron with the orange rickrack. "That's Charlie's job," Momma said.

"I don't mind, really," C.J. lied. "I'd just as soon be outside."

Momma snorted and headed back to the house. C.J. just kept shoveling.

"Look at you, your clothes all wet!" Her momma's angry words carried clear out to the yard. "Where have you been?"

C.J. latched the coop and headed to the front of the house. Through the open door she saw Momma wipe her hands on her apron, waiting. Charlie's relaxed look said he didn't see trouble coming.

"Me and William was just cooling ourselves off. It's blistering hot today." C.J. cringed.

"Well, it wasn't too hot for your sister to do your chores."

"I'm sorry, Momma. I didn't know it'd got so late."

C.J.'s momma moved toward the stove and lit the burner under a skillet. It seemed she would leave it at that. But she stopped, turned. Her wide-set eyes now took over her face. "Just how did you boys cool yourselves off anyways?"

"We had us a swim in the lake. That water felt mighty good."

"Tell me your daddy knows about this." Her hands folded across her chest in alarm.

"No, ma'am. Daddy was busy working."

"Lord, have mercy!" Momma's voice fluttered as it rose. Turning in circles, she muttered, "We did. I know we did." She reached for a chair to steady herself and looked Charlie dead-on. "I know your daddy and I taught you better than to think you can do as you please on the Wilsons' property."

C.J. could hear the onions sizzling in the skillet. She willed Charlie to take their momma's words quietly.

"But, Momma, Daddy's taken us fishing there so many Saturdays I can't count them no more."

"Charles Lewis Evans! Don't you know there's not a one of those times he didn't ask Mr. Wilson first, making sure they had no need of the lake for themselves?"

"Why would Mr. Wilson mind, Momma? He and Daddy were cutting pine trees near the barn."

"Son, it ain't about him minding." Momma's voice had gone low and slowed way down. "It's about knowing your place and staying safe."

Charlie's small face crinkled. "What you mean?"

"Mr. Wilson is Daddy's boss." Stooping to bring herself eye to eye, she grasped him firmly by both arms. "More important, Mr. Wilson is a white man."

Suddenly, Momma crushed Charlie to her chest, unaware of the smoke rising from the skillet. As if a powerful wind would snatch him away from her, she held on with all the might of her small round body. When the smoke turned black and thickened, C.J. rushed into the kitchen.

"Oh—Oh my!" C.J.'s momma moved toward the fire but never let go of Charlie.

"I'll take care of it, Momma," C.J. said. She clamped a lid on the skillet, turned off the burner, and opened the windows wider.

When Momma finally let go, she said, "Now put on some dry clothes and finish your chores. Daddy and I'll see to your punishment later."

The set of Charlie's jaw told C.J. he was peeved. The quiver of his mouth said he was worried. C.J. reached to give his shoulder a sympathetic squeeze. But he slouched away, leaving her alone with their momma. C.J. helped her into a chair and brought her a glass of water.

"Don't punish him too bad, Momma. He's just a baby."

"He's near a man and getting bigger every day." Her momma took tiny sips.

"What you thinking on doing?"

"First off, he'll apologize to Mr. Wilson. And I won't have him near that William. He can help your daddy 'til school starts back up. Daddy will know how to keep him out of trouble."

C.J. felt Momma's fear. Knew she must be thinking of her own brother, who'd disappeared. But summer was freedom. Even for a Negro child in Mississippi. C.J. knew all too well how quickly the days of summer gave way to years of work. "But, Momma, it was just a mistake!"

C.J.'s momma shook her head, causing the curls at her forehead to bob. "Daughter, hear me good on this. There's no such thing as mistakes with white folks, especially for boys. They don't get no second chances."

The next day, C.J. arrived home from the Harwells' to find Charlie lying in the yard like a dishrag, ready to complain that working in the field all day and coming home to chores had him too tuckered out for a catch or anything else she might suggest. She wasn't having it.

"Run, put on long pants and sleeves," she ordered. "We're going blackberry picking."

She was changed and holding two pails when he finally came back. They walked in silence until they reached the hill where jet-black clusters of fruit shimmered in the evening sun. Scarcely a trace of green or red meant the blackberries would soon be gone, as sure as summer.

Charlie tugged at berries, getting very few in his pail. "C.J.? I want you to do something for me. Will you?" He looked up at her with his emerald green eyes just like hers.

"Leave those that don't pull off easy. The easiest ones are the ripest and the tastiest."

"*C.J.*" He stopped picking altogether. "I want you to ask Momma can I go to work with you."

"Have you taken leave of your senses?"

"Just 'til school starts is all."

C.J.'s bucket slapped at her side as both hands went up in the air. "I wish *I* could go to work with you and Daddy."

Charlie jutted his chin forward. "Then let's trade places."

"Okay . . . let's pretend . . . we could do just that." Faster and faster, she flung berries into her pail until the mound neared the top. "You can scrub other people's toilets for twenty cents an hour and a lot of gum flapping. I'll spend the day in the fresh air with Daddy."

"Least you're making money. Daddy don't get extra for what I do. And you get to meet people and see different things."

"What I see is how boys got different opportunities and you ought to be grateful," she snapped. "Watch out!" She grabbed his arm and pulled him away from some poison ivy. "How many times have I told you? Leaves of three, let it be. That'll eat you up with the itching."

"Well, *you're* not Momma! I reckon you ought to stop acting like you are."

But C.J. suddenly saw herself in Momma's shoes, hurting for her brother. She held onto Charlie's arm, and her eyes glinted back at his. "I'm gonna act like Momma. Or tell you what to watch out for. Or do whatever needs doing. Momma has good right to be concerned. Did you know she had another brother, named Karl?"

Charlie shook his head.

"Momma was about your age. Her brothers went off for a swim in the creek. They cut across a white man's land. He hauled them down to the sheriff, said they were trespassing. Uncle Eugene was about ten and puny. But Uncle Karl was fifteen, big as a grown man and strong as a horse. That sheriff said Uncle Eugene best get on home and never let anybody catch him doing anything wrong ever again. But he saw a good worker in Uncle Karl. They took Uncle Karl to Parchman Farm."

"He want to go?" Charlie asked.

"Don't let the name fool you. It's jail, the Mississippi State Penitentiary."

"Uptown?"

"Naw, in the Delta, almost to Memphis. A huge farm, like a plantation. Men work like slaves."

"How do you know about it?"

"Momma sings about it when she's awful tired and sad: . . . *police'll catch and you're workhouse bound.*"

"He still there, Uncle Karl?"

C.J. didn't hear Charlie. She was remembering the letters she found in their momma's Bible. Every letter started the same. *Dear Sister, my friend Melvin is writing this. He got himself some schooling, so he writes for lots of us.* Some letters talked about the sun baking down on their backs as they stooped in the cotton fields, working from can-see to can't-see. Another letter mentioned the fool who tried to get away, but there were bloodhounds, trustees with guns, and no place to hide in the mile upon mile of flat, open land.

"*C.J.* Where is Uncle Karl?"

"That's just it, baby brother. No one knows. The letters stopped coming. And Momma, Uncle Eugene, Grandmomma and Granddaddy, not a one of them ever saw Uncle Karl again."

It all weighed on C.J. then, as she imagined it did their momma. The awful pain of never. Never seeing her brother again. Never knowing what happened. Never being able to help him know how to do right. Never seeing him grow up and have his own children.

"Still," Charlie said, trying but not quite managing to look tough. "You're not Momma, and—"

"And if I got anything to say on the subject, you're gonna follow the rules and stay safe. 'Cause you do that, and go after your opportunities, and your life's gonna be at least some better than mine. Now get to picking."

*   *   *

The first Sunday in September came, and with it Charlie's punishment ended, but there was no getting back the freedom he'd lost. As C.J. approached Hope Baptist with her family, her step was a tad slower than usual. School would resume in two days, effectively doubling her workload. Still, she smiled to see the chipping, peeling paint on the exterior. She knew just what Brother James would talk about today, how he would ask for a little extra in the collection plate and volunteers to do the painting. In a way it hardly mattered what he preached on. It was as much the rhythm of his voice mixed with the choir singing, the battered piano playing, and the tiny building resounding with "Amen, Brother" or "Praise the Lord" that she counted on each week to replenish her spirit.

"Welcome, brothers and sisters," Brother James said to settle the church.

Sitting between her family and the Willis family, C.J. shifted slightly along with everyone else. Part of Brother James's routine each Sunday was to pass on news to the congregation. Some didn't have electricity to run a radio. More than a few, including C.J.'s daddy, had never learned to read. Most who could read wouldn't waste their hard-earned money on a newspaper that only mentioned colored folks when they got arrested or killed.

Brother James paused, gathering their full attention. Finally, he said, "One of our children has gone on to be with Jesus."

"Home to Jesus," cried old Miz Miller.

"Sweet Emmett Till." Brother James closed his eyes.

"I don't know any family named Till. Do you?" Mae Willis whispered.

"Found drowned in the river."

C.J.'s eyes widened as she shook her head.

"From Chicago, he was visiting his great uncle up in the Delta. Perhaps he did whistle at the white woman, as they say he did."

"Who wouldn't know not to do that?" C.J. said a little too loudly. Momma leaned over to shush her.

"Somehow," Brother James continued, "this child was not taught, such that his way on this earth might be one of safety. For that, his life was taken in the most heinous of ways."

"What's he saying? What's *heinous*?" Mae said.

"It is not for us to understand. No, not in this world." Brother James raised his eyes to the heavens and smiled, like he could see a day when they would understand. Then he spread his hands, as if to pat the collective heads of all those assembled. "Today, parents, teach your children. Children, hear your parents."

C.J. shivered and reached for Mae's hand, wishing Charlie weren't sitting so far away.

"Let us turn to the book of Matthew and receive our guidance from Our Lord. Peter was confessing to Jesus, looking for an answer that would allow the disciples to carry on. They were feeling doubtful. Worried. Sore tempted to go another way.

"Jesus answered unto them, 'Every one that hath forsaken houses, or brethren, or sisters, or father, or mother, or wife, or children, or lands, for my name's sake, shall receive a hundred fold, and shall inherit everlasting life. But many that are first shall be last; and the last shall be first.'

"Hear the encouragement of Jesus," Brother James concluded. "Fix your mind. Hold it steady on his promise of the last being first."

C.J. tried to feel what had always come so easily. In her lifetime of Sunday services and Baptist Training Union classes, every word from every sermon and each learned passage of the Bible had done its job to comfort and give faith. Not so today.

"Amen," resounded the congregation. Miz Perry began to play "'Tis So Sweet to Trust in Jesus." Everyone was singing.

She wished they would sing louder. To drown out the fear always lurking in the distance. And the promise Brother James had offered once too often: Wait for a better time.

❊   ❊   ❊

B ut better times had seemed far off the day Miz Harwell wandered into the kitchen while C.J. was washing the floor.

"You hear about the new doctor in town?" Miz Harwell had begun, her gaze on the new neighbor's backyard.

"No'm." C.J. looked up but continued mopping.

"Of course people coming in, especially from up north, is never a good thing. And they do their worshipping at St. Stephen's—Catholic. But Poplar Springs is lucky, I reckon, to get someone so quickly to take over for old Doc Adams. We want to help Doc Barnes learn our ways."

C.J. couldn't imagine what that had to do with her.

"I told Miz Barnes you could help out. She just has the little girl, but I'm sure there'll be more kids directly. I'd rest easier knowing you were there and could tell me if anything seemed—well, not right."

"But Miz Harwell—"

"And I know you're the kind of girl who can keep her wits about her around Yankees."

That had settled it. And now, a month of Thursdays later, here C.J. sat in the back of Miz Barnes's car with the woman not one bit smarter about Jim Crow ways, insisting on driving C.J. home and each time determined to persuade her to sit up front.

Huge, fat drops pelted the windows, but Joan dozed peacefully in C.J.'s lap. She smiled, thinking that even this three-year-old seemed to know better. Each time her mother asked, Joan would put on one of her make-you-want-to-do-it-my-way smiles. "Please, Mommy. C.J. *has* to sit by me."

The child was smart and polite. All *yes ma'am, no ma'am, please,* and *thank you.* Even to C.J. And she minded well. She'd taken C.J.'s hand that first Thursday and walked her down the driveway, stopping halfway and pointing to the seam in the concrete. "This is the magic line."

"What's magic about it?" C.J. asked.

"I can't go over it. Not even my toe." Joan lifted her foot and waved it close to the line, then snatched it back.

"What if you do? Will you turn into a pumpkin?"

"No." Joan giggled, then became serious. "I have to sit in my being-bad chair."

"That happen much?"

"No, ma'am. Just sometimes." Joan had looked up at C.J. solemnly and added, "I won't be bad on C.J. days."

This evening's rain was one of those downpours that seemed to stop in frustration because it wasn't possible to make the air any wetter. Well before the car approached the point where paved road became a narrower dirt trail leading down to C.J.'s house, the late sun had blasted through the clouds and set to work wicking away puddles.

But standing water could hide the ruts. You had to be able to feel your way as if blindfolded, the way Uncle Eugene could in the wagon. As soon as the Wilson property was behind them, C.J. craned her neck, trying to determine the condition of the dirt road. "Miz Barnes, I really ought to walk the rest of the way today."

"Nonsense, dear. You'll get all muddy. I've driven roads like this many a time, on my parents' farm in Wisconsin."

"Oh, yes'm. It's tricky here is all I was meaning. Unless you know where the ruts are."

"Let's give it a try." Miz Barnes slowed but moved confidently ahead.

The road began to slope, past the neighbors' house, then Uncle Eugene's. C.J. gripped the hem of her skirt, twisting back and forth. They were almost there when Miz Barnes turned the wheel away from one puddle only to come immediately upon another. The car buckled like an animal with its front legs knocked out from under it.

Joan twitched but did not wake up. C.J. gently laid her down on the back seat, then opened the car door and looked for the best place to step. "I'll just fetch my uncle. He can pull you out with the mules."

"Wait, please." Miz Barnes met C.J.'s eyes in the rearview mirror. Her auburn movie-star waves lacked either bobby pins or the thick coat of hairspray that characterized southern white ladies' hair, yet held their own against the heat and humidity. "I'm sorry. I should have listened to you."

C.J. nearly fell out of the car. "Just sit here, ma'am," she managed to say. "I'll be quick."

She watched with Momma from the porch while Uncle Eugene coaxed the mules and the car back up to the paved road.

"Someone ought to tell that woman what's what," Momma sniffed. "Not knowing better than to drive down in the hollow after a rain or ask my child to sit up front in her car."

"I reckon she's just learned the first part, Momma."

"Well, better she'd do her learning somewheres else."

C.J. shook her head, thinking of Miz Barnes's apology, wishing her momma would let up some. Yes, one mistake by Miz Barnes could cost her and C.J. both. But Miz Barnes was a good person, just like the Wilsons. After all the years Momma and Daddy had worked for the Wilsons, C.J. just didn't see any danger with them for Charlie. She wanted to be able to trust Miz Barnes, too.

❧   ❧   ❧

"You know where Chicago is?" Mae asked as she and C.J. spread the contents of their lunch pails on the table. "Where that boy was from."

It was their second week at Booker T. Washington High School and Community College. C.J. was still getting used to the dilapidated yellow school buses that came into their neighborhood to take them the three and a half miles Metairie had walked until now.

She wanted to be happy, just the way Brother James said they should be. Money had finally found its way from the Mississippi legislature to Poplar Springs, money approved nearly two years earlier for new Negro schools, pay increases for Negro teachers, and buses for Negro children. Never mind that the legislature was trying to keep the separate by increasing the equal, or that the brand-spanking new buses had gone to the white kids. Better was better, as Brother James said.

But Emmett Till was still on everyone's mind. From one boy or another and what their fathers had told them, C.J. and Mae had pieced together the details Brother James left out. *Found that Till boy in the Tallahatchie, beaten so bad couldn't nobody recognize him. Had a bullet hole in his head, too. And a cotton gin fan tied around his neck with barbed wire. Talk is the white men who did it may not even go to jail.*

"I don't really even know where the Delta is," C.J. said.

"I asked her that, too, the librarian. Don't that just beat all, C.J.? We got us a librarian at this big school of ours." Mae slapped the table and grinned. C.J. could picture her questioning the librarian, seeming much bigger than her actual size because of her boldness. "The Delta is only four counties from here. But Chicago, you can get there in a day on the Illinois Central."

"That close?" C.J. shivered. She didn't much care where Chicago was, but the Delta suddenly sounded much too close for comfort.

"Yeah, the librarian showed me maps. She said Negroes been going there since the turn of the century. Making more money. Getting treated better."

"To the Delta? That boy sure didn't get treated better."

"Ain't you been listening, C.J.? I'm talking about *Chicago.*"

"Well, *I'm* talking about the Delta. It's too close. Momma was right."

"Right about what?"

"The rules, Mae. *We* can't make mistakes."

"Well, yeah. We always knew what to do. That boy should have, too. He was fourteen, same as us. I can't figure why he'd even want to come down here, him living in a grand city like Chicago."

"Fourteen. And here Charlie's just turned eight."

"Uh huh. Wonder what it's like up there—"

"Mae?" C.J.'s voice trembled. "How am I going to make sure Charlie gets on in such a world?"

"Not having a little brother my own self, I can't rightly say." Mae reached out to pat C.J.'s arm. "But I reckon you'll just be the best big sister you can be."

C.J. thanked her with a little smile for trying, but the place inside of her that needed to be filled up with wisdom still felt empty. "Up 'til now, I never much wondered why we got to follow the rules, any more than why we got to breathe. I liked it better that way. Knowing changes everything."

CHAPTER 4

September 1957
Old Habits

C.J. bent to wring out the mop, then stopped herself; old habits were hard to break. She squeezed the lever of the new Quickie Automatic Sponge Mop. Miz Harwell had pulled it from the broom closet just this afternoon, all proud, like it could do the mopping itself.

C.J. missed the rag mop. It was heavier, true, and harder on the back. But there was a rhythm to swirling the mop head in figure eights. Like the three years of coming and going to this house once a week. Scrambling to fit too much work into too little time. Waiting on one kind word, one penny extra an hour, anything more than a hint she could be trusted—and then only to keep an eye on someone Miz Harwell trusted less.

Opening the windows so the September heat could dry the kitchen floor, she moved on to dusting. Through the dining and living rooms and on to the parlor, she ran the rag over each curve and into every cranny, testing her memory of furniture styles learned from the book in the school library. The chairs with feet like lion's paws were Chippendale. The table next to it was—She gasped at the scratch that marred its ebony surface.

"Miz Harwell!" she cried as she ran. She found her sifting flour into a mixing bowl. "What happened to the parlor table?"

"*That* was Franklin Jr.'s doing. My grandmother on my daddy's side would turn in her grave." Miz Harwell sighed as she leveled flour in the measuring cup. "Just cover it with the doily."

The idea of hiding the precious wood made her sick to her stomach. "Oh, no, ma'am."

Miz Harwell looked at her in surprise, a frown creasing her brow. C.J. took a tiny step backward but held her ground. This family needed more grace, not less. If it could only come from the furniture, well that was a start. "That table's walnut, isn't it?"

"Well . . . yes."

"A surface scratch like that, I can fix it. Do y'all have a walnut tree?"

"No—"

"I know the Barneses do."

C.J. went through the back door and across the yard. Beneath the big shade tree, she gathered walnuts. Inside, she asked for a hammer and cracked one open. When she rubbed the nutmeat on the scratch, the oils erased it like a mark on a chalkboard.

"Miz Harwell, look!" C.J. turned and nearly bumped into her, leaning down, staring at the table. C.J.'s smile was as wide as the scratch had been.

"Thank you." The words came out quietly. But she heard them, and she thought Miz Harwell's eyes said more.

❊   ❊   ❊

The day the phone company came to the Evanses' house to install their first phone, C.J. made a mental note to be careful what she wished for. Her wanting a tiny show of respect and appreciation seemed to have landed her a lot more work, so much that Miz Harwell grew tired of relaying messages. Most of those now calling C.J. directly wanted occasional help with baking or cleaning before a meeting or party. But C.J. had also taken on the Thornhearts as regulars on Saturday mornings.

Reverend Thornheart was pastor of the big white church where C.J. left the bus to go to the Harwells', and master of the sprawling parsonage, with its wrap porch and dozen high-ceilinged rooms. Only when C.J. had finished every room but the reverend's study would she knock at his door.

".Enter!"

She nodded to the reverend and pulled the feather duster from her apron pocket. She circled the room, whipping up tiny swirls of dust, then pushed the vacuum around as if trying to catch them all before they landed. She reached to unplug the vacuum.

Sweet Jesus, let him leave me be today.

"Girl, don't you want to hear my sermon?"

"I best be getting that chicken frying so y'all's dinner won't be—" He lifted his page of scribbled notes and peered at her over his bifocals. "Yessir."

"You know about those troublemakers in Little Rock?"

Brother James had told them at Training Union about the nine foolish teenagers who'd challenged segregation at Central High. He'd said he didn't know about Little Rock, but the Negroes of Poplar Springs were lucky to have a high school as fine as Booker T. Washington. White folks in Little Rock had gotten so riled up that first day that the governor called out the Arkansas National Guard. Eventually, President Eisenhower had to send in troops to protect the children. Brother James had shaken his head sadly, adding that he knew none of his Hope Baptist kids wanted to be the cause of such trouble. C.J. felt saddest for the girl, Elizabeth, who walked up to Central High all alone, and most frightened for the three boys.

But one wrong word now and the reverend would be all in a flap. No, Reverend. Yes, Reverend. Perhaps repeating the point of his question, as if she were a parrot. These were the best ways to avoid trouble. She shook her head rapidly.

"Colossians tells us what we must remember in times like these." He loved to preach on God's order. She shut her eyes, hoping to be comforted by the familiarity of the passage.

"Wives, submit yourselves unto your husbands, as it is fit in the Lord. Husbands, love your wives, and be not bitter against them. Children, obey your parents in all things: for this is well pleasing unto the Lord. Fathers, provoke not your children to anger, lest they be discouraged."

The reverend paused, to emphasize God's words for C.J. and her kind. "Servants, obey in all things your masters according to the flesh; not with eyeservice, as menpleasers; but in singleness of heart, fearing God.

"Look at me when I speak!" he yelled in the very next breath. "Why must I always have my eye upon you if I am to be certain your work will be done well?"

C.J.'s heart was in her throat. Had the man taken leave of his senses?

"Do you not hear the word of the Lord God Almighty? Do I not pay you what is right and fair? One word from me and you would have no work in this town."

"Yes, Reverend, you pay me right and fair. I will do my best to serve the Lord."

"Then get to your cooking!"

She backed away from the menacing wave of his arm. In the kitchen, her hands shook so that she needed five matches to light the burners. Drawing deep, ragged breaths, she stirred chopped onions in a skillet until they were tender, then added okra, tomatoes, and seasoning. As it all began to simmer, her shoulders dropped back down, away from her ears.

When a few drops of water flicked into the other skillet made the oil sputter, she added battered chicken pieces. Under cover of the sizzling oil, she whispered from Ephesians: "Ye masters, do the same things unto them, forbearing threatening: knowing that your Master also is in heaven."

When everything was ready, C.J. let Miz Thornheart know, then set to work arranging each serving dish just so at the head of the table. When she was done, she took her place in the corner of the dining room to wait for further instruction.

The Thornhearts' son, Alan, and his younger sister, Charlotte, arrived first. They stood behind their chairs. C.J. still remembered the first time she'd seen Alan, playing catch with Franklin Jr. the day she started working for Miz Harwell. His hair and facial features made him seem to be the spitting image of his father. But Alan was taller and heavier, gentler and kinder. He'd looked at her with respect when she returned the ball, throwing hard and true. Something in Alan's eyes said he wondered whether, this time, his father's hatefulness would be directed at him or her.

Miz Thornheart rushed in ahead of her husband, nodding to her children. Everyone bowed their heads.

The reverend stormed into the dining room, rubbing his shin and hollering, "Again I ask, why must I always have my eye upon you?"

Too late, C.J. remembered the vacuum in the middle of the study, still plugged in. Involuntarily, her eyes met Alan's. He leaned forward, as if to come to her aid. That only heightened her fear. She shook her head, as imperceptibly as Alan had moved.

Reverend Thornheart's fingers bit into her arm as he dragged her outside. Down the winding path they went, toward the big white church. At the top of the marble steps, he let go to pull back the heavy double doors. They flew open like tiny birds. Her legs buckled. The reverend half carried her forward, dragging her knees on the floor.

"Beg the Lord Jesus to forgive you!" he bellowed as they reached the front of the church. Against the redness of his face, his pale hair glowed white as a star. As he drew back his arm to strike her, C.J.'s eyes met those of the white Jesus looking down from the stained glass window.

She flinched and closed her eyes, squeezing them shut so tightly that the face of Jesus blazed in all the colors of the stained glass. Then, feeling nothing, she dared to look up. The reverend was staring at his uplifted palm. "And lest I should be exalted above measure through the abundance of the revelations, there was given to me a thorn in the flesh, the messenger of Satan to buffet me."

He was reciting 2 Corinthians. *Dear Lord, the man imagines himself to be the disciple Paul!*

She watched him pivot and leave the church. Tears stung her eyes as she heard Jesus say, in the voice of Brother James, *But many that are first shall be last, and the last shall be first.* As her thoughts turned to Alan, her tears fell more freely. This kind boy had none of her blessings: a gentle teacher, the love she knew from her father, or the comfort she drew from being in her own home.

❊   ❊   ❊

As rattled as she was, C.J. took pride in continuing at the Thornhearts'. She never told her parents about what happened. There was comfort in the regular rotation of jobs: Saturday mornings at the Thornhearts', three and a half rushed hours at the Harwells' on Monday afternoons, five hours at the Barneses' on Thursdays plus babysitting Joan and the baby now and then. Special baking and cleaning jobs fit easily enough in between. And she was glad for the extra money, until Buddy Corrigan called.

At Mr. Corrigan's meetings, one man after another rang the bell until the living room of his ranch home overflowed with noise and cigarette smoke. Some men she knew by name or dress. Mr. Jimmy Harwell, of course, and Mr. Tommy Garret, the car dealer who was always working his Buicks into the conversation. The policeman who came in his uniform and the deacon who wore the handsome suits. C.J. walked among them, shrinking from their eyes and holding herself rigid when they leaned so close their hot, sour breath crawled all over her skin.

Tonight, as she dished out desserts, mixed drinks, and poured coffee, the men seemed more rambunctious than usual. Maybe it was the holiday season. Maybe because there was a new man among them.

"Y'all hear about that new nigger Catholic school?" he said, hitching up his trousers. "And those white Yankee nuns teaching up there?"

"Yeah," said another man. "It's bad enough they got the white school. Teaching them kids to worship the Pope and all. It's Communist is what it is."

"Well, we keep an eye on things, don't we, Jimmy?" Mr. Corrigan was using his now-now-don't-you-boys-be-worrying manner.

"Damn straight, Buddy," Mr. Harwell said.

While the others laughed, Mr. Garret took to pawing at C.J. until Mr. Corrigan called him off. She thought how lucky it was that she worked here rather than Metairie. C.J.'s body had begun to fill out, but she didn't think she'd ever have the womanly shape Metairie had.

"Go on now, girl," Mr. Corrigan said. "That's all 'til it's time to clean up."

C.J. rushed to the kitchen. She liked to pull a chair over near the back door and look out at the sky. On clear winter nights like tonight, the stars flickered softly through the bare trees. She imagined herself way up there, far away from the living room and whatever went on after she left.

". . . to the flag of the United States of America and to the republic for which it stands."

She turned, expecting to see Mr. Corrigan with an empty dessert plate to be refilled. A shaft of moonlight fell across the floor where no one stood. Dear Lord, she'd forgotten to close the swinging door when she came in.

"One nation under God, indivisible, with liberty and justice for all."

She needed to shut the door now, so the voices would be muffled like always. But she could not make herself move.

"Before we get down to business," Mr. Corrigan said, "let's recite our creed."

The men finished with "We believe that the crowning glory of a Klansman is to serve. Not for self, but for others."

Sweet Jesus, no matter what she'd suspected went on here, she'd never heard the word spoken. Softly, she sang: "Give to the winds thy fears. Hope and be undismayed. God hears thy sighs and counts thy tears. God shall lift up—"

"How about that nigger grocery store on Mill Road?"

The voice raged over C.J.'s song. She shivered and touched her arm, remembering the brush of a sleeve, the blue-black wool finer than any brand new Sunday-go-to-meeting suit.

"That'd do us fine," someone else said. She pictured a hand, with a farmer's dirt-stained nails, reaching for a dessert plate. "We just need to mess the place up some when nobody's there."

They were talking about Mr. Bishop's general store! C.J.'s family and friends and most of the members of Hope Baptist shopped there.

"Nothing much, now." The gravelly voice was Mr. Harwell's. "Just so's our new guy here can get his feet wet. 'Course we can keep some niggers on their toes while we're at it. They'll have a mess to clean up when we're finished."

The laughter resumed.

She had to shut the door. Mr. Bishop was a good man. He'd given her family and plenty of others items on credit during hard times. What if they hurt him? As she crossed the room, she bumped one of the kitchen chairs, toppling it over with a loud bang.

"Well, shit," Mr. Corrigan said. The laughter fizzled away. "Sounds like I need to go see to my girl."

It was too late. He would see the open door and know she'd been listening. Without righting the chair, C.J. shoved it over in front of a high cabinet, then snatched one of the plates with extra desserts and dumped it on the floor. She turned the faucet on full force, grabbed a rag, and fell to her knees. As Mr. Corrigan came in, she was busy cleaning up the mess and making as much noise as possible.

"I know you don't want any trouble." The words thundered overhead.

"No, sir. The chair . . . I slipped when I . . . I'll get this cleaned up directly." C.J.'s hands fluttered, raking a puree of brownies and sliced pound cake topped with strawberries back onto the plate. But her eyes never left his boots. Worn, with tarnished buckles, in need of a shine. The boots moved closer. Still, she did not look up.

"What goes on in my meetings is important business and not for anyone to know outside of us who's in them. Just keep your mouth shut, and everything'll be okay. You can tidy up now. We won't be needing anything more tonight."

"Yessir."

The boots walked away, leaving the swinging door swishing. Once again, the voices were low and jumbled. Or maybe they were overshadowed by the warning ringing in C.J.'s ears.

The next day at lunch, her stomach roiled and she had to remind herself to chew. It felt strange having something she couldn't share with Mae. But Mr. Corrigan had been clear that she wasn't to talk to anyone about the meetings.

There'd been no mention of anyone getting hurt, and yet dear, sweet Mr. Bishop—If he were to try to defend his store, he would surely be killed, and they would know she had warned him. And if she told her parents, she could be putting them in danger. Finally she'd decided to talk to Brother James on Saturday. She'd be at Hope Baptist with kids from Training Union who'd volunteered to decorate for Christmas. She could only hope it wouldn't be too late.

"You got to work tomorrow?" Mae asked.

C.J. shook her head.

"Reckon Miz Sadie would let you go uptown with me after school?"

That was ten cents for the bus, but it sounded heavenly. Going off for a little while, just the two of them, paying no mind to anything complicated. "I'll ask Momma tonight. What you need anyways?"

"I'm thinking I might get me a new fashion magazine." She posed, one hand to her chin-length, straightened hair.

"Well, listen at you. Talking like some white girl. *I* got to *save* everything I make."

"I'll probably just look, C.J. But Mr. King at the drugstore lets me have the old issue for half price if there's any left when the new one comes in."

"All I'm saying is, with what I got to go through for my money, I wouldn't be throwing it around on magazines, half-priced or not."

As Mae pouted into her sandwich, her long eyelashes brushed her cheeks.

"Okay. I'm sorry."

Mae brightened. "I want to learn *everything* about fashion!"

"Doesn't seem to be much call for that in Poplar Springs," C.J. said as kindly as she could.

"There's other places. Like Chicago."

C.J.'s forehead creased. "That's one place we got to steer clear of."

"Well, my cousin Alinda likes it fine. She sent me this letter." Mae pulled an envelope from her pocket and jabbed at the postmark.

"What's Alinda done a fool thing like going up there for?"

"She works for a white family. Cleaning, serving meals, looking after the children. Lives right in their house."

"In *their* house? Lord!" C.J. bit her lip and clasped her hands to stop them from shaking. God forbid, living with the families she worked for.

"C.J., what is it?"

"It's nothing."

"Come to think, you been not right all morning. Something happen?"

C.J. shook her head, hating the hurt in Mae's eyes. What else could she tell? Something bad enough Mae would believe that's what was eating at her. "I saw me the inside of that big old white church on Langley Road. You know, the First Baptist."

"You just went in?"

"No . . . the reverend . . . he carried me up in there. Got himself all in a tizzy when he tripped over the vacuum. Wanted me to ask Jesus could he forgive me."

Mae's eyes had gotten huge. "He hurt you?" she whispered.

"Not like that."

"Thank the Lord."

They finished their sandwiches and closed their lunch pails.

"Man sounds plumb crazy," Mae said.

"Yeah, some white folks would probably be a far sight better to live with than others."

Mae laughed. "I nearly forgot the amazing part. Hold your hat, girl. Alinda's making thirty dollars a week!"

"Every week? I've been saving most of a year to get that much. What's she say?"

Mae took out the letter. Her eyes moved down the page. "Here. She says, 'They're working us hard, but it's nothing I ain't done before. Strong girl like you, Mae, you could do it fine. I got an apartment with some other girls. We stay up there on our day off. Just a bus ride away from the L. That's what they call the train that runs up overhead—' "

"Wait a minute. Back up. Alinda asking you to come?"

"Well, sure. Alinda calls it a domestic program. There's an agency that matches up girls with families. The agency likes southern girls. Northern girls won't work for that kind of money. But, C.J., you got to come, too."

C.J. thought of Uncle Karl and knew her momma couldn't bear to have another loved one leave. "I just couldn't do it, Mae. I'd miss my family something fierce. And I got to look out for Charlie." As they stood, C.J. saw the excitement in her best friend's eyes. Already she felt the loss of Mae, like an awful ache in her chest.

❄   ❄   ❄

The ache was still there as C.J. stepped from the bus right into a puddle. Frigid water seeped into her shoes and crawled up around her ankles, sending a chill deep into her bones. Miz Barnes's car was nowhere to be seen. As she slogged her way up the hill, her coat took on water like bad news, heavy as the threat to Mr. Bishop's store and Mae's talk of Chicago yesterday at lunch.

Miz Barnes opened the door looking fresh and warm in a green woolen jumper over a soft beige sweater. But her face was a sweep of concern. "Get inside right away, dear." As she stepped aside, a tiny gold cross blinked from a chain around her neck. "Of all days for the car to be in the shop. Do forgive me for not meeting you at the bus stop."

"I'll just get to the kitchen floor while I'm wet, ma'am. Might as well make lemonade from lemons—"

"Hi, C.J.!" Joan called from the dining room. "Everything's ready for us. I filled the sprinkle bottle myself. Mommy let me."

Despite her mood, C.J. smiled. She walked into the dining room and found the child, dressed like a five-year-old version of her mother, stationed by the ironing board. "I'll wash the floor quick as I can, little friend."

"Betsy Wetsy and I'll be waiting." Joan held up her doll and helped it wave.

The floor seemed to mop itself. It sparkled up at her. C.J. glared back and returned to the dining room. She sifted through the basket of clean laundry, taking stock.

Joan busied herself with her doll, looking up now and then. When C.J. spit on her finger and touched the iron, it sizzled. She dampened a bed sheet and began moving the iron back and forth across it.

"What story are you gonna tell today?" Joan asked.

Joan loved the story about when C.J. was born, but what else could she tell? She recalled the day she sat next to Mae in Miz Clayton's classroom for first- and second-graders. What would Joan think of the little school on Mill Road, with its outhouse and four classrooms for eight grades? The kids had sat around a big table so they could more easily share the few reading and arithmetic books. C.J. had shared most everything with Mae ever since, and she couldn't quite picture Poplar Springs with Mae gone clear off to Chicago.

"What's wrong, C.J.?"

"Oh, I'm just feeling a bit down in the mouth today. Reckon it's the rain." C.J. watched Joan cradle her doll, alternately coaxing it to drink from a tiny bottle and checking its diaper.

"You need to play with Betsy Wetsy. It's so much fun. Feel this." She held up the doll. "My baby's wet her pants."

Miz Barnes walked by just as water leaked onto the floor. C.J. squatted to dab at it with her apron.

"Joan Olivia! How many times have I told you not to feed your baby on these hardwood floors? I know you don't want to have to sit in your chair and miss talking to C.J."

C.J. flinched, remembering Mr. Corrigan standing over her, saying, "I know you don't want any trouble." She reached in the basket for one of Mr. Barnes's white long-sleeved dress shirts. Outside, rain had dripped from the dark sky for nearly two hours now. Why couldn't it just stop? Or rain hard enough to be done with it? She thought of the night sky at the Corrigans' house, wondering if he meant to torment her one drip of fear at a time.

"C.J. C.J.!" Joan was tugging at her apron. "What's that smell?"

"Oh, my!" C.J. looked down and saw a dark scorch mark on the shirt. "Miz Barnes!" she cried, wanting to get her confession and whatever might follow over with.

Miz Barnes came running into the dining room.

"I'm so sorry, ma'am."

They stared together at the brown shape of the iron across one sleeve. The longer Miz Barnes was quiet, the worse C.J. felt.

"Is C.J. in trouble, Mommy?" Joan asked, looking wide-eyed.

"No, sweetheart. But would you go put your baby to bed in your room, please?" She unplugged the iron and set it in its metal holder. "C.J., please come sit with me."

C.J. followed her to the living room. She quickly checked the back of her skirt for dirt that might stain the light blue damask, then perched on the edge of the sofa.

"What is it, dear?" The voice was the warm and gentle one Miz Barnes used with the baby. "You haven't been yourself since you arrived."

"I'll pay for the shirt out of what you pay me," C.J. said, fully aware how long that would take.

"That's not what's worrying me. Something has you upset. Perhaps if you told me."

How comforting it must be to have this woman put a cool hand on your fevered brow or kiss your scraped knee. These were things her momma did, but C.J. wondered what it would be like to have a mother who could linger. "It's someone I work for. He might be fixing to —" She clamped her hand over her mouth.

"You can tell me," Miz Barnes urged, surely expecting a child's problem. C.J. recoiled from her words as if from a water moccasin that had crawled up in the yard.

A hurt look flitted across Miz Barnes's face before she crossed the room and pulled four child-sized books from the bookcase. She brought them to the couch, set two quickly aside, and studied the other two. "This one has the story of Saint Joan." She patted it tenderly. "But it's this one I want. I hope you might find some comfort in these stories. The one about Saint Zita in particular." She held out the book.

C.J. stared at the pretty picture on the cover of *Miniature Stories of the Saints, Book Four* and wondered at the meaning of the words saint and Zita. "I don't read much," she said.

"Of course, but these are *children's* books."

It's not that I can't, she wanted to explain. *But nobody I ever saw in a book has problems like mine.*

"May I tell you Saint Zita's story?" Miz Barnes asked. She explained how the girl had gone to work as a maid at twelve, to help feed her family. She was treated unfairly, even beaten.

C.J. was surprised by the things they had in common. "What did she do about it, Miz Barnes?"

"Because Zita held charity in her heart and kept her focus on her work, she gained everyone's trust and admiration. Just as you've gained mine."

"But Mr. Barnes's shirt—"

"Please don't give that another thought. Why don't you do the bathrooms now?" Miz Barnes moved as if she would try again to hand C.J. the book, but then stood. "I'll just set this by your purse. Keep it as long as you want. Maybe if you say a prayer to her, Saint Zita can help you better than I have."

Pray to someone other than the Lord? Is that what Catholics did? This was probably the kind of thing Miz Harwell wanted C.J. to tell her about each time she asked whether anything unusual went on at the Barneses' house. Her jaw tightened with the anger she'd heard in her momma's voice that day on the porch, when they'd watched Uncle Eugene pull Miz Barnes's car back up to the main road. She shuddered to think of something worse than getting stuck happening to Miz Barnes.

※　　※　　※

Saturday crawled by slowly. Miz Thornheart and her children stared at the pink Depression glass plates before them, waiting, as Reverend Thornheart served himself and passed the new potatoes to his right. While Charlotte took some and passed the dish to her mother, he spooned out okra and tomatoes. As the potatoes finally reached Alan, the reverend wielded the platter of fried chicken. Next came the biscuits and butter. Every Saturday, the same foods, in the same order, in the same silence.

C.J. itched to leave, to be with the other volunteers decorating Hope Baptist. She held her hands at her side, curling her fingers as if around the tiny figurines for the manger. When she was dismissed, she fixed herself a plate in the kitchen. She forked and swallowed without tasting. With each bite, she wished for change. Something new for dinner, a door she could close to shut out the dining room, time to concentrate on what to say to Brother James about Mr. Bishop's store.

"What do you children have planned for after dinner?" she heard Reverend Thornheart ask. "Charlotte, why don't you go first?"

Perhaps most of all, C.J. wished for change for Alan. If there was one pattern to what Reverend Thornheart did, it was his coddling of Charlotte and coldness toward his son. For months now, she'd watched him bear up under his father's cruelty and wondered at the goodness that still shone in his brilliantly blue eyes when they met hers. In C.J.'s eyes, Alan outshone his father. But she doubted Reverend Thornheart saw it that way. No, the reverend saw flaws. It was as if Alan were a mirror, reflecting his father's own sins back to him. Surely that was what drove Reverend Thornheart to distraction.

"Mommy is taking Missy and me for last-minute Christmas shopping," Charlotte said.

"That's wonderful, sweetheart. You ladies have a good time."

The silence expanded like a sponge dropped in water.

"Well, Alan." The reverend seemed to underline his son's name. "I'm sure you're up to no good."

"Actually, Ricky and I have a prayer session planned."

Though his words were uttered without tone, C.J. suspected he meant to mock.

"Aren't these biscuits delicious today?" Miz Thornheart said. "I must ask C.J. what she's done differently. Charlotte, pass the bread basket to your daddy so—"

"Prayer is your only hope of getting into college, that's for sure," said the reverend.

"And college makes a better man, right, Dad?"

C.J. winced as an edge crept into Alan's voice. He had nothing to fear from his father physically. Maybe that made him brazen. But it just as surely made things harder. She wished she could take him aside. Mr. Alan, she might say, the Jesus at my church would hear you if you asked for his help.

But even if the color of their skin didn't make that impossible, why would Alan believe her when he regularly saw his father mistreat her?

"Watch your tone. Your disrespect is no example for your sister."

"My influence on Charlotte . . . now, there's something that concerns me!"

"Honey, come to Daddy's study before you leave. I'll give you extra money for your shopping."

"Thank you, Daddy."

C.J. could hear forks scraping plates. She imagined the silverware was as anxious to complete its duties and be excused as the family was.

"My son," said the reverend. "Despise not the chastening of the Lord, nor faint when thou art rebuked of him: For whom the Lord loveth he chasteneth, and scourgeth every son whom he receiveth."

Reverend Thornheart's habitual repetition of Hebrews signaled dinner's end. Wearily, C.J. scraped her uneaten food into the garbage. Sunlight through the window seemed to backlight the pale pink plate like a cloud at sunset, giving it a rosy hue. She looked through the plate, trying one last time to see change, then yanked the curtains closed.

❊   ❊   ❊

Later that afternoon, after the others had left Hope Baptist, C.J. knelt before the manger, watching baby Jesus sleeping so peacefully, praying Brother James would somehow help her bear the burden of knowing about Mr. Bishop.

"Well, you sure worked hard today."

She looked up to see Brother James kneeling beside her. "If I tell you something, can it be just between you and me and God?"

"If you've done something, C.J.—"

"It's nothing like that. Suppose . . . you knew somehow that . . . something bad was going to happen. If you didn't tell, the thing would happen. If you did, something even worse could happen, maybe to your family." She sat back on her heels, her face straining to hope. "What would God want you to do?"

"You'll have to tell me what you know, C.J."

She squeezed her eyes tight against the memory of Mr. Corrigan's worn, dull boots. "I heard men talking about damaging Mr. Bishop's store."

"When, child?"

"They only said when nobody was there."

"It's not a life they're talking about taking?"

"No, but Mr. Bishop . . ."

"I think we must let it be. It's not something we can stop, and we don't want to make it worse."

"But how can we do nothing?" She'd taken a big risk talking to Brother James. And this was all he had to tell her?

"Recall Psalm 37. 'For yet a little while, and the wicked shall not be.' "

"A little while?" She knew he would probably say something like he had about Emmett Till, how it's not for us to understand in this world. But she asked anyway. "How long is that?"

"Pray with me, child," he answered. "Our Father, which art in heaven, hallowed be thy name."

"Thy kingdom come; thy will be done in earth as it is in heaven." C.J. joined him, but she silently prayed, *Dear Jesus, please let me do the right thing.*

"Give us this day our daily bread; and forgive us our debts . . ." *Please don't let anything bad happen.*

"For thine is the kingdom, and the power, and the glory, forever." *If it must, at least let it be nothing I knew anything about.*

"Amen."

Christmas morning shone clear and bright on the wreck of Mr. Bishop's store. The building stood, but canned goods, soap, penny nails, and bolts of cloth were strewn about amidst the splintered remains of counters and shelves. It was good the Bishops didn't live next to their store, Brother James told everyone. If they'd heard the ruckus and tried to defend their property, they probably wouldn't be here today.

C.J. had woken with hope in her heart and joined her family for breakfast. Everyday food made special by lingering over it together before giving in to Charlie's puppy-dog eagerness for opening gifts. Now her daddy's reassuring voice could be heard directing some of the men in rebuilding shelves and counters while the women and children sorted and swept.

She felt the broom, heavy in her hands. She stopped to stare at the remains of the big Mason jar that once held the penny candies and remembered Mr. Bishop letting her fish for a treat from that jar. The peppermints were her favorite. Tiny shards of red and white now sparkled amidst broken lemon sours and dust. She asked herself what she would do next time. All she could reply was to hope there was no next time, and a little sob caught in her throat.

Metairie was suddenly at her side, wrapping an arm around her waist. "I remember that jar, too," she said. "Ain't it just awful what comes over some folks?"

Together, the faithful of Hope Baptist salvaged what they could, then took up a collection to help Mr. Bishop restock. They worked into the twilight, then brought their Christmas dinners and desserts to the church to eat in fellowship.

Before they ate, Brother James asked everyone to stand. He acknowledged their weariness and praised their work. He walked among them as they recited the Lord's Prayer, pausing to place his hands on C.J.'s shoulders for the words "but deliver us from evil." And then they sang, finishing with "Silent night, holy night. Son of God, love's pure light. Radiant beams from thy holy face, with the dawn of redeeming grace. Jesus, Lord at thy birth. Jesus, Lord, at thy birth."

CHAPTER 5

April 1958
Craziness

On the Saturday before Easter, C.J. felt like a tornado as she whirled through the Thornhearts' house, snatching up all the dirt in her path. When dinner was served, she wrapped up a chicken leg and biscuit to eat on the bus and got straight to the pots and pans. She and Mae were meeting uptown, outside Lily's Ladies Lovelies. Their junior-senior party was six weeks away, but they were shopping early to give Momma time for sewing. Mae knew exactly what she wanted to buy. C.J. planned to just look, like she always did, to get ideas for what her momma could make for her. But right before she left home, she'd stuffed the entire forty dollars of her savings in her pocketbook. She clutched it protectively as she boarded the bus, wishing she hadn't been so irresponsible.

When the bus left Langley Road, it slowed, as if allowing C.J. extra time for viewing the white stores where she would not be shopping. They passed The Mademoiselle Shoppe and Meyer Jewelers, then the giant Bettelman's Department Store and J.C. Penney's. As Center Street narrowed, BJ's Diner, Thrifty Shoe Repair, and Kress gave way to the Greyhound station and train depot. The bus turned right, wobbled through a large pothole, and stopped at the edge of the colored shopping district.

Mae linked an arm through C.J.'s the minute she came down the steps. She carried her sketchbook so she could capture the details of any dress

C.J. took a liking to. They straightened their backs and raised their chins as they walked but were overcome by giggling before they got inside.

"Hey, Miz Lily," Mae said. "We need us some dresses for our junior-senior party. Mine's got to be pink."

Miz Lily pointed them to the rack with teenage styles. C.J. found the eights and riffled through them.

"You can't tell just on the hanger. Here." Mae thrust the armload of dresses she'd gathered at C.J. and moved to the eights. "Look. This one could be good on you, and these."

"But I don't like the colors or—"

"Come on to the dressing room."

C.J. hugged the wall, trying to stay out of the way as Mae tried on one dress after another. "How can you tell so fast?"

"Did you see that last one? I looked like a pink balloon on legs," Mae said from inside the folds of the next dress. When she pulled it down, though, she stood reverently before the mirror just long enough to say, "This is the one. Ain't it beautiful on me?"

The fitted bodice, square neckline, and short bouffant sleeves seemed perfect for Mae's small frame. She was trying to keep the softly gathered skirt afloat by twirling nonstop.

"You look like a princess," C.J. agreed. "But it's not pink."

"It's called white organdy. And this velvet sash is pink. I'll just get me some pink shoes, and it'll be perfect! Now, your turn."

The first dress made C.J. feel girlish. Mae shook her head. "You look too much like me."

They both laughed at the second dress. "It swallows me up like Daddy's old white shirt."

Dull and boring, C.J. thought when she saw herself in the next dress. "Now you look too much like good little C.J.," Mae said.

At Dot's Spot, Mae picked out even more dresses for C.J. to try, but the results were the same. At the Bargain Bin, she shoved the size eights from one end of the rack to the other while Mae found and paid for pink pumps.

Mae was quiet until they were outside. C.J. turned toward the five and dime, to look at patterns and fabric, but Mae pulled at her arm. "It ain't right," she said.

"What?"

"You got a kind of look about you, C.J. You're so tall and thin and serious. You know, sophisticated. Like Miz Clayton. Remember them dresses of hers? Finer than most we ever saw, and her wearing them every day up to the Mill Road School, just to teach."

"It's okay. Let's look through the pattern books."

"Miz Clayton told me once she shopped on Center Street. Said The Mademoiselle Shoppe was her favorite—"

C.J. planted her feet. "That'd be plumb crazy, Mae."

"We can't try anything on there anyways. Let's just go look, get you some sophisticated ideas for Miz Sadie's sewing." Mae patted her sketchbook.

A white man drove by like he was out for a stroll. Feed sacks were piled high in the bed of his rusted-out pickup, and a deer rifle filled the rear window. The man's eyes followed them, making C.J. feel as if she were at one of Mr. Corrigan's meetings. Some of the forty dollars in her purse came from what she got paid to walk among men such as this one. Bowing and serving. She suddenly wanted to walk through their stores, just to look. And so she allowed Mae to lead her toward Center Street.

Outside J.C. Penney's, white women took their children's hands and yanked them to the far side of the sidewalk. "Y'all best get on back to your part of town," said one.

"Let's go to Bettelman's," Mae whispered. "It's so big maybe won't nobody even notice us."

"I think I'd like to go there." C.J. pointed to The Mademoiselle Shoppe.

"You sure?" Mae seemed nervous now.

C.J. straightened her back the way she and Mae had outside Lily's Ladies Lovelies. Inside the small store, she could feel heads turning and eyebrows arching.

At the counter, the clerk smiled at a white customer. "I'm happy to take that return for you."

Slowly, gingerly, C.J. moved each size eight down the rod, from right to left. In hushed tones, she discussed them with Mae, all the while ignoring the white woman looking at the tens. Just before C.J. reached the plastic ring separating the two sizes, she heard a sharp intake of breath. As the woman snatched her hand away, her perfectly manicured nails flashed red. C.J. turned to stare at the woman's pouting mouth, drenched in matching lipstick. It was Miz Corrigan, looking as mean as she had the few times C.J. had come to their house to do baking.

She was just about to turn and run when she saw the most beautiful, perfect dress in the world. Emerald green like her eyes. She took it from the rack and walked to the side of the store. There, she held the dress at arms' length before smoothing it against her body, picturing the soft fabric following the lines of her figure, from the fitted bodice down to the slim skirt that stopped mid-calf. "Touch it," she urged Mae.

"It's called rayon crepe," Mae said. "The scalloped edges on the neck and sleeves and the slit in back are so sophisticated." She opened her sketchbook and began to draw.

C.J. checked the price tag—twenty-one dollars—then stared hard at her purse. "Here, Mae," she whispered, handing over the dress. "See is anything wrong with it."

"Why?"

"*This* is my dress."

Mae pulled herself up to her full five feet, studied the dress, and nodded. C.J. took it and walked to the counter. Only when she noticed Miz Corrigan watching did she begin to tremble.

"I'll take this, please, ma'am."

The clerk stared, then announced loudly, "That's twenty-one dollars and sixty-three cents."

"Yes'm." C.J. opened her purse, counted out exact change, and held it out.

The clerk jerked her head, indicating C.J. should place the money on the counter. "You know we don't take returns," she informed C.J. through lips that looked like they'd just tasted spoiled milk.

"That woman at the rack sure was giving you the evil eye," Mae said later, as the bus pulled back onto Langley Road.

"I work for her husband is all, serving at the meetings." She still hadn't brought herself to tell Mae the truth about them.

"I reckon Miz Sadie'll be mighty pleased she don't have to make you something." Mae said it like it was a question.

C.J. wasn't so sure Momma would be so *mighty pleased*. She reached into her shopping bag and traced the scalloped edge of one sleeve. What if she could get the dress on before her momma had time to ask questions? If Momma could only see, just the way C.J. did in her mind's eye, how perfect the dress looked on her . . . maybe then she could be happy, too. "I hope Momma isn't too mad at the price I paid."

"I wouldn't worry about that," Mae said a little too cheerily. She pulled some folded papers from her purse and slapped them against her palm, as if the sound made them more impressive. "This here's your ticket, C.J. All you got to do is send in this application."

"Where?" C.J. asked, rather certain she did not want to know.

"Chicago, of course. Alinda sent one for each of us. They were waiting in the mail box yesterday. I filled mine out already. I can help you."

C.J. wanted to laugh at the craziness, how alone Mae's wanting them to be together made her feel. Mae hadn't mentioned Alinda and the domestic program in months, and here she was with her application all filled out, practically stepping up into the bus. C.J. wasn't one to put her troubles on someone else's shoulders, even her best friend's. Working Klan meetings was a horror she knew better than to share with anyone. But she'd always believed Mae would be there, just in case.

"We haven't even graduated—"

"That don't matter."

"It'll matter to Momma. She's told us a million times all her children are getting theirselves high school diplomas."

"Can you imagine how rich we're gonna be?"

C.J. shook her head, but she took the application and put it in her purse before reaching to pull the cord.

Mae patted her hand. "I'll see you in the morning."

At home, Momma sat rocking on the porch. C.J. closed the door to her parents' bedroom so she could use their one mirror. She slipped her treasure from the bag, forgetting all about Mae and the application. Holding her breath, she disappeared into the silky softness, imagining what sophisticated would look like. She pulled the dress down, dared to look, and gasped. The dress in the mirror bagged out here, hung there.

Behind the person in the awful dress, C.J. saw her momma, her kerchiefed head barely reaching C.J.'s shoulder. Her momma's eyes moved between C.J. and the dress. She reached to brush a speck of lint from one sleeve. "My, this fabric is fine. But didn't you try the dress on?"

C.J. dropped heavily onto the bed. "No, Momma."

"Anyways, I thought we agreed you'd just look for ideas for my sewing. If we splurged, we could buy fabric like this. But I don't know could we find any that matches your eyes so."

C.J. looked crestfallen.

"I know, honey. It's your junior-senior party, and you want it to be special. I could make something a bit like this, but better suited to your figure. It's best you take this back."

"I . . . bought it on Center Street."

Momma drew a quick breath, opened her mouth, then closed it. C.J. felt her momma's weight in the silence even more than when she sat down beside her on the bed. But then she felt herself being drawn in, her head against Momma's chest, and rocked.

Finally, Momma lifted C.J.'s chin. "You're sixteen now, a woman. Gonna have ideas of your own. But, honey, why?"

"Mae got to talking about Miz Clayton, how she and I are so tall and thin and serious. Sophisticated, Mae said. And Miz Clayton shopped at The Mademoiselle, so why didn't we just have a look? But, Momma . . . I knew better."

"Not that. Why'd you buy *this* dress?"

"I thought it was me, Momma. I know I've disappointed you. And I spent half my savings—"

"This was a mistake." Momma absently fingered the touch of embroidery on the collar of her muslin dress. "But one I can probably fix. I'll get to it tomorrow, after Easter services."

C.J. reached to hug her, but Momma took hold of her hands. "Baby," she said, "knowing who you are, well that takes most folks a hunk of time. But I'm proud you're wanting to figure it out."

❋   ❋   ❋

As C.J. waited for Mr. Corrigan to answer his bell, she used her handkerchief to dab at the perspiration brought on by sitting on a crowded bus in the mid-May evening heat. When he finally let her in, his "You know what to do" sounded faintly like an apology. But he was back in his easy chair, covered by the newspaper and jiggling one foot to the song on the radio before she could reply.

She passed through the hall to the kitchen, thinking how she cherished her time alone there. The familiar tasks helped steel her for when the other men arrived. She would get through that part of tonight by thinking about the junior-senior party. She hummed the song she'd just heard, wondering what music would be playing Saturday night, and smiled to think of her momma's talents. Ever since Momma made the dress look the way she'd envisioned it in the store, she had been looking forward to the party.

She went straight to the pantry for the big coffee urn. On her way, she glimpsed skeins of yarn on the kitchen table. As she lugged the urn to the counter, she reminded herself to clear the yarn to make more work-space. Carefully, she measured water and ground coffee. A clicking sound startled her.

She turned to find Miz Corrigan sitting at the far end of the table. Nothing moved but her knitting needles. In. Out. Yarn inched from the table onto a finished square in her lap. C.J. dropped the measuring cup, splotching the counter with coffee.

"Don't let me bother you." Miz Corrigan smirked.

"Yes'm."

C.J. willed her pulse to calm as she lined up bottles. Smirnoff for the policeman. Gilbey's for the deacon. Two bottles of Early Times, most everyone else's favorite. She took out trays of ice and emptied them into the ice bucket, grimacing when one of the handles pinched her finger. She set out dessert plates, saucers, coffee cups. As she gathered silverware and folded napkins, the tiny, sweet rosebuds on the china grew large, like angry eyes. All the while, the needles clicked.

The doorbell was almost a relief. C.J. hurried to answer it. The men began to file in, either eyeing her in the way that made her squirm or, as she preferred, looking past her as if she were invisible.

She took drink orders and went to the kitchen to pour and mix. The needles clicked even louder. She tried to drown them out with her own sounds of clinking ice and stirring. When she returned to the living room with a tray of glasses, she was greeted with raucous laughter.

"Showed that uppity nigger, didn't they?" said the farmer, pointedly looking at C.J.

"Yeah, name of King, just like that trouble-making preacher," said the deacon.

"Crazy as a loon," said the man who wore the fine wool suit. His hand wrapped around C.J.'s as she tried to give him his drink, but he released it when he saw the look in Mr. Corrigan's eye.

"Damn straight," said the policeman, stepping into the sudden hush. "Thinking he could get into Ole Miss. Got him up at the crazy farm there at Whitfield where he belongs."

"What you think, girl?" Mr. Corrigan was suddenly standing very close. "Niggers in college. Don't that beat all?"

C.J. didn't know what had happened. But she was certain that if this group had any say in things, no Negro was ever getting into any white school. "Yessir. Crazy for sure."

"That'll be all," he said. "Close the door behind you." The men laughed again.

In the kitchen, C.J. could think of nothing to drown out the sound of the needles. She pulled a chair to the back door and looked out, concentrating on not screaming. Suddenly, the clicking stopped. The sewing basket clattered to the floor. The chair scraped as Miz Corrigan moved to pick up the basket.

"Let me, ma'am." C.J. put things back in the basket and picked up the knitted square that had also fallen. She stood there holding them both, trying not to stare at the woman's protruding belly. She was clearly pregnant, and that chair had to be killing her back. "It's beginning to get dark," C.J. offered, as an explanation for Miz Corrigan's clumsiness. "I'll turn on a light."

"No! Just put the things back on the table. And make me some tea and fetch me a piece of cake."

She tried to puzzle out why Miz Corrigan gave off hatred like an injured skunk. Returning to her chair and staring into the black, starless sky, she wondered why the smell was even stronger than what came from the laughing men.

Finally, Mr. Corrigan poked his head in the kitchen. "You can tidy up now. I'll carry you on home short—"

"Could you get one of the others to do that, dear?" Miz Corrigan's voice sounded like she'd dumped the sugar bowl into her tea.

Her husband's hand went to his chest as he turned toward the sound. "Good Lord, Nadine! Why aren't you at your mother's? I saw you drive away."

Miz Corrigan's eyes moved as fast as her knitting needles, back and forth between C.J. and her husband. But she was otherwise still. "I came back, Buddy."

"You know these meetings are for the men." Anger had shoved the surprise from his voice.

"What about *her*?"

"What *about* her?"

"*She's* not a man."

"She's nothing. She's a nigger!"

The spoon C.J. was using to rake coffee grounds from the urn made a screeching sound. Neither Corrigan seemed to notice. C.J. stopped moving anyway and stared at the pile of mush in the garbage.

"Don't seem that way. You driving her home, then coming home late yourself."

"I got business to tend to."

"That's my point, dear. You know where this girl shops? *At The Mademoiselle.* I saw her the Saturday before Easter, buying an expensive dress like some white lady with means."

"That's none of your concern."

"The baby's been kicking something fierce," Miz Corrigan went on, her voice controlled again. "I'd feel better if you were here. With *me.*"

Mr. Corrigan sliced off a hunk of cake and looked at C.J. "I'll carry you on home shortly," he repeated before stuffing the cake in his mouth and leaving the kitchen.

Good Lord, indeed! The woman was acting jealous. Wanting to avoid those darting eyes, C.J. filled the sink and began washing the dishes. But the woman stayed put, and she could feel her eyes bore into her back.

❅　❅　❅

The banner over the door to the Booker T. Washington High cafeteria proclaimed *Welcome, 1958-1959 Graduates.* C.J.'s Momma pointed to it and beamed, then headed to the table for chaperones. Cut flowers in jelly jars decorated each table. Mae immediately began circling the room, like a tiny hummingbird flitting from flower to flower. C.J. was left to stand awkwardly by the punch bowl. She served herself a glass and looked around, noting the white shirts and black pants on the boys and the dresses much like Mae's on the girls. As different as her dress was, she felt proud of the way she looked in it. Not even Miz Corrigan's hatefulness could change that.

Music streamed over the public address system, installed around the time the school buses began running to C.J.'s neighborhood. The music came from a radio, so it was interrupted now and then with talking. Boys approached C.J. for the slow songs, but she politely declined. She was a head taller than most of them, and just standing next to them made her feel gangly.

Mae's petticoat buoyed up her skirt as she sailed around the room with one boy after another. When Chuck Berry sang "Johnny B. Goode," Mae dragged her into the crowd. She began to relax and enjoy herself and finally accepted an invitation from Ronnie, the tallest boy in their class, to dance as Sam Cooke sang "You Send Me."

"You having fun?" Mae asked when they met in the restroom.

"I reckon I am at that." C.J. smiled. "Wonder what it's like for the seniors, with school ending soon?"

"Well, if they got plans like I do, they're happy, that's for sure."

The warm, relaxed feeling seemed to drain from C.J.'s body. "No."

But there Mae was, pulling yet another piece of paper from her purse. This one said she was assigned to a family in Evanston, Illinois and should be there for her first day of work on Monday, June 9.

"Well, what'd you expect, C.J.? 'Course they'd accept me, with Alinda's recommendation and all."

"I . . . just thought it would work out so we'd graduate together. Now I got to get through senior year without my best friend."

"But you don't! You just got to get Miz Sadie to let you go."

"Not much chance of that." C.J. turned to go before Mae could see the tears in her eyes.

Momma found her alone in the hallway, crying. "What's wrong, baby?"

She looked at her momma, accepted the handkerchief she held out, and blew her nose. It was hard to explain what was bothering her. She didn't want to go with Mae now, maybe ever. Yet she didn't want to be left behind.

"I was thinking about next year," she began.

"Your senior year." Momma's smile was as broad as the banner in the cafeteria. "I'll have me two high school graduates!"

"What if I didn't?" She blurted out the question, then followed it with details of the domestic program.

Momma shook her head. "Didn't you get yourself enough trouble listening to Mae about that dress? That girl with her crazy ideas is one thing, but to go putting them in your head—"

"But, Momma, all that money could really help the family."

"Some things are more important than money. This coming year, that's your schooling. Right now, it's your special party. Now dry your eyes, honey, and get on back in there."

As Momma led her back toward the cafeteria, Jackie Wilson began to sing "Lonely Teardrops," and C.J. had never felt a song more true.

By morning, Momma had softened just enough to agree to Mae's spending the night at their house. After supper, the girls headed for the Wilsons' lake. Flat on their backs on the bank, they watched clouds drift across the evening sky in the fading light. Mae pointed left and right, drawing comparisons to party dresses and corsages. C.J. thought the clouds looked like buses but pretended cheerfulness.

Three weeks until the big sendoff for Mae, and the days would all tick by until there was really only one more thing to count: minutes alone with Mae. They'd have to head back soon now, if only because the mosquitoes would start biting. "I'm gonna miss you something fierce," C.J. blurted.

"You're gonna talk Miz Sadie into letting you send that application come next spring, right?"

The truth was C.J. still couldn't imagine leaving her family to live in any white person's house. But she supposed anything was possible. "I reckon I'll wait for you to come home, waving your money and telling your stories, before I decide for sure."

"You got to get it *mailed* before the deadline," Mae snapped.

"Well, sure. But I'll see you at Christmas. That oughta be plenty of time for convincing Momma." Mae began to fidget with her shoelace, untying and tying it repeatedly. "How much time you think you'll get off for the holidays?"

"That's hard to say. But C.J. In the domestic program . . ." Mae's voice was fading like the light.

"Spit it out!"

"Okay. We can't leave Chicago—except of course for emergencies—until we worked there a year."

C.J. swatted at a mosquito. "Why didn't you tell me?"

"I was afraid it'd make you not wanna go. And you'd get upset."

C.J. nodded. She could understand being afraid and wanting to protect someone. "Aren't you scared to go? I mean Chicago must be awful big. And the people won't be like folks here, knowing how to behave to stay safe."

"Don't worry, C.J. I'm gonna do fine." Mae picked up a stone and skipped it across the water. "I reckon I am a little scared about going. But, truth is, I'm more scared not to." She stood then and dusted off the seat of her shorts.

If they went back now, the being absolutely alone would start right here. C.J. reached out and put her hand on Mae's sneaker.

"There's something I haven't told you either." She suddenly needed Mae to know. Somehow, with Mae far away but knowing, C.J. might not feel so alone.

Mae dropped back down, cross-legged, onto the grass. She stared out at the water, but C.J. could feel her listening. "Remember when I told you how the reverend dragged me up into the church?"

"You said he didn't hurt you. *Oh, C.J.*" Mae shuddered.

"He scared me near about to death. But, Mae, I told you about that, instead of what was really eating at me."

C.J. breathed slowly and tried to imagine she was a little girl again, walking the Wilson farm in her daddy's protective shadow or playing with Mae. Able to safely share whatever small worries she had, to feel her burdens carried off like field mice by the owls.

"The meetings I work . . . those men are the worst. I try not to look, but in my dreams I feel their eyes on me and hear them laughing." She told Mae what each night was like and, finally, what she'd heard through the forgotten door and what Mr. Corrigan said as she stared at his boots. "They trashed up Mr. Bishop's store on Christmas Eve. Remember? But they said they wouldn't hurt anybody, and they didn't. I figure that was them testing me, wanting to know I'd never talk."

"Good Lord! You been working Klan meetings?" Mae's whisper seemed to ring out across the lake.

C.J. looked around, then nodded. "There's more. Mr. Corrigan's wife, she's that lady who watched us in The Mademoiselle. And she's got the crazy notion in her head she can't trust her husband with me." She went on about the night Miz Corrigan snuck home to confront her husband. "It all keeps me antsy, you know?"

"C.J., it's *you* needs to be on that bus come June. What you gonna do?"

"Pray it doesn't get worse. And do like Momma says, don't make mistakes."

"You're acting like all that woman can do to you is ruin your reputation. But you got to know, ain't nothing meaner than a jealous woman. Mark my words. You give her time, she's gonna try something."

The moon was coming up, and the light made C.J. feel exposed. A dog barked somewhere on the farm. Mae gripped her hand.

"Promise me you'll send in your application, no matter what Miz Sadie says. You got to have a plan for getting out of here."

C.J. nodded. A plan was one thing, going against her momma quite another. "I think we'd best be getting back," she said. They ran, never letting go of each other's hands until they were back at the house.

CHAPTER 6

October 1958
Just Desserts

C.J. marked today as her eighteenth time coming to the Barneses' house since she'd seen Mae off to Chicago. She patted the pocket that held Mae's latest letter and reached into the basket for another of Mr. Barnes's shirts.

"You ever hear of a city called Chicago?" she said when Joan requested a story.

"Yes!" Joan sat up proudly. "Mommy went to college there."

"Well, that's where my best friend Mae's gone off to. She works for a family named Benton."

"Like you work for a family named Barnes?"

"Yes, but Mae lives up in their house and works there six days a week."

"Wow! I wish you lived with us. *That* would be fun."

C.J. smiled. "Anyways, on her day off, she stays at an apartment with her cousin Alinda and some other girls. They ride this train that runs on tracks up in the air. And they shop in the South Side. It's like the few blocks of Negro stores here stretched longer and wider than all of Poplar Springs."

She spritzed a sleeve, annoyed with Mae for her Chicago-this and Chicago-that letters. Didn't Mae know? C.J. was itching to hear what it was like living with a white family. And what she needed to hear most of all was how much Mae missed her. It was their senior year, and she could never have imagined hating it so much.

Joan looked up at her, then suddenly excused herself and went to the kitchen. C.J. could hear her talking to her mother but couldn't quite make it out. Then Miz Barnes said, "I think you should get started on your homework, sweetheart. I'll help you after dinner."

She reckoned family was pretty much all she had now. She dragged the iron back and forth, humming "They Can't Take That Away from Me," from her daddy's favorite Charlie Parker album. As she reached for a hanger, she noticed Miz Barnes leaning against the door jamb, smiling.

"Come take a break, dear."

The radio was on, but the kitchen looked like Miz Barnes was having a tea party and no one had shown up. A layer cake with crunchy golden icing sat in the center of the table. China plates and cups, silver, napkins, glasses, sugar and cream, a coffee pot on a trivet, and a pitcher of milk gathered around the cake.

"Please, sit with me while Andy's napping. That child still loves his naps. I wonder if that will change when he turns three in a few months."

C.J. stared at the thick wedge Miz Barnes put on her plate. Up closer, the golden stuff appeared to be pecans and coconut.

"I hope you like the cake. It's called German chocolate."

"German?" Making foreign food was no way for Miz Barnes to fit in with the neighborhood ladies. C.J. had overheard Miz Harwell more than once talking on the phone about how Miz Barnes's tea roses put everyone in the garden club to shame.

"Oh, it's not *from* Germany. That's the name of the baking chocolate. You can't open a ladies' magazine lately without seeing a recipe. I'm thinking of making it when it's my turn to host the garden club."

She poured C.J. a glass of milk and reached for the coffee pot. Slowly. As if feeling for it in the dark.

"Is something wrong, Miz Barnes?"

"Now, eat. You're looking so thin lately." Miz Barnes managed to pour the coffee. "It's just . . . His Holiness, Pope Pius the twelfth, died today."

"Ma'am?"

"The Holy Father, dear. The head of the Catholic Church, in Rome. I feel the loss, but no more so than the world. I remember when the Israeli Philharmonic Orchestra performed Beethoven's Seventh Symphony at the Vatican. Israel was grateful for His Holiness's help in protecting Jews from Hitler."

"I'm sorry," C.J. said, not understanding any more after Miz Barnes's explanation.

"Well, it seems we're both a bit down today." That must be what Joan had been telling Miz Barnes.

"Yes'm," C.J. admitted. "My best friend Mae's gone off to Chicago. I'm just missing her, I reckon."

"Ah, Chicago." Miz Barnes's eyes brightened. "That's where I went to college. Is that what your friend is doing?"

"No'm." C.J. dabbed at her mouth with her napkin to cover her smile.

"Now I do understand missing your best friend. I know how hard it can be to make a new one, especially in a new place. I'm sure Mae is missing you, too."

The radio suddenly got louder. "Holy cow!" screamed a man who talked a bit like Miz Barnes. "We're FOB!"

"Yes! Full of Braves!" Miz Barnes jumped up to turn up the volume. "My Braves have loaded the bases. I do so want them to beat the Yankees and take the series."

"You got a favorite?" C.J. asked. "My daddy got a ball once, in New Orleans, signed by Johnny Bissant."

"I'm quite fond of Warren Spahn. But that Negro Henry Aaron is awfully good."

"You ever seen him play, that Mr. Aaron?"

"No, I left Wisconsin before the team moved to Milwaukee, when Mr. Barnes was in medical school." Miz Barnes sounded wistful. "Have you ever seen that fellow who signed your ball?"

"No'm—"

The talking man became very excited again. Miz Barnes held her breath, then let it out in a sigh. "Turley got him. It's still two-one,

Yankees." She turned the volume back down. "More milk?"

"No, thank you, ma'am. I did enjoy the snack, but I'd best get back to the ironing."

"Today is just not a day for—" Andy had begun to wail. "All right, then."

Each time C.J. passed the kitchen carrying finished laundry, she thought Miz Barnes's attention to little Andy wandered a bit more. "Could I watch the baby while you listen to your game, Miz Barnes?" she finally asked.

Miz Barnes's shoulders slumped. "How thoughtful. But I'm afraid it's all over. The Yankees are the world champions. We had them three games to one and just handed it to them on a plate."

"Well, then, I'll just do my dusting."

"No. I have a much better idea. It might just cheer us both up."

She handed over Andy and headed for the living room. C.J. followed, hoping she wouldn't bring out more books. She was shocked to see her take a seat at the piano and arrange her skirt. Each time C.J. dusted the piano, she found its keyboard lid down, until she forgot to wonder who, if anyone, ever played it.

Without looking at any music, Miz Barnes played the song C.J. had been humming earlier. Not only could she play, but her fingers sped across the keys with such energy that Charlie Parker himself might have been accompanying her on his saxophone. She played as if to say there was something deep down inside she would hold onto.

✳   ✳   ✳

The windows of the Evanses' house were thrown wide, letting the sound of Charlie Parker and his sax carry out to the porch where Daddy and Momma rocked. Metairie was in Meridian with her boyfriend, George, visiting his family. The woodsy sweet smell of ribs slow-cooking in the yard drifted inside. C.J. stirred the black-eyed peas they ate every New Year's Day for luck, thinking maybe 1959 would be the year.

"What's this song called again?" her brother asked. He'd wandered into the kitchen and begun lifting lids, hoping to get early tastes of dinner.

He and Metairie were both named by their daddy. At nineteen, Daddy had enlisted in the U.S. Army, on the promise of seeing another part of the country and learning a skill. Stationed at Camp Leroy Johnson in New Orleans, he lived in barracks with other Negroes and took orders from a white sergeant. Their non-combat unit provided support to regular troops. Her daddy felt lucky to be selected for a construction crew, even though he'd lost the tip of his left pinky in an accident. Yet New Orleans, so similar to Mississippi in heat and humidity and conditions for Negroes, struck his ears differently. He fell in love with the rhythm of New Orleans jazz and the melody of the suburb named Metairie. When he heard the new style of Charles Christopher "Bird" Parker, though, Daddy switched his allegiance for the first and only time to what became known as bebop.

"It's 'White Christmas,'" C.J. said.

"I thought Charlie Parker was a Negro."

"You know he is."

"Wonder why he'd be wanting a white Christmas?"

Why, indeed, when a Negro Christmas could be so wonderful? Like this past week with her family. No work, no white people, no worries.

Even before the holidays, Mr. Corrigan had eased C.J.'s mind about the possibility of his wife sneaking back home again during a meeting and haunting her in the kitchen. He'd started driving Miz Corrigan to her momma's himself shortly before the men arrived. Then, with the baby and the holidays coming, the meetings had stopped altogether.

C.J. smiled at Charlie. "It's the snow, baby boy—"

The phone shattered the serenity like a rock crashing through the window. Charlie Parker played on. His namesake looked up at C.J. for an answer. She thought to ignore the phone, but it jangled insistently.

"Hello?"

"C.J.?" said a man's voice.

"No!" She reached over to swat Charlie as he tried to sneak a cookie, and the phone tumbled from the counter with a clang.

"Then call her to the phone," the man yelled over the noise, and she finally recognized the voice. It had that irritated tone Mr. Corrigan used on his wife.

"I mean, yessir, this is C.J."

"Well, all right, then. I need you every week."

"Time to eat!" Daddy called.

Momma held the door while he squeezed through with a pan piled high with ribs, like a skinny Santa ho-ho-hoing down the chimney with presents. C.J. made shushing signals.

"Are you there?" Mr. Corrigan said.

"Yessir." C.J. put her apron to her mouth. Her father made the best ribs in Mississippi. But the thought of working a meeting every week turned her stomach.

"For cleaning and such," Mr. Corrigan explained. "Since the baby, my wife could use some help. And I—uh—trust you."

The music sounded twisted and squeezed, like the hand-cranked, hand-me-down phonograph from the Wilsons had wound down in the middle of the song. C.J. opened her mouth to say she was so sorry, but she was already working every day.

"Miz Harwell says you don't work for anybody else on Fridays."

C.J. looked at the Grogan's Feed and Seed calendar tacked up on the wall. Nothing on its pages except the store advertisement, names of the months, and dates. Five minutes ago she'd have said the calendar was as full of hope as the New Year. Now, imagining Buddy and Nadine Corrigan written over and over again on each page made the Friday squares look like cages.

❊   ❊   ❊

The woman who answered the Corrigans' door the day after New Year's was recognizable only by her snake-eyed scowl. She wore blue jeans and one of her husband's faded shirts. A strand of dirty hair had come loose from her ponytail. Her face was bare of makeup.

"Buddy's left you a note." Miz Corrigan had to shout over Elvis belting out "Blueberry Hill." She stomped off to the den.

C.J. glanced at the living room. Scattered among movie magazines and overflowing ashtrays, she counted two pacifiers, three nearly empty baby bottles, one can of talcum, and one highball glass.

Elvis stuttered as the arm of the phonograph was yanked up. Then he sang even louder. C.J. glanced in the den as she rounded the corner to the kitchen. Miz Corrigan was on the floor doing sit-ups to "Mean Woman Blues."

The kitchen looked like her momma's well-tended garden overrun with weeds. C.J. sifted through the clutter on the counters, finally spotting an envelope addressed to her.

My wife has not been well since the baby came, Mr. Corrigan had written on the piece of paper inside. *Put some order to the place the best you can today.*

C.J. stuffed the note and envelope in her pocket. Soon, the washer hummed, Formica sparkled from beneath caked-on baby cereal, and dishes moved from the sink to the rack. When the washer stopped, she took the clothes to the backyard. Looking up now and then as she clipped a clothespin to the line, she tried to see the kitchen from the outside in, through the door whose window let her watch the night sky during the meetings.

How odd, she thought, passing through the kitchen on her way to the bathroom. She was almost positive that she'd left her purse on the chair, not the counter. She gathered cleaning supplies and bent over the toilet. As she lifted the seat, she felt eyes boring into her.

"What'd the note say?" Miz Corrigan demanded.

C.J. kept her head down. If Mr. Corrigan wanted his wife to know, he probably wouldn't have sealed the envelope. What could she say that wouldn't be a lie or offend or, worse yet, make the woman even more suspicious? "He said to help out the best I can." She looked up. "Is there anything you especially need done?"

Miz Corrigan studied her nails, then stuck them in C.J.'s face. She nearly gasped at the wreck, so unlike the hands that had flashed before her at The Mademoiselle that day.

"What I *need* is a manicure. Maybe lunch at the club. Things the way they used to be."

"Yes'm."

C.J. waited for her sneakered feet to clomp back toward the front of the house, then attacked the toilet. She was hunched over the tub, sprinkling Comet, when the baby started crying from the bedroom down the hall. With each minute Miz Corrigan didn't come, she scrubbed harder. Finally, the pitiful sound, so much like Charlie when he'd had the colic, was too much to bear.

In his crib, the baby flailed, red-faced and angry. She checked his diaper, then carried him to the rocker. Holding him belly down on her lap, she rubbed his back and hummed. The crying became muffled little sounds, then stopped altogether.

"That's a good boy," she cooed.

A shadow darkened the blue and yellow rag rug. C.J.'s head jerked up. "My little brother had the colic, too, ma'am," she stammered. "This stopped him fussing most all the time. I could show—"

"I'm sure I've *already* seen quite enough."

Gently, she laid the sleeping boy back in his crib and tucked the soft yellow blanket around him. "I'll just be getting back to my work, then." She took a step, but Miz Corrigan blocked the doorway. C.J. stiffened at the smell of whiskey.

"So you aim to make my baby yours, too?" Miz Corrigan hissed.

"No'm!"

Miz Corrigan dropped one shoulder, allowing her to squeeze past. She hurried back to the bathroom and scoured the tub until it gleamed, until she could see herself rather than Miz Corrigan.

Mae was right that there was nothing meaner than a jealous woman. Her prediction rang in C.J.'s ears: *Mark my words. You give her time, she's gonna try something.*

❊   ❊   ❊

It was late January, and the day's grayness was already being swallowed by the night. The wind chased its tail like a dog, winding through the bare-branched trees and around the Evanses' house. But the wood-burning stove made the kitchen toasty. C.J.'s momma had her shoes off and her feet up on a pillow on one of the kitchen chairs. C.J. knew her arthritis was bothering her, especially in her fingers. But Momma pushed and pulled the needle through a worn sock and hummed "Safe in the Arms of Jesus." She called doing the family's mending "resting," after a week on her feet at the Wilsons'.

Eight dollars the Wilsons paid her momma. C.J. boiled inside at the worthlessness of a high school diploma when she could make thirty dollars a week in Chicago. Knowing about the First World War seemed even more pointless. She nudged her history book aside and hunched over her notebook. She wrote the number thirty, underlined. Then she multiplied by fifty-two, twice to be sure. That was one thousand five hundred sixty dollars. Underline, exclamation point.

"What you ciphering?" Momma asked. "I thought you were doing history."

"Momma, has Miz Willis mentioned how Mae's been sending money home?"

"Twelve dollars a month." Momma shook her head. "Don't know how that makes up for having her only child run off and leave her."

"I know I could send more, really help the family."

"I'd worry myself sick. You up there, living with white folks." Her momma's needle worked faster, in and out.

"Miz Willis say anything bad happened?"

"You think that girl would let on if it did?"

"Maybe Mae hasn't said anything because folks up there are nice, like Miz Barnes. She went to college in Chicago."

"Humph. Fool woman doesn't know better than to—"

"Sometimes . . ." C.J. looked at her momma, willing her to understand. "The thing we think is keeping us safe is the thing we ought to worry most about."

Momma stopped in the middle of a stitch. "Sweet Jesus! Baby, has someone hurt you?"

"No, ma'am." C.J. got up to hug away the pain in Momma's eyes. "But the danger seems like it'll always be with me."

Her momma's body relaxed with relief. "You're a smart girl. I know you can get on in the world we live in. And family ought to stay together. Mae's done nearly broke her momma's heart, running off so far away. Can't even come for a visit for a whole year."

"Momma." It was C.J.'s best argument, and she'd saved it for last. "I could even start setting aside money for Charlie for college."

"The child is in the sixth grade! What he needs is his big sister around, keeping him on the straight and narrow. Lord knows he's a handful for your daddy and me. And Metairie's done gone all swimmy-headed over that boy George."

Through the window a squirrel scampered from branch to branch of the chinaberry tree, as if it, too, were searching for something else that might get through to her momma. When C.J. sighed and snapped her book shut, Momma added, "If your homework's done, I could use help."

C.J. fished in the pile of sad black socks. "I'd just as soon do one of Daddy's if it's all the same. Charlie's are too big a mess."

"But Charlie's are the ones need fixing."

As C.J. darned, she counted stitches in groups of thirty. And she recalled Miz Corrigan's meanness and Mae's warning.

Late that night, when the others had gone to sleep, she crept back to the kitchen. Outside, a dog barked and the branches of the chinaberry tree scratched against the window. She set to work filling out the application for the domestic program.

❄   ❄   ❄

On the last Friday in February, Miz Corrigan answered the door looking ready to go out or have a girlfriend over, except that her husband had the car and her black Capri pants and low-cut pink sweater fit her like white on rice. C.J. followed her through the spotless living room, past the equally clean den, to the kitchen. It practically gleamed.

"Y'all need me today?" She had a pounding headache and would just as soon go home.

"Of course," Miz Corrigan sniffed. "For once, I'd like the bathroom and bedrooms done right. And if the baby cries, well—" She waved her arm dismissively. "Do whatever that is you do. I'll be busy entertaining."

C.J. checked the bedrooms. They looked like a tornado had come through, leaving little standing but two baskets of clean laundry next to the ironing board. She was scrubbing the tub in tiny swirling motions when the doorbell rang.

Miz Corrigan almost instantly appeared overhead. "Show my guest to the kitchen," she snapped.

C.J. hurried to the front door and opened it. She blinked, more in response to the man standing there than to the afternoon sun. It was the new man from Mr. Corrigan's meetings.

"Bobby Ray," Miz Corrigan gushed from behind her. "How kind of you to stop by. Come right this way." She beckoned for C.J. to follow.

As they moved through the hall, Miz Corrigan swayed her hips. In the kitchen, she leaned across the counter next to the ice bucket and bottle of Early Times. Her pose made it nearly impossible for her breasts to stay below the neckline of her sweater.

"I do believe this is your favorite?"

He hitched up his trousers and squared his shoulders. "Indeed it is."

Her laugh said he was the funniest, cleverest man on earth. "Two whiskeys on the rocks then, girl."

While C.J. fixed the drinks, Miz Corrigan flirted. "Now how are things at the power company, Bobby Ray? I know they were so smart to promote you when the old manager retired." After C.J. handed them each a glass, Miz Corrigan put a hand on his arm and steered him toward the back door. Through the window, C.J. could see two chaise lounges set up by a small table.

When the baby began to howl, Miz Corrigan purred, "Do see to my sweet child, won't you, C.J.?"

On C.J.'s lap in the rocker, the baby thrashed. Against her shoulder, as she crisscrossed the rag rug patting and singing, he cried even louder. Finally, she took a light blanket, folded down one corner, and laid him on his back. She pulled the corner near his left hand across his body and tucked the edge under his back on the right side. Then she pulled the bottom corner up under his chin and brought the loose corner over his right arm and tucked it under in back.

He looked up at her, startled, and tried to wiggle loose. She was about to undo the swaddling, or try it again under the arms so his hands would be free, when he stopped crying. Gingerly, she laid him in his crib and backed away. Within moments he was sleeping.

But all the crying had only made her head hurt more. She really needed an aspirin. As she dug in her purse, she saw the envelope addressed to Mae. Inside, with a letter, was her completed application for the domestic program. The letter asked Alinda to write a recommendation for her, then send it on to the agency. She would mail it first thing tomorrow. She didn't want to work another minute for this shameless woman who would do the very thing she was accusing her husband of.

※   ※   ※

While she waited to hear back about her application, the first daffodils of March had sprung up outside the Thornhearts' kitchen window. Golden yellow, much like the cake that rested guiltily on the counter. Too nervous to eat, she eyed the perfectly frosted cake. Next to the pots and pans that held potatoes, okra, fried chicken, and biscuits, it seemed as foreign as Germany. Why couldn't she have just been grateful for the unending sameness of her Saturdays? No, she'd wanted change so badly, especially for Alan, that she'd asked Miz Thornheart if there was a dessert she could make.

Miz Thornheart had cringed. "We don't often eat dessert. The reverend has his routine."

But C.J. had persisted. "Another lady I work for made a delicious cake. She let me try it. It's called German chocolate."

"Ah, yes. I saw a recipe for that in a magazine at the beauty shop. The photo did make it look fabulous." Miz Thornheart looked up and to her left, as if remembering. "And my men—both my men—love coconut and chocolate. It's another thing they have in common. We . . . seem to have forgotten . . ."

"I was thinking"—C.J. jumped into the space left by Miz Thornheart's trail of words—"a good time to serve would be when you say, 'Now who'll have the last biscuit?' "

Now she was wondering if she'd made a mistake. "Charlotte," she heard the reverend saying in the dining room. "Have you made your birthday wish list yet?"

"Oh, Daddy. You sound like it's Christmas and I'm waiting on Santa."

"Nonsense. The day my princess was born was the best day of my life. Now tell Daddy what you're hoping for."

"Let me think." C.J. could picture Charlotte tossing her pale hair and affecting innocence with her eyes. "Well, maybe some new clothes."

"You got to think bigger than that, baby. Lord knows your brother would be the first to take advantage." And so began Reverend Thornheart's habitual cruelty toward his son. "How about a phone for your room?"

"Who'll have—" Miz Thornheart's voice cracked. She cleared her throat. "Who'll have the last biscuit?"

C.J. picked up the tray with the cake, plates, and a serving knife. She gripped it so tightly her fingers stung. In the dining room, she set it before the reverend's wife.

"Who wants cake?" Miz Thornheart asked as if she said it all the time, but her voice trembled pitifully.

C.J. served the first plate to the reverend. But, breaking order, she gave the second to Alan. The reverend sat slack-jawed, staring first at his cake, then at C.J.

"It's chocolate with coconut," Miz Thornheart rushed to explain. "For my men. Remember?" Her eyes had a pleading look.

C.J. watched anxiously while the reverend forked one bite, then another. Charlotte and Miz Thornheart took tiny, tentative bites. But Alan consumed his dessert with an interest C.J. had never seen.

"May I please have another piece?" He held out his plate.

"Take it away," stormed Reverend Thornheart. "Gluttony is a sin."

C.J. moved to clear the reverend's place, but he snatched up his plate. "I must get to my sermon right away," he said as he scurried off, taking the rest of his slice with him.

C.J. thought she might faint. The passage from Hebrews played in her head, the one Reverend Thornheart had spoken every Saturday she'd worked here, but had been distracted from tonight: "My son, despise not the chastening of the Lord, nor faint when thou art rebuked of him . . ."

Chairs scraped against the floor as the rest of the family stood to leave.

As Alan passed, he smiled at C.J. "Thank you. That was the nicest meal I can remember us having in this house."

❋ ❋ ❋

On Tuesday after school, C.J. rode the bus uptown and got off in front of the power company. Inside, the air-conditioning was already running against the spring heat.

"Afternoon, ma'am," she said to the clerk, a girl surely not much older than her. "The bill's in the name of Lewis Evans." She handed over their most recent statement and began counting out bills and coins.

The girl's expression soured as she pointed at the ledger. "Y'all got to pay every month, you know. There's four here unpaid." She jabbed her adding machine. "That comes to—"

"Yes'm." The Evans family knew enough folks who'd been harassed in similar ways that C.J.'s momma always kept receipts, and they made a habit of bringing a few when they came to pay their bill. "I have receipts for those months." C.J. handed them over.

The clerk looked back at the ledger. "My goodness. I've gone and read this wrong. It's eight months y'all haven't paid."

C.J. shook her head nervously as she took back her receipts. "That's all I have with me."

"Mr. Morrison," sang out the clerk. "I need you to see to this here girl."

A man swaggered over with his chest puffed out like he was fixing to fend off a mean dog. "Darlene, honey, how can I help?"

C.J. stared at Miz Corrigan's visitor, the man she'd called Bobby Ray, the newest member of Poplar Springs's Klan. Mr. Morrison glanced at C.J.'s money on the counter and twisted his mouth into a sneer. "Y'all owe way more than that. Wonder what I ought to do about this."

"I can bring in the other—" C.J. started, but Mr. Morrison talked right over her.

"What you think, Darlene?"

"Simplest thing would be to turn off the power," the girl said.

"That's a thought." He seemed to ponder her suggestion. "But I'm thinking I need to go see your daddy about this, offer him the courtesy of paying up."

C.J. struggled not to show her fear.

"Or, maybe your daddy's boss? Let him know what kind of a slacker he has working for him."

Now, she began to tremble. But maybe that would be okay. Mr. Wilson would tell Mr. Morrison that her daddy was honest.

"Yeah, that's what I oughta do. Who's your daddy's boss, girl?"

C.J. stammered.

"Now, as I recollect, it's Ernie Wilson. He and I go way back."

"Please, sir, can I pay this one bill, then bring in the other receipts?" C.J. tried once more.

"Sure, we'll take part today. But you got to bring the rest tomorrow." He handed over Darlene's adding machine tally and a receipt for one month.

"Yessir." C.J. took both and ran, equally certain Mr. Morrison intended to ignore any other receipts and that her family could never come up with so much money by tomorrow. She made her way almost blindly toward the bus stop two blocks away.

"Hey, C.J.," someone said. She turned to face Alan Thornheart. The sight of him caused the tears she'd managed to hold back to begin to flow.

"What's wrong?" he said gently.

They stood, just the two of them, on the street. For months C.J. had wished she could talk to Alan, offer him suggestions for making things easier with his father. Now she could barely explain what had happened.

He looked down, then back at her. "Seems like Buddy's got one of his boys bothering y'all."

"Mr. Corrigan?" She shook her head vigorously. "He's got no cause to do something like that."

"Didn't think so. But the deacons' wives do carry on after services." Alan's eyes were kind. "You know, how Miz Corrigan let the house go and all after the baby came. And Miz Harwell urged Mr. Corrigan to have you help out more . . ."

She held her breath, waiting for him to say more, to bring up the meetings. But maybe he didn't know everything.

"Must be that wife of his, then," Alan said, almost to himself. "Must've gone off her rocker some. Come with me. I know what to do."

"Hey, Darlene, Mr. Morrison. How y'all doing?" Alan said when he and C.J. were back inside the power company. "Look who I ran into." He used a voice she wished he would try at home—soothing and sure, subservient and suggestive all at the same time. "You know, the reverend thinks C.J. can part the waters. He'll just be so pleased if I can help straighten out this little misunderstanding."

Mr. Morrison sputtered at first, but it wasn't long before he caved. Alan waited patiently while Darlene stamped the ledger "Paid in Full" and handed over a receipt. Then he smiled. "See y'all on Sunday."

Mr. Morrison's eyebrows pinched tightly together, but he forced them back. "Yes. See y'all in church on Sunday, then."

Outside, C.J. thanked Alan profusely. "I don't know what we'd have done if . . . Well." She smiled. "I'd best get to the bus now."

Alan followed her and sat with her on the bench until her bus came. At first, neither of them spoke. Then Alan said, "One day we'll both be free of him. 'Til then, I draw strength from watching you."

She looked at him, unbelieving, just as the bus pulled up. He shook his head insistently. "I wouldn't say it if it wasn't true. And another thing I believe is things'll be better for you now, with Buddy and Nadine."

"The way you handled that in there . . ." She stood to go. "Thank you again for your help."

"You're welcome. Thank *you* for that cake."

As she climbed on board, C.J. felt a tiny chill run up her spine. Though she knew the likes of the Corrigans all too well, she wanted to believe what Alan had done would really make things better. She wanted to hope, and she had to start somewhere.

CHAPTER 7

April 1959
From This Place

While C.J. cut perfect white bread triangles, Little Miss Sunbeam smiled at her from the bag. She wondered if the ladies coming to Miz Thornheart's tea were all like that, nice when they were little and then...

Reverend Thornheart came through the kitchen for his car keys. "Let Miz Harwell take the lead," he was saying to Miz Thornheart as she nipped at his heels. "This one's tricky."

C.J. was suddenly listening more closely. She'd served at these teas for wives of men being considered as deacons before. Usually there wasn't much to them.

"Need to make it look like both men got a shot," Reverend Thornheart continued. "But Buddy'll be the one who—"

C.J. dropped the bread knife with a clatter.

Reverend Thornheart glared at her. He turned back to his wife. "Just see can you manage this girl and keep the ladies comfortable."

"Yes, Reverend," Miz Thornheart said as he hurried to the door.

C.J. had somehow spread the spiced cream cheese without ripping the triangles by the time the bell rang. On the porch, Miz Harwell stood front and center with several of the other deacons' wives.

While Miz Harwell organized them before the candidates' wives arrived, C.J. arranged serving trays. She worried what Miz Corrigan might do. But if her husband became a deacon, her standing in Poplar Springs would go way up. She could only hope Miz Corrigan's desire to impress would put her on her best behavior.

When the doorbell rang again, Miz Corrigan waited with a nervous-looking lady C.J. didn't know. Miz Corrigan had fought her way back to her pre-pregnancy figure, but she bore no resemblance to the tacky-looking woman who'd sweet-talked Mr. Morrison into harassing C.J. Her nail polish and lipstick were subdued. Her hat, suit, and shoes were all perfectly coordinated. Her single strand of pearls said sophistication. Without seeming to notice C.J., Miz Corrigan brushed past her and the other lady and made a grand entrance into the parlor. C.J. hurried to bring in the tea tray.

"Of course, both of these fine ladies joining us today are longtime members of First Baptist," Miz Harwell said as C.J. poured. "But we're doing the Lord's work, helping to select our newest deacon."

"Amen," said one of the deacons' wives. The others nodded.

"So," Miz Harwell continued, "let's pretend we don't know each other. I'll ask each of you to tell us about your husband. Nadine, dear, please go first."

"Oh, my. Where should I start?" Miz Corrigan was trying to sound light and breezy, but there was an edge to her voice. When C.J. held out a cup, Miz Corrigan drew in her breath, almost as visibly as she had snatched away her hand that day in The Mademoiselle. "Buddy"—she smiled her way around the room—"is so good at organizing and getting folks to go along. He could serve the Lord well as a deacon."

C.J. passed around sandwiches and teacakes and went to the dining room to wait, in case Miz Thornheart needed anything else. Through the window, the heads of climbing roses peeked above the porch rail. Yellow like those in the Barneses' yard, causing C.J. to wonder about white ladies and tea parties. Did Mae's white lady have tea parties? Was she like Miz Barnes, or cold and hateful like Miz Corrigan?

If her application was accepted—and the decision point was just weeks away—what would her new white lady be like? And—oh, Lord—how would she tell her momma?

Voices caused her to look up and out into the hall, where someone blocked Miz Corrigan's path. A fringe of white hair towered over one shoulder of her fine sherbet-green suit.

"Alan, honey," she said with the faintest hint of impatience. "I've just stepped out for a second to use the ladies' room."

"How nice that C.J. is helping y'all," he said casually.

"Of course." Miz Corrigan shifted her weight to the other high-heeled foot.

He reached out to touch the wall, taking over even more of the space between her and the bathroom. "It's like I was telling someone recently. Now who—oh, yes, Mr. Morrison up at the power company. My *father* thinks C.J. can part the waters."

"Alan, this has been a treat. I declare you're all grown up and handsome as all get out." Miz Corrigan had slipped into her Mr. Morrison voice. She leaned in close and laughed. "I'm sure a gentleman like you knows it's not proper to keep a lady waiting." She ducked under his arm and disappeared.

When Alan glanced her way, C.J. hid a shy smile. Was this what he'd meant at the bus stop about things getting better for her with the Corrigans? As unpredictable as Miz Corrigan was, his defense of her might send the woman into another tizzy. But it touched her that he would go out of his way to stand up for her again. She wanted to put her faith in him. And so, seeing Miz Corrigan teetering on the brink of becoming a deacon's wife, she let herself hope.

But on Saturday hope seemed beyond reach. As C.J. pulled the makings of the Thornhearts' dinner from the refrigerator, she recalled a letter where Mae explained how the domestic program moved the girls around several times during the first couple of years, weeding out those who couldn't adjust. Could their tests be any harder than what she had already faced? How wonderful to be able to move on so quickly. In Poplar Springs, there seemed no escape from year after year of Saturdays.

As she ate her own dinner, she pictured the serving dishes. New potatoes, okra and tomatoes, fried chicken, biscuits. No cake. She almost didn't hear the reverend signaling an end to the meal. So softly he spoke.

"My son, despise not the chastening of the Lord, nor faint when thou art rebuked of him." The way he had never spoken those words before, almost tenderly. "For whom the Lord loveth he chasteneth, and scourgeth every son whom he receiveth."

On her last trip between the dining room and kitchen, as she reached for the remaining serving dish, the reverend grabbed her wrist. "Behold the hypocrite!" he shouted. "Whom I have paid what is right and fair, so has she betrayed my trust, turning my son against me. Yet, in a little while, she will be among us no more."

Miz Thornheart gasped. Despite herself, C.J. stared at Alan. When he opened his mouth, his father brandished his hand to silence him.

"Much like a household, which relies on the wisdom of the head of the family, so is our relationship with God. Whether the question is how a man's dinner is to be served, or who sits in the front of the bus, or who will perish by his own hand because he has not been taught how to behave, God shows us the way."

The reverend, Charlotte, Miz Thornheart, then Alan. Alan always last, unless there was cake. Rosa Parks and young Emmett Till. Deacons like Buddy Corrigan, with wives like Nadine.

"Yessir," she finally said when he stared at her, unrelenting.

With his free hand, the reverend took coins from his pocket and flung them on the table. Everyone stared as the four quarters and two dimes spun and finally came to rest. C.J.'s pay for six hours at this house.

"We will no longer be needing your services!"

He released her wrist so forcefully that she stumbled backward. Suddenly, Alan was speaking. "Oh that I were made judge in the land, that every man which hath any suit or cause might come unto me, and I would do him justice," he quoted from the book of Samuel, looking at her with his kind eyes and somehow restoring her balance and reminding her to breathe.

"Silence!" Reverend Thornheart roared.

But his son stood, gathered the coins, and walked toward C.J. He moved as naturally as if, once he reached her side, they would wait together for a bus. He spoke from Exodus. "Remember this day . . . for by strength of hand the Lord brought you out from this place."

He took her arm and guided her from the dining room, stopping so she could gather her purse. She noted that his grip was at once strong and gentle and believed absolutely that it could anchor her in a storm.

At the door, she met his eyes. Hers expressed fear for him. His held a stricken look. "I only wanted to help. But all I've done is cost you your job."

"I'm grateful to you for trying." She wanted to offer him some hope, as he had her. But she knew the improbability that his father would change.

He smiled sadly. "Goodbye, C.J. One day, I'll be free, too."

*　　*　　*

On her first unemployed Saturday in nearly two years, C.J. wandered outside to the garden, the place that gave her momma purpose and hope for the future, if only for the next harvest.

"The okra and tomatoes look good," Momma said. She was wearing her "resting" dress—colored soft brown like a deer and looser fitting than her weekday work dresses—and an apple-green bib apron with giant pockets. "Maybe I'll fix them."

"Oh, Momma." She felt her stomach churn. "Could you make your tomato bacon pie instead? I don't think I can look at another plate with okra and tomatoes on anyone's Saturday dinner table ever again."

"'Course I can, honey."

C.J. pushed the tire swing in the big oak tree, imagining her little-girl self being sent skyward by her daddy, happy and carefree. And then she saw herself falling from the swing, alone on the ground, needing comfort. This week, she'd gone to work for each of her other employers, ready for them to fire her too. She'd wished Mr. Corrigan would let her go. But he'd said nothing, and Miz Harwell had said nothing. Reverend Thornheart had always said that if he were to tell others of her attitude, she would have no work in this town. And C.J. somehow knew she could never be sure when the other shoe would drop.

Only Miz Barnes had brought it up. She'd overheard Miz Corrigan talking at the beauty parlor. Miz Barnes then asked C.J. to work for them on Saturdays, too. Frightened for her if she got in the middle of it all, C.J. had wracked her brain for what to say. She'd finally thanked her and asked for time to think it over.

A dog barked, sending a chill down her spine, reminding her of the night she told Mae about the Klan and Miz Corrigan's crazy suspicions. Mae had been right that there was nothing meaner than a jealous woman. It had to have been Miz Corrigan or Mr. Morrison who told Reverend Thornheart how Alan tried to help her.

A slight breeze caused the leaves to rustle. They were turned silvery side up, waiting for the coming rain. The smells of freshly cut grass and everything blooming at once hung in the thick air. She pushed through and on, across the yard and up to the cluster of mailboxes on the main road. She tapped the side of theirs and listened. The likes of Mr. Corrigan's men had been known to put rattlers in folks' boxes. Snakes would strike the second they saw the light. Hearing nothing, she reached in for the stack of mail.

A letter from Mae smiled up at her. Hearing Mae jabber away in her letters was the next best thing to having her right here.

But the letter was so short it was hardly a letter at all. *Good news, girl,* Mae wrote. *I passed the first test in the program! I'm moving to Skokie.*

C.J. would have to go to the library at school on Monday and try to find Skokie on a map.

I can't hardly believe I've been gone a year. It'll be so good to see Momma and them. And YOU!!! Sunday, May 31ˢᵗ. That's when I'll be home!

Just fifteen days from now!

Got to be in Skokie on Monday, June 8ᵗʰ. If our schedules work out (See, I KNOW you're gonna get accepted), we can take the bus together to Chicago.

"Don't I wish?" C.J. murmured. "You were right, about me needing a way out."

She put the tiny letter back in its envelope and sifted through the others. The second Chicago postmark jumped out at her, almost as if there'd been a rattler in the mailbox after all. This letter was from the domestic program. Her heart started racing. *Your application has been accepted.* C.J.

looked down the hill at her momma, so happy. *The Powell family expects you in Skokie on Monday, June 8th*.

Good Lord, they assumed she was coming, just like Mae! . . . *three children, ages two to seven . . . six-thirty to eight, six days a week. Mr. Powell will meet you at the Skokie station. Send bus schedule to this address . . .* The details went straight for her heart.

She trudged toward the garden, reminding herself to breathe. "Momma?" she said to her momma's bent form. "I'll be graduating in just over two weeks."

Momma straightened, looking like an overripe tomato about to burst with pride. "Then I just got me one more child to push through."

C.J. ground her heels, as if to plant herself firmly against whatever her momma would say. "Remember when I said I could help Charlie go to college?"

"You're not talking Chicago again?"

C.J. looked at her feet. A small stone rested by her shoe. A stone like the one Mae had skipped across the Wilsons' lake before she left. C.J. understood now, how Mae was scared to go but maybe more scared not to. "I *have* to, Momma." She held out the letter.

Momma swiped one hand across her apron, then took the letter. She read, mouthing the words, then stared down at the dirt that streaked the tired green fabric. She took her time before looking back at C.J. When she did, fear and hurt had shoved the pride from her eyes.

"I'm sorry, Momma. Maybe I could still say no—"

Momma shook her head. "I reckon you can't take that paper back any easier than the dress you didn't try on down on Center Street. But this mistake I can't fix." She hugged her apron full of vegetables tighter to her chest and walked to the house.

❊   ❊   ❊

It was all happening too fast. Time—from graduation two nights ago, to boarding a bus two days from now—was squeezing C.J.'s goodbyes like the jaws of the vise in her daddy's workshop. Tonight, before

Mr. and Miz Barnes got home from the movies, she had to tell her little friend she was leaving for Chicago.

Other than her family, this was the hardest farewell. Joan had held a special place in C.J.'s heart since the day she'd met her. Almost a mix of Charlie and her, she had sometimes thought. Yesterday, when Joan had ordered her to serve lemonade, she'd thought her heart might break with disappointment.

She missed her little friend already. Watching Joan toy with her food at supper, she had wanted to reach out and hug her, tell her she understood how people just make crazy mistakes sometimes. But she didn't figure that would be best for the child.

Now, standing outside with Andy while Joan whispered with the Barbie-doll girls, C.J. wanted to snatch her away and give her a good shaking. When the white pickup crept down the street, C.J. saw it before anyone. The fogging trucks didn't run outside town where she lived. When Joan's friends chased the truck and she followed, C.J. lost sight of her. She knew parents let their kids run behind the trucks all the time, but she worried. And so, grateful for the encroaching darkness, she called out, "We have to get on back now, Joan."

It was the longest time before Joan emerged from the cloud. Even then, when her friends called out to her, she ran right back to them. Finally, she moved toward C.J., walking at a snail's pace, turning repeatedly to wave one more goodbye. The air, saturated with insecticide, hung heavily between them as they retraced their steps to the house. C.J. carried little Andy, keeping his face sheltered against her chest.

She got both children bathed and ready for bed. When Andy was down, she asked Joan to come with her to the living room. They sat on the blue damask sofa where Miz Barnes had lovingly patted the book with the story of St. Joan. From her purse, C.J. pulled *Miniature Stories of the Saints, Book Four*.

"Has your momma read to you about St. Zita?" C.J. asked.

Joan shook her head.

"Well, it's a long story. So, I'll just tell it to you." She told about the girl who had gone to work as a maid at twelve, to earn money to help her family. "I was twelve, too, when I started cleaning houses. Not much older when I met you."

Wearing her white baby-doll pajamas with the rosebuds, her damp hair held back by red barrettes, Joan sat with ladylike posture, listening.

"Many of the people Zita worked for treated her badly. Worse, I reckon, than folks have treated me. But she and I both tried to do right."

"I think I know this story," Joan said. "It's about charity, isn't it?"

"You know what that is?"

"Mommy said it's about helping people. And not thinking they're bad just 'cause we don't like what they do."

C.J. reached across the couch, encircling Joan with her arm. "That sounds about right, honey." Then, as gently as she could, she explained that she was going to live where Joan's mother went to school, to make more money. She would miss Joan very much and wished things were different so she didn't have to go.

Fat teardrops leaked from Joan's eyes. "Will I ever see you again?"

C.J. hugged tighter. "Now, that's probably not up to you or me. But we're the magic girls, aren't we? Me, being born like a magic trick, and you with your magic line on the driveway. Who knows what we might do someday?"

She turned Joan to face her, then wiped away her tears and handed her the book. "Will you keep this in your room and give it back to your momma for me? Tell her it helped me, and I thank her kindly. Now, let's get you tucked in."

❈   ❈   ❈

This Sunday was already unlike most C.J. had ever known; the bus schedule meant the family hadn't made it to services at Hope Baptist. Barely mid-morning, the handkerchiefs were out, mopping away the effects of the June sun and humidity. More menacing still was the clock in the tower of the Greyhound station. Its giant minute hand raced around its face, faster and faster toward departure time.

Her arm was locked around her momma's waist. She leaned in close, smelling her skin, hearing her softly hum "Safe in the Arms of Jesus." Charlie fished for change in the coin return slots of the Coca-Cola and candy machines. Metairie held the small, weathered satchel with essentials for the two-day journey: C.J.'s toothbrush and hair things, a change of clothes and a sweater, and her Bible. At the last moment, she'd added two things from her room: a delicate wooden bird her daddy carved long ago and a dresser scarf her momma crocheted for her twelfth birthday. Next to Mae's father, C.J.'s daddy waited to load his Army footlocker into the cargo hold. The trunk held everything else C.J. owned that she might possibly use during the coming year.

Mae stood with her mother, too. They were talking, and Mae was smiling. But Mae kept checking her watch and, now and then, got to tapping her foot and picking up her small suitcase and setting it back down.

I'm really going. Blinking back tears, she reached into the pocket of her dress and fingered a quarter. She traced its hard edge, remembering the dining room table in the Thornhearts' house. From the coins the reverend scattered there, she'd saved this one to remind her there were two sides to every situation. The good and bad of her leaving. But more than two ways to look at things, two ways to act—with cruelty like Reverend Thornheart or with kindness like Alan.

The belly of the bus seemed to swallow the footlocker whole. Daddy dusted his hands on the seat of his pants and joined them. He hugged C.J. almost fiercely, then stared hard into her eyes. "Don't go nowhere alone, baby," he said. "Leastways 'til you get your bearings real good."

Alone was all C.J. could see for an eternity, but she gave him her best smile. "I'll remember, Daddy."

"All aboard!" yelled the driver, starting the hugging and kissing all over again. But this time with the knowledge that the rest had been practice for now.

C.J. embraced her sister; wiped a tear from Metairie's face. "Now where's that boy got to?"

"Here I am," Charlie said, sneaking up from behind.

"Baby boy, you mind Metairie like she's me. Or I'll be back here in two shakes to see to it myself." She smothered him with kisses until he howled in protest, then she wrapped her arms around her momma and held on for dear life. "You'll be fine," Momma said. C.J. felt the strength and forgiveness that carried in her voice and tried to believe.

"C'mon, C.J.!" Mae yelled from the head of the line.

C.J. waved to her family over her shoulder as she inched forward. Once on the bus, she had to cover her nose and mouth against the smells. Most passengers had grocery sacks with food to tide them over until they reached the Chicago station's integrated lunch counter the next morning. The bag Mae carried was crammed full of Momma's fried chicken, Miz Willis's biscuits and cookies, peaches from the yard, and Mason jars of sweet tea. But it was the fading smell of their mothers' love that nearly made C.J. sick to her stomach.

Mae had found them a seat toward the rear. C.J. crawled over her and searched for her family. The faces of those she loved grew smaller, then disappeared as the bus pulled away. It was turning onto the highway when a storm cloud came up. As windows were closed, tiny rivers trickled down the panes.

CHAPTER 8

June 1959
Settling In

As one Thursday then another passed, Joan missed C.J. like an ache. It was her fault C.J. left, she just knew it. By now, though, she was certain C.J. hadn't told her mom what she'd done. And so, she put on a good face and resumed playing with Cindy and Sally Ann.

Then came the Thursday when her mom set up the ironing board and brought in the basket of clean laundry. "Would you like to fill the sprinkler bottle?" she asked.

Joan set the bottle on the ironing board just as the doorbell rang. "Be sure to show your good manners to Annabelle," her mom reminded.

"Pleased to meet you. We're glad you'll be helping us out," Joan recited dutifully as she stared, unsmiling, at the roly-poly woman.

When Annabelle reached out to pinch a handful of her cheek, Joan determined to stay clear of her. Later, though, she wandered into the dining room.

"What you up to, child?" Annabelle asked when she spotted her peeking at the ironed laundry laid out on the table. "You should be outside playing, not watching this old woman do her work."

Joan sniffed. That was one thing she and Annabelle could agree on. She had better things to do than hang around some Negro grandmother.

When Andy cried, Joan ran to help him out of his crib. Her mom had promised to take her fabric shopping as soon as she was certain Andy was comfortable with Annabelle. Joan knew just what she wanted her new shorts set to look like, and it had to be ready for Carol's Fourth of July party in Meridian. Though she saw more of the girls from the neighborhood during the summer, Carol was her best friend at school. And with no relatives of her own nearby, she was excited about being included in one of Carol's huge family gatherings.

Andy took to Annabelle like she was his best friend, climbing right up onto her lap the minute he met her. Her mom watched while Annabelle fed Andy a snack, then suggested she take the kids into the living room. Things were going well until Andy's ball rolled out of sight. He got down on all fours with his rear end pointed skyward, looked underneath the couch and pointed. Annabelle waddled over to help. She reached under, then pulled her arm back with a shriek.

"Owie!" said Andy as the three of them watched blood spurt from Annabelle's arm.

"Mom!" Joan yelled. Now they would never make it to J. C. Penney's. C.J. would have been smarter than to stick her arm under there. Everyone knew there was a spring that hung down from the hide-away bed.

Her mom came running. She took one look, snatched a freshly ironed dress shirt, and tore it into strips. When she'd wrapped Annabelle's arm, she bundled everyone into the car.

They parked on the street in front of her dad's office, a two-story brown brick building not far from St. Stephen's. Loblolly pines shaded the yard, and a green-and-white-striped awning spanned the front of the house. Old Doc Adams had lived upstairs when the practice was his.

Her mom helped Annabelle from the backseat and began urging her up the sidewalk. Annabelle kept stopping to examine her arm. Deciding each time that there was indeed more blood, she would sway from side to side and exclaim, "Sweet Jesus, don't let me faint."

Joan took Andy's hand. He tugged and strained to see where Annabelle was going.

"What's to see?" Joan grumbled. "Her hair poufs out in back like a blue jay fixing to fight. Her skin's got more wrinkles than the laundry after she fake irons it. We're not gonna be friends with this maid."

Andy tripped on a crack and went down with a splat. Joan picked him up and struggled to carry him toward the door, soothing his tears.

"*Joan Olivia*," her mom called. "I need you to take care of your brother and follow me."

Joan peered over Andy's head, surprised to see her mom walking around the side of the building. "But why don't we go the way we always—"

"We'll go *this* way to get your dad." Her voice sounded like Andy had dragged everything out of his toy box for the tenth time and she just didn't have the energy to pick it up.

They came to a door, the bright red of a stop sign. Her mom opened it and walked right in.

"Idella," she called to the Negro behind the counter. "Bring a nurse. Annabelle's cut herself rather badly."

Joan had never seen this woman or this doctor's office before, and she couldn't understand why they weren't taking Annabelle to see her dad.

From the metal folding chairs—not wooden with the padded seats—Negro eyes were upon them. Some of the Negroes coughed or sneezed.

Idella came back with a nurse. And not just any nurse, but one of Joan's dad's.

Her mom leaned down to whisper, "Stay with Andy. Don't let him out of your sight."

Joan's eyes opened wide and she mouthed the word "Here?" But her mom and Annabelle were already disappearing after the nurse.

How long had her dad been hiding this waiting room? The linoleum looked older than Annabelle. She couldn't even find a *Time* magazine, much less the Little Golden books her dad kept in the other waiting room.

She asked Idella for a piece of paper and a pencil, then helped Andy onto one of two chairs mysteriously vacated by men who now leaned against the wall. One small Negro girl tried to toddle over to draw with him. Her mother reeled her in like a fish.

An old ceiling fan batted at the muggy June air, unable to keep much of a breeze going even with the air drifting through the open screened windows. Joan shivered. This place was spooky. Not spooky like the witch in the *Wizard of Oz*, or a noise in the dark when everyone is supposed to be asleep. More like ghosts living right with you.

And why did C.J. have to go off to Chicago? Didn't she know her place was here in Poplar Springs? Joan had made no sense of it all by the time her mom and Annabelle reappeared.

Andy ran to Annabelle. "Owie gone gone?" he asked, his face all scrunched up with concern.

"Yes, sweet cakes." She sank into a chair and pulled him close.

Go on then, Joan thought, looking at Andy. *Don't listen. You'll get hurt too.* She scuffed the toe of her shoe, feeling her anger like a monster.

❈   ❈   ❈

June and July were marked by trips to the pool with Cindy and Sally Ann, jump-rope and other games, and adventures with their Barbies. Sally Ann even included Joan at her spend-the-night party.

August brought Joan and her dad to the Neshoba County Fair in Philadelphia, Mississippi, an hour's drive away. From the main gate, they made their way to Founder's Square, the center of it all. The Barneses had come once before, but this time would be different. Big Daddy Whitehead himself had invited them to his cabin. He said the real fair happened at the cabins that were handed down from one generation to the next, where neighbors caught up on each other's families and chewed the fat about Mississippi politics.

Outside the barns, quarter horses whinnied and pranced, eager for the race. A cloud of red-clay dust swirled around them. Already perspiring, Joan felt the dust on her bare arms, tasted it as it settled in her throat.

Dozens of cabins clustered around Founder's Square. The Whiteheads' cabin sat just to the south, on the short, narrow street named Happy Hollow. Joan spotted it first. Smoke from ribs slow-cooking in the yard since morning parted like a curtain, allowing them in.

"Hey there!" Big Daddy called out to them, waving from his rocking chair. "Look, y'all, it's Joey and the doc. Somebody run, fetch Carol." She dared a smile in his direction, even though he hadn't gotten her name quite right.

Big Daddy's shaggy white hair brushed the back of his collar. A colorful western bolo rested on his huge chest. He looked exactly the way he had on the Fourth of July, when she'd been Carol's guest at Highland Park. She'd seen him that first time, amid the crush of Carol's relatives, as if he were the only person there. "Who's *that*?" she'd asked.

"Big Daddy, my momma's grandfather. Let's see can he go with us."

Joan had grabbed the sleeve of Carol's T-shirt. "You mean your *great-*grandfather? How old is he?"

"I don't know. Near eighty, I reckon."

He'd tagged along behind as they made a dash for the carousel house.

"Why do you call him Big Daddy?" Joan asked as they ran.

"That's 'cause what *he* says really goes."

Once through the wide doors of the low white building, Joan had quickly chosen from the beautifully painted animals who strutted and bowed in time to the Wurlitzer music. With each rotation, she found Big Daddy and waved.

Back outside, as Carol walked on Big Daddy's left, Joan on his right, she'd darted her eyes between the rutted sidewalk and him, not wanting to trip but afraid he'd disappear. She had no idea how to behave around someone so old, but she very much wanted him to like her.

"You ever ride the merry-go-round, Big Daddy?" she asked.

"Sure did. I took my boy the year it opened. He'd just turned five." He put his hand on Joan's shoulder the way her dad did sometimes, the way she imagined her Grandpa Barnes would have. "I reckon near about *every* child who's been to Highland Park has ridden this carousel."

They passed some drinking fountains and turned toward the sound of children laughing and splashing in the pool. Joan and Carol laced their fingers through links of the fence, watching as a beach ball sailed across the water. Big Daddy plucked a blade of grass to chew on and wandered over to stand under a shade tree.

"I'm thirsty," Joan said.

She'd dashed off, Carol right behind her, but stopped short before the two fountains. Behind one, a sign commanded "Whites Only." The sign behind the other simply said "Colored." Otherwise, the fountains were about as similar, or dissimilar, as Joan and Carol. Each fountain looked a little like a metal birdbath, one taller than the other.

The nasty boy in the drugstore had said Catholics and niggers didn't belong. But Carol belonged even though she was Catholic too; Joan could tell. You couldn't have a million relatives around you all the time and not belong.

That's what gave Joan the idea. She persuaded Carol that they should try the colored fountain. As she backed away declaring, "It tastes just the same," a stick stung their legs in quick succession.

"Y'all know better than that." Big Daddy had pointed with the branch yanked from a sweet gum tree. "Sit yourselves down right here on this bench. And listen with your eyes." He'd loomed, hands on hips, waiting for them to meet his gaze. "Last I checked, isn't either one of you a nigger. And 'less you're wanting to turn into one, don't ever do such a thing. Everybody in his place is how things work best."

She'd thought again of the boy in the drugstore, and how that was really what he was saying. Maybe C.J. didn't belong. But Joan wanted a family like Carol's and friends like Cindy and Sally Ann.

Now, as she waited for Carol, she studied the porch of the Whiteheads' cabin. It was lined with rockers. Carol's dad, or grandfather, or uncle so-and-so gave up his chair to tend to the ribs or puff on a cigar, and Joan's dad sat down right next to Big Daddy. Joan longed to slip into place with the cousins playing checkers and slap-Jack. Big Daddy could be her very own grandfather for a day.

The screen door banged as one of the cousins darted through it. Joan looked into the tiny kitchen to see women shucking corn and stirring bowls of coleslaw and potato salad.

The door bounced again, this time on the heels of Carol's red Keds. "Hey, Joan," she said. "Let's go sit by Big Daddy."

"Been to every fair held in my lifetime," Big Daddy was saying to her dad. "This y'all's first time here?"

"Our first enjoying such hospitality."

"Well, you missed the cussing and hollering over in Founder's Square. You can imagine, what with the primary in a few days."

Joan's dad nodded knowingly.

"Got to get the right Democrat on the ticket, then kick the tar out of the Republican same as always. Mississippi ain't no place for Republicans, don't you agree, Doc?"

"No doubt about that." He shifted in his rocker and flicked at something Joan couldn't see on his pants leg.

"Who's your money on for governor?"

"Now I haven't put my money down yet, Mr. Whitehead." Both men laughed. "But economic progress is a big concern. And Lieutenant Governor Gartin has some ideas."

"True enough. But I reckon we got to put first things first. Ross Barnett is for segregation. Everybody in his place, like I always say." Big Daddy winked at Joan. "You want to go to school with smart kids, don't you, Joey? Not get dragged down by those not as good."

"Separation?" Joan said, bringing on snickers from some of the cousins.

Her eyes flashed, but she focused on Big Daddy, not wanting to lose his attention. Then she thought about the kids in her class at St. Stephen's Academy. They weren't all smart, especially Ray Henson. But he kept trying, and she admired him for that.

"I helped Ray Henson with his reading all last year. He really tried." She looked to Carol for support. "He was getting better, wasn't he, Carol?"

"Well, 'course y'all take care of your own at St. Stephen's. As it should be, folks taking care of their own." Big Daddy rearranged himself in his chair, like something wasn't as it should be.

"Most kids 'round here, though, go to the public schools," he continued. Joan remembered then that Big Daddy wasn't Catholic. "We got to consider what the coloreds would do to the public schools. Imagine if half the class was dim-witted like your Ray *and* shiftless both, like the coloreds."

School is your future, honey. In America, everyone can make their life better by working hard. Joan's dad had said that at least as often as Father

Frank had said Mass. But—her dad separated out the Negroes in his secret room. Oh . . . Joan shook her head sadly along with the others.

"Now, Doc," Big Daddy continued. "Barnett will make sure it's us in Mississippi that tells us what to do. Not federal troops invading us like over to Little Rock. As if those good people was Russians or some such evil."

"Well, I do believe those of us who live here need to be the ones deciding how things get done."

"Yessir!" Big Daddy slapped his thigh hard. "Don't need no damn Yankees for that."

Her dad's jaw tightened. Nothing moved for a minute but his eyes, reminding Joan of a squirrel treed by a dog. He slid in his chair like a squirrel might flatten itself against the branch. Big Daddy might say next, *You're not from here, Doc Barnes. You don't know our ways.* Or he might tell that joke that wasn't even funny: *You can take the Yankee out of the north, but you can't take the damn out of the Yankee.*

"Been that way for a hundred years now, since they walked the streets after the war." Big Daddy's eyes became a steely gray. He took a minute to rock. "I reckon I was about the age of the girls here when my daddy told this story to me." Some of the cousins perked up. "Only time I ever knew him to wipe away a tear, remembering what that Yankee bastard did to his mother. One of them sons of bitches knocked my itty-bitty grand-momma into a muddy street with the butt of his rifle. Just so's a nigger could pass on the sidewalk." He wiped at his eyes. "I reckon Ross Barnett understands, him being the son of a Confederate veteran."

Joan saw her dad rise up slightly in his seat, as if something needed saying. She felt the same panic she had when Cindy threatened to take her Barbie and leave if Joan didn't order C.J. to serve lemonade.

"Big Daddy?" she blurted. He turned in her direction, his face softening slightly. "Joey's a boy's name, you know."

He snorted. "I guess you didn't catch Miz Joey Heatherton on the *Perry Como Show.* Mark my word, she's gonna be big. And so will you."

CHICAGO

Each friend represents a world in us, a world not born until they arrive, and it is only by this meeting that a new world is born.

—**Anais Nin**

CHAPTER 9

June 1959
Brothers

C.J. woke to ringing that sounded so far off it could be coming all the way from Mississippi. Her hands fell to her sides, expecting the cold, hard vinyl of a bus seat. Instead, her fingers grazed softly ribbed fabric. She opened her eyes, saw the pale yellow chenille spread, and scrambled up. Swatting in the direction of the ringing, she silenced a small alarm clock on a bedside table.

Now she remembered. Mrs. Powell—that's what they called married ladies up North here . . . *Misses*—had pointed to the clock, suggesting a short nap would let her get right to work on dinner. That was after Mr. Powell had driven her here from the Greyhound station. In silence, as if he were delivering a package.

The somehow familiar blue and yellow rag rug beneath her feet was unsettling. She stepped quickly off it, onto the bare floor. Closer to the closet and the uniforms she was to wear.

Reluctantly, she put on one of the ugly black dresses. It swallowed her whole, just like the dress she'd bought at The Mademoiselle. No wonder. The tag said size twelve. She was certain she'd written size eight on the application.

This is a mistake I can't fix, Momma had said when she saw the letter assigning C.J. to the Powell family. And now she wasn't even here to try.

Blinking back tears, C.J. used one of the white aprons to cinch the dress at the waist.

Outside her room, she got turned around. She nearly walked into the master bedroom but finally found the back stairs leading to the kitchen.

The Joy of Cooking waited on the counter, next to the week's menu and four lonely canisters in a metal much like that of the sink. The late afternoon summer sun ducked in through thin horizontal slats where curtains should be. Everything else must be hidden away behind the doors of the light oak cabinets with no handles. C.J. reached out to trace the wood, hoping to figure how to open the door.

"Hi, I'm Molly."

She dropped her hand and pivoted toward the small voice. A pixie face, surrounded by a brown pageboy parted on one side and held back by yellow sun-shaped barrettes, shone up at her.

"I'm seven. Want to meet my parakeet?"

"Hi, Molly. I'd love to. But I'm waiting on your momma to talk about supper."

"Mommy can still see you. Come on."

Molly took her hand, pulling her around the corner to where a square metal cage with a rounded roof hung from a pole. On a little swing sat a small green-feathered body, interrupted only by a yellow blotch on its head, a putty-colored beak, and ink-dot eyes.

"C.J. This is Pedro."

C.J. smiled. In her Jim Crow Mississippi, she expected to forever be introduced to whites, never a white person to her. *Mr. So-and-so*, they'd say, *this is C.J., the one I spoke to you about.* Molly's dad had done the same thing—*Everyone, meet C.J.*, as if they wouldn't know who she was. Knowingly or not, Molly had shown C.J. the uncommon courtesy of introducing the bird to her.

"I surely am pleased to know you, Pedro. I hope we'll be friends."

"You can help me feed him sometimes," Molly said. "I know he'll like you as much as I do."

"*There* you are." Mrs. Powell placed one hand firmly on her daughter's shoulder and motioned with the other. C.J. followed her clicking high heels to the kitchen.

"I've kept it simple tonight—meatloaf, scalloped potatoes, buttered green beans, rolls, and leftover chocolate cake." Mrs. Powell waved at the cookbook. "You can cook to a recipe, can't you?"

"Yes, Miz Powell. I've had home economics in school and cooked for families I worked for back home."

"All right, then." The high heels clicked out of the room.

She moved as though there were bricks in her white lace-up shoes. But she prided herself on figuring things out in her head. The potatoes took the longest to cook. The potatoes and meatloaf had to come out while the rolls baked at a higher temperature. There was time to warm up the meat and potatoes, put everything in serving dishes, and have it all to the table at six thirty, but no time to spare.

"I need this pressed." Mrs. Powell was back, holding up a pink dress, collarless but with a skirt full enough to cover the dining room table. "The iron and board are in the tall cabinet by the back door. I'll be back in fifteen minutes."

The potatoes had to go in before then. C.J. pared and sliced furiously. Which would be worse—the family waiting on dinner or Mrs. Powell waiting on her dress? Surely King Solomon's decision was easier.

She tried to split herself the way he'd threatened to divide the baby. Set up the board, turn on the iron, grease a baking dish, layer potato slices, dredge with flour, dot with butter. Turn the burner on under the milk, iron the bodice, catch the milk before it scalds, add salt and paprika and pour over the potatoes, set the dish in the oven.

Five minutes before Mrs. Powell returned, C.J. maneuvered the skirt on the board, careful not to let the bodice drag on the floor. Back and forth, edging the point of the iron into each gather at the waist, murmuring thanks for all the practice ironing for the Barneses.

Mrs. Powell arrived to snatch the finished dress from her hands. C.J. hurried to mix the meatloaf. When everything came out on time, looking like it should, she sighed with relief.

"We're ready to be served," Mrs. Powell called from the dining room.

She gripped the edges of the platter, barely breathing until the meatloaf rested safely before Mrs. Powell. A flash of pink caught her eye as she placed the potatoes next to the meat. When she carried in the beans and rolls, she looked closer. Mrs. Powell's dress was pink, but this dress had a large white collar.

She shrugged inwardly. "Will there be anything else, ma'am?"

Mrs. Powell surveyed the table as if she were about to do very important work and everything must be precisely so. Then, looking squarely at C.J., she adjusted her collar. "That will be all until dessert."

C.J. fixed herself a plate and sat down at the red Formica dinette set. She should have known nothing would be different here. Mrs. Powell couldn't be any clearer if she'd had Mrs. Corrigan do the talking. She swallowed without tasting. As she studied tomorrow's menu, she listened, in case Mrs. Powell changed her mind again.

"What did you do with yourself, dear, not having to make dinner?" Mr. Powell asked.

"You make it sound like I had a day of leisure, Walter. I have three young children, you know."

"C.J. had to take a nap just like Joey and Jessica," Molly said. "I waited for her so she could meet Pedro. He really likes her, too."

"You'll get the hang of it, I'm sure, Evelyn."

"Is C.J. going to take a nap every day?"

"Heavens, no. Just today, after her bus ride. Walter, how were things at the office?"

"Why? Was it long?" Molly asked.

"I'm not sure, Molly." Mrs. Powell's voice was taking on an edge. "Walter?"

"A day maybe," he mused about the bus ride.

"Tatoes!" screamed little Joey.

"They are good, aren't they? Different than yours, Evelyn."

"I went swimming, Daddy!" Jessica said.

"That's wonderful, sweetheart—"

"A whole *day* on a bus?" Molly sounded horrified. "How'd she sleep? I could never sleep on the school bus."

"I'm sure it wasn't that bad. Now *let* your father finish."

"The Bridges deal is eating up all my time. If I can pull it off, though, there may just be a promotion."

"Oh, how wonderful, dear!"

Mrs. Powell took her time calling for the cake. It was well after nine when, excused for the evening, C.J. stumbled up the back stairs and into her pajamas. She started to crawl into bed, then reached for the dresser scarf and wooden bird. Standing on the blue and yellow rag rug, clutching the remnants of home, she cried, as inconsolably as the Corrigan baby in his nursery.

❋　❋　❋

Sunday came slowly, without mention of C.J.'s day off. The agency letter had said *six-thirty to eight, six days a week.* But Mrs. Powell didn't seem to have gotten the same letter. She had C.J. getting to know the house inch by inch, on all fours, cleaning wood floors that looked plenty clean to start with. Mae had warned that it could be a while before their days off matched up. She'd explained how the twenty-four hours off could start on Friday night or Saturday evening and would likely be unpredictable in the beginning, or if your employer wasn't very considerate. C.J. was aggravated, though not sure whether to be more put out with Mrs. Powell or with herself for not asking.

For the Powell family, today was a day of rest. With morning Mass and an elaborate mid-day meal behind them, Joey and Jessica were napping while their parents lounged in the family room with the *Tribune.* Bone tired and stuffed into one of the child-sized chairs at the table in the playroom, C.J. struggled to keep her eyes open.

"Wha—" A small hand resting on hers sent C.J.'s eyelids up.

"Mommy said you wouldn't need any more naps." Molly sounded more worried than accusing.

She smiled at the child, touched by her concern, then let her gaze roam the room. Cheerful bunnies pranced on the border circling above the baseboards. High windows spanning one wall allowed the light in without danger the kids could reach them. Since she arrived six days ago, she'd been reading *Alice in Wonderland* to Molly. They'd gotten through the first chapter, where Alice shrinks, then grows too large. C.J. imagined herself as too-large Alice, and Molly, surrounded by an abundance of toys and games, as the miniature.

"C.J., why didn't you take Communion this morning?"

Molly was a sweet child, but her questions had the kind of answers that had to be weighed carefully. Truth be told, that made C.J. more tired than the housework.

"It's my job to look after Joey and Jessica so—" She struggled to come up with an explanation, not certain why Mr. Powell wanted her there when Mrs. Powell clearly did not. "So you and your parents can keep your minds on your Mass."

"I know *that*. But we could take turns. I could sit with them while you go."

C.J. squirmed, feeling at once cared about and pushed. Finally, she just admitted, "I'm not Catholic, Molly."

"Oh! You'll have to be *sooo* careful then."

Such a strange thing for the child to say. In Mississippi, it was being Catholic that made a person careful. She couldn't help asking why.

"If you die, you can't go to heaven."

She almost laughed. Despite all the things she'd been kept out of in her life, she'd never once thought about being excluded from heaven. "Is that what they teach in your church?"

"If you're not baptized, you can't go to heaven."

"Well, don't worry then. I was baptized back home, on a beautiful summer day."

"You remember?"

"Yes, very well. The creek was high because we'd had so much rain. I was a little scared to walk in. But then Brother James reached out and held my hand."

"Walked? Weren't you a baby?"

"I was twelve."

"That's pretty old." Molly scrunched up her face. "But then—if you've been baptized—you *must* be Catholic."

"No. I'm Baptist."

"Do you believe in God?" The child's eyes had taken over her face.

"Yes, honey." C.J. remembered how she could sometimes turn Joan Barnes's attention with questions and asked the first thing that came to mind: "Have you ever had anyone helping your family out before, like I do?"

"Babysitters, but . . . not like you."

"You mean because I live in your house?"

"No. You . . ." She could almost see the wheels turning in Molly's head. "Wear a uniform."

She did indeed. Mrs. Powell had instructed her not to leave her room unless she was wearing one of the hideous, two-sizes-too-big black dresses.

"Mommy said it's important so you don't get lost."

So she didn't forget her place was more like it, C.J. figured.

"And, C.J., what's Negro?"

"That's what I am."

"I thought you were Baptist." Molly looked like she was about to cry in frustration. "Negro must be bad. Mommy said she doesn't trust it."

"Let's read," C.J. suggested, afraid she, too, might cry. Loneliness pierced her heart. Hundreds of miles and three hundred fifty-eight days stood between her and her family. She had no idea when she'd be allowed her day off, see Mae or the other girls, attend a church she might call her own. She'd heard the congregation this morning offering up prayers for the Pope, their families, and everyone at Mass. But surely no one other than Molly meant to include C.J.

"Should we start chapter two of *Alice in Wonderland*?"

"I don't really like that story. It's scary." Molly dashed to the bookcase and back, holding out *Cinderella*. "Can we read my favorite instead?"

C.J. recalled the book Mrs. Barnes had lent her about Saint Zita and sighed, wondering why white children so often read about poor girls doing housework for someone else's family.

❖   ❖   ❖

Thirteen days since C.J. waved goodbye to her family, twelve since she saw Mae's or any Negro face other than her own. From Skokie and the Powells' to Hyde Park, she prayed for guidance in getting on and off buses and the L at the right time. Finally—still wearing her uniform because she'd been uncertain whether Mrs. Powell would allow her to change out of it before she left the house—she stepped from the bus onto the University of Chicago campus.

Heavy-looking buildings gathered around large rectangular areas of grass, guarding the space for the college students who sat here and there, in jeans or shorts, laughing and talking. Their voices rolled over one another, louder and louder. High overhead, towers, steeples, and grotesque devilish creatures jutted from the buildings. Their ivy-covered walls, appearing so thick that nothing could penetrate them, loomed menacingly. C.J. hugged her satchel against her chest to hide the ugly black dress and walked faster and faster, until she was running, like in a nightmare.

A car horn stopped her from darting into the street when she saw the brownstone. She bent over on the sidewalk, gasping for enough air to carry her up the stairs to Mae on the third floor.

The girl who opened the door of apartment ten wasn't Mae, but her Negro face—set off by a fringe of soft bangs and a floral print headband—was so warm and friendly that the tears threatening in C.J.'s eyes never fell.

"Is this the apartment Mae Willis shares? I'm her friend—"

"It's C.J., y'all!" The girl reached out to pull her inside.

"I'm Sissy," said another girl sporting red cat-eye glasses. She hurried over to take C.J.'s satchel. "And this here's Emily."

When Mae bounded from the bedroom, C.J.'s joy was complete. "Hey, girl." Mae grinned as if they'd never been apart.

"You eat yet?" Sissy asked as soon as C.J. and Mae stopped hugging.

C.J. wanted nothing more than to sit here looking at these faces. "No, but I'm not really—"

"Oh, you got to eat," Emily said. "Run, change out of that uniform."

The minute C.J. returned, Mae steered everyone out the door and down the stairs. They walked in the simmering evening sun to 55th Street and

Jimmy's Woodlawn Tap. Emily said it was a popular hangout for working folks and professors and students.

"Y'all know any? College students, I mean." C. J. couldn't imagine.

"Naw." Sissy laughed. "They ain't too much for socializing with the maids."

Inside the pub, she shrank from the din and the sea of mostly white faces. "It's okay? Us being here?"

"It's fine, C.J." She knew that's what Mae said. Still she heard, *I know what I'm doing. I can teach you how to stop being small town.* Just the way Mae had said it on the bus ride from Mississippi, when C.J. had been afraid to sit up front after they crossed the Illinois state line.

She shook off the hurt as best she could, relishing her hamburger and Coke and enjoying sharing stories of the families they worked for. Finally, she could no longer keep from yawning, and the girls took pity on her.

Back at the apartment, Sissy and Emily took the couch and gave the bedroom to Mae and C.J. The radio, tuned to WGES, whispered soothing sounds. The voice was definitely Negro—maybe Ruth Brown—the music rhythm and blues.

Mae's breathing in the other bed reminded C.J. of a lifetime next to Metairie. She fell asleep easily, but stirred throughout the night, agitated by gargoyles riding buses.

❖   ❖   ❖

A break in the August heat wave was predicted, and C.J. intended to follow suit. She was going to church in the morning, and she wouldn't be dragged out anywhere tonight.

None of her roommates were much for church, save the mysterious Flo who she had yet to meet. She'd walked around the South Side with Sissy and Emily on Sunday mornings, a few times now, while they pointed out the block-long South Center Department Store and Walgreen's, with its soda fountain running the length of the store. She'd marveled as groups of strangers came together and drifted apart in ever-changing patterns, like the kaleidoscope in the Powell children's playroom, and snatches of conversations floated by—". . . dancing at the Savoy . . ." ". . . a fine dinner at the Palm . . ." ". . . heard them up at the Regal . . ."

For Sissy and Emily, the South Side felt like home. They loved it there, thought it grand. Yet it struck her as cruel that such a place could exist in the same city as the house where she expected to spend nearly every day of the coming year. In the South Side, every face was black, and it seemed possible to do or buy anything. In the Powells' house, she was sometimes startled to see her face in the mirror. So white was everything around her that she could almost forget she wasn't white, too. But in her uniform, like Cinderella in her rags, she could never forget she did not belong.

Alinda was their sixth roommate. C.J. knew her from home but had spent no real time with her here—she was always out with her man, Roger. When the couple went to clubs, Mae joined them. C.J. always declined invitations to go along. Of course, her momma would be appalled. But, even more to the point, she had no intention of letting Chicago change her like it seemed to be changing Mae.

So this Saturday evening, when C.J. left the bus in Hyde Park, she went into the first diner she saw. She ate slowly, watching the evening sky dim and trying to figure how to find a Baptist church. Alinda's book of places to see in Chicago might help. Or the campus might have a church.

At the apartment, light from the lamp they left on when they went out shone under the door. As she turned the key, everything was quiet. She almost didn't notice the girl sitting so still on the couch, largely covered by *The Chicago Daily Defender*.

"I've been wondering when we were gonna meet." Flo's smile was welcoming. She folded her newspaper, aligning the edges just so before standing and holding out her hand.

C.J. took it, all the while fixated on Flo's eyes. In their emerald green, she could almost see herself. She and Flo were precisely the same height. Flo's dark olive brown skin closely matched hers.

She returned Flo's smile. "Did you get my note some time back?" On Sissy's urging, she'd borrowed one of Flo's dresses from the closet. It was smart but tasteful, and fit like something Momma had made for her.

"I surely did." Flo sat down and patted the seat next to her. "I'm glad the dress worked for you."

"Fit me perfectly. So, maybe you'll borrow something of mine sometime." She nodded. "Maybe so."

"Anyone else got Sunday off?"

"Yeah. You missed your chance. Emily went with Alinda and Roger to hear some music."

"I don't mind. Sometimes I just like doing nothing. But here, where I kind of feel—"

"At home?"

C.J. laughed. "At home." As she sank back into the couch, a heavenly smell hit her. She crinkled her nose with pleasure. "I could believe my own momma was in that kitchen cooking."

Flo beamed. "I made my macaroni and cheese. Come have some with me."

"I stopped off on the way here, but it smells so good. Can I just have a bite?" She pulled herself up and followed Flo to the kitchen.

"What you up to tomorrow?" Flo asked as she dished up a large serving. Noodles crowned by molten cheese with crispy brown edges.

"I mean to find me a church." She shook her head and pointed to her plate. "This is wonderful."

"I've got me a mind to try Olivet Baptist. Want to come?"

"Well, sure. Something special about that church?"

"Mahalia Jackson. It's one of the places she got started singing professionally. You know her?"

"I saw her in *Imitation of Life* with Emily right after I moved here."

"I saw that, too! We go way back, though—that is, me liking her. Miz Jackson used to perform at churches all over. When she came to Birmingham, my momma got to sing with her."

"You're putting me on."

"I wouldn't." Flo looked serious, almost hurt. "It's my mother put the love of gospel in me, teaching me Miz Jackson's songs."

"Well, we never had anything quite so exciting at Hope Baptist. But it was Momma taught me all my hymns, singing me to sleep and while she worked."

"You know this one?"

Flo sang "Take My Hand, Precious Lord" and C.J. joined her, finishing with the refrain. As they ate, silence fell like choir robes around their shoulders.

Sunday morning did indeed dawn cooler. As the final notes from the choir and piano faded away after the service, C.J. took the last two steps of Olivet Baptist at once, hopping to the ground like an excited schoolgirl. Attending church again had felt so good.

"Looks like Jesus done lifted you." Flo grinned and hummed "Love Lifted Me." "You might could walk faster than the bus. But I'd rather save my feet for wandering around if it's all the same to you."

"Well, sure." C.J. grinned back. "The bus is here anyways."

They got off near the Maxwell Street Market. It felt like a party, folks sweating in the summer sun to the cool beat. Everything from fish to vacuum cleaners seemed to be for sale from one street vendor or another.

At the corner of Halsted and Maxwell, they saw a makeshift stage. The twang of a guitar took them home again.

"Wonder what that smell is," C.J. said.

"Polish sausages. We got to try us one before we leave."

"This here's the kind of thing I wish I could show my little brother," C.J. said.

"Me, too. Freddie always did love this sound. He got him an old beat-up guitar for Christmas when he was ten and started picking. Barely could reach the chords."

"My Charlie's twelve. Smart, but a handful. Got this friend who's always putting ideas in his head."

"Yeah." Flo sounded like she'd wandered on back home in her mind. "What'd you think 'bout church?" she asked after a while.

"It was so big! I reckon every church-going Negro in Chicago was there. But Reverend Jackson put me in mind of Brother James at my tiny little church in Poplar Springs."

"That so?"

"It's how he counseled us to live, I reckon. Kind of like Reverend Jackson was doing."

"What you mean?"

"When trouble would come, Brother James always said to fix our minds on God's promise of the first being last and the last first."

"He one of them waiting-on-heaven preachers, then?"

C.J. raised an eyebrow. "I don't know as there's a special name for it. He preached about staying alive and taking care of our families is all."

"Nothing's going to change, just—staying alive." At the corner, Flo looked both ways, then darted across the street just ahead of an oncoming car.

"I reckon your little brother doesn't require quite as much looking after as mine," C.J. said when she caught up.

"I reckon not."

"When Miz Parks wouldn't get out of her seat, Brother James reminded us how we needed the bus to get to work."

"Well, there's all kinds of things we need," Flo said stiffly.

"Like?"

"We *need* to be treated with dignity. I don't cotton to what Reverend Jackson said, criticizing Dr. King's civil disobedience. And his book, too, 'bout the bus boycott right there in Montgomery."

The part of C.J. that had so enjoyed the day until now longed to say what she felt, what she'd kept mostly to herself. How it was more than fear that set her mind this way. More than Buddy and Nadine Corrigan or knowing what people could do to each other and fearing they would. How it was her belief that freedom came from within and couldn't be given or taken away.

"I think I just may have to go to the library and read me that book," Flo went on. "*Stride Toward Freedom*, didn't he call it?"

They'd come full circle back to Halsted and a stand whose sign said: *Jim's Original, Serving Chicago Since 1939.* Flo handed over money and received two buns, each stuffed with a fat red sausage and grilled onions. "Looks mighty interesting, don't it?"

Who said she wanted to try this anyway? C.J. could get know-it-all from Mae, and it was a mite easier to swallow coming from someone she knew cared about her. Flo had seemed all right. But she was a book reader, and C.J. had never come across a book that dealt with the kind of problems she'd experienced. Flo's talk was dangerous.

A man, reaching to toss his empty wrapper in the trash barrel, bumped into C.J. Her Polish slipped in her hands, threatening to fall to the ground. When the man apologized, his face so close to hers, the smell of onions was overpowering. She let go of her sandwich.

❈   ❈   ❈

Four months later, C.J. leaned on the brownstone's door, closing it tight against the wind and snow that had whistled and skittered around her all the way from the bus stop. In the sudden quiet and stillness, she felt like a figurine in one of those snow globes at Marshall Field's—one finally righted and allowed to come to rest. This was what she needed. Time with her friends. Two whole days where nothing changed.

She unknotted her scarf, the pale blue one Molly had gifted her for Christmas. Mrs. Powell had given her Thursday night to Saturday night off. How unusual to be off on a Thursday, with two glorious days of freedom stretching before her! But then, it was the season of miracles. Mrs. Powell had also delivered the news that the family was moving to St. Louis. In less than two weeks, C.J. would have a new family. Mae had warned her this would happen, and as much as she disliked Mrs. Powell, she couldn't help worrying what the Uptons would be like.

Things were changing in Poplar Springs, too. C.J. had read and reread the long letter packed with the gifts from home, pressing the pages to her face, trying to smell the soap her family used, faint traces transferred from each person's hand as they wrote. But she couldn't, any more than she could convince herself things were as she'd left them. *I'm being good*, Charlie claimed in printing more assured than her daddy's, *but I don't much like school. George and I got engaged*, Metairie reported. *We're planning the wedding around your summer visit.*

Upstairs, C.J. found Alinda and Mae. The others dribbled in until all six crowded into the tiny apartment. Almost immediately, they were debating who would be in charge of which dish for their southern dinner.

"Ain't no Mississippi girl ever barbecued ribs as good as us in Alabama," Flo opened boldly, considering she was outnumbered five to one.

Sissy adjusted her glasses and shot back, "Y'all ought not to even call what you do barbecue."

"When y'all taste my grandmother's sweet potato pie . . ." Emily folded her hands over her chest and closed her eyes. "You'll believe you've died and gone to heaven."

"C.J. makes the best cornbread," Mae said.

"What about the ribs?" Flo said. "That's what *I* want to know."

"I say let's vote," Alinda suggested. "Who wants Alabama ribs, raise your hand."

"Sorry, Flo," Sissy offered. "But we'd love your macaroni and cheese."

"Guess I'll go get the mail, then. If *that's* all right with the five of y'all."

"Go on." Mae laughed and waved Flo out the door. "That leaves black-eyed peas and collard greens for us, Alinda."

When Flo came back, she was clutching the pile of mail like a rag doll.

"All that for you?" Alinda asked in the same teasing voice she'd used to call for a vote.

Wordlessly, Flo walked to the couch. She disappeared into one corner, like a turtle going into its shell.

"Flo? You all right?" It was then that C.J. noticed Flo's vacant stare. "Is it bad news?"

She shook her head. "I didn't mean to."

"Mean to what?" Emily came over to sit by Flo and pat her hand.

"The white boy . . ."

C.J.'s skin prickled.

"He was standing behind me, waiting to get at his box. When I turned around, I bumped into him."

"He give you trouble?" Sissy asked softly.

"He commenced to picking up the mail." Flo shook her head in disbelief. "When I apologized, he said, 'Don't worry about it, please.'" She drew a deep, shuddering breath.

"Flo, you got to tell us what this is about—"

"C.J., don't interrupt her," Mae whispered.

The roommates were moving like a well-oiled machine, like the ladies of Hope Baptist rallying around the sick.

"Then he said, 'I'm Zach Bernstein. Where'd you get that wonderful accent?' I figured he was mocking me. My drawl must have got even stronger . . . remembering."

Remembering seemed to stick in Flo's throat like a bone. The look between Emily and Sissy said it was more than the fear and anger of a lifetime of stepping out of the path of white folks. Yet C.J. somehow got the feeling they didn't know exactly what it was.

"Did you tell him your name?" Sissy asked.

"I said I was Flo Thomas from Birmingham." Flo uncurled her body. She seemed to be coming around. "'Alabama! Really?' he says, all excited like. 'I hope we can talk sometime.'"

"He from Alabama you reckon?" Alinda asked.

"Naw." Flo shook her head again. "He got a Yankee accent for sure."

"What you gonna do?" Emily asked.

"Keep my distance is what. Y'all'll be getting the mail from now on."

The girls smiled with relief, and the tension seemed to dissipate in the room.

"I surely do agree with you on that position," C.J. said. "It's best to stay out of the path of trouble."

Everyone was up early the next day, smiling and hugging and wishing each other "Merry Christmas." By around six that evening, they had pulled together their feast. Into the night, they ate and talked.

"What y'all want to be doing some years from now?" Mae asked.

"I'm gonna be warm again!" Sissy scooted closer to the radiator. "I've 'bout had my fill of snow. And, Lord, if the wind don't blow hard enough here to break your bones."

"I'm longing for something that may never be." Flo's voice was hushed and reverent, easy and joyous, as if in gospel hymn.

"Yeah, good ribs in Alabama," Alinda teased.

"Naw, I'm serious." Flo lifted the plate of sweet potato pie from her lap and stretched out her long legs. "A better Alabama. Where I can vote and make decent money. Where crow is forever out of season."

"You think that can be?"

"Folks braver than me been trying. I think about Miz Rosa Parks in Montgomery every time I get on the bus here and sit wherever I please."

C.J. watched Flo's energy, the way she leaned in toward them. She appreciated what Mrs. Parks had done as well as anyone. But couldn't Flo at least spare them her civil rights preaching on Christmas? A lonely car horn sounded from below, reminding her how few of the students who shared the building must be around over the holidays.

"Miz Ella Baker started the Southern Christian Leadership Conference with Dr. King in Atlanta to get Negroes registered," Flo continued.

In a huff, C.J. moved to the window. Staring out at the icy whiteness, she imagined herself as a snowflake, drifting to where the words couldn't reach her. She could almost count the stars through the bare branches. Just like at Mr. Corrigan's house, where the men planned what to do about people like Flo was talking about.

"I reckon we'll see what comes," Flo finished.

"I want to go home, changes or not," Emily said. "Back to where I don't have to wear no uniform."

"I sure do hate that uniform." C.J. perched on the arm of Mae's chair and took her hand. It was warm and familiar, like a piece of home on a cold, faraway holiday night.

"*So* fashionable." Mae laughed and let her hand rest comfortably in C.J.'s.

"It's like we got to wear it so they can tell us apart," C.J. went on. "We didn't need one in Mississippi."

"Well, I plan on staying right here," Alinda said. "I like the big city. Restaurants and clubs, something always going on. And *fine* Chicago men." She closed her eyes and pretended to swoon.

"Like that Roger who's always underfoot?" Flo teased. Then, more serious, "Y'all know this ain't no paradise either. Just try to buy a house in Skokie or go someplace like Riverview."

"My family carried their kids up there last summer," Sissy said. "It's an amusement park, ain't it?"

"Yeah," Flo said. "Y'all hear about the dipping game? Negro men hired to egg the crowd on until they get dunked. It's worse than some white man play-acting Jim Crow."

"Well, I ain't going back either," Mae said.

Mae's words hit like a baseball, knocking C.J. right off her platform into the cold water. She listened for more, like *leastways not until I get my fill of going to clubs.*

"After I save me enough, I'm going to New York City," Mae said instead.

C.J. looked down at her. "For a visit, right? Who you know there?"

"To work in Rose Morgan's House of Beauty. I read about her in *Ebony.*"

"You just gonna show up there expecting her to give you a job?"

"'Course not. I'm gonna do like Miz Morgan. She came to Chicago from Mississippi, too. Studied at the Morris School of Beauty."

"You could have a beauty shop in Poplar Springs."

"Miz Morgan's place is a *salon.* They do your hair, sure. But they also do your wardrobe and get your body looking fine. They even give massages."

"What's that?" Sissy asked.

"Here, let me show you." Mae began to knead Sissy's shoulders.

Sissy wriggled in delight. "I could sure pay good money to get this after a hard day's work."

C.J. felt the muscles in her neck and back tighten. She wasn't blind. She'd seen Mae changing ever since the bus ride up from Poplar Springs. Yet she'd always pictured herself growing old with Mae. The prospect, arthritis and all, delighted her. "I just always thought we'd go home together."

Mae let go of Sissy to give C.J. a hug. Remembering when they were schoolgirls, C.J. hugged her back. But she saw Mae in King's Drugs, talking the owner into letting her have old fashion magazines for half-price. It began to dawn on her that, even then, Mae had been thinking about what she wanted and how to get it.

"What *you* want, C.J.?" Mae asked gently.

She pulled away. This was the second thing Mae seemed to have known for a while but chosen not to share. "I'm gonna work some years and take money back to Mississippi. Set my family on an easier path. I want my kids to grow up with small town ways, feeling they belong."

The distance between them seemed to expand like the silence in the room. But C.J. couldn't help adding, "It appears I'm going by myself. Back to where we got to make do with beauty *shops*."

❖   ❖   ❖

Saturday saw Mae, Emily, and Sissy leave the apartment early, hunting for after-Christmas bargains and running errands before returning to work. C.J. reprimanded herself for being snippy with Mae, yet couldn't quite make herself apologize.

"Y'all have fun," she called as Alinda left now with Roger. Flo waved from behind the *Chicago Daily Defender*.

The door closing left only the sound of the newspaper rustling and, sometimes, Flo sighing or groaning over what she was reading. She gave no sign that anything upsetting had happened two days ago, much less that she'd like to talk about it.

C.J. turned on WGES. Lying back on the couch, hands behind her head, she wiggled her toes in time to LaVern Baker. Left foot, she should try to get Flo talking. Right foot, she should respect Flo's privacy.

"You gotta see this." Flo was laughing now. She brought the paper to C.J. and pointed to a cartoon strip called "So What?" A lady stood on a scale, explaining to her friend how she's not really overweight, she just needs to be four inches taller.

C.J. laughed, too. "I can see the practicality in that." She hated to spoil Flo's mood. If she and Flo got to be better friends, whatever had caused such a strong reaction at the mailboxes would probably come out sooner or later.

"Speaking of eating, there's not a scrap of leftovers from last night. We're gonna have to go out. You hungry?"

"Yeah, but I just can't drag myself up right—" C.J. was interrupted by a knock.

"Alinda must have forgot her key," Flo said, crossing the room to the door.

The song ended. For a moment, no one spoke. Not the DJ, or Flo, or Alinda. C.J. looked up. A white boy filled the doorway. Flo, facing him, looked somehow small, though she and this boy appeared about the same height. He had to be the one who'd so unnerved her. C.J. slid to the edge of her seat, ready.

"Hi, Miss Thomas." She could see how Flo might have felt mocked. "I'm Zach Bernstein. We met downstairs. Remember? I could really use your help with something."

"I'm spending time with my friend today." She could feel Flo fighting to keep her voice even, civil. "Is it an emergency?"

C.J. stared at them—Flo waiting for Zach, Zach with his mouth slightly open. The aroma of baking cookies crept in from across the hall, filling the silence with memory. C.J., waiting in the Thornhearts' dining room, the smell of her freshly baked teacakes hanging in the air, while Alan blocked Mrs. Corrigan's path through the hall to the bathroom.

"Well," Zach said finally. "I guess that depends on how you look at it. I'd like to talk to you about Alabama, for my class." He waved the notebook in his hand. "I wondered if you'd let me buy you a sandwich while we talk."

Talk, he said. Zach Bernstein didn't look or sound like Alan. Curly, dark hair ringed his face. His features were sharper, his accent strange. Yet C.J. thought of Alan's kindness. They'd exchanged a few words that time outside the power company and again the day Reverend Thornheart fired her. But so many other times, she'd wanted to have a simple conversation, knowing that was impossible. Would it be any different here?

"Like I said, I'm pretty busy."

Zach shuffled his feet. His eyes darted away from Flo. "I'd be happy to have your friend join us."

C.J. went to stand beside Flo, meaning to offer extra moral support. But she heard herself saying, "Hi, I'm C.J. Evans. Flo, I wouldn't mind getting out for some lunch, would you?" She felt squeezed like a nut in a nutcracker between the looks turned on her—Flo's angry stare and Zach's warm smile. She focused on Zach. "Of course, we'd have to talk about where to go."

"There's a place I like several blocks over. I don't know how you'll like the food, but I'm sure you'll be comfortable. It caters to students and faculty."

He'd understood her subtle reference and gracefully addressed it. "What do you think, Flo?" She leaned slightly toward her. "We can always leave if it doesn't feel right."

"We got to eat, I reckon," Flo snapped. "But we'll meet you there."

Zach opened his notebook and scrawled a map. "I think you'll like this place. It doesn't hold a candle to most delicatessens in the Bronx, in New York where I'm from. But it does fine."

Flo practically slammed the door in Zach's face, then turned on C.J., one hand to her forehead. "Now I do recall you saying—let me see, can I get this right—*it's best to stay out of the path of trouble.*" Her green eyes flashed. "Weren't those your exact words? What in the name of heaven's got into you?"

C.J. suddenly remembered herself down on the Corrigans' kitchen floor, cleaning up the dessert she'd dumped, trying to act like she hadn't overheard the conversation from the living room. "I can't rightly say, Flo. But sometimes we do it to ourselves, putting the fear there when it doesn't belong. I just got a feeling it'll be okay."

Silently, they grabbed their coats and purses and went downstairs. The wind shoved them along. C.J. leaned back into it, trying to keep her balance. When they turned the corner, Zach was waiting outside the deli, doing a little dance to keep warm.

"Good. You found it." He held the door for them.

The wind followed them inside, stirring up a host of unfamiliar smells. Zach stood for a moment, searching for a table. C.J. peeked around him like a child taking refuge in her mother's skirts. But the people seemed more interested in their food and conversation than in the three of them.

The deli had the warm feel of a place that had been around for some time, crowded but well cared for. Photos lined one wall. What looked like giant sausages hung from pegs behind the counter. Feeling herself thawing like ice in a just-brewed pitcher of sweet tea, she took off her coat.

"Zach! Arein!" called out a small bearded man delivering a tray loaded with food.

Zach led them to a table and held out a chair for C.J. She watched Flo's mouth gape open and realized she should close her own. Flo hurried to seat herself before Zach could reach her. He took the chair across from Flo, next to C.J.

"Would it be okay if I order for us?" he asked. "There are a couple of things I'd like you to try."

C.J. glanced at Flo, then let her gaze wander to the menu board over the counter. Scattered among some familiar items were other foreign-sounding words: lox, matzo ball soup, egg creams, knishes, kasha, kishka, kugel, knockwurst, potato latkes, blintzes.

"It would be a relief," C.J. admitted. Zach smiled and went to the counter.

She closed her eyes and sank into the background buzz. It sounded like any group of people—a class at Booker T., Wednesday night social at Hope Baptist.

"Well—I'll tell you this *one* thing for true." Flo hadn't said a word since they'd left the apartment. C.J. opened her eyes to find her cross-armed and glaring. "You put me between a rock and a hard place, saying you wanted to go after I said we was busy. I'm here now. But I'm not spending my whole afternoon with no white boy from New York."

C.J. checked on Zach at the counter. He was filling a tray with Cokes, a knife, napkins, plates, and a small red plastic sign with a number on it. "All right, Flo," she promised. "When you think we been here long enough, just say we got to be getting home, and I'll make sure we do."

"And mark my words," Flo whispered as Zach turned back toward the table. "This ain't a good idea."

Zach's chair was still scraping the floor when Flo asked, "So, what is it you'd like to know about Alabama, Mr. Bernstein?"

"Please, call me Zach—both of you."

Up close, C.J. noticed Zach's eyes. She'd been looked at by many a white man. All those eyes looked past her or roamed her body, judging. These eyes reached out and held hers, gently but firmly. These eyes were piercing blue like Alan's.

"Your accent is lovely, too, but different. Are you from Alabama like Flo?"

"No, Mississippi." Now that she was here, she wasn't sure what to say. Her conversations with white people had been mostly with little girls, or their mothers. At least she and Alan had been in the same grade in high school and might have been able to talk about that. This boy was in college. "Our friend Mae has plans to work in New York someday," she said. "What's it like?"

"A lot like Chicago, really, only bigger." Zach shook his head. "The food in New York, though, is something all its own."

He had a dimple on each side of his mouth. She liked how his smile conveyed confidence without a trace of conceit. "Something in particular you miss?"

"Oh, yeah. *Bagels*. They get close here, but New York bagels are the best. How about you?"

"My momma's cooking. It's—"

"If you don't mind my asking," Flo said abruptly, "why didn't you stay in New York for college?"

"Well, I plan to work in government, to help it do more for people." Zach appeared not to notice Flo's tone. "UC has a strong political science program."

C.J. studied them. Flo's glare said she should stop asking questions; Zach's manner suggested he was among friends. "What made you want to work in government? That where your father works?"

"Oh, no. Pop's always worked with his hands." Just like her daddy. "He's been operating an acetylene torch since before he married my mom. His crew was on the new TIME-LIFE building. Just finished it this year. Forty-eight stories tall!"

"New York sounds like the place for Mae, doesn't it, Flo? Everything so big, just the way she likes it."

Flo grunted and sipped at her Coke. C.J. shifted in her chair, ever so slightly, until Flo's face blurred in her peripheral vision.

"But that was just your second question," Zach apologized to C.J. "Why government? It has to do partly with growing up without much money."

"I reckon we all got that in common."

"And mostly with being Jewish," Zach finished.

C.J. flinched with the memory of the men's voices at the meetings— "... no good Jew bastard ..." "... Commie ..." "... nigger lover ..."

"All my life, I've watched Pop going to work, doing the best he could for us, then coming home after another day of being made to know he didn't belong."

Zach scooted his chair in closer and wrapped his hands around his Coke. He leaned toward them both, but his eyes met C.J.'s. "Big ways. Like tampering with his equipment, trying to get him in trouble with the foreman. But little ways, too. Telling him to find another spot away from the rest of the men to eat his lunch."

"Y'all got Jim Crow in New York?" C.J. asked.

"That's *exactly* what it's like," he said, then flushed. When he added, "I'm sorry. I don't mean to presume," both girls lowered their eyes.

Gradually C.J. had begun to distinguish familiar smells. Chicken broth steaming on a passing tray, the starchy sweetness of potato wafting from a nearby table. Just then the man who'd greeted Zach arrived with a tray piled with sandwiches. "Ess gesunt!" he said, beaming at Zach.

"That's Yiddish for 'eat in good health,' " Zach explained. He cut the huge sandwiches carefully in thirds. Tuna salad, it looked like, and some reddish meats. "Try some of each," he urged. "We have my favorites—pastrami and corned beef. And tuna salad, just in case you don't like those."

Flo immediately reached for the tuna salad. C.J. wavered but chose the pastrami. Biting cautiously, she was struck all at once by smoky, sweet, and peppery flavors. Zach attacked his share of the corned beef.

When he'd swallowed the last bite, he looked at Flo. "That's why I wanted to talk to you. We're studying the Montgomery bus boycott."

"There's a book you could read by Dr. King," Flo said. "I reckon that would tell all about it." She wiped her hands on her napkin, suggesting nothing more needed saying.

"Yes." Zach wiped his hands and carefully folded his napkin. "My professor had us read that. He says the boycott was a turning point for civil rights. I guess what I'm curious about is how *you* saw it. Someone who lived through what it was all about."

"First off, I was in Birmingham." Flo was still using her voice that could prick a porcupine. "There's lots of Alabamas in Alabama, you understand."

"I imagine so. Maybe it's too hard to talk about if you lived it? My grandmother never could talk about losing her brother in the concentration camps."

The compassion in Zach's eyes touched C.J., reminding her how her momma couldn't really talk about Uncle Karl. Flo seemed to disappear inside herself for some moments, almost the way she had when describing meeting Zach at the mailboxes. But then, her voice noticeably softer, she said, "I reckon how it was with the bus was a bit like your daddy might've felt. Every day we went to work or uptown, we got humiliated going and coming."

C.J. thought Zach had touched some memory in Flo, too. When Flo reached for a section of the corned beef and peeked under the bread, C.J. was certain.

"My cousin had a friend named Claudette who got arrested for not giving up her seat. That was in Montgomery but before Miz Parks. I don't know why Miz Parks pushed things to where they got to."

"That's what we're studying," Zach said. "The thinking, the timing—the politics."

"Order up!" yelled a voice from the kitchen.

"I like it." Flo held up her sandwich to show the bite she'd taken. Now C.J. could definitely hear the iciness in her voice melting. "What does your teacher say?"

"He has a theory. They needed someone with a spotless record, to make the case strong in court. Mrs. Parks was educated, in the NAACP, well respected. Your cousin's friend, though—Miss Colvin, I believe—was only fifteen."

C.J. could feel Flo relaxing into her favorite topic. But this wasn't what she'd had in mind at all when she thought about having a simple conversation with a white boy. She pushed the uneaten portion of her pastrami to the far edge of her plate and switched to the tuna salad.

"Don't you like it?" Zach looked worried.

She glanced at her sandwich. "Doesn't seem like what went on in Montgomery did much good is all. Especially in light of the danger."

"But," Zach argued, "it led to the Supreme Court outlawing Montgomery's segregation laws. In effect, they said segregation on city buses is illegal everywhere."

"They said that about schools a long time ago, and Greyhound buses and the like. I guess what they say doesn't mean much in Mississippi." She folded her arms across her chest. "Besides, folks got to stop asking for freedom and know we get that from inside."

"This isn't bad either," Flo said after trying the pastrami.

C.J. looked at her in disgust and pushed her entire plate aside. Through the window she could see snowflakes swirling in the wind, just like in a snow globe. She could almost feel them bumping into her as she tried to right things, to bring them to rest. "Flo," she said. "I think we got to be getting back now."

CHAPTER 10

February 1960
Changes

The smell of sausage and beans simmering in the girls' kitchen crawled under the door and climbed right up on the bed where C.J. lay at the start of her twenty-four hours off, arms crossed over her chest. Too cranky to sleep, she propped up on one elbow to stare out the window. Clouds hung low and heavy in the February sky, like a soufflé gone flat.

She was sick to death of it all. Practicing for Mrs. Upton's fancy French affairs, preparing one pretentious dish after another under her new employer's reproachful eye, only to have to throw it out over some imagined imperfection and start again. Trying to get along with Flo, to have a conversation without her launching into her civil rights preaching or bringing up Zach and how he'd turned out to be okay after all. Wondering why, when she knew full well it wasn't a good idea for her or Flo to be talking to that white boy, she found herself thinking of him now and again.

She'd made herself offer to help Flo with dinner anyway. But Flo had shooed her away, saying she looked tired and ought to lie down. C.J. pulled the spread over her and let her eyes droop closed. But a knock at the apartment door sent them flying open. She crept across the room to listen.

"Finally, you're home." The voice could only be Zach's. "Is C.J. here, too? I've got news."

Before C.J. could lie back down, Flo was in the doorway. "Good! You're awake," she blurted, blind to C.J.'s shushing motions and head shaking.

"I'll be out in a minute." She took her time, though, listening.

"You reading Dr. King's book?" Zach asked.

"I surely am." Flo sounded proud, like she fancied herself a college student. "Y'all talking in class about the sit-ins this week at the Woolworth's in Greensboro?"

"Quite a bit. Seems the attention they're drawing just might lead to changes."

Boycotts. Civil disobedience. Who knew how long the two of them might carry on about it all? C.J. figured she'd best find out Zach's news and be done with it. She put on one of her momma's disapproving faces and walked into the living room.

"C.J., hi!"

His grin was kind of goofy. But she saw, too, how his eyes twinkled— just like in the deli, maybe more so—and his dimples had popped out.

"*Changes*," Flo said. "That's what I'm thinking, too—"

"Did I hear you have news?" C.J. interrupted, still stony-faced.

"Well, yes . . ." He looked from her to Flo, like he wondered whether to jump into the fire or stay put in the frying pan. "I wanted you both to know I got an A on my paper, thanks to your help."

"Now that's real nice," Flo said.

"Yes, nice," C.J. echoed.

"I've been stopping by all week, trying to catch you. You must be really busy with classes."

"Oh," C.J. said. It came out more like a long, sighed *aah* as she considered what to say next. *I can see how you might mistake us for students, especially Miz too-big-for-her-britches here. But we take care of white folks' houses.* That ought to put an end to Zach coming around.

"Actually, we're not students." She glanced Flo's way. Flo had taken up watching the pot of beans, as if it were a baby about to crawl into danger. "We're maids." There, she'd said what needed to be said, considering how he and Flo had practically picked up the conversation where they left off in the deli.

Silence crowded into the room, shoving aside smells from the kitchen. Flo's gaze fell to her feet. Zach looked around the apartment as if searching for a way out. He looked everywhere but at C.J. and Flo, until he noticed the battered piano, overrun with family photos and knickknacks.

"Does one of you play?" he asked suddenly.

"What?" Flo sounded confused. She followed C.J.'s eyes to the piano. "Naw, it's just been here since any of us moved in."

"Can I try it?"

Flo bent her head C.J.'s way. Her look said, *You're the one always wishing you could play. Tell him it's okay.*

"Go on, then," C.J. said. "But none of us have shown those keys the light of day, so it's got to be way out of tune."

He folded back the keyboard cover. The expanse of black and white keys startled her somehow. She found it hard to believe it had been there all along. One sat lower than the rest, as if held down. But the others looked ready to work together. Zach tested the keys, cringing a couple of times at sour notes, then launched into a performance that made them dance—ragtime, he called it.

Flo clapped her hands. "What else can you play?"

"I love all kinds of jazz. And I know some popular music. Name someone you like."

"Sam Cooke."

He played "Summertime," then looked at C.J. "Is there someone *you* like?"

"Oh, I—"

"C.J. *loves* Charlie Parker."

"A genius on the saxophone." Zach's tone was respectful. "But I'm afraid I don't know any of his songs."

He looked so crestfallen that C.J. admitted, "I did like Nat King Cole in high school."

His playing pulled her back home. Yet, at the same time, it yanked her forward, forcing her to see him differently. No longer simply the white boy who frightened and annoyed her with his civil rights talk, but someone who could coax amazing sound from a neglected instrument.

"Well? How was that?" He turned toward C.J. but seemed to get tripped up by Flo's frown, every bit as stern as C.J.'s earlier look. "Didn't you like it, Flo?"

"Don't think much of the man myself."

"Well, he influenced your Sam Cooke."

"He might could've influenced more by not playing segregated clubs." Flo was getting wound up. "*Dr. King* says anyone who accepts evil without protesting helps keep it alive."

Zach opened his mouth but closed it without saying anything.

"Oh, dear," Flo said. "Smells like those beans could be overdone."

"I should be going." He stood to leave. "Thank you again for your help. And the use of your piano."

"The others won't believe that old thing could sound so fine," C.J. said, suddenly wishing he would stay.

"Maybe sometime I could play for them, too." And then he was gone, leaving her to stare at Flo and wonder what to talk about now.

❊   ❊   ❊

C.J. was wrapping smoked salmon around dill gherkins when Mrs. Upton came for the ruler. Day to day, Mrs. Upton trusted her eyes to tell her the plates were the right distance apart and the silverware lined up exactly with the table's edge. But she'd fallen back on her ruler for dinner parties. And this one, with five couples invited and two of the guests on the hospital board, had her all in a flap.

C.J. rolled her eyes at Mrs. Upton's back. The table had been set for two hours. As perfect as the drawing in the *Joy of Cooking*.

"Let's go over the wines," Mrs. Upton said, returning the ruler to the drawer. She nodded as C.J. pointed out the Merlot and Cabernet Sauvignon to be served with the tenderloin and cheese platter, the Sauvignon Blanc and Sauternes chilling to accompany the soufflé and dessert. She peered at the Tarte fine aux Pommes, ready to bake while the guests ate, and left.

After peeling and slicing potatoes, C.J. started two hamburger patties for the boys. Nathan and Eli—not an ounce of goodness between them.

More than once, they'd opened the oven door to collapse a soufflé. While she assembled the gratin, sprinkling grated Swiss and nutmeg between each layer of potatoes, she kept one eye on the sizzling patties, as if they couldn't be trusted any more than the boys.

The phone rang just as she called for them. Mrs. Upton rushed in behind her sons. "The Millers will be late. They can't say how late." Her voice climbed to a high-pitched whine. "I can just see the soufflé collapsed in a cold heap." Both boys snickered.

"I know what to do." C.J. turned her eyes briefly skyward in appreciation for the time she'd spent studying the *Joy of Cooking*. "We can serve a timbale."

Mrs. Upton wrinkled her nose. "That doesn't sound French."

"It's a fine custard dish that will even submit to the indignity of reheating." C.J. quoted the cookbook. "That way, the Millers won't get a cold entrée."

"Well, if you're sure . . ."

When the bell rang, Mrs. Upton waltzed to the door with her husband at her side. C.J. carried hors d'oeuvres to the living room. As each couple arrived, she scuttled back and forth, collecting coats and serving drinks.

Two ladies sitting in the window alcove held out their glasses but kept right on talking. "Nancy, that can't be!"

"Oh, yes. The hospital might as well shut its doors if this passes. I'll definitely be voting *no* next week."

C.J. was gathering ingredients for the tenderloin when the Millers arrived. They declined drinks and drifted toward the others standing about. As she waited for their coats, one of the other men greeted Mr. Miller. "Glad you could make it."

"Business is hopping, don't you know?" Mr. Miller clapped him on the back. "Now, Myron, I need to give my two cents on that matter before the board. Nancy will be voting yes, I hope."

She rushed away with the coats, right past the dining room table where Mr. Miller's place card sat next to Nancy's. She took the steaks from the refrigerator but just stared at the white paper. She'd watched the butcher wrap them in suet to keep them moist. Hadn't she? What if Nathan and Eli had somehow turned the suet into bacon to get her in trouble?

"This is a Jewish house!" Mrs. Upton had screeched the time C.J. unwittingly brought home steaks wrapped in bacon. "I will not have an ounce of pork in it. Is that clear?"

C.J. peeled back one corner and peeked inside.

"*C.J.?*"

She nearly knocked the steaks to the floor. But the barding was indeed suet. "Ma'am?"

"Are you ready to serve your timbale?"

C.J. opened the oven. The knife inserted in the center of the mold came out clean. If only there were such a foolproof test for deciding whether to speak up about the seating arrangement.

"The timbale looks perfect," she said, somehow reassured. "But, ma'am—I think I should . . ."

"What *is* it? We need to get seated."

"That's just it. I think I should tell you some of your guests have strong opinions on the matter before the board. You might ought to move Mr. Miller so he isn't next to Miz Nancy or her husband."

"I can't stop them talking about it."

"No'm, but if they get to discussing things, it's liable to take the spotlight off the main course. Perhaps the disagreeing could at least get delayed to dessert."

Mrs. Upton's eyebrows shot up. "That's good advice. I'll just shuffle a couple of place cards and call everyone to the table. You can serve shortly."

As the evening progressed, C.J. cleared dishes, served the next course, assembled the cheese platter, baked the tartlets, and tried not to get too far behind with cleanup. Still, when everyone had gone, she faced a mountain of dirty dishes. As she dried the last one, she realized there'd been no time for her to eat. Too tired to care, she turned off the kitchen light and headed for the stairs.

"C.J." The voice from the darkened living room startled her. As her eyes adjusted, she spotted Mrs. Upton in an armchair by the window. Did the woman expect her to clean the living room tonight? "I just wanted to say it all . . . went quite well." The effort seemed to tire Mrs. Upton. "Your dinner was excellent."

"Thank you, ma'am. I'll go upstairs, unless you need anything more." She waited a moment, then turned to go.

"Mr. Miller could have spoiled the evening in more ways than one. But your quick thinking—well, it surprised me."

That sounded like a left-handed compliment at best. C.J. bit her tongue.

"I guess, with you coming from Mississippi . . ."

Now C.J. was certain she was being insulted. She pushed past her fatigue, drawing herself up straight and tall. "Yes'm. That was a big part of my job back home. Knowing what to do when a problem came up."

"Did they come up often?"

"Yes'm. They surely did."

❊   ❊   ❊

The South Side often made C.J. feel like Alice gone down the rabbit hole. Whenever she approached from Washington Park, she immediately noticed more Negroes, until suddenly she saw nothing but. The very buildings were different. Large wooden apartment buildings battered by Chicago's winds hugged the streets for comfort. Today an old man in a tattered chair watched from the litter-strewn strip of dirt between a building and the sidewalk as she and Flo passed.

Yet today, under the gray, wind-whipped sky where winter hung on like a dog to a bone, C.J. felt at home here. She glanced to her right and realized that was Flo's doing. Whether they were going to church, walking around Lake Michigan, or shopping for a bargain—and despite their tendency to argue—she felt at home with Flo.

Their day of leisure stretched before them. They giggled as each, in a grand and gallant gesture, tried to hold the doors of the South Center Department Store open for the other. Then they hurried inside.

"C.J.," Flo called from her dressing room a few minutes later. "I'm right next to you, I think. How're you doing?"

"Not so good." She'd already ruled out the green dress with the broad white collar and matching cuffs. The skirt flaring out from the hips drew too much attention to her small waist. And the rusty red dress with brown and beige stripes was no better. She sighed and shoved all the dresses with stylish swing skirts aside. Better to stick with what worked. She reached for the sleek navy suit dress. "I've got one more to try, though."

"I found me a great one, just right for Sundays," Flo called as C.J. smoothed the soft wool over her hips. "It might even do for something special now and again."

C.J. turned this way and that. The pencil skirt suited her figure. She gave her reflection a satisfied smile. "Me, too! C'mon over and show me."

Suddenly, there were two identical images in the mirror. C.J. blinked, then burst out laughing. "What's that they say about great minds?"

Flo laughed, too. "You know, the way we share clothes, we probably don't need but one of these." She pulled a coin from her purse. "I'll flip you for who buys."

"Tails," C.J. called as Flo caught the coin and slapped it against the back of her hand.

"Sorry, C.J. I'll buy next time."

"Lunch is on you then."

They hurried from the department store to Walgreen's and took seats at the counter. Mixers whirred, blending chocolate syrup, vanilla ice cream, milk, and malt powder. A man seated to their right received his patty melt, still sizzling on the bread.

"Too cold for a shake today," Flo said. "A patty melt sounds just right."

As water glasses appeared before them, C.J. looked up into kind eyes in a face surrounded by thick, curly black hair, shorter on the sides and longer on top. Were it not for his perfectly squared bowtie and jauntily set white cap, she would have said the counter clerk looked almost exactly like Little Richard. "We'll have two patty melts, please. She's buying."

"Have a milkshake, too, then." He winked.

A flush crossed C.J.'s cheeks. She glanced sideways, but Flo was looking in the mirror, at the store behind her.

"Maybe come spring. *If* it ever does," she said, sending the man on down the counter with a friendly smile. "Flo, you all right?"

"I don't know could I sit that still."

"Huh?"

"You know, the students. In Greensboro."

The last trace of C.J.'s smile fled. Why couldn't they get through one afternoon without trouble?

"I mean *think* about it. Feeling all them eyes watching. Climbing up on that stool anyways." Plumb foolishness. "Then just sitting." Flo patted the counter, like it was a child. Ever so slightly, she twisted the stool one way and another. "See? It's almost impossible to sit still."

"I have read about it, you know." C.J.'s voice was as stiff as her back. "The Uptons take the *Tribune* and the *New York Times*. Some say we bring trouble on ourselves. And some"—she lowered her voice reflexively, even though everyone in the Walgreen's was a Negro—"how maybe we finally got mad enough about Emmett Till."

"Yeah, mad. The *Defender* says Woolworth's got picked on account of it being a national chain that Negroes all over the country shop at."

"The papers I read got stories about places been showing their support. Like the University of Chicago. And especially Alabama." She touched Flo's arm. "People are getting sit-in *crazy* in your Alabama."

Their patty melts arrived. C.J. peeled the bread away from the oozing yellow cheese and reached for the ketchup.

"The *Defender* says young Negroes are turning against the old ways. Using non-violence, mind you, but demanding our rights."

C.J. took a loud, crunching bite out of her pickle and set it down. "All *I* know is how to pull my own self up one day at a time. Not waiting on somebody else to give me something." She bit into her sandwich.

Flo reached for the mustard. "Don't you want more?"

C.J. counted the times her jaw moved up and down—ten—before she swallowed. She wiped her mouth carefully, then looked hard at Flo. "More might be fine for folks like Mae. But you and me, we're going home some day."

"When we go home—" Flo sliced her sandwich and waved half of it in the air for emphasis. "Don't you want to vote? Send your kids to good schools? Get a better job?"

C.J. studied the counter clerk. His was a job no Negro could have back at King's Drugs. He seemed proud of it, too. Then a shadow in the mirror reminded her of Mr. Corrigan's men. She felt them crowding around her as if she were sitting somewhere she didn't belong. Knew how easily the hatred in their eyes could turn to murder. "Isn't a bit of that seems worth it if someone gets killed." Her voice came out hard-edged like the counter.

Flo looked at her plate for the longest time, as if it held the secret of the ages. Did she wipe away a tear before counting out money for their lunch?

Outside again, the March afternoon sun seemed to struggle to reach them. Most people walked purposefully, on their way to someplace warm. Still, there were children tossing a baseball. It flew past one boy, toward C.J. and Flo. Flo ducked, but C.J. scooped it up and shot it back, hard.

"Ain't you just the biggety one?" Flo said.

C.J. scowled. "My daddy taught me to throw like that."

"Not the ball." Flo rolled her eyes. "How many times you gonna do this? I ain't never met someone I got more in common with. *Or* someone more stubborn."

"I'm not—"

"We could be twins, C.J. Separated at birth. But then we just showed up in Hyde Park at the apartment. You gonna ruin that 'cause we got one thing we can't agree on?"

She heard her momma admonishing Charlie. *It's about knowing your place with white folks.* "That *one* thing—it's not like I want ketchup and you'd rather have mustard. It's a big—"

"It ain't big unless you make it big. Unless we can't talk 'cause we're afraid of disagreeing."

At the corner of 47th and South Parkway, C.J. stopped, remembering Sissy saying if you stood here long enough you'd meet everyone who'd left Mississippi before you. It was indeed amazing how she and Flo had come to know each other. Her fingers tightened around the handles of the shopping bag, reminding her of the dress they'd agreed to share and the friendship she wanted to share. She held out the bag but kept a grip on one handle. When Flo took the other, they walked on down the street, swinging the bag between them.

❈   ❈   ❈

It seemed to her that things were suddenly moving faster again. Summer, kicked off by their first nearly ninety-degree day, was upon them. Zach had been stopping by a lot. And the moment C.J. thought would never come, when she would see her family again, was now little more than a bus ride away. Yet, here she stood in the tiny Hyde Park kitchen, nearly motionless with inactivity.

She watched a puff of flour escape through the seam of a brown paper bag as Emily shook chicken pieces. Sissy dabbed at her cheek where juice squirted from the tomatoes she was slicing. The batter for the spoon bread had cooled. It waited for someone to add milk and eggs, but C.J.'s were the only available hands. Sissy began coaxing the pineapple-upside-down cake free of the pan. Onto the plate slid a golden creation with pineapple and cherries crowning its caramelized top.

That did it. C.J. grabbed a wooden spoon. "I can at least finish this, y'all. I'm going back home in the morning. That makes me happy, not helpless."

She was washing the bowl when they heard the knock. Sissy wiped her hands on her apron and went to the door.

"Hi, Sissy," said the voice that, by now, all the girls of number ten recognized as Zach's.

"I declare, that white boy is underfoot more than my daddy's favorite hunting dog," Emily whispered. "Delivering the package the mailman left for Alinda. Asking do we need anything when he's going to the market. And getting his friend to fix that old piano."

"Wonder what it is this time?" Emily finished.

"Is C.J. here?" she heard Zach ask.

Emily and C.J. raised their eyebrows at each other. Ever since the first time he played their piano, C.J. could scarcely pass it without adjusting a photo or lifting the keyboard lid to peek at the keys. Each time, she thought of Zach. She'd hoped she could get on the bus for Poplar Springs without running into him. She was sure once she was back at home with her family, she would forget all about him. Now, she'd just have to make this quick. By the time she got to the door, she had smoothed her dress and slowed her breathing. But the sight of him—dark curls grown thicker, arms tanned by the June sun— caused her face, like some unmanageable child, to fan out in a smile.

"I learned a Charlie Parker song!" Zach grinned back, looking a lot like her little brother when he caught a big fish or a high, fast ball.

"Which one?" C.J. asked.

"It's called 'Now's the Time.' "

"Well, come on in," Sissy said. "We got to hear us this song."

Zach seated himself and folded back the keyboard cover as if this would be any one of the times he'd played for them over the past few months. But today, before his fingers flew and the newly tuned piano with its liberated key tried to keep up, he looked only at C.J. His eyes seemed to say *What you like is important to me.*

A part of *her* flew home, to rock with her daddy while the music she'd loved her whole life poured outside to the porch. But another part stayed busy right here, comparing the sound of Charlie Parker and Zach. It struck her then that the things Zach had done lately might be for all the girls, no one more than another, but this was Zach doing just for her. She hoped Sissy and Emily didn't notice.

Resting his hands in his lap, he turned to her. "How'd I do?"

"Not bad," she admitted, more surprised than stingy with her praise.

Sissy clapped her hands. "C.J. ought to know, but I say it was wonderful."

The smells of all the foods nearly ready seemed to rush in at once to fill the silence.

"Don't let me keep you from dinner." Zach stood to leave.

"Let us thank you for all you been doing lately by asking you to stay to supper," Sissy said.

"Sure," Emily called from the kitchen. "We got plenty. Southern girls don't know how to cook just a little."

Again Zach looked to C.J.

"I reckon you got to try Mississippi food, since you fed Flo and me those Jewish sandwiches."

Sissy dipped collard greens into a serving dish. Emily cut into a chicken leg to test it. C.J. added another place setting to the table and set out the tomatoes. As she sliced spoon bread, she heard breathing so close she thought it was her own. When she looked up, inches separated her and Zach.

She recalled shadowing him at the deli—curious but unsure what to expect. "Over there, in that cabinet," she said, needing him to move. "Can you take down some glasses? I'll get the tea."

"Let's eat," Emily said as she piled crispy golden chicken on a platter.

Zach held out chairs for Sissy and C.J. He waited to seat Emily, then took the chair to C.J.'s left. "It smells wonderful."

C.J. had to agree. If she closed her eyes, she could easily believe she was in her momma's kitchen. Home.

"This is my chicken," Emily said. "We fry most anything you can shake a stick at."

"And Sissy's collard greens boiled with ham hocks." C.J. passed the bowl to her left. Zach's hand brushed hers, causing the tiny hairs to stand on end. He was looking at her again, as if searching for something and trying to see right inside her to find it. The way he'd looked at her in the deli, when she felt a wave of empathy for his experience growing up—Jewish! How could she be so stupid? "I'm sorry," she stammered. "Of course you can't eat that."

Zach's fork stopped halfway to his mouth. "Why not?"

"The ham—Miz Upton won't have any part of a pig in her house. You said . . ."

"Oh, that I'm Jewish? It's okay."

"No, you don't need to eat it to be polite."

"Y'all got rules about eating, too?" Emily asked. "The O'Shea family I work for, they're Catholic. Can't have no meat on Fridays."

"Well, I'm not actually Jewish. My dad is, but not my mom."

"But you said . . ."

"I'm sorry for confusing you. I call myself Jewish because I like Jewish beliefs about how to treat each other. But I don't follow Jewish laws strictly."

C.J. watched Zach finally taste the collard greens. "What do you think?"

"They're delicious. Now, what I'm wondering is this." He flashed a dimpled smile. "Do you ladies cook like this all the time?"

"No, tonight's a bit special," Emily said on her way to the refrigerator. She took an ice cube tray from the freezer and pulled up on its handle to release the cubes. "We're sending C.J. back to Mississippi in the morning."

The cubes clanked in the tray. As Emily slid them into the pitcher, tea sloshed over the sides. It was only a little spill. But Zach's look reminded C.J. of how she'd felt when he was about to eat the ham. All she'd wanted was to stop him.

"You're going home?"

"I've been here a year now. It's time for a visit."

"Oh. Just a visit then."

C.J. sent the spoon bread back around the table—to the right—and took another tiny bite of her food. To watch and listen to the three of them, one would think they sat down to supper together all the time. But her stomach felt oddly unsettled.

"I just *can't*," Zach moaned when Sissy tried to give him more chicken.

"Dessert, then," Emily announced.

How fitting. A dessert as upside down as the sight of the four of them in this kitchen.

"A small piece, please," Zach said.

Emily cut a big piece for Zach and only slightly smaller ones for everyone else. The cake was one of C.J.'s favorites, but she toyed with it.

Zach pushed his empty plate slightly aside and looked at C.J. "I see why you miss home cooking. That was fabulous."

Home . . . missing home . . . Right now, returning to Poplar Springs didn't seem as wonderful as it had just a while ago.

"Now please, ladies, let me help clean up."

"If you'd play some more, that'd be even better," Emily said, and he nodded.

After several songs Sissy said, "Zach, you play so fine. Reckon you could teach someone else? C.J.'s always had a hankering to play."

C.J. pictured Mrs. Barnes helping her daughter at their piano, leaning over the bench from behind and placing her hands over Joan's, and panicked. She stuffed her hands in the pockets of her dress. "Oh, no. Y'all don't want to hear me when you got someone knows what he's doing."

"Sure!" Zach said. "Here's one we can do together, C.J. It's called . . . um, 'Chopsticks.' "

Her hands felt clammy. She rubbed them against the fabric. It would be a month of Sundays before she would be persuaded to take her hands out of her pockets.

But Sissy grabbed another chair and pushed her into it. And she had to free her hands in order to maintain her balance, to keep from falling right in Zach's lap.

He showed her where to place her right hand, then had her follow him. Before too long, C.J. had mastered the melody. Zach then added chords, and they performed the duet over and over until the others pleaded with them to stop.

"Thanks, everyone," he said, pausing at the door before he left. "And, C.J. Travel safe."

In the kitchen, Emily handed C.J. a sponge. She didn't want or need a boyfriend. If she did, someone like the counter clerk at Walgreen's would be who she should be thinking about. She washed dishes with a vengeance, as if the caked-on food were her own misguided thoughts, as if getting them done sooner would get her on the bus and back home that much quicker.

CHAPTER 11

June 1960
Now's the Time

"Momma tell you we're moving to Meridian after the wedding?" Metairie asked.

"What?" C.J. looked up from the table. It was her first night home and they were finishing supper. She'd been remembering the day her daddy brought the table into the house from his workshop. Before Charlie was even born. Just look at her brother now. If he kept eating the way he had tonight, he'd soon shoot up taller than her.

Metairie rested a hand on George's well-muscled arm, as if measuring his biceps, and brought her chin up slightly. "My man's got on with the city, driving a truck."

George's barrel chest puffed up a notch as Metairie sang his praises. He was a rather short man, though plenty tall for Metairie. His face was like so many others, yet graced with kindness. C.J. couldn't help comparing him to Zach, who was kind to a fault, with a smile that could warm the sun. She loved to watch his hands and forearms when he played the piano. Best of all, and the thing that made her most comfortable, was his height. Perfect to bring her emerald green eyes in line with his azure blue ones. She cringed at how uncomfortable everyone would be if Zach were here, talking jobs with George. The Walgreen's counter clerk was tall, too. She reckoned he and George were both lucky, having jobs no Mississippi Negro could take for granted.

"I start on Monday," George said. "Momma and Daddy helped us move most everything over last weekend."

Momma and Daddy? George was more in the family than she was, and he and Metairie hadn't even tied the knot yet. "That's great, y'all." She stood and stacked several plates before Momma stopped her.

"I'll have *none* of that, girl. You're here to rest."

"I'm family, Momma, not the Queen of England." She leaned over Charlie from behind and wrapped her arms around him. Were those little muscles she felt beneath the sleeves of his T-shirt?

"Ah, C.J." He sounded as if she'd wiped his face or tousled his hair, but he made no move to break free.

"I got to work on your sister's dress," Momma said. "And your daddy's got to pick a melon for dessert. You go on outside with him. Let the others do them dishes."

Daddy put one of his albums on the old phonograph and motioned to C.J. She walked with him to the garden. Stooping, he thumped and patted the larger melons until he'd selected the ripest. Cradling it like one of his children, he carried it back around front.

Through the open windows, the music was blowing and bopping. C.J. and her daddy settled themselves in rockers. He reached out to pat her hand. In the unrelenting heat and humidity, they watched the orange-yellow sun begin to slide down the horizon like a riff.

"Charlie sure has grown, hasn't he, Daddy? I couldn't believe my eyes when I stepped off that bus."

"I reckon so. I don't notice day to day. With summer here, I'm carrying him up to the Wilsons' with me. Mr. Wilson's paying him to help."

"Now I know that makes Charlie proud."

"Happier, too. During the school year, we stayed on him 'bout studying." Daddy looked up as Momma joined them. "Especially your momma."

"Well, that's one thing hasn't changed." C.J. smiled fondly at her mother arranging her sewing basket and Metairie's dress in her lap.

C.J. had an image of the dress she'd like some day. Long and straight, like her. In white satin. With short sleeves, a round neck, and a little flare to the bottom. Metairie's dress was white, of course. But it was full and flouncy, like Metairie. Sadly, the dress C.J. was to wear as her sister's bridesmaid had similar lines.

"I got to get this lace on tonight," Momma said.

"Momma, you got to let me know how I can help."

"I don't rightly know. The ladies at Hope Baptist are cleaning the church and making the cake. Miz Wilson is letting us take flowers from her garden."

What in heaven's name had gotten into the lot of them, herself in particular? Since when did she have to *ask* to help? "I'll get things for the watermelon," she said.

But as C.J. pushed up off the arms of the rocker, Metairie came out, carrying napkins and trailed by George with the saltshaker. They sat together on the porch steps, staring into each other's eyes. C.J. sank back into her chair and scowled at this change in her family. No longer just the five of them, but George, too, in every picture.

Charlie bounded onto the porch like an overgrown puppy, banging the screen door behind him. "Here's the butcher knife, Daddy. Let's have at that melon."

Her daddy pulled himself up from the chair, a little more slowly than C.J. was used to seeing. In one clean stroke, he slit the melon in half lengthwise. He sliced three-inch rounds and cut those in half.

Charlie grabbed the first piece. Juice dribbled down his chin as he chomped. Metairie and George helped themselves. C.J.'s momma set the wedding dress carefully aside and moved over to the steps, where George served her.

"Here, girl." Daddy held out a slice to C.J. "Surely you can't get nothing this good up there in Chicago."

"'Course not, Daddy. Your melons are the best anywheres."

"What you wanna bet I can hit that tree more times than you?" Charlie challenged George.

They arced seeds from the porch to the sweet gum tree, until Metairie gave George a look that said that's enough of that. "You win, little man," George said.

C.J. was smiling on the outside. But inside, her irritation was growing. She was sure it was good for Charlie to have the influence of another strong, hard-working man in his life. But she wanted to be important, too. She slipped into the house, returning with shopping bags.

"What's in them sacks?" Charlie said almost immediately.

She handed out the wrapped gifts first. A box of Frango Mints made right in Marshall Field's on the thirteenth floor for Momma. A poster she'd found in an old bookstore for her daddy, from a concert Charlie Parker did in New York. The intricately embroidered tablecloth she'd chosen as Metairie's wedding gift. Then, she pretended the bag was empty. Charlie's crestfallen look made him seem eight again. "All right." She took out the White Sox cap and slapped it on his head with a laugh.

Daddy balled up one fist and twisted it in his palm. His faraway look said he was feeling the ball he'd caught at the New Orleans Pelicans game.

"Wow! The majors." Charlie took the cap off and traced the emblem. "What's it like?"

Metairie crinkled her nose when C.J. mentioned the stockyards near Comiskey Park. Charlie smacked his lips at the hotdogs. Momma smiled as if the sunshine shone on Daddy in one of the cheap seats. But her family looked at her blankly when she spoke of the mix of Negroes and whites sitting and playing together.

"Well, I got to go. Me and William got plans," Charlie announced.

"Be back by nine thirty," Her momma said, too matter-of-factly for C.J.'s liking. She opened her mouth to object, but instead reached out to straighten Charlie's cap.

"George and I are gonna take us a walk down by the lake," Metairie said. "We got a few things to talk about before the wedding."

Alone with her parents, C.J. moved into the empty rocker between theirs. Momma's needle and thread seemed to work faster as the daylight dwindled. Daddy got up to put on another album, then stood in the doorway rolling a cigarette.

"Momma, Daddy. I got y'all one more thing." She held an envelope out to Momma.

Momma fingered the envelope. "Daughter, you ain't said two words about your work. Is it what you been used to?"

"Pretty much. Only the money's better. I've been setting some aside in a bank in Chicago for Charlie, to help him go to college. Take a look."

"Good Lord, girl!" Momma said when she saw the balance on the bank statement. "This *and* what you been sending us each month. Your daddy and I are mighty proud."

Daddy's soft "Mighty proud" floated on the familiar smell of his tobacco. C.J. closed her eyes, steeping in the feeling of her parents' praise.

Around the side of the house, mosquitoes buzzed and slapped themselves against the window screens, trying to get at the light inside. But the air on the porch was mosquito free, thanks to the castor bean plants Momma had put in around the rail. C.J. rocked to the beat of the music.

But, suddenly, Charlie Parker was delivering his version of "Now's the Time." She saw Zach's hands on the keyboard, heard him breathing so close while she sliced spoon bread. And all she wanted was to be back in Hyde Park.

No! What she needed was a plant that could keep away such thoughts. *Now* was the time. She was home with her family, where she'd longed to be for some part of every one of the last three hundred seventy-one days. Where she would be for good, once she saved enough money for Charlie.

She looked at her parents. Her daddy had moved into the rocker on the other side of Momma. He gazed at her while she worked, as if she were eighteen and they'd just met. "Momma? You think Metairie and George have the spark?"

"The what?"

"Like you and Daddy. He still loves to talk about the very first time he—"

"Saw the girl of my dreams, standing in the church yard in a cloud of pale lavender, like you was sent from heaven," Daddy finished, exactly the way C.J. remembered it.

"The way you look at each other. You can see it in the photo from y'all's wedding day, too. I always called it the spark."

"What you really asking?"

"Maybe how'd you know you were in love and ought to be getting married."

"We did like to look on each other. Your daddy was so handsome, especially fine in that uniform. But I knew soon as I looked in his eyes, 'cause I could see all the way to heaven." Momma reached out to pat his hand. "This man moved into my heart that day and never left."

C.J. watched her daddy crush the cigarette butt beneath his boot, heard him softly hum to the record. "Then what happened?"

"We talked and figured we thought the same ways 'bout making a family and a life together. I reckon what you see in that picture is the hope." Momma paused to tie off a knot. C.J. felt suddenly more tired than she could ever remember feeling. "And what you see today, that's us blessing God that we was right."

"Thank you, Momma. I think I'll go on to bed now."

"Daughter?" Momma sounded alarmed. "You met you someone up there in Chicago?"

"Oh, no'm." Her cheeks flushed and she blessed the rapidly falling darkness. "It's nothing like that." *Nothing* like that. She pecked her momma on the cheek and gave her daddy a squeeze. "I'll see y'all in the morning."

❧   ❧   ❧

Throughout that week, C.J. found ways to help at home and at church, baking and decorating. Still, being at home reminded her of the aimless feeling she'd had when Reverend Thornheart let her go, and her little church felt like a doll house after the ones she and Flo had visited. When the ladies of Hope Baptist asked what Chicago was like, she told them Sissy's and Emily's view. She had trouble looking Mae's mother in the eye, wondering if she knew about Mae's plans to move to New York City. And with a conflicted heart, she watched the clock tick down the hours until she would be back on the bus, taking solace in helping her daddy carve and decorate the wedding broom.

At four o'clock sharp on Saturday, C.J. walked down the aisle on the arm of George's best man, Albert, feeling her dress like a weight. She and

Albert took their places with Brother James and George, looking out at the assembled congregation. Family, every one of them. From Nellie, who'd seen the Evans kids into the world, to Miss Clayton, to Mr. and Mrs. Bishop. They'd all turned out for Metairie. Would they do the same, some years down the road, if C.J. were to be married here?

Metairie practically floated toward them on the cloud of her dress, tethered only by Daddy's steady arm. He released her carefully to George.

Brother James then asked the bride and groom to take seats across the aisle from each other in the front row. Metairie bowed her head, but her face held a perpetual grin as he spoke about marital relations and responsibilities and God's place in their lives. To C.J.'s horror, he recited from Colossians: "Wives, submit yourselves unto your husbands, as it is fit in the Lord. Husbands, love your wives, and be not bitter against them."

Mrs. Perry began playing "O Perfect Love" to bring the bride and groom back before Brother James. C.J. smiled bravely through her tears, seeing Zach at the piano. And she felt small for envying her sister.

C.J.'s momma put her handkerchief in her pocketbook, snapped it shut, and adopted a smile that would not leave her face again that day. Her oldest daughter, married to a man with a good job and poised to deliver grandbabies.

Metairie turned toward C.J. and held out her bouquet. Stargazer lilies, Shasta daisies, and yellow tea roses from Mrs. Wilson's garden, nestled in a spray of honeysuckle from the fence behind the Evanses' house. C.J. moved quickly to her side, happy to have Metairie and George between her and Albert. Her first thought on meeting him was relief that he was tall enough to be her escort. From her new vantage point, she had to admit that he was also a good-looking man. Still, too much had been made, by too many, of the possibility of Albert and C.J. getting to know each other better. She looked away, thinking of the possibilities of men from A to Z she might one day find herself next to, wearing the straight white satin wedding gown.

The couple exchanged vows and were pronounced man and wife. Daddy brought forth the beautiful broom he had carved. The congregation uttered "Amen" and "Praise Jesus." He laid it before his daughter and son-in-law, surely thinking of slave ancestors who, forbidden to marry and live together, jumped over a broom to signify their commitment. C.J. thought of the African symbolism of sweeping all past problems away and wished for a broom of her own.

❊   ❊   ❊

On the trip back to Chicago, C.J. had almost wished she could stay on the bus forever. She'd felt out of place with her family, yet dreaded returning to the Uptons; wanted to see her friends, yet known Flo's and Zach's talk would rile her. In the two months since, her habit of wishing herself backwards or forwards, here or there, had only gotten worse. She'd concluded that "Now's the Time" ought to be her theme song.

This Saturday, she was part of the throng of spectators attending the annual Bud Billiken Parade, held every year since 1929. Like a cat birthing a giant litter, it spit them out in Washington Park—thousands of Negroes, some of whom had participated in the parade, all of whom had thrilled to the sight of their heroes of stage, screen, and radio and now eagerly awaited the show on Picnic Hill. Mae marched C.J. and Flo to a prime spot and settled herself on the grass. Legs angled to one side, neckline adjusted, ready to see and be seen.

"*The* heavyweight champion of the entire world shook *my* hand, y'all!" Mae said. "Floyd Patterson just leaned right down—" Mae stopped to wave at a girl who then motioned her over. She stood up and left.

"You know we ain't *never* gonna hear the end of that!" Flo said.

"Yeah." C.J. laughed. "And Mae's doing so much waving she should've been in the parade her own self."

The crowd stirred as someone approached the microphone. "Who's the music host who loves you the most?" he shouted.

"Daddy-O!" Flo yelled back with the crowd.

"You know him?"

"He's on late nights on WMAQ."

Daddy-O began to work the crowd, ticking off the list of scheduled performers, talking up each one. Big Maybelle and the John Coltrane Quintet. Oscar Peterson, Roland Kirk, and the headliner Dinah Washington.

"You listen to him much, this Daddy-O?"

"Yeah. He talks about the cause, in between spinning jazz and blues records."

C.J. sifted out "the cause" like a lump in flour, wondering if Zach listened to WMAQ. *I love all kinds of jazz,* he'd said the first time he played piano for her and Flo.

"A day like today—it's a time to be proud of being Negro." Flo leaned back on her arms and tilted her face to the early August sun.

"Weren't those kids something?" C.J. shook her head. "Marching down the parkway with their chests all puffed out, looking so proud of their costumes."

"I can see them marching with Dr. King."

"I reckon they were just happy to be seen. For a change."

"I reckon they were at that."

Big Maybelle took the stage, all soft and round with a smile as wide as her face. As she sang her hit "Gabbin' Blues," her bosom heaved, just as Mahalia Jackson's would—C.J. and Flo exchanged smiles—just like Momma's did when she sang at Hope Baptist.

Flo's smile lingered as the next performer, eyes shielded by dark glasses, was led on stage and helped into a chair. Three saxophones hung from his neck.

"Scoot over," Mae commanded, rejoining C.J. and Flo. "I got all caught up with my friend. Her cousin is studying at one of Madame Walker's beauty schools. The schools are run by Miz Joyner. *The* very same Miz Joyner who chairs this parade."

Daddy-O interrupted, instructing the crowd to prepare for a sight and sound to behold. C.J. gaped as Roland Kirk played the three saxes simultaneously. She could only describe as magic the way a note from each horn constituted a chord. *That's near about as impressive as the sound Zach gets from our old piano.* She opened her mouth to offer her joke, but found herself stuck on the word *magic.*

She'd come into this world, to hear her momma tell it, like a magic trick—a strong girl, with a mind of her own. *Aren't we the magic girls? Who knows what we might do someday?* That's what she'd said the last time she saw Joan Barnes, the smart little girl, with her magic line that she knew not to cross. And yet she had. Joan had been bad on a C.J. day, despite her promise. Why was she thinking of Joan now, feeling the anger she thought she'd left behind the night she bid her little friend goodbye? She tried to shake it off.

"Now, here from their debut at New York City's Jazz Gallery"— Daddy-O's voice rolled across the grass like a brewing storm—"the John Coltrane Quintet!"

C.J. jumped to her feet to get a look. She listened, amazed, to the sound of Coltrane's tenor sax, his rapid runs seeming to spew forth hundreds of notes. Coltrane put down his saxophone. Someone handed him another one. He began to play. A new sound. Not tenor, but soprano. She wondered what had caused him to take up the new instrument. As he played more, she heard the difference—reaching higher registers, notes coming even faster—a good change.

She wished Zach were here, to ooh and aah with her, to talk about it. "Don't you know Zach would eat this up?"

"I know he would," Mae agreed.

"I reckon he wouldn't even hardly notice his was the only white face in a sea of darkness," Flo said.

C.J. felt stung, brought up short, as if the music had suddenly stopped and the party ended. That night when she'd eaten watermelon on her parents' porch, she'd seen how George dropped into her family like he was a piece of the puzzle meant to be there all along. And, yet, she'd kept thinking of Zach when she should have been enjoying being with her family.

"Maybe not. But Zach would stick out here like a pumpkin that wandered into a watermelon patch."

"Someday . . ." Flo added.

Someday, my eye. Not likely in her lifetime. There were lines that shouldn't be crossed. There was magic that wasn't quite enough.

"What you thinking?" Flo asked.

"'Bout the differences in saxophones."

But she was really thinking about the differences in lives. The twists of fate that set her on one path and Metairie on another. She saw it now. Her thoughts in Mississippi were pure foolishness. It wasn't even possible for her and Zach to be more than friends in Chicago, much less back home in Mississippi.

❈   ❈   ❈

Two days after Labor Day, C.J. sat in her room at the Uptons' house reading a magazine. The temperature had broken one hundred today, and it promised to be a tough night for sleeping. But as soon as Mr. and Mrs. Upton got home, she would give it a try. Just then, a shadow crossed her open door. She tensed. When it fell on the pages of her magazine, she sprang from the bed, ready.

"Can I—" Eli's voice came out in a high-pitched squeak.

"Where's Nathan?" She peered around the corner. "Y'all are supposed to be watching TV."

"Downstairs. I want to ask you something without anybody else hearing."

Ten-year-old Eli stared up at her with the same curious look he had the first day she came to the Uptons' house. She'd winked at him then, and he'd almost let himself smile. Now his almost pretty face seemed etched in sadness.

She sighed deeply and sat back on the edge of the bed, wanting to believe he wasn't the troublemaker Nathan was. "Come in, then."

He stepped across the threshold as if the floor on the other side might give way beneath him. "Why haven't you told on us? For the things Nathan and I've been doing."

That was what she called being between a rock and a hard place. "Tattling doesn't usually fix things. It's best to work out a problem directly with the one you have it with."

"Even kids?"

"Ones who are old enough to know right from wrong."

"What if the thing you might tell is . . ." Eli searched his shoes for his next words. "Is really bad and hurts you?"

"Hurts you how?"

"Makes you really sad . . . and scared." His shoulders drooped.

"Is someone hurting you, Eli?" The child was slight, and it wasn't hard to imagine bigger kids picking on him.

As he took a deep breath, he let out a little hiccup. "It's kids at school. At recess they make fun of my nose and try to trip me."

"Can't Nathan straighten these boys out?" She was certain he wouldn't let anyone pick on Eli if he knew.

"It's girls, too," Eli whispered. A tear escaped one of his watery eyes. "They call me Jew boy."

No good Jew bastard . . . Commie . . . nigger lover . . . She let out a soft "Oh." Her mouth felt stuck around the sound. She patted the bed. "Come sit. Let's see can we figure something out."

Eli gulped air and sat down. He accepted the handkerchief C.J. pulled from her pocket and dried his huge brown eyes.

"I heard a story once," she said, "about a boy and a wolf. The boy started yelling mean things at the wolf. The wolf yelled to the boy to stop." Eli raised an eyebrow. "In this story, wolves could talk."

"Wasn't he afraid the wolf would eat him?"

"Nope. The boy felt really brave."

"*I* wouldn't have." Eli's eyes widened.

"This boy was way up high, somewhere the wolf couldn't get to him. *That* made him do something he wouldn't usually do." She looked hard at him. "It's like that when people are in a crowd."

"You sure?"

"Very sure. I can't tell you how many times I've seen it happen like that."

She leaned down close to him. Heads together, they whispered until they had hatched a plan.

"Now, promise me," she said firmly. "If things get worse, you'll tell your parents."

"I promise."

She stood him up and held him at arms' length by his shoulders, feeling his breathing even out. "Go on and get ready for bed now."

At breakfast, Eli looked bleary-eyed, like he'd stayed up late studying. Yet his manner, as he polished off his eggs and cinnamon toast, said he was ready for the test. When C.J. winked at him on his way out the door, he nodded.

As the morning wore on, she caught herself several times wondering how Eli was doing. She moved a load of bed linens from the washer to the dryer and went upstairs for the boys' dirty clothes. As she gathered Eli's little shirts and pants, she pictured Charlie—the way she guessed she always would—and smiled.

In Nathan's room, she opened the hamper and sniffed. There it was again, fainter than the tobacco mixed with perfume on his mother's clothes, but still noticeable. She would wring Charlie's neck if she caught him smoking. What could these parents be thinking?

The laundry was out of the dryer and back in the dressers by the time the bus brought the boys home. C.J. was in the kitchen mixing up an apple cake.

"I did it," Eli reported. "Recess went pretty well." Nathan gave his brother a sideways glance but then shrugged.

"Anyone want to lick the beaters?" C.J. held them out.

"Naw, that's for babies," Nathan said, stomping off.

Eli climbed up on one of the stools at the counter and slurped happily until Nathan's door slammed upstairs. "Miss McCarry let me speak to the class in morning meeting time."

"That so?" C.J. spooned batter into the pan.

"I said bullying was going on during recess. And I wouldn't want to, but I'd have to let the bullies' parents know if it didn't stop."

"That did the trick?"

"I think you were right." He took another lick. "I watched the biggest bullies while I was talking. Joe Spivey kind of slid down in his desk and crossed his arms. Betsy Parsons flicked her braid over her shoulder and stared at her fingernails."

"I think that was mighty clever. I reckon Miz McCarry was watching same as you. She surely knows now just who's been causing the trouble."

"Thanks, C.J." Eli's voice carried a note of admiration. He left to do his homework with his shoulders back up where they belonged.

She smiled, as grateful she'd helped as that Eli had thanked her. *Please, Lord*, she prayed. *Let someone be there to help Charlie if he needs it.*

She was settling the cake in the oven when Mrs. Upton opened the back door. She passed right on through without a word but was back quickly, motioning for C.J. to join her at the table.

"I must speak to you on a serious matter," she began abruptly. "Someone has been taking cigarettes from my room for weeks now. I do not like to think you would do that, but I don't know what else to think."

So Mrs. Upton didn't know about Nathan. If C.J. simply led her to his bedroom, told her to sniff, she would smell—only the lemony freshness of clothes barely out of the dryer. Her face burned with the shame and humiliation she'd witnessed when Eli told her about being called Jew boy.

"Miz Upton," she said. "I do not smoke."

"All right, then." Looking anything but convinced, Mrs. Upton got up and left.

Later that evening, C.J. took a bite of kasha, remembering when she'd first seen the word on the deli menu board. Now here she was eating it for supper. She made it with onions and almonds, the way Mrs. Upton required. She wondered how the small bearded man at the deli made it.

". . . cigarettes." Mrs. Upton's voice from the dining room called C.J. to attention. "*Boys*," Mrs. Upton continued. "I need to know who is taking them."

"It's got to be C.J.," Nathan said.

"Mom?" came Eli's small voice. C.J. strained to hear. "I don't think C.J. would do that."

"'Course she would," Nathan said. "She's hired help *and* a—"

"Why *not*, Eli?" Mrs. Upton said.

"She's smart *and* a nice person."

"Since when?" Nathan said.

"Well, she helped me with kids at school." Oh, dear. She knew she should have insisted he go to his parents for help. "She said people do bad things sometimes when they think no one's going to tell on them."

"So, she told you to be a tattletale?"

"No." Eli sounded irritated. "She helped me figure out how to get it to stop without tattling."

"Get what to stop, son?" Mr. Upton suddenly chimed in.

"Some kids were picking on me is all. It's no big deal."

"Why, honey?" Mrs. Upton said.

"Just name calling."

"Well, you shoulda told me. *I'm* your big brother. Not *her.*"

"What *kind* of names?" Mrs. Upton asked.

"Nothing."

"Probably Jew boy and stuff," Nathan said. "I used to get that until I punched a few kids' lights out."

"Joel, we're going down to that school tomorrow. You—"

"Mom! I told you, I can handle it."

"That's my boy," Mr. Upton said.

"*Joel*..." Mrs. Upton's voice had started to growl. "Change your schedule if you need to. I won't have my child in a fist fight."

"Son," Mr. Upton said. "You'll let us know if you need help?"

"Sure, Dad."

"Then let's give this a little more time."

C.J. strained again but heard not a sound from the dining room for a full thirty seconds. Then Mrs. Upton called, "C.J., you may bring in the apple cake."

The next morning, Mr. and Mrs. Upton rushed around as usual while C.J. tended to the boys in the kitchen. Mrs. Upton pecked them each on the head and went to the counter near the back door for her car keys.

"Nathan!" she yelled. "What is your jacket doing in here?"

"I don't know, Mom," he sputtered, his mouth full of toast. "I hung it in my closet like I always—"

Before he could finish, she was standing in the kitchen holding a lighter in her hand. "And what is this I found in the pocket?"

C.J. watched Eli's head swivel between his brother and his mother. She could have sworn his face held a look of satisfaction.

"Nathan Upton, we did not have that big party for your Bar Mitzvah just to have you pick and choose among the commandments that suit you. So, I'll ask you once more. Have you been taking my cigarettes?"

"Yes," he mumbled.

"It will stop *now*. We'll discuss consequences later."

Nathan glared. First at C.J., then at his brother, then at his mother's back as she left the room.

※   ※   ※

C.J. faced Mrs. Upton across the kitchen table. They'd already talked, several times. Already said all there was to say. The Uptons were moving to Lake Forest. Since Lake Forest was outside Cook County, the employment agency wouldn't allow C.J. to stay on with them. Mrs. Upton had tried persuading her to leave the agency. Though C.J. was flattered, she'd said no.

Mrs. Upton peeled the cellophane from a pack of Lucky Strikes. In all the months since Nathan admitted taking his mother's cigarettes, C.J. hadn't noticed even a hint of smoke on his clothes or his mother's. She watched Mrs. Upton slide a cigarette back and forth between her fingers as if she were feeling fine silk, saw her nose twitch slightly. "This new agency simply does not understand," Mrs. Upton said to the cigarette.

Skokie had surely never seen so many Negro women going in and out of one of its finest houses, not one interviewee coming close to satisfying Mrs. Upton. But C.J. hardly saw how that affected her.

The cigarette tapped the table. Faster and faster. "I want you to talk to them."

C.J.'s brows pinched together. She certainly knew Mrs. Upton was picky. Had known it since the day the agency assigned her to this house. It had taken longer, but she'd come to know that Mrs. Upton was pretty satisfied with her work.

"I don't know what else to—" Mrs. Upton looked down at her cigarettes, cleared her throat and began again. "A nice tea service should keep that pretentious Miss O'Connor occupied. You'll sit in the kitchen with the girls. She'll assume you're just keeping them company while they wait to talk to me."

The furnace clattered on, sending a burst of air from the register by the counter, kicking up the smell of the coconut macaroons cooling there. Mrs. Upton had insisted C.J. bake them this morning. Suddenly, she thought she might gag. *In the kitchen . . . with the girls . . .* She watched her hands clenching and unclenching atop the table where she'd taken her meals for the past year. To Mrs. Upton, she was little more than a belt in a vacuum cleaner, to be replaced when it wore out, with the main consideration being to get the right size and no need to know how the belt made the vacuum work.

"I'm talking about finding the right girl. Miss O'Connor will be here any minute with four more of them. Can you handle this?"

"Yes'm." She stuffed both fists in her lap. "I'll just get to that tea tray now." *And sit in the kitchen, doing as I'm told. But my next family—well, change can't come fast enough.*

As she assembled the tea service, she realized what she needed to do. Less for Mrs. Upton and more for herself. She needed to understand the value she brought, whether or not Mrs. Upton ever did.

When the doorbell rang, C.J. pointed the first girl to Mrs. Upton in the dining room and seated the others at the kitchen table. Miss O'Connor's ears went back when she spied the full tea service and *Ladies Home Journal* waiting in the living room. She arranged the skirt of her inexpensive suit just so on the gold damask while C.J. poured.

While each girl took her turn with Mrs. Upton, C.J. tossed out questions to the others. What was the hardest part of their jobs? What did they like best? How did they handle difficult children?

"I do believe it's best to work out problems with the one you've got them with," Althea said. C.J. tried not to grin at the trim woman whose hands rested comfortably where her own had been just minutes earlier. Althea's hands were worn and chapped from work, but the whites of her nails made perfect little quarter moons. "Some of the kids I've looked after have been a handful. But I've got a few tricks up my sleeve."

Soon, Mrs. Upton was coming through the doorway with Miss O'Connor on her heels. C.J. handed out coats and led the way to the door. When she returned, a plate of macaroons and two cups of coffee were clustered on the table, like leftovers someone forgot to put away. Mrs. Upton was taking deep drags on a cigarette.

"Do you understand what I require?" Mrs. Upton stubbed out her cigarette and leaned forward through the haze. "It's *you*—or someone just like you."

C.J. almost laughed at this woman and her left-handed compliments. "Yes'm."

Mrs. Upton's frown relaxed. "Have a macaroon," she said, as if toasting her return to confidence. "Now this Maisie has done French cooking. And she seems like such a cooperative girl. Don't you think?"

The Maisie C.J. had observed had blabbered on about her soufflés being divine and sashayed back and forth from the dining room like she had this job in the bag. C.J. reckoned she'd just tell Mrs. Upton what she thought. "Well, ma'am. Besides the problem with her being biggety—"

"Biggety?"

"Full of herself."

"Oh."

"Besides that, I don't know as she could get all your work done to your liking. She'd probably be tuckered out before noon from all her sweet talking."

"Well, who then?" Mrs. Upton pulled another cigarette from the pack but just twirled it in her fingers. "Surely not Cleo."

"No'm. She's definitely too antsy."

"Etta June?" Mrs. Upton shuddered.

What a sight that would be, Etta June serving Mrs. Upton's guests in her too-short skirt and buttons about to pop from straining to hold in her bosom. C.J. shook her head. "Too tacky."

"That leaves Althea. A nice enough girl, but she just doesn't have Maisie's experience."

C.J. sipped her coffee. It had gone cold and tasted bitter. She saw herself in Althea, and she knew Mrs. Upton didn't understand either of them. Althea didn't deserve to be stuck with Mrs. Upton, but this mattered. "No'm, she doesn't. But more important—"

"*More* important?"

She straightened, sitting tall in her chair. She would just tell Mrs. Upton this, too, a thing or two about herself. "Althea's got gumption. And she'd do to ride the river with."

Mrs. Upton peered over the rim of her cup, looking like a schoolgirl considering whether to raise her hand to ask another question. For a moment, C.J. was a schoolgirl herself back on Mill Road, the day she first realized how, to Miss Clayton, her teacher, every question was an opportunity.

"It's the two things I reckon made my being here work out," C.J. explained. "A cool enough head to solve problems when they come up. And trustworthiness."

"You're sure?"

She was quite sure about Althea. But Mrs. Upton's guest lists could challenge even the most capable girl. Somehow, C.J. had to look out for Althea, too. "I think, especially if you were to bring in extra help for the larger affairs, Althea would come on just fine."

Mrs. Upton crushed the unlit cigarette in the ashtray, then handed the pack and her lighter to C.J. "Get rid of these, please. I'll just go call the agency about Althea."

CHAPTER 12

January 1961
The Sound of Hope

The January wind was howling in Evanston, and the house shivered in the early morning darkness. C.J. set her toothbrush in the pretty glass Mrs. Gray had brought to her room last night, right after she went for the extra blanket.

Someday she might recall moving from the Uptons to the Grays and laugh. Mrs. Upton, practically pleading with her to prepare dinner, "One last time, just in case you're wrong about Althea." Fussing over Coquilles St. Jacques while Mrs. Upton watched President Kennedy on the television. And, from the moment Mrs. Upton had deposited her at the Grays', Mrs. Gray, hovering over her as if she were a houseguest.

She added a sweater to one of the uniforms Mrs. Powell had bought a year and a half ago and hurried downstairs, a touch of lightness in her step. The two Chicago families under her belt gave her a pretty good idea what to expect. She just needed to get her bearings in the kitchen before the Grays were up.

At the base of the stairs, she smelled coffee and something burnt. She rushed to the dining room, praying she would not meet the rest of the family this way, having gotten their own breakfast on her first day here.

The dining room was empty. She followed the sound of piano music to a small radio on the kitchen counter. Mrs. Gray sat at the table, her brow furrowed in concentration. A plate of burnt toast and a coffee cup seemed forgotten among papers, a ledger, and an adding machine.

"I'm so sorry you had to get that for yourself, ma'am."

"Oh, no, dear." Mrs. Gray waved away her concern. "I often work on the books for the store before anyone else is up. Don't let me bother you."

Now that was about as likely as breakfast making itself. Determined not to ask where things were, C.J. searched for flour. The pretty canisters behind the lineup of framed photos—the whole family; Mrs. Gray cutting a ribbon before a store whose sign said GRAY JEWELERS; a boy and girl wearing uniforms and holding musical instruments—were empty. The pantry was overwhelmed by an assortment of breakfast cereal. But way up on the top shelf, she spotted things for baking.

While she measured ingredients, Mrs. Gray's pen scratched at the paper. She reached for the pastry cutter and began twisting her wrist, making clumps of flour and shortening.

"It's a great day for the family." She turned to see Mrs. Gray push her glasses up on her head and pick up a half-eaten piece of toast. Her smile seemed almost as sad as the blackened bread. "As you see, toast can be a challenge."

C.J. set the oven to four-fifty. "I'm partial to biscuits my own self."

"Oh, I hate for you to go to all the trouble. Toast would be fine."

The clumps became pea-sized as C.J. twisted harder, unable to decide what to make of the remark. In between rolling out the dough and cutting circles to drop into the greased and floured cake pan, she watched her new employer. She'd never seen such hair. Bright red, almost like the inside of a watermelon, and curly. Mrs. Gray wore it in a knot at her neck, seemingly held back against its will.

The oven beeped, sending C.J. across the kitchen with the pan of biscuits. As she lined up strips of bacon in the skillet, she suddenly felt Mrs. Gray watching her.

"C.J., what *are* you wearing?"

"It's one of my older uniforms." She moved a stack of unopened mail off the counter next to the stove to make room to work. "I hope you don't mind. I wear these for housework and save the newer ones for when you have guests."

Mrs. Gray scrunched up her face the way she had when she frowned over the numbers in her book. Again, the glasses popped onto her head. "I just didn't expect—I told the agency no when they asked if I wanted to buy any uniforms."

The bacon began to sizzle. Still, C.J. felt Mrs. Gray watching her. Slowly and precisely, she transferred the bacon onto paper towels, then cracked eight eggs, added milk, and whisked.

"Wait," Mrs. Gray said, just as she held the bowl poised over the pan.

"Ma'am?"

"We've never had . . . help around the house before. But I just don't like the idea of a uniform. Could you run upstairs and change?"

"Change to what, ma'am?"

"Anything that makes you comfortable. I want you to be comfortable with us." Mrs. Gray bent her head to her books, using one hand to write while the other moved in time to the music, like a conductor.

That evening, C.J. yawned, eager to complete her first day in this house, to be past the newness. She carried a bowl of potatoes but saw Mrs. Powell, adjusting the collar of a different pink dress than the one she'd demanded be ironed. The next bowls held green beans and rolls. Yet, somehow, they resembled Mrs. Upton and her ruler. Each time C.J. entered the dining room, she expected to be handed a look or a test—like a dirty dish. Each time, she found the Grays facing their place settings as they might total strangers. The crystal stemware, Wedgwood china, and silverware—all taken down and cleaned that afternoon—sparkled in the silence. On her last trip, she set the platter of crispy golden fried chicken before Johnny.

"What'd you do with the trays?" Johnny's voice bounced off the walls, nearly causing her to lose her balance. He reached for a chicken leg and took a chomping bite.

"Excuse me?"

"You know, the metal trays the TV dinners come in," Jenny answered for her brother.

"These are my recipes. I hope you like them . . ."

"Wow! This is good," Johnny said. "Since Mom and Dad started the store, our fried chicken comes from a box."

C.J. cleared her throat. "Will there be anything else right now, ma'am?"

Mrs. Gray's face now matched her watermelon hair. "No, thank you," she managed.

"Yes'm. Call when you're ready for dessert." C.J. turned away, but added over her shoulder just to be safe, "Or if you need anything sooner."

She set her lonely plate on the cold kitchen table, felt the quiet. Now and then one of the Grays murmured something about their day. C.J. took small bites, chewing deliberately and toying with her food until it clustered around the plate's edge, exposing the bouquet of wildflowers in the center. She smiled then, sadly, rested her fork on the plate, and let her mind wander on home to walk the Wilson farm with her daddy.

"I don't think we can put it off any longer." She looked up as Mrs. Gray seemed suddenly to have found her normal voice. "We're going to *have* to get a television for the store."

"Oh, good!" Jenny said. "When we're there, we'll have something fun to do."

"Now hold on, everyone," Mr. Gray said. "There's not a lot of time for TV watching at the store."

"That's true, dear. But first we missed the inauguration. Then, last night, we were busy closing up when President Kennedy spoke to the press corps."

C.J. paid closer attention, wondering. What did this family think of the new President? How did they feel about him being Catholic? And what was their religion? With bacon in the refrigerator and no crosses or pictures of Jesus on the wall, she had no way of knowing.

"We did hear about it today from customers," Mr. Gray said. "And we can read about it."

"Looking at pictures in *LIFE* is one thing," Mrs. Gray argued. "But I've got to keep a close eye on *my* President. If—oh, dear. On my husband as well, it seems. I've never seen you eat so many rolls."

"They're wonderful."

"Anyway, I want to see for myself."

"My friend Rita's mom thinks Mr. Kennedy is *sooo* handsome," Jenny piped in again.

"Is that why you want to see him, Mom?" Johnny asked.

"No, son. Dad and I voted for him because we like his ideas on getting our economy going, keeping us safe, and helping the poor. Now, if we're going to help like he's asked, we have to pay attention."

Very quietly, C.J. scraped most of her dinner into the garbage can. In her experience, it was the church that helped poor folks.

"I want to see Mrs. Kennedy's beautiful clothes," Jenny said. "Wasn't her ball gown gorgeous?"

"All right, ladies," Mr. Gray said. "What I'd like is dessert."

C.J. took down plates, then spun around, trying to remember which drawer held a knife she could use to cut the cake.

"You go ahead," Mrs. Gray said. "Having Earl Wild perform at the inaugural concert has inspired me to practice my Gershwin." She poked her head in the kitchen to say, "Just three for dessert, dear."

As C.J. did the dishes, she listened to the music. Mrs. Gray played so beautifully. Why, then, did she stop repeatedly to go over a passage, as if diligently ironing out a tiny wrinkle no one else could see?

❊   ❊   ❊

"Had enough?" Zach asked as C.J. pushed her nearly empty plate across the black Formica table at Harry's Deli.

"Too much. I reckon I eat more with you than the whole rest of the week."

A habit strangely come by—these weekend meetings. She recalled the first one, if only for the weather. Early that Saturday in March, up before Mae or Alinda and intent on getting breakfast, she'd stepped outside into drizzle and nearly forty-degree temperatures. Fog had rolled in over the lake, causing the sky to press downward heavily, obscuring much of the view. She'd bumped squarely into Zach, pausing on the steps of the apartment building to adjust his collar against the damp chill and also on his way to breakfast. They'd gone together that morning and, later, around five o'clock, as C.J. returned to Evanston at the end of her day off, a tornado struck south of the University of Chicago campus, killing one person and devastating a thirty-block area of the South Side.

Zach held the door for her now as they left Harry's. After discovering that they were both early risers, they'd begun bumping into each other more and more often when C.J. had Friday evening to Saturday evening off. Eventually, even her occasional Sundays off, like today, became habit, though those were always lunch after church when Flo wasn't around.

She buttoned her jacket against the October wind. Without either suggesting it, they turned east, toward the lake.

"C.J.?"

Zach sounded serious. "Yes?"

"I have a feeling today's the day. It's the Yankees' last game of the season, and Roger Maris didn't hit a home run Friday or Saturday. But I think he will today."

She grinned. "You called it, saying Maris would be the one to break Babe Ruth's record. Here he is, just needing one more home run."

"Yeah, it was close until Mantle got sidelined with his injury last month."

"Them both being Yankees, though, you really couldn't lose."

"So . . ." He drew out the word. "Will you spend the whole afternoon with me today?" He rushed to add, "I mean, looking back, some years down the road, we're going to want to remember where we were on this historic day, October 1, 1961."

"Well, I'd think you'd want to be home, listening to the game on the radio, but all right. I reckon we can find a pay phone and call Miz Gray if it looks like I'll be getting back there too much later than usual. Just so she won't worry."

C.J. suddenly recalled the first professional baseball game she'd ever been to, shortly after she moved to Chicago. The White Sox versus the Indians. She'd watched the outfielders twitch in anticipation, imagining how the grass felt beneath their feet. Zach's invitation had her feeling just as she'd believed those ballplayers must have.

"You know, most Yankee fans don't really want the record to be broken. If it is, they'd rather Mickey be the one."

"Well, I'm rooting for what you want."

Sprawled before them, Jackson Park's Wooded Island held every tree imaginable. They glimmered honey-gold and scarlet in the sun. But from the moment C.J. spotted the ancient burr oak, she ignored the rest. Acorns crunched beneath her feet as she ran. She stuffed a handful in her pocket before stepping onto the branch that reached out to the ground like a friendly hand. She pulled herself up into its arms with practiced ease and looked down. Just as she had from her favorite tree on the Wilson farm, where, sheltered in the tangle of branches and leaves, she felt less afraid.

Squinting from beneath the visor of his Yankees cap, Zach held up his hands to make a sort of viewfinder. "I wish I had a camera," he said.

If she had a picture of Zach, where would she keep it? Not even the girls of number ten, who'd adopted Zach as one of their own, would understand. She gathered images. Dark curls springing from beneath the cap. Achingly blue eyes peering up at her. The remnants of a tan where his neck and forearms peeked from beneath his sweatshirt. Dimples like two tiny suns brightening his smile. C.J. blinked, snapping them all at once to store in her mind.

She watched, surprised, as the dimples disappeared. Figuring that sitting in a tree could cure almost any bad feeling, she motioned. "C'mon up."

"Oh, no." He shook his head. "That's okay."

"You scared of heights?"

No . . . No, I'm not."

"Please. You can feel Mississippi up here." *The only way you'll probably ever know it.*

Zach moved toward the tree's friendly hand. It was the way he gripped the branch overhead that made her realize he must have had precious few trees to climb growing up in New York City. "That's right. Step there to your left," she coached.

She guided him until he reached a branch opposite hers and perched there. Even then he was silent. Overhead, two squirrels chattered and chased each other.

"You worried the season will end without Maris breaking the record?"

"It's just . . . time." He sounded tired. "Babe Ruth set the record of sixty home runs in 1927. My pop was just a boy when he saw him play. Seems like not much has changed since then."

C.J. thought of her daddy. How they would come in from playing with the rag ball to stand before the curio cabinet, awestruck by the beauty of the real baseball inside and the signature scrawled across it. "He ever catch a ball—your pop?"

"Not that I know of."

"Charlie and I sure knew about the one Daddy caught. 1938, while he was in the Army."

"Who'd he watch?"

"You probably never heard of them, the New Orleans Black Pelicans. He caught it off Johnny Bissant."

"I don't know the Pelicans. But Pop taught me about the legends of the Negro Leagues. He saw some of them when the championships were in Yankee Stadium."

"Wonder why he wanted to go to those games?"

"More exciting, he said. Stolen bases. Everything faster."

C.J. pulled an acorn from her pocket. She felt it in her hand like the rag ball and pitched it at an old log. It hit square on.

"Cool Papa Bell, fastest man ever to play pro baseball," Zach said. "Satchel Paige. Maybe the best pitcher ever lived. And Oscar Charleston—they called him the black Ty Cobb."

"Seems kind of insulting, being called the black somebody." She threw another acorn and another. Both hit their mark.

Zach whistled. "I think it was kind of a measurement. Comparing the best to the best. They called Josh Gibson the black Babe Ruth. He hit eighty-four home runs in 1936, and some say he was the only man to hit a ball out of Yankee Stadium."

An acorn finally fell short of the log.

"That's what I mean, though." He scowled again. "About not much changing since Babe Ruth. My pop always said Gibson should have been up against him."

"Johnny Bissant wasn't well known like those you've named. But *my* daddy always said you got to catch the ball that's thrown to you, not be pining after some other one. Look at the Negro players all over the white teams now. One of them will do it."

"Not just *baseball*, C.J."

"That's where you're wrong, Zach. I think *everything* has changed. I'm in Chicago, up a tree with you. Talking about what a sight it woulda been, Gibson and Ruth chasing the home run record like your Maris and Mantle—"

"Hey, man! Did you hear?" The boy passing by was attached to a transistor radio by its earpiece. "Maris broke the Babe's record!"

Zach climbed down to talk to the boy. "How'd it go?"

"First inning, Stallard tricked Maris with an outside pitch. Maris flied out to Yastrzemski. It was scoreless through the third. Bottom of the fourth, Maris steps to the plate, and the crowd begins to chant. Stallard throws high and outside for ball one, low and inside for ball two. Next pitch, Maris pulls a fastball into the right field stands. Man, what I'd give to have seen it!"

"Yeah. Thanks for telling me."

Zach seemed lost in thought. Robins sang their clear, cheery songs while a pair of feisty crows flapped their way to the crown of the giant oak. As the crows landed, he held up his hands again and peered through them at C.J. "A sight indeed. But I still wish I had a camera."

She climbed down from the tree and stood facing him.

"Well, the home run race is over," he said, "but I'm not ready to go home. Can we walk some more?"

She nodded and kept silent pace with him. As they skirted the shoreline heading northward, she wracked her mind for a new subject of conversation. "There's another race we got to keep our eyes on, you know."

"Yeah?"

"Now, I got my own bet I'll make you. I say we'll have a man on the moon before the Soviets."

"Why so sure?"

"First off, it's the way the President talks. He makes me believe."

"Kennedy's inspirational, that's for sure. I can only hope to develop a fraction of that talent."

"You thinking of running for President?" C.J. teased. She'd never considered what Zach might do when he finished college. Realizing suddenly that he would graduate in two years and surely disappear from her life, she felt sad.

"Maybe something a little less ambitious the first time out." His dimples appeared then, the way they did when he was about to tease her. "Would you vote for me?"

"Well . . ." Voting was something else she'd never really thought about. "Of course—"

"Of course you couldn't even register in Mississippi." His dimples had vanished. "Please forgive me," he said, as if he'd done something far worse than remind her of the way things were.

"I was *going* to say I'm not even old enough yet. But"—she smiled, wanting to tease him back into a good mood—"I'd like to be able to vote for you. When the time comes."

As they left Jackson Park, west winds pushed birds against the lake in a crush of color and motion. A pair, gray and white with bright yellow crowns and wing patches, landed on a branch overhead and erupted in wheezy song.

"Warblers," C.J. said. "You can tell, my daddy says, 'cause they can't carry a tune in a bucket."

"Did you spend a lot of time together, growing up?"

"Every day, while Momma fixed supper, us kids got Daddy to ourselves. We'd walk the Wilsons' property while he taught us about nature." She looked around, half expecting the buttercups, clover, daisies, and morning glories. "Saturdays, when his work on the farm was done, we'd go fishing."

"Good times?"

"The best. Especially when I'd slip out to the lean-to off the chicken coop and watch him making toys and furniture. I worship the ground my momma walks on. But . . . Well, Daddy's little girl, I reckon."

A lone bird flew after them. C.J. suddenly felt watched, aware that the occasional mix of whites and Negroes seen nearer campus had disappeared.

"Now here's the rest of my argument. It was all the Soviets this and the Soviets that in 1959. But last year, we started matching them accomplishment for accomplishment. And look what all we've done just since President Kennedy's announcement. Gus Grissom was our second person in space, in a spaceship named the Liberty Bell, no less. Last month we had the ship that orbited Earth. Next month, there's a chimpanzee going up!"

Zach waited as the bird ascended and finally disappeared. "Maybe we *can* be first on the moon," he said. "But should we?"

"Of course! Think of the danger if they get there first."

"That's billions of dollars the President's asking for. Money that could feed the poor."

She smiled patiently. Crossing Lake Shore Drive, they were dumped out in Promontory Point Park. They followed the land that jutted into the lake. To the south lay the 57th Street beach. To the north, the skyline of Chicago's Loop.

"My pop taught us we're obliged to help the poor," Zach continued. "For Jews, *tzedakah* is the highest commandment."

"We have to stay safe first."

"You want safe?" He took her hand, pulling her along. She was startled, confused by the sensation of her hand in his as they ran. "There," he said when they stopped before a fence. Inside, towers reached skyward, dwarfing the turret of the nearby field house.

"What *are* they?"

"Army radar towers, for the missiles. In case the Soviets attack Chicago."

"Good Lord!"

"It's gone beyond occupying the lakefront parks. The newer missiles can carry nuclear warheads."

They walked on, to the revetment that protected the shoreline, and stood looking out at the gray-blue expanse of Lake Michigan. A wave splashed against the terraced limestone, misting their faces with fishy-tasting water. Backing away, C.J. slipped. Zach caught her, then drew her toward him the way the wind pressed the birds against the lake.

Her mind rolled like a wave against the wall. *Step away now.* Only when Zach touched her face did her feet obey.

"Reckon it's like this, out there in space?" she sputtered. "All wide open and strong and beautiful?"

Zach's silence overpowered the slapping of waves. He reached out, as if to take her hand, then let his fall.

We're friends. *Talk to him like a* friend. "Places like this are good. Where God splashes us in the face, just to be sure we don't get too full of ourselves."

Zach nodded. "Places like this *are* good."

But there was more in his voice than those simple words. It was faint as the earlier taste of algae and fish, yet ominous as the tornado that struck the South Side the first time she'd allowed a change in their relationship. It sounded like hope. She touched her lips, brushing it away.

CHAPTER 13

December 1961
New Music

After leaving Chicago blanketed in snow, C.J. found the warmth of Poplar Springs disconcerting. She'd forgotten somehow what the temperatures would likely be and brought all the wrong clothes. Charlie's fit her best, his legs having finally caught up to his arms.

He had her leanness now as well. "The both of you standing together near about makes one good-sized body," Momma had said when C.J. hugged her brother at the Greyhound station. "Lord, if I don't have my work cut out this coming week, putting some meat on y'all's bones."

Charlie had seemed glad to see her at first, but had gotten more and more standoffish ever since. "I prefer being called Charles," he announced as the family, minus George, who was at work, lingered over the noon meal the day after Christmas.

"Oh, do you? After fourteen years, you expect me to just up and change—" His indignant look stopped her. "All right, then."

Eight-month-old baby Anna sat on her mother's lap. Metairie stared at the child all goo-goo-eyed, the way she'd stared at George the last time C.J. was home. How had a year and a half flown by so fast?

"C.J., I wish you could have seen it," Momma said. "This young-un popped her head out like a daffodil calling an end to winter. She's been turning that big fat sunny baby face on us ever since."

"She sure looks adorable in that dress," C.J. said.

"*This* little dress, C.J., is one we wore! Momma saved all our baby things. If Anna doesn't run it ragged, I'll keep it ready for you."

"That'd be nice, Metairie," she forced herself to say. She expected to stay in Chicago at least three, maybe seven more years to make enough to get Charlie through college. What if it was too late by then? To come home, find someone to marry, and have children to wear Anna's hand-me-downs.

At the stove, she reached out, meaning to trace the dimpled side of the coffee pot, dented so long ago when her momma threw it at a dog that was threatening one of her children. C.J. had to jerk her hand away from the hot pot. But she reached out again, her hand at a slight distance, imagining the feel of the dent. Close, but far enough away to study—the same way, it seemed, she now needed to keep her family, to try to figure out what was different about them.

"Wasn't the Christmas music beautiful at church?" Momma asked. "Miz Perry does a fine job on that old piano she's stuck with."

Old. Was that all it was? No. They were older, but so was she. *Stuck.* The things and people of home were stuck in time, unchanged. But despite her determination not to let it, Chicago had changed her.

"I've been learning to play a bit myself," she said, just to keep the conversation from turning back to Metairie and her precious baby. Maybe she would just tell them she had a white friend.

"Your white lady let you play her piano?" Metairie asked.

"My—" C.J. stopped herself from saying she hadn't referred to her employer that way now in going on three years. "Well, it's got to be dusted," she said instead, a bit too stiffly. "But, we got one in our *apartment*, too. One even more pitiful than the one at Hope Baptist." She laughed then, trying to recover from her peevishness. "One of the college students in the building brought a friend over to tune it. We help out like that, taking each other's mail and whatnot."

"Well, ain't that just like home, all friendly," Momma said, giving C.J.'s hand a pat. C.J. squirmed inside as she watched Metairie fuss with Anna's hair.

"They got Negroes going to the college there in Chicago?" Daddy asked.

"Sure, Daddy."

"That where you're thinking on Charlie going?"

"College?" said Charlie. "Y'all know how I feel about high school. Maybe William and me will head off somewheres. Or I could join the Army like Daddy."

"Ain't you told him?" Momma asked. "Your sister is putting away money so's you can go to college. Now ain't that wonderful?"

"Maybe we could get a car!" Charlie said. "William's cousin's sending his family money to get them a car."

Ungrateful boy. She'd had a plan since the first day at Mrs. Harwell's. Charlie would have a better life.

"So, what's her name?" Daddy said.

"Who?" C.J. said, twisting the bracelet she'd bought herself while doing her Christmas shopping.

"Your friend, this Negro *college* student."

"Oh, the student. He's—"

The phone jostled the very air.

"Momma," Metairie said. "George wants to know when should he pick us up. I said we'll be cleaned up here pretty soon."

"No, just tell him come on for supper."

"He's just a boy we know," C.J. finished. Of course she couldn't say, *Zach's a white boy, y'all.* Knowing that brought on an even greater feel of separateness. It was beginning to hang in the air now like the unaccustomed weather.

"Well, now." Her daddy squeezed the point of his chin between his thumb and forefinger. "My daughter's rubbing shoulders with college folks."

"Better be careful," Metairie said.

"Huh?" C.J.'s head jerked up. It had gone down, with the shame of letting everyone think this friend was a Negro.

"This boy might turn you *all* the way into a Yankee," Metairie said. "And turn your head, too, so's you don't ever want to come home."

She would never turn into a Yankee, and she would always want to come home. But she wished she could talk to Zach. Somehow she knew that he would understand how lonely she felt.

"There's gracious plenty Southern still left in me, I'll have you know," C.J. snapped. "And I'll be home soon as I've saved enough to put you through college, *Charlie*." She jabbed her finger her brother's way and nodded at her mother, who nodded back. The baby began to cry.

❋   ❋   ❋

C.J. stirred but kept her eyes closed. The air was fresh and damp, the way it felt on Sunday mornings when Charlie stepped from the wash tub set up in the kitchen, shaking his head like a dog. When she would struggle to comb out his thick, stubborn hair while the smoky sweet smell of bacon floated through the cabin, calling the family to breakfast.

"C.J.," someone said insistently.

She squeezed her eyes shut, trying to hold onto sleep. But as the happy memory was yanked away like a blanket, she opened them to see Flo blotting her hair with a towel.

"I got breakfast made. I set you out a plate."

While Flo finished her hair and dressed, C.J. ate. Slowly, still in her pajamas, studying the mismatched dishes before her. Forest green Fiestaware plate, juice glass from the Oxydol detergent box, coffee cup from the remains of a china set one of the girl's employers had given her. She'd been back in Chicago nearly three months now and was more confused than ever.

As she cleaned up after eating, the plate slipped from her hands and crashed to the floor. She threw the dish towel over one shoulder and stared at the broken pieces, thinking the plate couldn't stand hearing Flo hum one more hymn either.

Flo came running. "I'll clean that up," she said. "You go on and get ready."

C.J. took a dress from the closet without bothering to look. She stepped into it and went to the mirror to check her hair. Her reflection, in the blue wool suit dress she'd bought to share with Flo, brought on a scowl. She rummaged in the closet, snatched Alinda's fluffy yellow sweater and a skirt, and changed. From Mae's jewelry box, she took large gold-colored earrings.

"You're not wearing those to church?" Flo asked, although it came out as more of an order.

C.J. snapped on the earrings and added a matching bracelet. The sweater, which set off Alinda's every curve, was more forgiving on C.J.'s much leaner frame, but still tighter than things she usually wore. She adjusted its V.

"And that's Alinda's sweater she wears when she wants Roger to do something her way," Flo harped. "We're going to Sunday services, girl."

"I'm thinking I might not." The idea seemed to shatter and smash in her head like the plate she dropped.

"Might not what?"

"Go to church."

"You feeling all right?"

"Matter of fact, I'm hungry. Let's go to 47th. We can eat at Walgreen's."

"After that big breakfast? Don't be ridiculous, C.J. Now hurry up and change."

C.J. patted the soft angora where it clung to her hips. "Well, if you won't go with me, I'll just go on by my—"

"You cannot traipse around by yourself looking like that. I'll have to go with you."

Along the way, children played stickball, a sign spring was breaking out despite the chill that lingered in the March air. The little bell over the door to the Walgreen's jingled merrily as they went in. C.J. bounced right up to the counter and claimed three of the empty stools, laying her coat on one. Settling herself required more effort. Keeping the point of the sweater's V from falling too low, stopping the jangling of the earrings when she turned her head—how did Alinda and Mae manage all this?

The blender whirred under the direction of the counter clerk, indistinguishable from any other until he came their way carrying water glasses. The perfect alignment of his bowtie contradicted the slant of the cap atop his pompadour.

"Looks like Little Richard is working this morning," Flo whispered, sending them both into giggles over the private nickname.

"What can I get you ladies?" He smiled disarmingly. "You've beat the lunch crowd. So, the grill's all yours."

"We're usually at *church* this time of the morning," Flo said.

"Can't get there every week myself. What with my hours here. Which one y'all go to?"

"We go all over," C.J. said brightly, feeling the earrings swat her cheeks. "Just to try different ones. Lately we've been going to the First Baptist, over by the university."

"Y'all live over that way?"

"Yes," Flo said. "And I reckon we'll both have us a patty melt and a shake."

He winked as he left. The second he was down the counter, Flo demanded, "Girl, what *are* you doing?"

"Just being friendly."

"Well, I suggest you *and* Alinda's sweater and Mae's jewelry be a mite *less* friendly. That is, unless you're after something here."

"What you mean?"

"The way that boy is eyeing you, it wouldn't be no surprise to *me* if he was to ask you out."

C.J. looked in the mirror, then down at the sweater, suddenly seeing herself as Flo must. She pressed her hands against her chest where the neckline plunged. "Flo, I just wanted to do something my sister wouldn't do. Something I can do because I'm *here*."

Flo removed her scarf and handed it to C.J. "You ain't said much about your trip home. Something happen?"

C.J. wrapped the scarf around her neck and tied a knot. "Seems like there's a clock running is all."

The young man set patty melts before them on the counter.

"Oh, ketchup, please," Flo said.

"Metairie's using up the baby clothes Momma saved for the both of us. I don't even know—"

He was back in a flash, leaning toward them on his elbows.

"Mustard, too, if you don't mind," Flo said.

The counter suddenly began to fill up as it got closer to noon. The young man dropped off the mustard without even stopping.

"You in a hurry to get hitched and start having babies?" Flo ignored the ketchup and mustard and started on her sandwich.

C.J. twisted the bracelet. "Every night, I'm sitting all by my lonesome in the kitchen. With some family not ten feet away. When I go in there, I half expect to see my own momma and daddy. Metairie, with her husband and my momma's grandbaby. And Charlie."

"You wishing you was back home?"

"Yes. No." She yanked off the earrings and put them in her purse. "It's not . . . quite right . . . when I *am* there."

Flo nodded. "That's one reason I don't go back much."

C.J. tried to eat. But come to think of it, she couldn't recall one time Flo had gone back, couldn't imagine letting so much time pass without seeing her little brother. She set her sandwich on the plate. "Don't you miss Freddie?"

"It's just too soon is all." Flo wiped her mouth and meticulously re-folded her napkin. "For now, I think you and me both got churches to visit and people to get to know. Question is, do you want that boy over there to be one of them?"

C.J. offered a half smile. "I suspect I need to get to know my own self first."

"Then we might should come back another time for those shakes that got lost somewheres." She tucked money up under her plate, grabbed their coats, and steered C.J. to the door.

❊   ❊   ❊

C.J. spit on her finger and touched the iron. The little sizzle told her it was ready. A white dress shirt rose from the basket, as if connected to the thousands of others she'd ironed. A spritz to the collar, then back and forth. As the sounds of Jenny's French horn and Johnny's saxophone drifted to the Grays' kitchen, she tried to imagine the twins were her children. She swelled with pride at the way they did their practicing without being reminded, even on a gorgeous July morning.

Another shirt, another spritz. Jenny and Johnny finished their scales separately, then began playing a piece together. Jenny's sound was mellow with long, sustained notes. Johnny's melody floated brightly above her sound. C.J. beamed with pleasure, all goo-goo-eyed like Metairie over baby Anna. But here and there, Jenny would play a wrong note, or the sound of her French horn would disappear when she didn't get enough air. Now and then, Johnny's sax would screech. Each time, C.J. tensed, until her smile was gone. She chided herself over how ridiculous she must have looked. The manner was wrong on her, just as there was something wrong with her pretend children.

"Can I fix y'all a snack?" she'd asked before they went upstairs. "Y'all have to leave for the school soon."

"Oh, no, thanks," Jenny said. "You're busy." Cupboards banged, the refrigerator door slammed a couple of times, and the twins were off to their rooms.

They were *too* polite really, just like their parents, never wanting to impose. And when they got back home, there would be no hugs, no excited stories of their day. There was no closeness, no love.

"C.J.! What's that smell?" The voice came from somewhere deep in her memory. She saw a triangular burn mark on white cotton.

"Miz Barnes!" she opened her mouth to say, carried back to that day when the dark, cloudy Mississippi sky dripped fear. When her worry over what Mr. Corrigan and his men would do to her family kept her from minding her ironing. She set the iron in its metal tray and picked up the shirt, examining first one sleeve, then the other. She was certain it was the sleeve of Mr. Barnes's shirt she had burned. But where was the brown shape of the iron?

Then she saw it, like a muddy toe print, on the shirt tail. Not Mr. Barnes's shirt at all, but Mr. Gray's. If the shirt were tucked in, the mark would never show. But she would still have to tell Mrs. Gray. Would Mrs. Gray take her aside, as Mrs. Barnes had, to ask what had her upset? Perhaps give her some book like the one about St. Zita? Heavens! Having things relax a bit between Mrs. Gray and her would be one thing, but a heart-to-heart would just be too much.

Down the street, a bus clattered over a manhole cover and wheezed to a stop. The twins dashed out the door carrying their instruments. C.J. felt herself jounced along Poplar Springs' Langley Road, past the chain gang, their backs stooped in the simmering heat. On to the sleeve, back and forth, erasing wrinkles and time.

When she'd finished ironing, she checked the wall clock shaped like a rooster. The house couldn't be any cleaner, and it was way too early to start supper. She could be spending the better part of her days in the bed, with hardly a chance the Grays would ever know.

It was warm today. And still. Without even a hint of a breeze coming this way off the lake. She slid a finger around the neckline of her work dress, lifting it off her skin.

"I want you to be comfortable with us," Mrs. Gray had said on her very first morning in this house.

C.J. snorted. Well, then. Maybe she would have herself a glass of sweet tea and put her feet up. She filled a tall glass with ice, poured. Gathered a stack of Mrs. Gray's magazines, so crisp and unruffled they had surely never been opened. The rooster clock ticked, and the glass began to perspire while she sat, ignoring the magazines.

Her first day working here had been her last day wearing a uniform. Until this moment, she might have said the uniform didn't matter one way or another. But she began to think of it as more than a work dress. In Mississippi, she'd worn her fear like a uniform. At the Powells', where the whiteness of life shocked her, the black dress grounded her. She'd made her way through the months at the Uptons' by imagining their behavior was directed at the uniform rather than her. With the Grays, it was almost as if *they* were the ones wearing a uniform, they were so doggone solicitous. Now, she had no uniform, no fear haunting her. Now, feeling awash in uncertainty, she had to restrain herself from running upstairs to put on one of the ugly black dresses.

She picked up the first magazine, *Good Housekeeping*. It offered "125 ideas you can really use to save time." More time was the last thing she needed. She could use 125 ideas, though, about what to do with herself each day.

For the first time since she moved to Chicago, the new year hadn't brought a change of address. If she had indeed finally passed probation, she might stay here, in Evanston with the Grays, until—God only knew what would cause her to leave.

Her hands started to shake. She balled them into fists and massaged the small of her back, then continued flipping through the magazines. On the cover of *Family Circle* was an enticing backyard setting for a summer cookout. Inside, Donna Reed, Dick Van Dyke, and Alan Young showed how they did cookouts.

C.J. was inspired. She could cook out, too, surprise the Grays on Friday night. She'd seen a grill in the garage. The table would need flowers, just like the picture on the magazine cover. The yard was full of lovely flowers waiting to be picked. She could learn how to arrange them, maybe get a book from the library tomorrow when she went into Evanston to the market. She hummed as she jotted a list for shopping. Suddenly, there was scarcely enough time to get everything done.

❊   ❊   ❊

Saturday, C.J. faced Zach across the black Formica table at Harry's Deli. He'd been fairly warned, when she agreed to join him for breakfast, that she was ornery.

"So," he said. "Did you have a good week?"

"Not hardly, but thank you just the same."

"What happened?"

"I know it looked every bit as fine as the cover of *Family Circle*." She barely noticed his confused look. "The shish-kebabs had those little cherry tomatoes. There was corn and green salad and lemonade. Even strawberry rhubarb pie with ice cream. And the flowers—now they may not have been the exact same ones as in the picture. But they *were* in a basket. Beautiful yellow Gerbera daisies. I cleaned up the lawn furniture and the backyard—"

"So you had a cookout for the Grays? It sounds great."

"Miz Gray said it surely was lovely, but she just hated for me to work so hard. Then she asked would I like to have more days off for the summer. Now there's a fine how-do-you-do."

"It sounds like a very nice thing—"

"I did *something* wrong. I just know it."

"C.J., people don't reward you with time off for doing something wrong."

"Miz Gray, she kept shooing me back inside."

"Maybe they just wanted time to themselves."

"I felt like a gnat she was trying to brush off. I don't know why they hired me if they don't want me there."

Zach seemed to ponder his answer. "You've said the Grays never had help before. Could be they're still getting used to things."

"It's been more than a year! Good Lord, if white people don't take the longest time getting used to the easiest things." She hung her head. "You're not—I didn't mean you—"

"Has anything else happened?" Zach's voice was somehow soft and strong, gentle but unwilling to be lost in the sounds of the deli. "Any problems?"

"Not a one. And I'm not accustomed to there being no problems."

"Why not?"

"It's unnatural is all—"

"Zach!" A pretty dark-haired girl flounced over to their table. "Where *have* you been?"

Zach looked up, swallowed. "Summer job. Saving for next year."

This girl's clothes said she never had to worry about that.

"Class is *so* much more fun when you're there," she purred. "Let's—"

"*Sarah*. This is my friend C.J."

"Well, hello there."

Sarah's words seemed to pat C.J.'s head as though it were a child's.

"Isn't Zach just a mensch?" Sarah fluttered her eyelashes at him. "Always doing mitzvahs. Oh—" She turned. "Of course, you don't . . . Isn't Zach just the *best*? Always doing *good deeds*."

"The best," C.J. agreed.

"Now, I'm interrupting your breakfasts, aren't I? Zach, let's get together *before* we run into each other in class."

"Thanks for stopping by, Sarah."

Harry arrived with a fresh plate of babka and coffee.

"A dank!" C.J. said when Harry filled her cup. "This pastry is wonderful."

"A sheynem dank!" Harry beamed at her as he left.

She watched him lovingly straighten one of the photos that lined his walls. Customers or friends from days gone by. Who would be in Harry's photo of Zach, years from now, when Zach had settled down? Surely someone like Sarah. A smart college girl. And Jewish, not playing at speaking Yiddish like she was.

"*C.J.* Where were we? Oh, yes. You were saying nothing bad happened—"

"So, you and Sarah have classes together?"

"A few. She's a political science major."

"She's very pretty."

"I guess. Way too short, though." He finished his last bite and began counting out money.

C.J. did the same, her orneriness turning to obstinacy. "Momma tucks right up under Daddy's arm. Like they were made for the fit. I got my daddy's big bones, though."

Zach rose and, as always, helped her from her chair. He stood close, blocking her from stepping away from the table, and reached out to her with his startlingly blue eyes. "*I* prefer looking eyeball to eyeball."

She searched the flecks in the black Formica as if one had suddenly gone missing. Hadn't she had the very same thought? "Metairie, too. She's that way with George."

Zach sighed and stepped away. He said nothing as they walked to the door. Outside, they headed east, toward Jackson Park.

"Well, if it's height that's important to you," he said suddenly. His voice had taken on an edge.

For the life of her, she could not figure why. She tried for a teacher-like tone. "Of course, there's more important things."

"Such as?"

"Religion. Work. And . . . heritage."

"Then I ought to introduce you to Henry."

"The one who's always cutting up and making y'all laugh at the warehouse?" She shook her head. "This isn't something to joke about."

"Huh?" Zach looked as confused as she was. "I really should introduce you, because—" He held up one finger. "Henry's Baptist, I believe. He's a good worker, doing honest work." Up came a second finger. "Oh, yes." He snapped his fingers. "He's a Negro from Georgia. And he's, I don't know—" He squinted and held one hand above his head. "A good six inches taller than me."

"I told you that's—"

"Is *that* how you're going to pick your partner in life, C.J.?" Zach's voice came out very low.

"I'm going to do like Momma and Daddy. They talked and figured they had the same ideas about making a family and a life together."

"Well, there you go." He put both hands firmly on her shoulders, stopping her. "The Yiddish word for that is bashert. *That's* how I intend to choose. I'm going to spend *my* life with my soul mate."

She shrugged off his hands and quickened her step. He kept pace and kept quiet as they approached the West Lagoon. They arrived at the beach and made their way to the damp sand along the water's edge. With each step, C.J. sank in slightly. She flexed her calf muscles, working to stay on top of the sand. She stepped on something hard and stooped to pick it up. Some sort of fossil.

"Like I said, there being no problems is unnatural. Take this beach for example. Nothing to stub your toe on, no reason to ever look down." She handed the stone to Zach.

He turned it over and over in his hand. "But the problem you have now—I still don't get it."

She stared out over Lake Michigan, all the way to where there was no shoreline, only water as endless as the routine of her life. "I've been trying to come up with something to earn my keep, to maybe get them to like me. I've tried near about everything I can think of, from fondue to flower arranging."

"Sounds like that's all for them, though. What about you?"

The wind whipped at her hair, blowing it into her eyes. Almost tenderly, he brushed it aside.

"What *about* me?" she snapped.

"Maybe you could take a class or something. Northwestern's right there in Evanston. It's awfully expensive. But maybe a junior college."

"And what do you figure they teach in college that I need to learn?"

"What would you *want* to learn?"

"Well, if there *was* something, Evanston is not the place. I can't even get a library card without being cross-examined. I fit in at the market, with the others shopping for their employers. But that's it."

She glared at him and turned her back, watching the wind skid across the massive lake. Each time the water tried to just be, the wind stirred it up again. She dropped down heavily on the sand and hugged her knees to her chest.

Zach reached again to push back her hair. "I'd really like to know what's important to you."

Without looking at him, she began to talk about Charlie and her determination to make his life better. Only then did she get up and start walking again.

Zach followed her. "I—" he began, but she shushed him.

She held out her hand to take back the stone. He laid it in her palm and curled her fingers around it. They turned together, into the wind, and walked on.

❊   ❊   ❊

The sun was up on another relentless summer day. Alone in the kitchen, C.J. ran her forefinger down each column of the classifieds. Jobs. Used cars and furniture. There—people offering to do work.

Zach's suggestion that she go to college was just plain craziness. What she could do was learn to play the piano. It had crossed her mind to ask him to teach her. But she pictured Sarah batting her eyes at Zach, worming her way into spending more time with him, and simply couldn't do it.

Behind her, coffee burbled, splashing muddy brown against the little glass knob on top of the percolator. Yard work. Window washing. Piano lessons! But the lady advertising lived in Kenwood Park. That would never work.

She jumped at the sound of heels as Mrs. Gray breezed past her. "Don't get up. I'll just pour myself a cup of your delicious coffee and start on my books."

C.J. folded up the newspaper. "That's all right. I didn't find what I was looking for."

Mrs. Gray took her mug to the table and reached for the sugar bowl. "You're not unhappy here, I hope."

The rooster clock squawked the half hour. C.J. agreed. The question was ridiculous. Any of the girls of number ten would be thrilled to have her job. And none of them would be feeling the way she was. "Oh, no, ma'am. It's not a job I was looking for."

"Well, can I help?"

"It was a silly idea. I hadn't even asked if it would be okay." She pushed herself up from the table, wishing she'd pushed the entire conversation with Zach out of her mind.

"If what would be okay?" Mrs. Gray tucked a wayward strand of watermelon hair back into the clip.

"*Really*. I'll just get started on breakfast."

"That can wait." Mrs. Gray's tone was insistent. Her glasses perched on her head.

"It's the piano," C.J. blurted. "I thought maybe—if you didn't mind—I could take a lesson now and then. I've been dreaming up new things to try, but I just can't seem to stay busy enough every day."

"Well, I don't see why—"

"Of course not. It was wrong of me. I apologize." She felt suddenly very hot and uncomfortable in her work dress and thought of running upstairs to change.

"I was about to say I don't see why that couldn't work. This household has never run so smoothly."

"Thank you kindly, ma'am. But, like I said, I couldn't find anyone in the ads."

"I might be able to help." Mrs. Gray went to the living room and returned with her glasses on, holding out a book. "I used this with the twins. Neither of them took to the piano like they have their horns. But I'd be happy to help you. We'll just spend a few minutes a couple of times a week, perhaps before the others are up. Then you can practice whenever you have your work done."

C.J. stared at the cover of Michael Aaron's *Piano Primer for the Early-Age Beginner*. Now Mrs. Gray was getting too close, just like Mrs. Barnes. "On your piano?" was all she could think to say.

"Well, of course. Where else?"

"I was planning to practice on the one at our apartment."

"Well, you can do that too. But there's also a perfectly good piano sitting right here."

"Your piano . . ." Her hand, at her side, moved back and forth, feeling the gleaming wood when she dusted it. "It's the most beautiful piano I've ever seen."

"All the more reason it should be used."

"But—" C.J.'s eyes cast about for a way out, landed on the *Family Circle* sitting right where she'd left it on the counter. "I thought . . ."

"What, dear?"

"It's seemed—especially since the cookout—almost like you wished I wasn't here."

The glasses moved back onto Mrs. Gray's head.

"I wish a lot of things," she said finally. "That I could be here *and* at the store. That I could manage the house as well as you do. My word, that cookout was so perfect—" She waved her hand at the counter. "It could've come straight out of one of those magazines I never find time to read."

So perfect? Mrs. Gray looked so perfectly sad.

"But C.J. Most of all, I wish we could both be comfortable with what is."

"I'm—"

"No, that's not right. That *I* could be comfortable with what is. I hope you'll stay with us until the twins are off to college at least."

❊   ❊   ❊

C.J. measured out two cups of grits and closed the bag she'd lugged from Poplar Springs. Like Indian summer, the grits were almost gone.

"I reckon you'll be going home just in time to get another bag." Flo glanced at her, went back to peeling white butcher's paper from a half pound of shrimp.

She closed her eyes, imagining this was the smell of the ocean at high tide on a summer day. It probably would be totally different than what she expected, though. Just like her trips home. And she didn't relish another disappointment. Suddenly, her mind was made up. "Actually, this year I'm spending Christmas with my friends."

"I see." Flo was bent over the shrimp, expertly pulling back the pink translucent skins and digging out the black grainy veins. "So, how are those piano lessons going with Miz Gray?"

"I'm looking forward to a book that's not for little kids. 'Twinkle, Twinkle' and 'Yankee Doodle' are my big songs."

"At least we won't have to listen to 'Chopsticks' forever. I, for one, can appreciate hearing some new music."

"It's crazy, though, Miz Gray teaching me piano."

"I guess I never told you how I learned to read. One of my momma's white ladies used to help me. If she could see me now, sitting up here reading *The Defender*." Flo laughed so hard she snorted.

C.J. laughed just as hard, as much at Flo as at her joke. "Anyways, I reckon Charlie *has* to go to college now. I was thinking to use some of his money on myself. But with Miz Gray teaching me, well, the Lord's saying help your brother— Flo, you're crying."

Flo shook her head and pointed to the cutting board. "Onions'll get you every time."

"Here." She handed her a couple of kitchen matches. "Put these in your mouth."

"Speaking of the papers, you been reading about the riots at Ole Miss?" Flo·sniffed and tapped the matchsticks on the counter. "They can send a man round the earth. But try to have a Negro enroll in a white school . . ."

C.J. concentrated on dicing the boiled ham. "Two people *died*, Flo. And hundreds were hurt. I got to ask why."

"Maybe so your brother has a choice when the time comes for him to use your money."

"The kind of choice my brother wants is what kind of car for me to buy him," C.J. snapped. "But I'll be satisfied seeing him in any of the Negro colleges in Mississippi."

Squeezed between Charlie's lack of ambition and Flo's overreaching, she searched for a way to change the subject. "And what about your brother? You talk more about Charlie than your own Freddie."

In the silence while Flo did not speak, olive oil sizzled loudly in the pot. Bits of pepper and celery thwacked against the metal as C.J. dumped them in. Flo added the chopped onion, her knife scraping the cutting board with a harsh, grating sound. She used her apron to wipe away more tears.

Finally, she said, "That ain't in the cards for my Freddie."

C.J. studied her. "You know, the matchsticks really do work."

"Next time."

"All right, then. Pass the shrimp, at least what there is of it."

"Ain't it just a crime? Back home, we could get near about a whole grocery sack, trucked fresh from the coast, for what this couple of handfuls cost."

This was the Flo that C.J. knew, happiest when she was in a flap about one thing or another. C.J. added the ham, shrimp, and milk, stirring to keep the milk from scalding. Flo chopped tomato and minced garlic. C.J. blended in the grits.

"Two ingredients left," C.J. said. "You want to grate cheese or chop green onions?"

"Oh, no more onions today."

When Flo had a big pile of cheese, she looked at C.J. "What *if*? What if you took that money you're saving for Charlie and used it on you?"

C.J. chopped harder. "Don't be ridiculous."

"I'm serious. What would you do?"

"I don't know. What would you do?"

"That's easy. I'd be a gospel singer like Mahalia Jackson. I'd go all over making people feel God's love. Every now and again, I'd go back home and sing in the choir with my mother."

C.J. savored the heavenly aroma of their jambalaya and imagined. "Maybe I'd buy a little flower shop. Like the one near the market in Evanston." She added the onions and cheese and stirred. "But then I'd have to stay in Chicago. So, of course, that's—"

"I know," Flo said as they watched the cheese melting. "That's ridiculous."

CHAPTER 14

December 1962
Anne's Christmas

"Emily, crack a window. It's gonna get way too hot in here . . . Alinda, put that man of yours, Roger, to work. We got to borrow Zach's table and chairs . . . Sissy, Flo, y'all move the coffee table into the bedroom . . . Mae, fold these napkins . . ."

"Take a breath, C.J.! It's Zach's sixteen-year-old sister joining us from New York. And it's the same supper we have every year 'round Christmas."

Exactly—not nearly special enough. She looked at the kitchen table, where her day's work rested beside Emily's never-fail sweet potato pie. Cinnamon laced the bread pudding's golden crust, and pecan halves marched in perfect circles atop the pie's caramel-colored filling. She breathed in the Mississippi mud cake, its cocoa as strong and dark as the earth back home, and trusted in dessert.

"C.J.," Alinda called as Roger and Zach edged the table through the doorway. "Where you want this?"

"There." She pointed. "We'll eat in here and lay out the food in the kitchen."

Roger and Zach righted the table and set it down. And there stood Anne. Roughly the same height and weight as Mae and equally over-dressed, her blond hair wild and kinky looking. Mae's hair, smooth and straight, gave C.J. the impression each had tried to fashion herself after the other and met somewhere in the middle.

"Mae, there's one more chair in the hall," Alinda said.

Mae ignored her. "Where *did* you get that outfit, girl?"

Anne raised her Saks Fifth Avenue bag and smiled. Her eyes twinkled. Though they were brown, not the astonishing blue of Zach's, they took in the entire room and sent out energy at the same time, just like his.

"More food for the feast," she said brightly. Leaving Mae standing there, she walked straight to the center of the room. "*You* must be C.J. Where should I put these?"

"The kitchen is this way. Just help your—" But Anne was already pushing the desserts out of her way and pulling things from her bag—bagels, cream cheese, lox, and Mandelbrot.

"I really am the big brother," Zach said, suddenly at C.J.'s side. "But Anne has a way of taking charge wherever she is."

"She's a very pretty girl. She's got your dimples, well, one anyway—oh, dear." She wrinkled up her nose. The tanginess of the barbecue sauce, sweetness of the cornbread and melted cheese, even the sharpness of the collard greens were being outdone by the smell of something burning. She pulled dishes from the oven like rabbits from a hat and lined everyone up to fix themselves plates.

She found the sole remaining chair between Anne and Mae. Mae was busy eating, but no sooner had C.J. lifted her fork than she leaned around her. "Tell us about New York City, Anne. You know, from the feminine point of view."

"It's just the biggest and best of everything." C.J. could hear Mae as surely as if Anne had mimicked her—*Girl, you know it's the biggest and best!* "That's where I'm going to school next year—New York University."

"Now, Anne," C.J. said. "Are you going to be a politician like Zach?"

"Oh, no. My brother's going to change the world with words. I'm going to do it with my camera. Like Charles Moore. I just adore his work. Y'all saw his photos in *LIFE*, I'm sure." Anne looked around the table but seemed to miss Alinda mouthing "y'all."

"You know," Anne said when no one answered, "pictures of the trouble at Ole Miss when James Meredith enrolled."

Zach sent a back-and-forth shake of his head his sister's way. "Anne—"

"Do you realize? The press shapes history just by documenting it. You just have to look at how things are done from one place to the next. The New York papers and magazines, the southern ones, the *Chicago Defender*."

"You read the *Defender*?" Flo didn't quite conceal a look of amusement.

"Of course. For my American history class."

"Well, I love the New York magazines," Mae said. "I'm going to study in New York my own self, at Miz Rose Morgan's House of Beauty, so's I can open up a salon just like hers one day."

"Then, Mae, you've got to start learning right *now* to appreciate good bagels." Anne stood and disappeared into the kitchen.

"Switch places with me, C.J.," Mae said immediately.

C.J. moved over with her food and turned her attention to the other end of the table, letting the chatter between Mae and Anne slip into the background. She smiled at Flo just as the sound of carolers reached them from the street below. ". . . *Noel, noel. Born is the King of Israel* . . ." She grimaced, knowing that Christmas sometimes got the better of Zach. She snuck a peek at him, only to find him looking at her.

"Zach," she said, flushing. "You're almost through another Christmas season. How're you doing?"

"I'm hanging in there. More people to do things with this year than last." When he looked right at C.J., she flushed all over again.

"What y'all gonna do, Zach, while Anne is here?" Sissy asked.

"*Zach.*" Anne pouted. "Didn't you tell C.J. what I want to do?"

C.J. shook her head, somehow certain she did not want to hear.

"Anne wants to experience authentic Chicago blues—"

"*Not* what I've heard in New York." This girl more than looked and sounded like Mae. She had Mae's swagger. "Even when the Chicago musicians play New York, I don't think it's the real thing."

"You're probably right about that," Roger said. "Different audience and all."

"I told my sister this is Christmas. *Maybe* this weekend."

Anne set down her glass and locked eyes with Zach. "I love you. But I'm here to see the blues."

"We'll see."

"I know where we could go," Mae said. C.J. nudged Mae with her elbow, to no avail. "Theresa's. Tonight's Blue Monday."

"What's that?" Anne asked, clapping her hands together.

"Something I haven't gotten to see yet my own self. On Mondays, a lot of the great blues musicians just drop by and sit in with Junior Wells and the house band."

Forks began to clank, coming to rest against plates. C.J. thought about the desserts on the kitchen table.

"I've been wanting to take you there, too, sweet face," Roger said. Alinda beamed at him.

"You reckon they're open tonight, Roger?" Mae asked.

"I expect so. It'd take at least a blizzard to shut the doors at Theresa's."

C.J. studied her plate, pushing the remaining foods away from the bare rib bones, feeling her plans falling apart. "Roger, you think it's okay and all?"

"Well, you won't find too many . . . others . . . at the clubs. But anybody who loves the music seems to be welcome most everywhere I've been."

She dropped her napkin onto her plate, right on top of her unfinished food. There would be no lingering over her desserts, no watching Zach at the piano. "I'll just start the coffee. It's early for dessert, but . . ."

"Y'all got *my* sweet potato pie," Emily said. "Make sure you don't miss it in there with all the things C.J. made."

"C.J.," Zach admonished. "You said you wouldn't go to any extra trouble for us."

"It's just a few desserts. So, we'd have plenty while we talk after dinner—"

"Oh, I'm too excited to eat another thing," Anne said. "How soon do we need to leave? Zach, we should go change."

"Anne—"

"It's all right, Zach, really. Y'all go. Have a great time." C.J. struggled to keep her voice even. "I'll take care of things here. The desserts will keep." Well, they would and they wouldn't. They would all taste nearly as good tomorrow as tonight. But the evening was lost, and she wanted something for that. "In fact," she said, almost before she knew what would follow, "I'll wrap some up and bring them down tomorrow."

"Yeah, y'all have fun," Flo said. "I'll help C.J."

"C.J.," Mae said. "Sometimes you and Flo can wipe the smile right off a person's face with all your practicalities. We should all go."

"Oh, I don't think on Christmas Eve . . ."

"Well, there won't likely be another Christmas Eve like this for a while," Sissy piped in. "I say let's give it a try."

C.J. looked around, helplessly, as Flo shrugged and Zach smiled.

❊   ❊   ❊

When the two jitneys deposited their group before a yellow-brick apartment building, C.J. thought surely they were at the wrong place. But a sign hanging from chain link fencing said *Theresa's*. They took the steps to the basement. Alinda and Roger led. Anne crowded behind Roger.

Inside, the air was hazy with smoke. Packs of cigarettes were stacked against the wall of the bar, like cords of wood waiting to stoke the fire. Theresa herself rested on her elbow and forearm, in an apron and goggle-like glasses, chatting with a customer. Christmas lights were strung overhead.

The nine of them moved as one until they found two tables to shove together. Roger ordered Cokes for Anne, Flo, and C.J., beers for the rest of them. They settled into their seats—C.J. between Zach and Mae, with Anne on the other side of Mae next to Roger. Roger slung an arm around Alinda. Flo chatted with Sissy and Emily.

C.J. thought about how long it had taken Mae to get her into a club. Now that she was, it felt oddly like church. People stomped their feet and called out to the singer. Mae whooped it up, too. Anne kept one eye on Mae, clapping when she did but mute all the while. When the commotion got especially loud, Anne inched her chair closer to Roger's. Zach clapped like he was at a ballgame, like a white boy.

C.J. was busy sneaking glances at him when Anne tugged at her sleeve. "I need to go to the bathroom."

C.J. was up in a flash. "I'll go with you."

Inside, she hurried to finish so Anne wouldn't be alone. The door opened, letting in more of the music. She flushed, jumping at the loudness of the whooshing.

When she exited the stall, C.J. stiffened. Standing in front of one Negro girl, Anne was facing down three others. The music came to a screeching halt, as if it had been shoved in a box and the lid slammed shut. No one moved or spoke. Then, suddenly, the music spewed forth again, and the three were talking and waving fists.

"You stay away from my man!" yelled the biggest girl. Anne held her ground.

"Crazy white girl," said another.

"Yeah, let's go," said the third.

The door swept them neatly back out into the bar.

"Are you all right?" Anne asked the small girl who stepped from behind her.

"Yeah. They're my friends, really. Rhonda just had herself too much to drink." Over her shoulder on her way out, she added, "Thanks."

C.J. stared at Anne. "Do you know what a fool thing that was to do?"

"They were coming at that little girl, the three of them." She turned her back and walked toward the sink.

"I don't care what *they* were doing." C.J. stepped around in front of Anne. "What *you* were doing was crazy. Y'all may be crazy in New York City, but that's not how it's done in a place like this."

Anne shrugged. "There's no need to tell Zach. He's a typical big brother. He worries." When C.J. took her time washing her hands, she added, "All right, *please.*"

C.J. met Anne's eyes in the mirror. "Don't take another swallow tonight. We're not coming in here again."

"What took so long?" Zach asked as they returned to their seats.

"Too many people in there is all." C.J. tried to match her breathing to the gentle beat of the music. She kept her eyes turned away from Zach. But as the singer proclaimed his love, they both reached for their drinks. Zach's hand brushed her arm, telling her once again it was a mistake for them to be here.

She avoided Zach and Anne all day on Christmas. When it was almost time to leave for Evanston, she gathered her things. A knock at the door sent her head up, but she continued packing. Then the knocking came louder, faster, as if someone needed help. She strode to the door and yanked it open.

"Can I come in?" Anne said breathlessly. "Just for a minute? Zach's taking a shower. So I haven't got much time."

C.J. stepped back. Inside, Anne waited for her to close the door.

"I just wanted to thank you again for not telling Zach what happened. If there's ever anything I can do . . ."

C.J. shook her head. "Just remember your brother loves you. If anything was to happen to you . . ."

"Okay then." Anne turned to go. The square of her shoulders, topped by her wild blond hair, irritated her even more than when Anne had walked away from her in the bathroom at Theresa's.

"Wait," C.J. ordered. "On second thought, there is something."

"Really?"

She ignored the hint of amazement. "I know your father is Jewish. But what does that mean?"

"I don't understand."

"Do y'all go to services? If you're going while you're here . . ." If Anne could demand to be taken to a club on Christmas Eve, she could certainly ask this. "Well, I'd like to go with you."

"I still don't understand."

"It's how I know people. Seeing how they are with their religion."

"And you want to know Zach?" Finally, Anne looked as if she did understand. She clapped her hands together, just as she had when Mae first mentioned Theresa's. "You care about him, *don't* you?"

"Of course," C.J. snapped. "He's my friend—"

"He'll be so happy to know—"

C.J.'s look was withering. "He can *never* know."

Anne nodded slowly. "I don't know that Zach has somewhere he goes," she said finally. "I'll suggest it to him, though."

✻   ✻   ✻

On the last Saturday of 1962, C.J. surrendered her coat to Zach as he whispered, "I'm glad you wanted to come." From the corner of her eye, she caught Anne's pleased smile. She turned away from them both and began to search the sea of faces around her. If there was one other Negro here today, that person must be hidden away like the choir. Yet she took for granted that Zach's God was her God.

She guessed the congregation of Hope Baptist could fit in the synagogue's choir loft. If they were there—faces and hands freshly scrubbed, wearing their threadbare Sunday-go-to-meeting clothes—they might well have collapsed the balcony by now with all their stomping and swaying. The people who surrounded her in high-backed seats, just like at the movies, sat as still as the air, murmuring together from the Union Prayer Book, never calling out "Amen!" or "Praise the Lord!" Only what was written. Their smells were of perfume and fine wool.

Uncomfortable in the comfortable chair, she missed the pine pews sanded smooth by time. Winter sun streamed through intricate stained glass windows, glancing off brass menorahs on the walls, striking marble and gleaming wood. C.J. squinted. When she next looked at her prayer book, she'd lost her place.

Then her fingers found the silent prayer. And as she read, *O Lord, I shut out the din and fret and littleness of things that I may feel myself alone with Thee in the silence*, the massive temple with its still air seemed to make sense.

She read on and took solace in the wisdom that things happen for the best. The words were more beautiful than any poem. She could almost hear Brother James reading along with her, his voice shimmying up and down the scale, its highs and lows perfectly timed. Flo might call him a waiting-on-heaven preacher, but she took the meaning of this prayer to be similar to what Brother James preached.

She watched as scrolls were brought from behind the heavy doors of a cabinet on the platform and paraded around the room. Listened as the rabbi told how the Israelites safely crossed the Red Sea before the waters closed behind them, drowning the Egyptians who had enslaved them. Imagined the Israelites rejoicing and Moses looking up to see God crying because the Egyptians were his children, too.

"You shall not oppress a stranger, for you know the feelings of the stranger, since you were strangers in the land of Egypt," the rabbi read. Zach's people, her people . . . slaves.

The choir sang again just before the rabbi stepped to the high pulpit to begin his sermon. Finally, C.J. relaxed into the chair and went back to her childhood, half dozing between her parents while Brother James preached. She'd grown accustomed way back then to letting the words wash over her, secure in the knowledge that the most important ones would ring a bit louder.

"It is the destiny of the Jewish people," said the rabbi, "to champion justice, brotherhood, and peace for all mankind."

These words put her in mind of Flo's and Zach's leanings, not Brother James's. Even so, they sounded more like the Pledge of Allegiance than something a person might get out of bed in the morning planning on doing. She glanced at Zach. Where would their lives take them? What if they had met in another time?

"Dr. Hirsch taught that 'The Jew assumes for himself the historic post of a soldier . . .' A soldier 'of righteousness and justice.' "

Suddenly, C.J. could hear the old piano at Hope Baptist as its congregants sang, "Onward Christian soldiers, marching as to war . . ." Whenever they sang that hymn, Brother James would read from 2 Timothy, "Thou therefore endure hardness, as a good soldier of Jesus Christ." Destiny . . . soldier . . . war. No longer words of encouragement, but a call to action. And all she could smell was danger.

The rabbi's words blew up her fear until it filled the sanctuary. The massive building seemed suddenly fragile, as if the waters of the Red Sea might close, knocking down the walls and drowning them all. The songs and prayers no longer comforted her. She wished they were all said in the language the Uptons had sometimes spoken and there was no translation in the prayer book. She wished she did not know Zach's destiny.

"C.J.," she heard, as if someone were calling to her from the choir loft. She felt Anne tapping her arm. "We're leaving now."

She followed Anne and Zach outside, threading their way through the people who stopped to chat. She was anxious to get away, but Zach took her and Anne by the arm.

"Why are we stopping?" Anne asked.

Zach had turned to gaze at the inscription above the colonnades. "Mevakshei Tzedek," he said. "What *exactly* does it mean?"

"Well, my Hebrew isn't much better than yours. But I think it means 'those who pursue justice.'"

"That's what I thought."

C.J. hugged her coat tightly around her. On the walk here, the excitement of learning more about Zach had kept her warm. Watching him now, staring at the inscription, she felt chilled to the bone. Something had drawn him back to look at it. The call of the rabbi's message.

❊   ❊   ❊

The winter wind circled the brownstone, knocking at the windows, asking for a warm place to spend the night. The others had all gone out to various New Year's Eve celebrations. C.J. sat on the couch, wrapped in a blanket. She wore thick wool socks and a heavy sweater over her favorite sweatshirt, the faded pink one, slightly frayed at the neck and sanded smooth by years of wear. The macaroni and cheese Flo had made for her was heating in the oven.

When "Auld Lang Syne" came on the radio, she switched stations again. But the melody stuck in her head, sending her to the piano to try to pick it out. Frustrated, she scowled at her beginner lesson book and returned to the couch. If only she *could* forget certain people. Mevakshei Tzedek had been two days ago. She'd been out of sorts ever since, rejecting invitations from Zach, insisting he spend time alone with Anne.

The sound of knocking took a while to reach her. She dragged herself up, opened the door. It was Zach, just as she'd feared, probably aiming to talk her into doing something with him now that Anne had gone home.

"I was afraid you wouldn't be here." He took a deep breath. His shoulders slumped with relief.

She stepped aside to let him in but then looked hard at him. "Zach, I've already said no to the parties and all."

His brow crinkled in confusion. It was then she noticed how red his eyes were and how drawn he looked, as if he'd aged in the short time since she'd last seen him.

"It's not that. It's Anne."

She checked her watch. A little after nine. Anne should be home by now, talking her parents' ears off about her visit.

"I called. You know, to make sure she got home." He paced toward the piano, then back again. "My parents were about to leave for the hospital. Anne's bus skidded on the icy roads just outside the city and crossed over to the oncoming lane. They don't know . . . anything more yet."

"Oh, Zach, what can I do?"

He seemed not to hear her at first, but finally said, "I need to stay by my phone. Come wait with me."

"Okay." She touched her hair, not certain she'd even combed it today, then threw off the ratty sweater, only to remember the sweatshirt underneath. No time to change. "Wait," she said, running to the kitchen to turn off the oven. As she locked the door, she realized she hadn't left a note. But Zach was steering her toward the stairs.

Inside Zach's apartment for the first time, all she could focus on at first was the phone. He rushed to it, picked it up, heard the dial tone and set the receiver back down. Gradually, as if her eyes needed to adjust to the pale yellow light, she took in the room. It seemed somehow bigger and nicer than the girls' living room. Perhaps it was the lack of clutter that made the identical fabulous high ceilings and crown molding pop out, or the idea of all this space being for one person. In place of a piano was an old door laid over cinder blocks. The work surface was neatly organized with books and papers. She moved to the sofa and perched there uncertainly. Zach went to the window.

"Nothing ever happens to Anne. She gets by on her spunk," he said as if to someone passing by on the street below. "Just this morning, she said—"

The clock on the mantel chimed three times, startling them both. A quarter to ten. Zach pulled a scrap of paper from his pocket. He stared at it, then at the phone, then at the clock. When the clock chimed again, he dialed.

"Hello, I'm calling about the status of a patient," he said for the third time. "Anne Bernstein. She's my sister."

C.J. held her breath while Zach listened.

"Please tell them I called," he said and hung up.

Standing across the room, Zach seemed so far away. As far as the distance between Chicago and New York, or Chicago and Mississippi. If she were waiting for news about Charlie, she could hardly be more nervous.

"The hospital will only give out information to my parents," he said finally. "So, we wait some more."

She thought to go stand by him, just to be closer. Perhaps to take his hand. But neither of them moved. She gripped the hem of her sweatshirt and closed her eyes now and then to pray, all the while waiting for the next chime of the small wooden clock. Sometimes when she opened her eyes, Zach would be at the window. Once he was hovering over a record player, looking sorrowfully at the albums stacked next to it in a crate, as if music must wait. Another time, he had sunk into the armchair by the table with the lamp. His hands were in front of his face, his fingers spread like the leafless limbs of trees before the circle of the moon.

She left him like that, in the chair, at a quarter to midnight, to go to the bathroom. As she dried her hands, the phone rang. She walked quietly to the living room. Stopping in the doorway, she watched him curl the phone cord nervously in one hand.

"Surgery?" he said.

In the silence, he twisted the cord enough to pull the phone toward the edge of the small table. She reached out to catch it.

"Yes, Mom," he repeated, blinking back tears. "I love you, too. And, Mom . . . kiss Annie for me the second they let you see her."

C.J. held out the phone. He set it back on the table and took hold of her hand, stroking her fingers as if he drew comfort from them.

"It's pretty bad. She has a concussion and broken bones. And internal injuries . . . We won't know about those until she's out of surgery."

He looked into her face just long enough to say, "Thank you for being with me tonight," then turned his attention back to her hand.

C.J. trembled as Zach traced its curve. She watched him, unaware of time until the chimes sounded midnight and the new year. He pulled her toward him then, touching her face the way he had her fingers. She closed her eyes, afraid to let them meet his. She felt his lips on hers and, unable to stop herself, kissed him back.

When she pulled away, it took all her strength. Zach led her to the couch, where they sat, wordlessly, waiting, finally drifting into a half sleep. His arm never left her shoulders. Now and then, his hand caressed the smooth pink of her sleeve. She scarcely heard the chimes of the clock over her own heartbeat. But the ringing of the phone was as loud as thunder.

Zach was across the room in an instant. "Mom?" He listened, then exhaled loudly. "You said it's her spleen?" He began to twist the cord again. "How bad is her leg?" C.J. leaned forward, ready to jump up and catch the phone. "When will she be awake?" He nodded into the silence. "Mom, don't be ridiculous. You and Dad are going to need help. I'll call to let you know when I'm coming, as soon as I've spoken to my professors."

He said goodbye and returned to the couch, but sat on the edge, hands clasped, shoulders slightly hunched, looking at C.J. "The concussion isn't bad, thank goodness. But . . ."

"Oh, Zach."

"Annie's spleen was ruptured, but they were able to repair it. It's the recovery I'm worried about. Her lower left leg and her right arm. She won't be able to use crutches, and Mom and Dad have to work."

Time seemed to speed up after that.

He looked at his desk. "I'll have to leave school for a while, at least for a quarter."

"If there's anything any of us can do while you're gone . . ." She could feel at once his kiss on her lips and her Cinderella ball gown turning to rags. "Try to rest," she urged, moving toward the door. "I'll just go on up by myself."

"C.J., I—"

She turned. "Flo and them have got to be worried."

He hesitated a moment, then nodded. "Happy New Year, C.J."

Inside number ten, C.J. leaned against the door as if the wind were trying to blow it down.

Flo rushed from the bedroom. "Are you all right? You didn't leave a note. The macaroni I made you was still sitting in the oven, not a forkful gone."

C.J. walked to the couch where she'd tossed the raggedy sweater some five hours earlier. "It's Anne," she began, pulling the sweater around her. The story spilled out of her then.

"But she'll be all right, won't she?"

"Zach says it'll take time. But yes."

"Then what is it?"

"It was terrifying is all. Sitting there waiting and wondering."

"There's something more. You was pushing that door closed like the boogeyman himself was on the other side."

"I think I'll have me some of that macaroni now."

Flo walked quickly to the kitchen. She turned on the oven, took the pan from the refrigerator, slapped it down on the oven shelf, and slammed the door. "Now we got nothing to do but wait for it." She sat down at the table.

C.J. dragged out a chair and slumped into it, remembering Zach sinking into his armchair. She'd watched him in the moonlit glow of the table lamp, wanting only to comfort him. That's all the kiss had been.

"Zach . . . kissed me."

A grin conquered every bit of sternness on Flo's face. C.J. held up her hands in protest. "It was just him being relieved that Anne would be okay and all. Just finding some comfort in a friend, not being alone and all."

"Friends? Humph. *Friends* is you and me. And I reckon what friends are for is to tell you what you can't see."

"Zach and me, we're friends is *all*." She shook her head as tears slid down her cheeks. "You know that's all we can ever be."

"I don't know any such of a thing." Flo took out the macaroni, served her a plate, and handed her a fork. "Now eat."

C.J. stared at the plate, still feeling Zach's touch. She remembered walking along Lake Michigan with him a year ago, when she'd thought to worry about him disappearing from her life after graduation. Now he was gone for who knew how long. And his kiss had made her want more.

CHAPTER 15

June 1963
Justice Like a Hammer

"That picture of the sit-in at the Jackson Woolworth's could've been taken right here." Squinting the way he once had at her up in the giant burr oak, Zach framed a view of the diner's counter seating.

Six months of not seeing him, while he stayed in New York supporting Anne during her rehabilitation, had seemed an eternity to C.J. It hadn't been long enough to forget their kiss; she'd known that before she agreed to come. She never would have risked it if Flo wasn't with them. It was clear that Zach hadn't forgotten either. His eyes walked her face the way she would the Wilson farm, cherishing the familiar while searching for the new.

C.J.'s eyes flitted everywhere but to Zach's, settling on the brownish-yellow splotches caked on the handle of the mustard spoon. Suddenly, wiping it clean seemed the most important thing she could do.

"I saw that in the papers," Flo said.

So had C.J. The faces crowding behind the three at the counter had the looks she remembered on Mr. Corrigan's men, like dogs who had cornered rabbits.

"Can you imagine?" Zach said. "Trying to ignore the crowd while they dumped mustard and sugar on your head?"

"It's a brave thing they did, those three from Tougaloo," Flo agreed.

Here C.J. had thought Tougaloo was a fine Negro college, maybe the right one for Charlie. But if folks there got involved in sit-ins, she would have to think again.

"The girls and their professor, that white man," Flo went on.

Reverend Thornheart, Brother James, her teachers, and Mrs. Corrigan suddenly gathered in C.J.'s head, all shouting, *Remember Zach is a white man!* His kiss—as far from the groping and leering of Mr. Corrigan's men as she was now—had made her forget.

"I don't know could I sit there so calm," Flo said.

"Something *I* don't know," C.J. said, "is what possessed them in the first place—"

"What'll it be?" The unsmiling waitress jutted one hip forward, letting the table prop her up.

Zach ordered a cheeseburger. Flo looked up hopefully. "What I'd really like is a BLT on toast."

The waitress scowled and thumped her pencil against her order pad. "It's got to be on the menu."

"All right, then. Give me a minute—"

"Ma'am, there's no reason we can't get a BLT." Zach's voice held the forced patience C.J. had heard when he called the hospital about Anne. "Everything it takes to make one is on the menu."

She quickly scanned hers. "I'll have the number four breakfast, with an extra side of bacon and toast. Zach, you give Flo your lettuce and tomato. There, that's it, I think." She smiled at the waitress. The woman snorted and left.

"There comes a point," Zach said, "when it's just too much."

"It's only a sandwich," Flo said.

"Not your BLT." He laughed, but his eyes didn't cooperate. "Anne has made me see that."

Something about the way Zach said *Anne,* rather than *Anne's accident,* and looked straight at C.J. made her edgy, as if it had something to do with her. He'd told them a little about the months in New York while they walked to the deli. How painful Anne's physical therapy had been, but how she'd been the one to keep everyone's spirits up. And how she'd admonished him to keep up his synagogue attendance once he was back in Chicago.

"I found a synagogue near Anne's hospital. Got to know some folks who liked to talk about what's happening. Bull Connor using fire hoses and dogs on demonstrators in Birmingham. President Kennedy calling for his civil rights bill one day and early the next morning, Medgar Evers shot dead outside his home. Now, a big march on Washington—"

"Why?" C.J. croaked. Her fear, big enough that day to fill the Mevakshei Tzedek sanctuary, now sucked the air from the deli. She wiped harder at the stubborn splotches.

"It seemed so important to Anne."

Not why did you look for a synagogue in New York! she felt like screaming at him. *Why are you giving in so easily to the pull of your destiny? Don't you see the danger?*

"Anyway," Zach continued. "Look at it all, just in these past few months. It's too much. What else could the Jackson folks do?"

She watched the ceiling fan circle diligently, yoked like a team of mules—each doing its job, each knowing its place. "But breaking the law?"

"It's sometimes necessary with unjust laws. That's how the Jews were freed from slavery in Egypt and how America came to be."

The surly waitress reappeared, balancing all their food on her arms. C.J. passed her sides of bacon and toast to Flo.

"Don't you just feel like you need to do something?" Zach handed Flo his lettuce and tomato and reached for the mustard jar. "Maybe Washington." He slathered mustard on his burger and began to eat, nodding now and then, absorbed in some private conversation.

Suddenly he pushed his food aside and leaned toward C.J. "Anne said you . . . I need you to come with me."

She could barely hear him, so loud was the sound of her momma's voice. Saying, *This man moved into my heart and never left,* the day she asked how her parents knew they loved each other. But she thought she'd made it clear that Anne could never tell Zach she cared about him.

Zach touched C.J.'s shoulder, so close to her heart. She looked at his hand, then up, up, into his eyes, unable to look away.

"C.J., I said I need you to come with me."

"Come with you where?" She could no more keep quiet now than she could stop herself from kissing him on New Year's Eve.

"Washington, D.C. For the march Dr. King announced this week to bring attention to President Kennedy's civil rights bill."

Her mind raced. She clutched at the table and tried not to duck as dueling forces assaulted her, as if the blades of the ceiling fan had spun free. Zach's destiny, now trying to pull her toward danger, too, and him away from her if she let him go off without her. How could she stop this?

"Can anybody go?" Flo asked.

"I don't even know. But I'm going to find out."

"Zach," C.J. said, low and controlled. "You've asked me 'bout folks I worked for back in Mississippi. Now might be the time for me to tell you."

Now that she'd opened things up, she wasn't certain what to say. She decided to begin with Mrs. Barnes. "There was this Catholic family. The wife was from Wisconsin, sweetest lady you'd ever want to meet. But, being a Yankee and all, she didn't understand how things were. Whenever she'd drive me home, she'd ask didn't I want to sit up front with her. And once, she drove right up to my door in the rain and got her car stuck. My uncle had to pull her out with his mules."

"You said . . ." Zach hesitated. "Being a Yankee, she didn't understand."

Now she'd gone and insulted him. She blushed but did not apologize. "*Everybody*, if they want to stay safe, needs to be following the rules. This lady didn't even know there were rules."

"Maybe she knew and chose not to follow them. I mean, my parents taught us rules aren't sacred. Few should be accepted without question—"

"Oh, did they? And what kind of rules did they teach y'all to break?"

"Mostly those saying one person is better than another because of something like religion or race."

"I guess you and Anne are lucky they didn't send y'all south for a visit then, like Emmett Till." Her voice whipped at him. "*My* parents been teaching us how to stay alive since—" She studied Zach's face, wondering whether foolishness or ignorance made him say such things, needing him to know what Emmett Till somehow hadn't. "Since way before that Yankee boy came down from Chicago and got himself killed."

"I just think I might do the same as your Mrs. Barnes, C.J. Say something about what's not right."

Of all the high-minded talk, thinking he had known trouble and could handle it better. She fought back tears. "Well, aren't you the biggety one?"

"C.J.," Flo interrupted. "It *is* too much, what all's happened. Especially in my Birmingham. I want to go to Washington. Will you come with us?"

Even louder than her mother's voice or Zach's, C.J. heard the slow whap-whap of the blades overhead and covered her heart with her hands. "You know I can't."

❊   ❊   ❊

On her hands and knees, C.J. inched her way backward across the kitchen in tiny swirling motions. The ridiculous rooster clock had scratched its way to noon, an hour and thirty minutes still to wait before the TV would be showing the march.

"We'll look out for each other," Flo had tried to reassure her.

Still, in her dreams, she saw Flo flailing helplessly against the force of a fire hose, Zach caught in the biting grip of a police dog.

All summer her fear for their safety had grown, fed by the TV and papers predicting riots worse than any so far. Now, she had to wonder. Would Flo and Zach sleep on the bus, one or the other nodding off, head coming to rest on the other's shoulder? As they marched, would they hold hands or lock arms?

She couldn't stop worrying that things would change between her and Zach. Goose bumps prickled her skin as she remembered Zach's hand holding hers on New Year's Eve. His firm grip on her arm had guided her along the windy streets of Chicago so often she could feel it now. Her heart beat as if held back only by her rib cage. No! It should be *her* head resting on his shoulder, *her* hand he took.

She threw the sponge at the bucket. It landed smack dab in the water, rocking back and forth like a tiny boat tossed about on the waves, sloshing dirty water over the edge. "Now look what you've gone and done," she snapped.

She stared at the floor. If anything, the last few tiles she'd washed looked dirtier than before. She carried the bucket to the laundry room, watched the water swirl down the drain. While clean water rose to the top, she touched the lapel of her work dress.

For the twelfth time that morning, she unpinned the little white button, one of thousands sold to finance the march, and studied it. *March on Washington for Jobs & Freedom. August 28, 1963.* The clasped hands, one black, the other white. When she'd bought the button, she felt like she was doing something. Now, scrubbing a floor and waiting to watch on TV, she felt as small as the button, as small as the quarter she paid for it.

From the moment the broadcast finally began, C.J. watched for three things: police dogs, a glimpse of Zach and Flo, and trouble.

CBS had canceled its afternoon shows, from *As the World Turns* to *Secret Storm.* Cameramen looked out from the stage to show the nation's capitol. President Lincoln watched their backs from within his temple.

The towering Washington Monument cast its shadow across the Reflecting Pool. C.J. squinted, trying to make out the blurry mass surrounding the water. The cameras moved closer, closer, to . . . people! Negro and white, young and old, dressed for church and the fields. Her hand flew to her mouth. Zach and Flo were lost among hundreds of thousands of people.

The program began. While first one person then another spoke, she willed the cameras to scan the crowd. She cringed at each policeman, but saw no dogs. Everywhere, whites and Negroes stood shoulder to shoulder. But none were Zach and Flo.

Mrs. Medgar Evers and Mrs. Herbert Lee were among the women honored as freedom fighters. C.J. ached for them, losing their husbands to killers. But it was the others who fascinated her. Rosa Parks, starting the Montgomery bus boycott. Daisy Bates, leading the nine Negro students who desegregated Little Rock's Central High. Diane Nash Bevel and Gloria Richardson, sitting-in in Nashville and demonstrating in Maryland. Didn't *these* women have husbands, children, brothers?

Seeing Mahalia Jackson made C.J. smile with happiness for Flo. Hearing her left C.J. stunned.

Then Flo's Dr. King stood at the podium, microphones jutting up toward his face. The policeman by his side wore a hat and sunglasses. But Dr. King looked out unblinking, his voice rolling like cotton puffs rippled by the wind in the fields of Mississippi. He spoke of his dream, and it sounded wonderful. But when he had finished, C.J. remembered only how he insisted nothing would be still until the fight for equality had been won.

That single idea danced on the sunlight that shot through the living room like arrows. That single idea swirled madly until each of Dr. King's words had been spun out into its individual letters and merged with a particle of dust. And still, that single idea reverberated in her head: *no rights, no rest.*

C.J. struggled to fill her lungs. The air, unwilling to be contained, rushed out with a low, shuddering moan. In that moment, she accepted the inevitability of the fight. From the final view the cameras presented of the crowd—most of them Negro, all of them braver than her—she understood the scope.

Whether or not she would be part of it, she knew Zach would. She clasped her hands in prayer. "Sweet Jesus, watch over us all."

❊   ❊   ❊

On the Saturday before Halloween, C.J. smiled as the last child, clutching his bag of candy, filed out of the activity room at the Hyde Park Neighborhood Club. She, Flo, and Zach had volunteered to help with the party, held on Saturday so the kids could trick-or-treat next Thursday night.

She was excited about seeing him again. When he'd entered law school in September, he begged off their Saturday breakfasts, explaining that his study group met then. Sunday lunches, too, had fallen mostly by the wayside. But Zach was trying to manage his volunteering here. He'd gotten involved through the university and enlisted her and Flo.

C.J. liked coming to the club, seeing the shining faces of the kids as they relaxed within the safe play space and basked in the attention of staff and volunteers. She appreciated the history—this was one of Chicago's earliest settlement houses, modeled after Hull House and dedicated to all Hyde Park's underprivileged children. And this was her idea of a good cause—neighbors helping neighbors, just like at Hope Baptist.

She began sweeping while Flo cleared away Kool-Aid cups and Zach took down decorations. But as he peeled away paper ghosts and goblins, the words on the poster reappeared one by one, bigger and more glaring than when C.J. had covered them. WANTED: THOUSANDS OF MARCHERS—TUESDAY, OCTOBER 22, FREEDOM DAY SCHOOL BOYCOTT.

She focused on the pile of multi-colored curly-cued crepe paper gathering beneath her broom, then looked back at Zach, still somehow surprised he'd been part of it and not wanting to talk about it. "Isn't it special Ricky was the one to hit the piñata?"

She and Zach had met Ricky at a softball game, struggling to connect bat to ball. Afterwards, they'd worked with him until he gained confidence and ability. At her reference to one of their favorites, Zach beamed just like Ricky had. She leaned on the handle of the push broom, knowing to keep the rest of her thoughts to herself. Boycotts. She could still hear Brother James, during the Montgomery bus boycott, reminding his flock that they needed the bus to get to work.

Flo dropped the last Styrofoam cup in the trash and studied the poster. "Now, Zach, *The Defender* and the TV made it sound like this Chicago march was near about as big as the one on Washington. What you think?"

C.J. clenched her teeth, preparing for Flo and Zach to start carrying on about being in Washington together.

"It's hard to say, Flo. But walking down LaSalle, with people ahead and behind me as far as I could see, I couldn't help remembering walking with you."

"Was there music?" Flo asked, then, without waiting for his answer, "Remember it all? Besides Mahalia Jackson, of course, I liked that Peter,

Paul, and Mary. Standing on the steps of the Lincoln Memorial, wishing for nothing more than a hammer, a bell, and a song."

"C.J., you've got to hear about Flo and the flags around the Washington Monument."

She smiled halfheartedly.

"When I told Flo there was a flag for each state, she dragged me by the arm to look at every one of them. We were nearly full circle when she started counting. 'Forty-eight, forty-nine, fifty,' she said. 'Well, I swan. There it is. My Alabama *is* part of this country after all.'"

She'd heard the story at least once. Flo and Zach just couldn't seem to remember what they had and hadn't told. Now she saw again the images that had tormented her while she scrubbed Mrs. Gray's floor and waited to watch the march on television. Flo and Zach, resting their heads on each other's shoulders on the bus. Flo and Zach, holding hands as they marched. Flo and Zach, together in a way she had missed out on and could never get back.

Desperate to steer the conversation away from these thoughts, she asked about the Chicago protest. She knew *what* it was about. Chicago Negroes standing up against Superintendent Willis for better schools. So she asked *why* instead. "Why did you get involved in *this* march, Zach?"

"I didn't think I would at first, but then a couple of guys I know mentioned it. They're both in Chicago Area Friends of SNCC. One was going to teach Negro history to the younger kids at a Freedom School that day, at one of the local churches, but the other was going to the march."

Zach began to recall Dr. King's speech then—how he'd repeated the word "justice" and spoken of whites who recognize the connection between their destiny and that of their Negro brethren. "You know, I think I've been in this since that day Anne got us go to Mevakshei Tzedek. 'Those who pursue justice.' Remember?"

C.J.'s heart pounded.

"But I assumed the really important work to be done is all in the south. Until I read my friend's protest sign. *Willis—Wallace, what's the difference?*

It's barely been four months since Governor Wallace stood in the doorway to block Negro students from registering at the University of Alabama. I mean, think about it."

C.J. breathed a tiny sigh of relief. "Well, good then. It's best you get involved here. The thought of you trying to do something in Alabama or Mississippi just scares me senseless." She put her hand over her heart.

But in the next weeks, she couldn't help thinking more about Dr. King's speech. He'd said that now was the time. After the march he wrote that the marchers summed up everything in that one word—*now*. President Kennedy's civil rights bill was working its way through Congress. It would mean she could vote when she went home. She believed the President when he said the U.S. would win the space race. Maybe she should believe in his civil rights bill, too. She wanted to, but it made her jumpy.

She was doing laundry when the phone rang on November 22. "Miz Gray? Are you there?" C.J. cradled the phone between her ear and shoulder, straining to hear as she folded the sheet, still warm from the dryer, in half.

"Yes, I—I don't know how . . . It's the President. He's been shot. He's . . . dead."

"No, ma'am. Not the *President*." The sheet fell from her hands. People might be killed every day, but not the President. She believed that absolutely. And he had things to take care of.

"C.J.? *C.J.*, are you there?"

"Yes'm."

"Jenny and Johnny will be home soon. Perhaps they've heard. But, if they should turn on the television, I didn't want them to be startled—or you, dear. But, oh . . . that's just what I've done . . .'"

"Miz Gray, should I tell them not to?"

"That's all right. But please sit with them until their father and I get there. We'll try to close the store early."

When C.J. moved to hang up, she stepped on the sheet. Gently she gathered it up and brushed it off. In the laundry room, she concentrated on making the folds precise. Each time she reduced the sheet by half, she ran her hands over its cool smoothness until there were no more wrinkles.

Finally, she set it on top of the basket just as the school bus screeched to a stop.

The November chill followed the twins inside. "Did you hear the president's dead?" Jenny asked, turning her tear-stained face to C.J.

"Yes, honey." Her thoughts raced through things said in the face of death, violent and untimely death at the hands of white people. As each platitude came to her, she offered it out loud. "He's gone on to be with the Lord . . . We have to put our faith in Jesus . . . It's not for us to understand why."

The twins stared at her as if she were a creature from outer space. Of course, none of those sentiments was right for this family who seemed to be not Catholic or Jewish or Baptist, but . . . *nothing*. What would they do in the face of death? Who, if not the extended family of their church, would bring the casseroles and cakes and sit with them while they cried?

"Y'all's momma and daddy will get here soon as they can," she tried instead. "Why don't you two help me in the kitchen?"

There was leftover roast beef. She would make something simple for the Grays to eat in front of the television. She pulled the cover off the mixer, and oil and a cake mix from the pantry, then set the oven.

"Jenny, can you mix this?" C.J. handed her an egg. "Johnny, would you like to slice or peel?"

"Huh?"

"Tomatoes, cheese, and meat or the potatoes?"

He reached for the peeler. C.J. started eggs to hard-boil and went to work on the tomatoes. When the oven beeped, everyone jumped.

"The principal made announcements over the public address system," Jenny said. "Starting with President Kennedy being . . ."

"Shot," Johnny finished. "People were praying, I guess. I saw Maggie crossing herself."

C.J. nodded. "You'll want to rinse those soon as you're finished peeling."

As the boy ran cold water over the colander, his parents arrived. Peter and Donna Gray went straight to their children and hugged them. It took

C.J. a moment to realize that Mrs. Gray had reached out to hug her, too. Involuntarily, she stiffened.

"C.J." Mrs. Gray drew back but kept her hand on C.J.'s arm. "Mr. Gray and I talked about this on our way home."

My Lord, that was the way her first two employers began their announcement that she would no longer be working for them. Surely not now . . .

"This loss is one we share. We'd like you to sit with our family tonight as we mourn together."

"Thank you, ma'am." Her voice caught, as if stuck somewhere between the shock of physical contact and relief—over not being let go, but just as surely over not being alone.

"I'm going to turn on the television," Mr. Gray said.

Mrs. Gray steered C.J. to a chair, then gathered her children on the couch, hugging them as if they might vanish. They watched the casket being lowered from the plane at Andrews Air Force Base. While Lyndon Johnson asked for the help of God and America in the role thrust upon him, Mrs. Kennedy stood alone in her blood-spattered clothes.

How devastating for the Kennedys, losing their husband and father. How heartbreaking for Mrs. Gray, losing her President. But C.J. realized she'd caught Mrs. Gray's feeling some time ago. President Kennedy had become *her* President, too.

❋   ❋   ❋

They huddled near the radio as if before a crackling, dancing fire. Now and then, someone recalled what they'd been doing when they heard the news. The clunky radiator and the body heat of the six women made the room toasty cozy. Yet Flo hunched in a blanket, hugging her long legs to her chest and rocking slightly.

A knock on the door made them jump. Sissy got up, patting Flo on the head as she went by.

"Hi, everybody," Zach whispered into the hushed room. "I've been watching TV at the student union all morning." He told of seeing former

President Eisenhower, the first dignitary to pay his respects in the East Room of the White House, where the President's body lay. Of accused assassin Lee Oswald paraded through the halls of the Dallas City Jail. "I thought maybe you'd like to watch with me."

"That's right thoughtful of you," Sissy said. "But we're keeping up with it all on the radio. And it's warm in here."

Mae and Emily nodded.

"I usually prefer the radio myself," he said. "But there's something different about this. We've gotten to know President Kennedy through TV. They're showing some of his speeches, even some Kennedy family home movies. It feels like being there, with the whole country watching together."

Flo's head jerked up. "I want to go."

'Course you do, C.J. couldn't help thinking.

Flo threw off her blanket. "C.J., you'll come, too. Get your things."

"Well—all right." She looked around the room.

Alinda held up her hands. "Zach, you don't need to be marching onto campus with an army of Negro maids."

Flo unwound her legs and stood. C.J. hesitated. Mrs. Gray had asked her something yesterday, something she'd promised to consider.

"Wait," C.J. said. "I need to talk to y'all."

"Should I leave?" Zach asked.

"No, you might can help."

Flo sat down but stretched her legs into the circle, making the room seem more crowded than cozy. "What is it then?"

"It's about the family I work for. I've told y'all they're sort of unusual, not even wanting me to wear a uniform and all."

C.J. paused, considering how best to tell the story. She began with how Mrs. Gray came home yesterday and went straight to the twins, but then reached out to draw her in, too. Alinda raised an eyebrow. Mae coughed. C.J. told them next about sitting with the family while they watched the reports on TV. In the circle, each girl shook her head. C.J. moved on to the Thanksgiving invitation. "Such a word coming from this woman's mouth. *Tell, expect, need.* I've heard me all of those before. But invite?"

"You saying this white lady's invited six Negro girls to sit down at her table for Thanksgiving dinner?" Emily screeched.

"This ain't no time for fooling," Sissy said.

"I'm serious, y'all. Miz Gray said plain as day, 'you *and* your friends, however many you like.' "

"She crazy or just some naïve do-gooder?" Sissy asked.

"I said, careful as can be, that it might not be wise. That's when she snapped, 'This is not Clybourne Park in the fifties! No harm will come to us if we do this.' Got so mad I finally promised I'd ask y'all and let her know could anyone come."

"*She* got mad!" Emily waved her hands around, punctuating her words. "She's put you between a rock and a hard place, asking you to sit at her table one day, then go back to eating in the kitchen."

C.J. noticed Zach then. He sat so still, as if not to call attention to himself, but one hand stole across his body to scratch his other arm.

"Wonder what it'd be like—being a guest at a white person's home," Mae said.

"You can't be serious, girl!" Emily said.

"It'd be plumb loony is what," Alinda pronounced.

"You know," Mae said, "Zach's the one we ought to be asking."

Zach dropped the hand that had been doing the scratching, as if it had brought on the punishment of being forced to weigh in.

"You know I can't speak for all white people, if that's what you're asking." He sounded a bit testy. C.J. pursed her lips in apology.

"You'll have to judge what was in Mrs. Gray's heart when she asked, C.J."

"I reckon she surprised herself almost as much as me. But she did seem sincere."

"Let's start there then."

"But Emily's right," C.J. wailed. "Going back to the kitchen after sitting with them in the dining room? And if I don't do it, there'll surely be bad feelings between us. She said she didn't know what my life was like in Mississippi, but she'd surely like to, and how she gets impatient for things to happen when they seem right. So, I should talk to y'all, of course, but she truly hoped we'd say yes."

The radiator sputtered in sympathy.

"Can we let some of this heat out?" She opened the window before anyone could answer.

"Lots of bosses have their employees over for dinner," Zach said. "But those employees don't usually work in their bosses' homes." He rubbed his forehead while everyone looked at him. "Is there anything that could make the situation okay?"

"Sure." C.J. tapped one foot furiously. "It just needs to be clear what the rules are. And after *that* happens, I'll just go out and buy myself a new car with all the money I've been getting overpaid all these years."

Alinda snorted amid the girls' laughter. From the street below, a car horn hooted along with them. Zach did his best to ignore it all.

"I don't know," he said. "What if somehow it could be clear? Here's one situation, and here's another."

Watching Zach try so hard, C.J. wanted to help him. "Maybe if I wasn't alone? If someone was there who wouldn't be, come dinnertime the next day."

Zach leaned back like his work was done. The girls looked at each other.

"You know I'll do it if it's what you want," Mae said.

Alinda held up her hands again. "I'm spending the day with Roger."

"I got to work," Sissy said.

"Me, too, thank the Lord," Emily said.

C.J. knelt down by Mae and hugged her. Mae patted her back and looked around her, right at Zach. "Now, what if you was to go?"

"Wait a minute," he said. "I doubt the invitation included me."

"Miz Gray was surely thinking about my roommates," C.J. agreed. She rested on her heels, considering. "But she did say my friends. And how nobody should be without family right now."

"C.J., that's crazy," Emily said.

"But it'd be such a help if you came, Zach. You'd know better what to do. Wonder if I couldn't say something like I'd understand if her invitation was only for my roommates, but we don't want our friend to be alone either?"

"Well, I guess I'm with Mae," he said. "I'll do it if it's what you want. But when you tell them I'm a student friend who lives in your building, mention my full name just so there's no surprises."

"Thanks, y'all—so much. I've been sick with worry." C.J. got up and stepped toward the closet.

Flo had been sitting silently the whole time. "I want to go," she said.

"I'm getting the coats, fast as I can."

"Good. But I mean to Thanksgiving dinner."

"Really?" C.J. turned to look at her. "You don't have to, you know."

Flo nodded. "Reckon we got us a history, C.J. Going with each other where we don't want to. And I think I just got to see this with my own two eyes."

The next day, C.J. left for Evanston earlier than usual. She'd sooner clean the whole house tonight than talk to Mrs. Gray. But she was determined to get it behind her. All the way there, she rehearsed her answer.

Inside the back door, the smells of spaghetti sauce and garlic bread greeted her. Mrs. Gray loose in that kitchen—good grief! Now C.J. would have to clean up a huge mess *while* she asked about Zach. What she saw, though, surprised her. The family's dinner dishes neatly stacked by the sink. The counters spotless. Mrs. Gray emptying marinara into a Mason jar.

"Oh, C.J. You startled me."

"Yes'm, I . . . uh, about your invitation . . ."

"Please, sit. Have you eaten? I'll just grab a plate. The meal is still warm."

"Let me do that, ma'am."

Mrs. Gray waved away her offer, leaving C.J. to fidget at the table while she did all the work. Humming and clattering about, as if waiting on the help were normal. Getting silverware, a napkin, and Parmesan from the refrigerator. Dishing out noodles, sauce, and garlic bread.

As Mrs. Gray finally sat down, C.J. blurted, "Most of my roommates have to work or already have plans. But Mae and Flo can come."

"Excellent." Mrs. Gray smiled. "How's the pasta?"

C.J. forked and chewed, nodding and smiling back, trying to remember how she'd planned to say things.

"We have another friend, Zach. He's—"

"Goodness. I haven't given you anything to drink. What would you like?"

"Just water, ma'am. Thank you." As the rooster clock announced the half hour, she felt her carefully prepared speech flying out the window. "*Miz Gray*, Zach can't be with his family either."

"Then Zach must join us as well."

C.J. suddenly realized she hadn't been prepared for Mrs. Gray to agree. "Then, ma'am," she sputtered. "What can they bring?"

"Not a thing. I'll do all the cooking."

Didn't that just beat all? She'd talked her friends into coming for burned toast and fried chicken from a box!

"Oh, no'm."

"The pasta's not *that* bad I hope." Mrs. Gray laughed. "I can cook a few stand-bys. When I have the time, like at the holidays, I even enjoy it."

"It's just—" C.J.'s cheeks burned. "Our mommas would have a conniption if we was to go to dinner without bringing something."

"Now, I do understand that. Is there a special dessert from home?"

"I'd say sweet potato pie."

"*Wonderful.* And perhaps Zach can bring a bottle of wine."

"Yes'm."

"That's settled then. We'll gather at noon and eat about one. Now you finish that while I get back to the dishes."

❖   ❖   ❖

"I'll get it!" Mrs. Gray yelled when the doorbell rang.

C.J. forced herself to stay seated in the living room with the other Grays, pretending to care whether the Lions or Packers won. *Unusual* was Mrs. Gray's word when she'd made her invitation. *Perhaps this is unusual, but yesterday our world took on an unusual quality.* Well, that word was at least a couple of sizes too small to cover this morning. They'd worked right alongside each other, saying little beyond "Excuse me" when they went for pans from the same cupboard or C.J. reached for the oven door to put in her cinnamon buns just as Mrs. Gray tried to baste the turkey. The family sat down to breakfast in the dining room while C.J. ate in the kitchen and cleaned up after them. Then Mrs. Gray declined help with dinner, firmly shooing C.J. in to watch the Macy's Parade.

Absently, C.J. ran a hand over the soft navy wool of the suit dress she and Flo had bought together. She wished for a uniform, to put on and take off at the right times throughout this day. Even Jim Crow, unwritten yet unconfused. Anything to clearly signal her position.

The sound of Mrs. Gray greeting her friends traveled from the kitchen. "Oh, doesn't this pie look delicious? Thank you for the wine. Let's meet the others."

C.J. grabbed the arms of the chair and leaned forward like one of the football players on the TV, ready to spring into action the second the ball was snapped.

One by one, her friends came into the living room. Mae, looking like a much shorter, less expensive version of Mrs. Gray, who wore black wool slacks, an emerald green sweater set, and a strand of pearls. Flo, dressed perfectly for any Baptist church in Chicago. And Zach, handsome as ever in his sports coat and tie.

"C.J., would you do the honors and introduce your friends?" Mrs. Gray asked.

She was at Mae's side in an instant, taking her hand. "This is Mae Willis. We've been friends since first grade. I wouldn't be here today if it wasn't for her." She reached to pull Flo from behind Mae. "Flo Thomas is another roommate, from Birmingham."

"Are you *really*?" Jenny asked. She came to stand by C.J., close enough for a better look, but not too close. C.J. could almost see Jenny's mind at work on more questions.

"I really am." Flo's mouth just did manage to curve up in a little smile.

"I read the story in *TIME* about the bomb—"

"Now, Jenny, you're interrupting C.J.'s introductions," Mrs. Gray said firmly.

C.J. reached out to Zach but quickly dropped her hand. Oh, no. She'd never told Mrs. Gray his full name.

"This is our friend Zach Bernstein, from New York City." Jenny looked at him all swimmy-headed. But if anyone else reacted, they concealed it. "He's a student at the University of Chicago."

Mrs. Gray introduced her family, then invited everyone to make themselves comfortable. "How was the parade?" she asked, to start the conversation before returning to the kitchen.

"It was nice they went ahead with it," Mr. Gray said. His attire—corduroys and a cable knit sweater—seemed to underscore his usual calm, confident manner. "Jenny and Johnny have watched it since they were tiny."

"We watch it now for the bands," Johnny said.

"Yes, *really*, Daddy." Jenny sat up a little straighter and tossed her hair over her shoulder.

"Do you play an instrument?" Zach asked.

"Yeah. We're in the marching band at our high school. I play sax, and Jenny plays French horn."

Zach occasionally ran one index finger between his neck and shirt collar and fidgeted with the knot of his tie. But he talked easily with the twins about which college band was the best in Chicago.

"Daddy would say the University of Illinois," Jenny said. "That's where he went."

"So you'll be cheering for the Illini to beat the Spartans, sir."

C.J. had been right to press Zach to come. He knew just how to talk to Mr. Gray.

"Absolutely." Mr. Gray turned to Mae and Flo. "Do you girls enjoy football?"

"This'll be my first time watching a big game like this," Flo said.

"I'm more of a baseball fan my own self," Mae said. "You got to love those White Sox. So close in fifty-nine."

"Yes," Mr. Gray agreed. "This year, too. Second place, after falling all the way to fifth last year."

"Still chasing the dream," Mae said.

On the television, the two teams had moved scoreless into the second quarter after three failed field goal attempts by the Lions and four by the Packers. C.J. wondered if they felt a little like her, watching for her chance to get in the conversation. When they began to score, she envied them both, despite the six-six tie at the end of the half.

Brass horns glinting in the sunlight and drums rat-a-tat-tatting shifted the focus from the cautious conversation in the room. Marching back and forth in kaleidoscope formations, the band never missed a beat or stepped out of place. Zach oohed and aahed with the twins. With the final notes, Mrs. Gray appeared. Like a drum major, she led her family and guests to the dining room.

C.J. sank into the chair between Zach and Jenny, grateful for Mrs. Gray's place cards, and looked longingly at her water glass. Her mouth felt dry from lack of use.

The turkey sat before Mr. Gray, who began to carve and stack light and dark meat on a platter. Mrs. Gray passed the potatoes to Zach on her left. Soon all the serving dishes moved like dancers rising and bowing to the tune of the serving utensils.

Zach offered to pour the wine. In the absence of conversation, the dark red liquid seemed to crash into the glasses. C.J. looked at Flo, wordlessly asking, *What in heaven's name are we doing here?* Flo smiled reassuringly. With the glasses filled, Zach raised his in a toast.

"To express our appreciation for the bounty we enjoy, we say in Hebrew: *Baruch atah, Adonai Eloheinu, Melech haolam, borei p'ri hagafen.*"

"We have a family tradition," Mr. Gray said as he started the platter on its way around the table. "We take turns sharing something we learned in the past year."

"If you want pie, you have to do it," Johnny said.

"I'm thinking we might try something a little different this year," Mrs. Gray said. "Could we talk about a favorite Thanksgiving in the place we're from?"

"Aw, Mom," the twins said almost in unison.

The adults nodded, but something so quick C.J. almost missed it flickered in Flo's eyes. Wariness, perhaps? Well, C.J. figured she was the one who ought to be wary, what with Mrs. Gray's pushing to get to know her.

"I'll get us started," Mrs. Gray offered. "But please, everyone eat." She took a bite of turkey and buttered her roll.

"Now this stuffing doesn't use cornbread like we do back home," Mae said, "but it's delicious."

Mrs. Gray smiled. "Well, here goes. I'm from Peru."

"Peru?" Zach said.

"Oh, not the country." Mrs. Gray laughed. "A very small town just south of Chicago. I remember the Thanksgiving my father let me help him build a dollhouse for my cousin. Dad was an electrician. This house had wiring that plugged in and tiny light bulbs in each room. That was such a special time with my father."

Such a fancy house for dolls. The things C.J. watched her dad make were beautiful but sturdy and simple. Things he could barter, for milk from a neighbor's cow or a visit to the doctor. Mrs. Gray might truly believe she wanted to understand her experience. But C.J. feared even the Evanses' cabin, with the lean-to off the chicken coop where her father worked, might test Mrs. Gray's understanding.

While Mae bragged about Mississippi barbecue and tried to get a rise out of Flo, serving dishes again made the rounds. Others took seconds of this and that. C.J. chewed without tasting, trying to figure what part of home she dared talk about.

Zach volunteered to go next. "I'm from the Bronx. My favorite grandmother—Bubbe, we called her—lived with us. Every Thanksgiving we made her special cookies together. The year I was nine, I'd broken one of my sister's toys."

C.J. had been nine the year they moved into their own house. She would tell about that.

"My parents decided I couldn't help bake. In her soft voice that everyone paid attention to, my Bubbe said to my dad, 'You don't need to punish me. Please find another way.' I got to bake cookies, and I'll always remember that year because she got sick a few months later and that was our last time."

Across the table, Flo smiled wistfully. C.J. knew she should take her turn now, before she lost her nerve.

"When I was very young, in Poplar Springs, Mississippi, we lived in an old cabin on the property of the folks my parents worked for. When I was nine, we moved into our own house that my father and uncle built."

Mrs. Gray leaned forward in her chair. C.J. closed her eyes for a moment, drawing strength from the memory.

"'Course I knew even then that Poplar Springs had much grander homes. But, to me, this was the most wonderful house in the world. That first Thanksgiving, every one of us would've said the same thing if you asked what we were thankful for. It's usually warm in Mississippi that time of year. We just opened up the doors and windows and sat around delighting in that house."

"Now being warm at Thanksgiving, that is another fine memory," Mae said.

"Can someone pass the gravy?" Johnny said.

"Everyone, please help yourselves. We still have enough to feed a small army." Mr. Gray smiled at his wife, then turned to his daughter. "Sweetheart?"

"Well, Johnny and I were born in Evanston. The Thanksgiving I remember best is when he choked on a turkey bone. He's a brat sometimes, just like any other little brother—"

"I'm three *minutes* younger."

"But being a twin is really special. I'm glad he didn't choke to death."

Flo coughed.

"Are you all right, dear?" Mrs. Gray asked. "Perhaps a drink of water would help."

Johnny wolfed down the rest of his food and pointed to his empty plate. "I like how we always watch football and get hungry for pie."

"All right." Mrs. Gray laughed. "You two go on."

Johnny pushed back his chair, leaving Jenny seated.

"But I want to hear about Birmingham. Did you go to that church where those girls got killed, Flo?"

She cleared her throat. "I did. A long time ago, before I came here."

"We heard it happened because they were having meetings about civil rights."

Flo's eyes asked C.J. for help.

"Yeah." Johnny sat back down, looking interested. "The KKK probably."

"Now, Johnny," Mr. Gray said. "You shouldn't talk about what you don't know."

"But, *Dad*, we can ask *them*."

Silver scraped the plates.

"It's something we live with there," C.J. said.

"You *know* them?" Johnny's eyes widened, resembling the funnel end of the tubas in the halftime show.

"Yes and no." Against her will, she traveled back to the meetings at Mr. Corrigan's house. "People I worked for . . ."

"You worked for them! Why?"

Zach put his hand on C.J.'s arm. She could feel how much he wanted to help her.

"Johnny, that might be hard for C.J. to talk about."

"Lots of bad stuff happens there, doesn't it?" Jenny asked. "Is that why you left? All of you?"

C.J. looked to Mae, then Flo. As Flo put down her fork, she bumped her glass. C.J. tried to right it through sheer force of will. But it fell, red wine seeping into the tablecloth and spreading like a river.

"Oh! Your tablecloth!" Tears gathered in Flo's eyes.

"Now, don't worry about that," Mrs. Gray said. "We'll just clear things off and set it to soaking. I'm sure we were all about to eat too much anyway."

Everyone jumped up and grabbed dishes to carry to the kitchen. They were very quiet.

On her way to the sink with the tablecloth, C.J. grabbed a bottle of milk from the refrigerator. She stopped up the drain and poured in the milk. When she turned, everyone was staring at her.

"Milk will keep that wine from setting in," she explained. "It's the fat that absorbs it." Only then did she notice Flo crying. She went to stand next to her and put her arm around her. "What is it?" she asked softly.

"It's just . . . *Every* Thanksgiving was my favorite until—I left Alabama. And I miss my little brother."

A sob escaped Flo's throat. And then C.J. saw that Mrs. Gray was crying.

"C.J.?" Mrs. Gray reached out to take Flo's hand. "May I borrow your friend for a few minutes?"

"Well . . ." She looked at Flo, who seemed willing to go almost anywhere to escape the moment. "I reckon."

"Peter," Mrs. Gray said. "Would you take the others back in to see how the game is going? I'll serve dessert in a while."

In the living room, the fourth quarter was underway, the score still six to six. C.J. half watched, half listened, fighting her curiosity and concern as hard as the Lions and Packers pushed against each other and the clock. Zach certainly didn't seem worried. Sitting on the floor between Mae and Jenny, he exchanged sports talk with Johnny and Mr. Gray, then leaned left or right to explain. Only Mae occasionally met C.J.'s eye. The way she crinkled up her face and shook her head slightly seemed to say, *Let's not worry.*

"Touchdown, Packers!" shouted Mr. Gray. "We almost missed it!"

What if Mrs. Gray was yelling at Flo? But Mrs. Gray wasn't a yeller, and she'd told Flo not to worry.

"A relentless effort by Bart Starr," reported the announcer. "Sixty-one yards in nine plays. And now it's Earl Morrall's turn to move the Lions."

Mrs. Gray had cried, too. Maybe it was a very special tablecloth. But then Mrs. Gray had taken Flo's hand. C.J. felt Reverend Thornheart taking her arm, dragging her into the church to repent for leaving the vacuum in his way. Flo had come here for her. She should go find them, see what was happening. But, just as in Mississippi, she was unable to move.

"With sixteen seconds on the clock, the Lions have scored! Seventeen plays this time," said the announcer.

"What a game!" Zach said.

Just then Mrs. Gray appeared with a pie in each hand. Flo followed with plates, forks, and napkins. Her face seemed to have softened. She no longer held her body rigid; it must have gone okay. C.J. watched them work together, Flo cutting a slice of apple, Mrs. Gray adding a piece of sweet potato, until everyone had a plate with both kinds.

"Flo, Mae." Mrs. Gray pointed her fork at her plate. "Your pie is absolutely delicious."

"They're both good, Miz Gray," Flo said.

In fact, Flo seemed more than okay. She was talking, looking comfortable for the first time since they went in to dinner. But Mrs. Gray was C.J.'s. And C.J. couldn't imagine ever being as comfortable with her.

"What happened with the game?" Mrs. Gray asked.

"Thirteen-thirteen," Johnny grumbled. "Can you believe it?"

When the plates were empty, Flo said, "I think we'd best be heading on back to Hyde Park now."

C.J. didn't want to see her friends go, but she needed to move, to do something. So she went to the closet for their coats. While they bundled up, Mrs. Gray disappeared into the kitchen. She returned carrying packets of foil.

"Flo and I made care packages. Turkey sandwiches and pie."

The Grays said their goodbyes, then moved to the living room.

"Thank y'all for coming." C.J. looked hard into the eyes of each of her friends, wanting desperately to be a guest like them, free to go. She put her hand on Zach's arm, hoping he could feel her gratitude the way she'd felt his support at the table. She hugged Mae first, then clung to Flo.

"I'm okay," Flo whispered. "I'll talk to you soon as we get together again, I promise."

C.J. waved until they were out of sight, then leaned heavily against the door until she could gather enough strength to return to the living room. There, she looked at the faces of the people who, until today, were just one of the families she worked for.

"Thank you." Her voice wavered, seeking a note that appreciated the day without sounding presumptuous. "For making me and my friends welcome in your home. I'll just be going to my room now."

Tomorrow morning would come early, and she felt suddenly more afraid than she could remember with any of the others.

CHAPTER 16

December 1963
Responsibilities

C.J. clutched her coat around her and hurried the last few blocks from the all-night market in Hyde Park. In the small paper sack was a quart of eggnog and a tiny jar of nutmeg. She'd insisted on running out for something to make tonight special while Flo checked on her macaroni and cheese and finished setting the table. Inside the lobby of the brownstone, she leaned against the door and caught her breath. She turned toward the stairs, then changed her mind. Slowly, she walked to Zach's door.

An entire year had gone by since he'd asked her to wait with him for news of Anne. She'd been annoyed when he showed up at her door on New Year's Eve, assuming he wanted her to go out somewhere when she'd already said no. She'd been nervous about being in his apartment, feeling helpless against his anxiety. But with him in New York now for the holidays, the distance couldn't seem greater. Gingerly, she reached out to stroke the face of his door, then hurried upstairs.

"I got something for us to try," she called out with forced cheeriness. "The man at the market said it's got to be heated and spiced." She took off her coat, revealing the faded pink sweatshirt she couldn't help wearing tonight.

She and Flo hadn't had time alone since Thanksgiving at the Grays' house. Mae had admitted that Flo talked to her about what happened, but said the story was Flo's to tell. With the others all gone out to parties, C.J. and Flo were dancing around each other, pretending they were about to sit down to an ordinary supper. But C.J felt talk coming as surely as judgment day.

"Wonder how Zach's doing back home?" Flo said as she dished out the macaroni.

"I reckon I wouldn't know," C.J. snapped.

"Well, then." Flo took a small step backward. "I sure hope you're hungry."

C.J. gave her a weak smile. But she was suddenly ravenous. "Yes, I surely am."

They ate in silence. C.J. dug into the delicately browned crust of cheese and savored the perfectly cooked macaroni. She considered taking more, wondering if she could just keep eating all night, then pushed away her empty plate.

"It was very good, Flo. Thank you."

Flo's food sat half-eaten. She batted a clump of cheesy noodles around with her fork, occasionally opening her mouth but then closing it without speaking. C.J. wished she could help, but all she could do was wait.

"Your Miz Gray, she's very nice," Flo said finally.

Too nice—that was surely Mrs. Gray's problem. "I reckon."

"Did the wine come out of the tablecloth okay?"

"It did."

"You know, she was crying herself."

"Uh huh."

"She held my hand near about the whole time, until we went back to the kitchen. We must've sat that way ten minutes, nobody saying a word. I told her then—I'm sorry, C.J. I should've told you sooner—about Freddie."

"It's okay, Flo," C.J. said. But she couldn't be certain Flo heard. Flo proceeded—her eyes set, her voice soft—as if following a dimly lit path to a place that both frightened her and pulled her toward it. C.J. sat back in her chair, out of the path of the words.

"Freddie was with me, same as always. I remember him begging extra hard that day, 'Flo, just today, let me go off with Walter and Johnny.' But I thought he'd be safer with me."

A chill climbed C.J.'s spine as she recalled Charlie and William and her determination to keep her own little brother safe.

"It was winter and already turning dark. We were coming home from the store, getting something Momma needed. The man came right out of the shadows. Grabbed me. Didn't seem to see Freddie. Just pulled me in the bushes and started yanking at my clothes."

C.J. felt herself shrinking from the eyes of the men at the meetings, zigging or zagging as one or another reached out or edged up against her. Thanks to Mr. Corrigan, things had never gotten out of hand.

"When I saw Freddie coming at that white man with a tree branch, I yelled at him to run. The man saw him, just before Freddie hit him in the head and knocked him cold. We ran all the way home. That night, they came and took Freddie away."

C.J. meant to reach out to Flo, but her hand went instead to her mouth, holding back every question she'd started to ask, or asked only to have Flo change the subject. At the Maxwell Street Market, when Flo mentioned how her little brother loved the sound of the blues—*how old is Freddie?* That first Christmas, when she clutched the mail like a rag doll and told them about bumping into a white boy—*why is there panic in your eyes?* When the Birmingham 16th Street Baptist Church was bombed—*wasn't Freddie lucky not to have been right there with those four little girls?*

Finally, C.J. looked at Flo, expecting her to seem a thousand years old, her eyes hollow as if she'd retreated far behind them. But she seemed so unburdened she might float up off the chair.

"Miz Gray said it wasn't my fault. I said of course it was. Nobody else to blame but me. Me thinking I could keep that boy safe. Me taking responsibility for his every move. *That* made me responsible."

C.J. shivered. "What else did she say?"

"She told me how she killed her brother. At least that's how she looked at it for a long time. She was driving the car when there was an accident." C.J. was crying now, for all the big sisters and little brothers. "She asked me then, did I love Freddie. I said more than life. She said that's how she knew I wasn't to hold myself responsible. That I needed to forgive myself."

Flo stopped talking then. But after a while, a smile took over her face. "Zach saw them, too." She laughed. C.J. touched the shoulder of her sweatshirt and ground her teeth, waiting for another Zach-and-Flo story from Washington.

"I pointed at a man in a brimmed straw hat holding hands with a woman and a boy." Flo described the three of them, standing slightly apart from anyone else. The man wore overalls over a T-shirt that sparkled white against his dark olive brown skin. His biceps strained against the sleeves. The woman's eyes were closed, and her thick lashes rested on the smooth skin of her face. The boy, eyes bright and lips parted, stared toward the Lincoln Memorial.

"I couldn't believe Zach could see them, too. 'The boy has the face of an angel.' Those were his exact words, mind you. I'll never forget."

Flo nodded and closed her eyes, looking just like the woman must have. " 'Daddy . . . Momma . . . Freddie,' I cried out. Zach asked if it was my family. When I said yes . . . no . . . it can't be, that's when I know he got to worrying about me just a touch."

It was beginning to dawn on C.J. that what she'd been envying since August was somehow all tied up with Freddie.

"Poor Zach." Flo laughed again. " 'Momma! She's here,' I started yelling when they introduced Miz Mahalia Jackson. Zach was bouncing from one foot to the other, wanting to get me water and out of the sun. But I wouldn't budge. When she'd finished singing 'I've Been 'Buked and I've Been Scorned,' I used my free hand to loosen the grip Zach had on the other one. Then I touched his chest, right over his heart, and said, 'This feeling—Zach, that's you knowing C.J.' "

C.J. felt small. Small and mean—for being jealous of Zach's and Mrs. Gray's attention to her friend. Small and powerless—to help her friend, much less keep anyone safe. Finally, her hands found Flo's. They sat that way for the longest time, each staring at their clasped hands, until Flo spoke again.

" 'Course those people weren't my family, but I kept hoping to see them together like that, one more time. There was a man dressed the same as the one who could've been my daddy. And he did collapse in the heat, like Zach was worried I would, right when Dr. King got to talking about his dream. But then two white men wearing suits tended to him. The one took out his handkerchief, dipped it in the Reflecting Pool, and gently dabbed the Negro's brow." She squeezed so tightly that C.J.'s fingers began to tingle. "That was a sight to see, C.J. Gave me hope. Him, too, I reckon, 'cause that's when his voice rang out like a song, saying, 'Seventy-five years now I been living in this country. But today's the one I become a man.' "

C.J. understood then. Surely all Flo meant by her civil rights talk was the hope that she could stop what happened to her family from happening to anyone else.

Finally, Flo looked up and searched C.J.'s eyes. "The boy . . . who looked like Freddie—I never saw him again. Oh, C.J.," she sobbed. "My Freddie is dead."

Ever so carefully, C.J. led Flo into the bedroom and told her to lie down. She covered her with a blanket and patted her hair until she fell asleep.

❊　❊　❊

C.J. tossed and turned on the couch in the Hyde Park apartment, Sissy and Emily asleep in the bedroom, wondering if missing Zach was an ache that would go on and on and on. Valentine's Day would surely come and go next week with her still not having laid eyes on him.

She could scarcely remember the last time she and Zach had done anything, just the two of them. As she crossed her arms over her chest in frustration, a faint sound, like the scratching of a mouse, caused her to bolt upright and scan the room. In the pre-dawn shadows, a patch of white glimmered just inside the door, resembling the moon on a starless night. She lunged at it, snatched it up. The envelope bore her name. She switched on the dim light over the stove and read.

Dear C.J.,

I've missed talking with you, too. Besides law school, my new job takes up most of my free

*time. Could we have breakfast together EARLY
next weekend, say 7:00? Please leave me a note
saying which day you have off. I'll skip my study
group this once if necessary.*

Your friend,

Zach

Certain sleep would not return, C.J. put on coffee. While it percolated, she stared happily at the words *Your friend, Zach* as relief flooded over her. Relief that he was okay, had missed her, too, had gotten her note, and had not been too put off by it to reply.

She scrounged in a drawer for paper and pen and scribbled an answer, saying Saturday would work. She made it to the stairs before she realized what she was doing. Zach was probably still awake, and here she was in her pajamas. She would bring her note another time.

The week crawled by and it was Saturday morning again, scarcely enough time to figure out what to wear. In lavender hues, the first streaks of daylight followed C.J. to the bedroom closet.

Her hand landed first on Alinda's clingy angora sweater with the low-cut V-neck. C.J. blushed and tried again. She took out the emerald prom dress, imagining Zach reaching out to help her on with her coat. But this certainly was not a date. She snapped the hanger back in its place on the rod. In one of the twin beds, Alinda stirred.

No, this was only breakfast, and Zach was fitting her in before work. Something simple and comfortable, then, like jeans and her favorite sweatshirt. She stroked one worn, pale pink sleeve the way Zach had, shivering at the memory.

Surely in all these clothes there was one thing she'd never worn when with him. Something that still made her feel good about how she looked but said *friends, nothing more.* She saw it then, another of Alinda's sweaters. Fresh and new, like the dew-dappled, just-bloomed petals of a pink rose. Tied stylishly at one shoulder. It would be just right with jeans.

It was precisely 7:00 when Zach knocked quietly on the door. She opened it so fast he must surely know she'd been waiting on the other side. The unfamiliar way, full of urgency, in which his eyes swept over her caused her to suck in her breath so sharply that she let out a little hiccup. Just for an instant, she thought he might reach out and gather her up. But then he put one arm on the door frame and leaned into it.

His eyes moved to the piano, where new, more difficult sheet music and lesson books from C.J.'s practicing cluttered the music stand. "Looks like you're really moving fast with your lessons with Mrs. Gray. Will you play something?"

She hurried him out the door, whispering, "Maybe later. Alinda's asleep in the bedroom."

"I was thinking of the little coffee shop you like so much. You okay to walk? The wind's wicked today, but it's a crystal clear morning."

She caught herself smiling. Crystal clear. The words sounded like tinkling bells when Zach said them, making her imagine how her full name would sound on his lips.

"I survived getting here from Evanston last night. I reckon I can walk a few blocks."

In the lobby, he helped her on with her coat, adjusting the tie on Alinda's sweater, almost as she'd imagined. Then, all too quickly, he moved away to put on his jacket.

As they stepped outside, the wind came at them immediately. She noticed his longer hair—it made him seem older, more street smart—and his oh so blue eyes. He took her arm to steady her. Using her free hand to keep her coat firmly bundled around her, she focused on not stepping too close. He released her arm only to open the door of the coffee shop.

The waitress gave them a half smile of recognition before scribbling their order and jamming her pencil back behind her ear. Scurrying from one customer to the next, she reminded C.J. of a performer on *Ed Sullivan* who balanced spinning plates on poles. Now that she was here with Zach, she wanted time to slow down.

"Eggs, sausage, bacon, hash browns, and hotcakes." She ticked off things he'd ordered on her fingers. "Wonder how many plates it'll take to hold it all?"

He leaned back in his chair and smiled. The way he always did when she teased, yet differently. Like a boy who was looking at something shiny and new, perhaps a marble won in a shooting contest. "I didn't get dinner last night. Too busy working."

"Your note said *new* job."

"Yes, I had to quit the warehouse. First-year law makes it pretty tough to handle a job. But money's still tight. I was lucky that my constitutional law professor could bring me on as a research assistant."

"Now that sounds like an honor," she said as their food arrived. Zach accepted one plate after another while she stared at hers. Whipped cream in the shape of a heart cradled blueberry compote atop her waffle.

"The cook was doing that all day yesterday, for Valentine's Day." The waitress shrugged. "Guess he's still got love on his mind."

A flush crept across C.J.'s cheeks. She darted her eyes at Zach, who was suddenly very busy with his hotcakes, buttering and pouring syrup. She grabbed her fork and swirled the toppings. Satisfied there was no trace of the heart, she relaxed into the conversation.

"I forget to eat sometimes myself when I'm busy. I can't forget anymore, though. Leastways, not breakfast or supper."

"Why's that?" His question was garbled by trying to talk with his mouth full.

"It's Miz Gray." C.J. raised her coffee cup to her lips but then absently returned it to its saucer. "She's up and decided I should take my meals in the dining room, with the family."

"Wow! We talked about what it might be like after Thanksgiving dinner. But I wouldn't have guessed something like *that*."

"We started to know each other on Thanksgiving, Miz Gray says. That was trouble for me in Mississippi when Miz Barnes got too close. This is way beyond that, with me living up in their house and her teaching me piano."

Zach watched her intently but remained silent.

"We got to see that through, Miz Gray says. So, she asks me questions."

"Like what?"

Zach's food was nearly gone. C.J. slid her half-eaten waffle aside.

"Things people ask when they've just met. About my family, school, work I did in Poplar Springs. But I've always got the feeling she's getting ready to ask something really hard."

"C.J." He leaned across the table. "They seem like good people. *Maybe* you need to trust a little in that. Try to follow her lead. Ask about the jewelry store and how school's going for the twins."

She started to say more, to insist that this was a bad thing. But then Zach checked his watch, and she suddenly realized she hadn't given a thought to him. "I'm sorry. I haven't asked about school, or your holidays with Anne."

Did Zach blush? Again, just like in her apartment, his eyes gathered her up. She squirmed under his gaze and waited.

"Anne says hi," he said suddenly. "She asked if we'd been to synagogue again."

"Have you?"

He frowned pointedly. "Yes. Did you want to come?"

"It was j-just that one time," she stammered. "I like to see how folks are with their religion. It's how I know them."

"And you want to know me?" he said, in an eerie echo of Anne that day after Christmas.

"'Course," she snapped. "You're my—"

"Friend?" he finished.

She nodded, watching him twirl his fork through the remnants of her whipped cream heart.

"Anne told me, you know." C.J.'s heart skipped a beat. "What happened in the bathroom at Theresa's."

"Oh, that." C.J. cleared her throat. "She was lucky."

"I think she knows that." He smiled sadly. "She's had to grow up a lot this past year. Me, too, for that matter. It's different for her and me, though. Finding out she's not invincible has made her more cautious."

The waitress arrived with more coffee and the check.

"Being careful, now that's a good thing," C.J. said.

"The thing is, no one's invincible. And there's so much to be done. All my life, I've wanted to make the world a better place. That's what brought me to the university. And . . . and . . ." He seemed to have lost his train of thought, then reached out and touched her shoulder. "That sweater—Pink is your color, I think. And, C.J., it brought me to *you*."

His words were like a kiss, bringing her back to New Year's Eve. And yet, they were like a splash of ice water, waking her up. Lord help her, Zach cared about her, too.

"I have to know," he went on. "Why didn't you come to Washington with me?"

"Part of me wanted to, because *you* asked," she told him truthfully. "But I couldn't. My parents been teaching us how to stay alive since—"

Without looking at Zach, she resumed a long-ago conversation, where she'd told him about Mrs. Barnes and following rules. She began to talk about the others. Her very first employer, how nothing was ever good enough for her and how she asked C.J. to spy on the Catholic family. The minister who dragged her into the sanctuary of the First Baptist Church and called her a sinner. And she did not stop until she spoke of the meetings, the threat to her family, and the woman whose jealousy made her as deadly as a rattlesnake. "There's an order to things. We don't have to like it. We do have to admit it's there."

"Oh, I admit it, all right. And I definitely don't like it. I'm going to fight for—"

"That's *not* what I mean, and you know it." C.J. let her voice rise, just as the waitress came by looking for them to pay up. They both threw down money.

He helped her on with her coat. They walked in silence, with determination. Once inside the brownstone, Zach followed C.J. upstairs. She opened the door and allowed him in. They stood for moments, squared off against each other, neither one speaking.

"I'm going to fight for us," Zach said. "For a world where we can be—whatever we want to be to each other."

"I know you're gonna fight," she said, near tears. "I knew it when I saw the march on TV. But, Zach, I beg you to stay safe—"

He put a finger to her lips to shush her. "Play something for me, please? Something hard and new, that I've never heard you play before."

She seated herself at the bench, then turned to him. "There *are* some things I can do for you. But they have to be mine to decide."

She flipped through the scores, thinking, *I can't, I just can't. He'll have to understand. Oh, if I lost him as a friend* . . . Ultimately, she closed each one and replaced it on the stand. Mrs. Gray could play by ear. She'd figured out a song C.J. asked for and helped her memorize it. This song would say what C.J. couldn't.

She began to play Nat King Cole's "Smile." She played as if Zach were sending the music through her hands. As if the four years that had passed since he first played for Flo and her—a Sam Cooke song for Flo, then one by Nat King Cole for her—were but heartbeats. She sang silently to herself, feeling her heart aching just like the song said. But she could not smile, could not even bear to meet Zach's eyes. When she had finished, she placed her hands in her lap and continued to face the piano, willing him with everything in her to understand and accept.

Zach leaned over and kissed her hair. Then he let himself out.

✳   ✳   ✳

On Thursday night, the last day of April, C.J. carried the platter of fried chicken into the dining room and placed it before Johnny. She smiled at the boy as she took her seat between Jenny and Mrs. Gray.

"Might as well set that in front of you, Johnny. I know you're gonna eat most of it." He grinned back at her and immediately helped himself.

It still wasn't easy, eating with the Grays. C.J. wasn't a guest, wasn't one of the children, wasn't the wife, and was no longer just an employee. What exactly she was, she still couldn't quite say. But the awkwardness had eased considerably since the first time she'd served them a meal and sat down to join them. Truth be told, she'd stopped counting the days since Mrs. Gray decided Thanksgiving had gone so well they might as well make a habit of it, in favor of counting days since she'd seen Zach. She was up to seventy-five.

"You had a game today, didn't you, son?" Mr. Gray said.

"Yeah, we played Sacred Heart."

"Who won?" C.J.'s voice croaked like a baby bullfrog's, but she finished. It felt like butting in, like very poor manners or worse. But she'd found it best to talk as soon as an idea came to her, rather than thinking about it too much. The more she thought, the less likely she was to speak and the greater the likelihood she'd get beaten to the punch by someone else.

"We slaughtered them." Johnny's chest puffed out a bit. "So bad Coach even put some freshmen in for a few minutes. I got a hit, but I got left on base."

"That's fantastic, son. I'm proud of you," Mr. Gray said.

C.J. nodded and smiled, as much to congratulate herself as the boy.

"Thanks, Dad. And C.J., I told Richard about you—after I quit razzing him about us beating them."

"Now that's your friend from Winnetka, isn't it?" Mrs. Gray asked, just as C.J. was opening her mouth to say, *Me?*

"Yeah, Richard's got this boy, Obie, staying with his family this week, from the South Side. I said we got C.J. all the time. Now you're eating with us and everything."

C.J. put her napkin to her mouth, but her eyes darted around the table. Johnny beamed, just the way he had when telling about his hit. Jenny's face mirrored her brother's. Mrs. Gray's mouth hung open.

"Dear?" Mrs. Gray said finally.

"Well, uhm." Mr. Gray cleared his throat. "Why is Obie staying with Richard's family?"

"Not just Obie. A bunch of seventh graders from the Raymond School are spending this week with families in Winnetka and going to school at Sacred Heart."

"Really?" Mrs. Gray said.

"It's like an experiment, I guess. They're wanting to get to know each other."

"Yeah, Mom," Jenny said. "Like you told us we are with C.J."

All the forks were resting on the plates now, afraid to make a sound, while the four Grays and C.J. looked at each other. It's what had bothered

C.J. most about eating with the Grays—this feeling she was some sort of project for Mrs. Gray.

"I did. I certainly did. I . . ."

Mrs. Gray sounded like a stuck record. Someone needed to stop her. C.J. reckoned she should be the one. She thought hard. About Obie, twelve or thirteen and plunked down in some fancy white home and school for a week, probably frightened and fascinated at the same time. About Richard's family, trying to do . . . whatever by having Obie there. About herself, coming to this table for who knew how long, never going back to the Grays' kitchen. She twisted the napkin in her lap. Angry at being considered an experiment. Angry at the need to have one.

And then she thought of Mrs. Gray, maybe wanting nothing more than to get to know her. All C.J. knew for certain was that she didn't want to be the reason the experiment turned out badly.

"The wanting," she heard herself say. "That's a good thing."

Mrs. Gray blessed C.J. with her eyes. The forks, no longer afraid, began to move.

"Richard said we could read all about it in the *Winnetka Talk*," Johnny said.

"Well," Mrs. Gray said. "Then we'll have to find a copy."

❖   ❖   ❖

On Monday, C.J. arose early, in order to get breakfast partially made before Mrs. Gray came down for their piano lesson. As she crisscrossed the kitchen, she stopped to glance at the papers strewn over the kitchen table. Mrs. Gray must have spent Saturday at the library. Copies of articles, mostly from *The Winnetka Talk*, went all the way back to 1959. From the mess, she was trimming and pasting into a black notebook.

That earliest article told about a developer who tried to create an integrated housing subdivision in the village of Deerfield, north of Evanston, and met with white resistance. Then there was a full-page advertisement from early last year. Folks who signed the ad asked North Shore residents to help eliminate racial injustice. Beginning early this year, there were articles about things people in Winnetka were doing, including a human rights club at New Trier High School and tutoring Negro kids on the West Side. Another article was accompanied by a photo of Raymond School kids boarding a bus for their week at Johnny's friend Richard's school.

Mrs. Gray's heels tapping on the hardwood floor of the living room announced her arrival. C.J. gathered her music just as Mrs. Gray appeared in the doorway, beckoning her. Mrs. Gray had her warm up with scales, then moved to the piece they'd started about a month ago: Bach's "Minuet in G Major." C.J. was excited. After weeks of practicing hands separately, today was the day she would put left hand together with right hand.

"Let's do hands separately once more," Mrs. Gray said. "Pay close attention to phrasing."

C.J. obliged, chafing a bit inside. She focused on Mrs. Gray's adage about proper phrasing. *Think about where you're going in each phrase. How do you feel as you go? How do you feel as you arrive?* She tried not to rush toward the end of the piece.

"Where are we going, C.J.?" Mrs. Gray asked suddenly.

"Is it my phrasing?" C.J. looked accusingly at her hands.

"I was so sure of myself that day I told you we're not living in Clybourne Park in the fifties."

Oh, no. Mrs. Gray had lapsed into what she called being philosophical. C.J. called it loquacious.

"But Johnny's talk last week got me thinking. From what I've been reading, we have a mess on our hands, not just elsewhere in our world, but right here on the North Shore."

"Yes'm."

From the kitchen, the rooster clock clucked the quarter hour, bringing Mrs. Gray back to the piano. "No, dear, your phrasing was fine. Let's try hands together."

C.J.'s heart raced. She'd tried hands together by herself, despite Mrs. Gray's advice that she wait. She pictured her hands working in harmony all the way to the end and began to play. Mrs. Gray stopped her after sixteen measures.

"That's a good start," she said, sounding anything but believable.

C.J. knew she'd fouled things up completely. Her shoulders slumped. Mrs. Gray left the bench to stand behind her. "You've lost steadiness, added unnecessary pauses. But we can fix this," she said.

C.J. heard what Mrs. Gray was saying, but she was suddenly feeling Zach standing behind her as she played. Right after he'd said, *I'm going to fight for us, for a world where we can be whatever we want to be to each other.* Right before she answered him with a song and he kissed her hair and left. She began to tremble.

"Now, now, dear," Mrs. Gray cooed. "This is perfectly normal. It happens to everyone learning a new piece."

But C.J. wasn't convinced. She didn't even want to put hands together, did she? She knew she and Zach could never be.

Somehow, much as on that long-ago day when C.J. found herself telling Mrs. Barnes about Mr. Corrigan, she was suddenly talking about Zach. "I worry when much time goes by without running into him, what with Anne's accident and all."

"Of course you do. But Anne's all right, isn't she?"

"Yes, but Zach—it's been almost three months."

"Law school must certainly be very demanding."

"Yes'm, and he has a job, too."

"There you go," Mrs. Gray said cheerily.

"But I'm—h-he's—I don't . . ."

"Ah. Now I have an idea." Mrs. Gray returned to her place beside C.J. on the bench, rested her hand on C.J.'s arm. "You've come so far. We can fix this. The thing to try next is playing at half speed. Let me show you."

C.J. forced her attention back to the Minuet, captured the tempo and all the nuances of Mrs. Gray's playing in her mind, and tried again.

"Much better!" Mrs. Gray pronounced. "Yes, things will be much better now. From the beginning, please."

Once again, C.J. obliged, trusting in Mrs. Gray and losing herself in the music.

But four weeks and seven piano lessons later, Mrs. Gray threw C.J.

another curve ball. No sooner had she relaxed into the routine of eating with the Grays, than Mrs. Gray asked her to set an extra place for their company. She wished Mrs. Gray would take her own advice about slowing down to half speed.

At the sound of the doorbell, C.J. spun around and wiped her damp palms on her apron. She was about to find out who the Grays had invited. Who she was expected to serve, then sit next to, making conversation as if situations such as this happened every day. Feeling as shaken as a chicken leg in a bag of flour before it was dropped into the frying pan, she reached for the bottle of dressing to toss the salad.

"Zach, how nice to see you again," she heard Mrs. Gray say. The bottle crashed into the sink and shattered. "Go on in the kitchen and see if C.J. needs any help."

C.J. left the broken glass, grabbed a knife, and pretended to touch up the icing on the chocolate layer cake.

"My favorite." Zach rested his hands on the counter and smiled at her.

"I didn't make it for you," she snapped, telling herself he had *not* gotten more handsome in the one hundred two days since she'd last seen him.

"Well." He coughed into his hand to cover his lingering smile. "It's still very good to see you. I've—"

It's still so good to see you, too, she thought. But her peevishness got the better of her. "I would have figured you to be too busy."

Just then Mrs. Gray stuck her head in the kitchen. "Is everything about ready?"

"Yes'm. Y'all can take seats."

"I'll help serve," Zach offered.

C.J. slid six custard dishes under the broiler and stomped around the kitchen gathering mayonnaise, ketchup, and Worcestershire for a make-shift dressing. She tossed the salad and shoved it into Zach's hands. When the timer rang, she loaded a tray and delivered the Coquilles Saint Jacques to the dining room. The salad bowl traveled one direction as she moved in the other, setting a custard dish at each place.

"How are your courses, Zach?" Mrs. Gray asked.

"Well, law school is tougher than political science. But I'm doing well and loving it."

C.J. stabbed a forkful of lettuce and chewed furiously while Mrs. Gray carried on the conversation she would have liked to have herself—in private. Where she could catch up on Zach's life, tell him how meals with the Grays had gotten better—until tonight, pretend she hadn't driven him away.

"Has C.J. played the piano for you lately, Zach?" What was Mrs. Gray doing, talking about her? Why was Zach here? "She's coming along so nicely with her lessons."

"Yes, ma'am. Last time we—" His voice grew husky as he stole a glance at C.J. "Uh, got together. I'm sure she's even better now."

C.J. was horrified. *You didn't!* she wanted to scream at Mrs. Gray. *Surely you did not call up this man and tell him he should come join our ridiculous collection of diners because you think I said . . .*

"This stuff is good, C.J.," Johnny said. "Is there more?"

"It would just take a few minutes—" She leapt from her chair.

"You sit, dear," Mrs. Gray said. "Let's all save room for cake."

"Well, I have some news," Zach said.

C.J. could feel him looking at her. Deliberately, she forked another mouthful of salad.

"What, dear?" Mrs. Gray asked.

"This spring I learned about something called the Mississippi Summer Project. From my friends in Chicago Area Friends of SNCC." He looked at C.J.

Her head had begun to pound with the thought of her worst nightmare—Zach in Mississippi. She counted the times her jaw moved up and down before she swallowed. Eleven, twelve . . .

"Anyway, the project will be staffed by volunteers, including college and grad students." He went on to explain what she already knew—how the rabbi's sermon at Mevakshei Tzedek had gotten him thinking, and how Dr. King's call to action in Washington and Anne's accident had crystallized for him that he wanted to take part in this country's fight for justice and change. C.J. felt like throwing up. She'd been relieved when he found a way to help in Chicago; now, she sensed the story was about to explode out of control.

"What would these volunteers be doing?" Mr. Gray asked.

"Well, sir. It's really all about registering Negro voters." Her heart lurched. Surely he would not have anything to do with something so dangerous. "The project is also setting up community centers and summer schools throughout Mississippi. Those will help get the word out and get folks committed. I have the brochure if you want to take a look."

He pulled a folded paper from his pocket and handed it to C.J. From the cover peered a boy who could have been Charlie or Obie, Freddie or Emmett. He looked skittish and sad. His lips were parted, as if he might speak to them. She handed the little pamphlet to Mr. Gray without looking inside.

"It says here they need contributions."

"Yes, sir. We certainly do."

"So you've volunteered, Zach?" said Mrs. Gray.

"Yes, ma'am. Volunteered and been accepted." He drew himself up tall, like a soldier. "We each have to bring five hundred dollars, for expenses and . . . bail. That's another thing that's kept me busy lately. I've taken on more hours at work."

We. Zach was one of them now, swept up as if in an embrace. Pulled toward this from the moment *she* asked Anne to take her to synagogue so she could know him. Mevakshei Tzedek—*those who pursue justice.* She should have run from there that day, dragging him away with her.

C.J. picked up her plate. "I'll just bring in the cake now."

Alone in the kitchen, she felt the knife wobble slightly in her hand. She sliced six pieces, including a tiny sliver for herself. Zach appeared with the salad bowl and a stack of dirty dishes. She'd forgotten all about clearing the table. She handed him plates and filled a carafe from the percolator, not meeting his eyes, not saying a word.

Back at the table, the Grays fired questions at Zach. The twins, with their fascination with things done by college students. The adults, as if

Zach were going on a vacation. C.J.'s cake had a dry, sharp taste, what she imagined dirt would taste like.

"Zach, would you help C.J.?" Mrs. Gray asked when the plates were all empty. "Johnny and Jenny, you'd better get to your homework."

Zach followed C.J. into the kitchen. He watched her put the top on the cake saver and wrap up the leftover salad. "You've been very quiet tonight," he said.

"I told you it's not easy for me, eating with the Grays." She stuck out her lower jaw. "For them to up and invite company, then you to show up . . ."

"Oh—You didn't . . . know . . . it was me, did you? Mrs. Gray said . . ."

"What *exactly*?" She met his eyes. "Tell me what Miz Gray said."

"Well, that you were worried, hadn't seen me in ages." He shifted his weight awkwardly from one foot to the other and dropped his chin. "That she knew seeing me was just the thing to lift your spirits."

"I have been worried," she admitted. "None of us have seen you, heard from you, even gotten a note in over a hun—in over three months." She concentrated on sealing the edges of a Tupperware container and burping out the air in little gasps. "Little did I know how worried I ought to be."

"So, you think what I'm doing is a bad idea?"

She laughed bitterly. "I think being friends with all of us in number ten should've made you smarter."

"I think it has."

"You don't have the slightest inkling what you're getting into. The people you're going to fight would sooner kill you than look at you. And for what?"

"C.J." She heard the longing in his voice. "Don't you know it's because of all of you—especially you—that I have to do this?"

More than the splash of ice water she'd felt when she realized Zach cared for her, what C.J. felt now was ice water coursing through her veins. It was the chill of death—Zach's unless he was very lucky; their friendship's as she realized what she must do.

"You're gonna fix things for your Negro friends, then? By going to Mississippi? You can stay right where you're at. There's plenty to fix in Chicago. Just ask your Miz Gray."

"I—"

"You?" Her voice had climbed an octave. "*One* person?"

"Dr. King says if we don't protest, we're helping keep evil alive."

"Don't blame him! It's me you should be blaming. I twisted Anne's arm about going to the synagogue. Look how things have just spun out of control ever since."

"No." He was shaking his head. "It is because of you that I have to do this. But, oh C.J., I don't *blame* you. I thank you."

"That's ridiculous."

"Didn't I tell you I was going to fight? To make this world one where you and I can . . . where we can . . ."

She clutched her apron in her hands and began to wring its folds. "I'm begging you to think this through. And, whatever you do, do *not* say it's for me. I couldn't bear to be responsible if—"

He reached out and drew her toward him. She sank into the tide of his embrace, for just a second, then shoved him away with all her strength.

"Don't ever do that again!"

His expression was inconsolably sad. "You're right. This has to be totally my decision and my responsibility. I should go. I'm sorry . . . about tonight. Will you tell Mrs. Gray I'll call to say thank you?"

Helplessly, she watched Zach's back, as if he were boarding the bus this very minute.

"Was that the door?" Mrs. Gray asked as she came into the kitchen. "Did Zach leave?"

C.J. shook her head and cried.

❉ ❉ ❉

The darkness in the Hyde Park apartment was interrupted only by the flicker of the streetlight outside the open window and headlights that arced up to their floor when a car turned the corner just so. The silence was broken only by the hum of traffic and an occasional frustrated mosquito bouncing off the screen. Today was the twenty-fourth day since she'd watched Zach walk out of the Grays' kitchen, the twenty-fourth day since she'd spoken to him, hoping against hope that cutting herself off from him would save him from himself. C.J. lay on the bed and waited for morning.

Tomorrow was the first day of summer. She would be in church, but the time for praying Zach would come to his senses would be past. She knew with a certainty that seemed to crush her chest that he would board the bus for Ohio, where he would get some kind of training before going on to Mississippi. They might even tell him in this training how dangerous it was for him to go. But he would no more listen to them than he had her. Flo was right when she'd said, "I reckon the Zach who cared more for himself is no one you could care about so."

She admired Zach's commitment to his beliefs. But she would never understand how he could go if he loved his family the way he said he did. Didn't he know how devastated they would be if anything happened to him? She murmured a prayer. "Yea, though I walk through the valley of the shadow of death, I will fear no evil." If God had plans for Zach, He would keep him safe.

She wondered how Zach was saying goodbye to Chicago in spring. She pictured him in all the places they'd been together—laughing at something she said, sharing an idea he learned in school, smiling with his eyes. She clenched her eyes shut against the memories.

"I'm going out for a while," Flo called from the living room.

C.J. listened for the gentle thud of the door. But the noise was followed by footsteps. Probably Flo back to say, for the umpteenth time, "If you won't admit you love him, just run on downstairs and say goodbye. Leastways, let him know you wish him well, before it's too late."

She slapped her hands over her ears but bolted upright at the sound of music, coming ghostlike from the piano. The style was pure Charlie Parker—fast, furious, free. It was a song she had never heard before. Or had she? Was the song itself familiar but the playing of it somehow different? Her heart seemed to race in time with the music. She listened, unable to move, feeling her father's presence more than fear.

Keep your head about you, he would say, when something rustled in the brush as they walked the Wilson farm, or when he came to comfort her after a bad dream. She surrendered to the song.

Just as startling was the sudden sound of silence. Was it all a dream? Had the force of her sadness caused her to conjure up Zach? She dared not go to the living room to look. She sat, perfectly still, for an eternity. And then she heard the door shut.

"Flo?" she called out. "Is that you?"

When no one answered, her feet finally found the floor and carried her into the living room. Bathed in the weak light of the lamp with one bulb burned out, the black and white keys of the piano twinkled. Poised over middle C was an envelope. *To C.J.*, it said, in Zach's familiar hand.

She held the envelope to her face, breathing in the smell of Zach, already growing faint, vanishing into the air as he had seemed to. Finally, she broke the seal and pulled out his letter.

Dear C.J.,

I'm sure your father knows the song I've chosen—"Thriving on a Riff." He might tell you a riff is a short rhythmic passage often repeated in improvisation.

The song is a wonderful one, loved by Charlie Parker's fans. I selected it for that—I am and will always be a fan of yours—and because of the title. If we substitute one letter, we have "Thriving on a Rift." It is my hope that you and I will surmount the rift in our friendship and thrive as before.

With best wishes always for your happiness and well-being, I remain your friend.

Until the fall,

Zach

FREEDOM SUMMER

For to be free is not merely to cast off one's chains, but to live in a way that respects and enhances the freedom of others.

—NELSON MANDELA

CHAPTER 17

Monday, July 13
Welcome to Meridian

Zach tugged at his shirt where it clung to his sweaty skin. The laughter of some of the younger Meridian Freedom School students wound its way around the building from the playground. He envied those on the swings, managing to get a breeze going on themselves.

It felt like a hundred degrees in the shade, but that record high thus far for 1964 had happened on June 21, the day three fellow volunteers came up missing. James Chaney was from Meridian. Mickey Schwerner and Andrew Goodman were from New York like him. The three had left Meridian to investigate a church bombing in Neshoba County. Zach had been in Ohio then, gathered with the second group of volunteers for orientation. Bob Moses had delivered the news staring, dazed, at his feet: "They haven't come back, and we haven't had any word from them."

It was July now, *twenty-three days missing*, the haunting new way of telling time. The mosquitoes were at bay, resting up for dusk. Zach had brought his Negro History class outside and gathered them under the broad leafy arms of the huge live oak, away from the other kids. Eleven to seventeen years of age, their faces were bright with desire to learn, or at least commitment to the cause, and their demeanor was at once grateful and expectant. Sometimes the hubbub and enthusiasm inside the three-story brick building, now retired as a Baptist seminary school, was too much for him. At those times, he would quietly hum one of his favorite freedom songs—"We Shall Not Be Moved," "Ain't Gonna Let Nobody Turn Me Round," or "We'll Never Turn Back," the ones that spoke of an unshakeable resolve that sometimes deserted him.

The kids settled themselves, facing him, on the grass that covered Mississippi red clay like a balding man's head. Boys in long pants and short-sleeve button shirts drew their knees toward their chests and leaned forward. Girls in sleeveless dresses angled their legs and tucked their skirts around them. Only he could see the boy moving up the street, striding at first, then slower and slower, as if looking for something under the tree. Finally, the boy stopped altogether, almost hidden by the tree's thick trunk.

Zach fingered the book in his hands. It presented a different history than these kids, or Zach himself, had studied in school. On a whim, he set the book aside, thinking there was plenty of time another day to talk of slave rebellions on the Amistad or Negro heroism during the Civil War.

"Can anybody name the first Negro professional basketball player?" he asked.

A few girls rolled their eyes. Most of the boys sat up a little straighter. "I heard 'bout somebody goes by the name of Wilt the Stilt," one said. "Reckon it coulda been him."

"My cousin lives in Detroit," said another. "He says Bill Russell got it all over that Wilt the Stilt."

"Bill Russell plays for the Boston Celtics," Zach said. "Anybody know the rest of their starting lineup last season?"

The faces stared.

"Ever heard of K.C. Jones?"

Head shaking.

"Sam Jones? Tom Sanders? Willie Naulls?"

More shaking.

"Can you guess what they have in common?"

"My cousin says Bill Russell ain't got nothing in common with a bunch of white guys."

"But—all five of these guys are Negroes."

"Naw," said shy Lynette, causing the boys to laugh. "Well, even a girl knows that."

"It's true. The Celtics drafted their first Negro player, Charles Cooper, while you guys were in diapers. They're also the first NBA team to have an all-Negro starting line." Zach picked a blade of grass. "Anybody know how Russell changed the game?"

"He's a great rebounder."

Heads turned toward the unfamiliar voice as the boy stepped around the tree into view. He, too, wore long pants. But his shirt was brown, with an emblem over the pocket.

"That's right. Suddenly defense is getting as much attention as offense—"

"What about baseball?" asked the boy in the uniform.

"Same question?"

"Naw, too easy. Everybody knows Jackie Robinson changed baseball playing with the Dodgers. Who was the first Negro in the American League?"

Zach looked around.

"I reckon he's asking you," Theo said with a mischievous grin.

Zach nodded Theo's way. "All right. Larry Doby."

"Last major league team to sign a Negro player?" the boy shot back, looking Zach straight in the eye.

Zach's pulse quickened. He wanted this for C.J. From the moment the organizers in Oxford, Ohio told him he would be teaching, not registering voters, he'd feared all his students might be like her. Accepting, always accepting. "Boston Red Sox, 1959, Pumpsie Green."

"You ever seen the great Robinson?"

"Sure have. '55 World Series, stealing home against the Yankees."

"What was he like?" The boy sounded less challenging now, more genuinely curious.

"Like lightning. Made the game about speed. And big. Bigger than players who spit on him as he ran the bases, or his own teammates who tried to keep him from playing." Zach nodded his head. "Bigger than life, I'd say."

"Isn't a one of these Negro athletes a woman?" asked Rosalee, just as the boy sat down, looking eager to soak up anything Zach could offer.

Rosalee was one of the most enthusiastic of the two hundred registered students. But—that look on the boy's face. This pretty girl with the searching eyes had caught his attention, Zach was almost certain.

"Thanks for reminding me of a woman named Althea Gibson, Rosalee." He stressed Rosalee's name slightly. Sure enough, the boy stared at her like a lovesick puppy.

"Women don't play any of the sports you been talking 'bout," Jackson protested, rubbing his hand over his closely cropped hair.

Rosalee glared at him.

"Maybe not yet," Zach said. "But Miss Gibson played—"

"Now you talking 'bout a white woman," Jackson said. "Calling her Miz."

"It's the respectful way to refer to a lady if you don't know her well, or she's older than you."

"You seen her—this Miz Gibson?" Rosalee asked.

"Not playing tennis. But there was a big parade in her honor, in New York City in 1957, when she won women's singles *and* doubles at Wimbledon."

The exchange wound down as the sun dipped lower in the sky. Zach sent the kids to gather their things and head home or to the community center. As he swept the classroom, he sensed someone watching and turned.

"I ain't much for school," said the boy in the brown work shirt. "Probably move up north after a friend of mine, soon as I save me some money."

"Well, I'm glad to see you here," Zach said, suddenly aware he was feeling more than an automatic response to try to enlist another student.

"Yeah, well, I usually got work."

"Oh?" He forced himself to stand still, even as his mind danced. This boy might want to be pulled, but he couldn't be pushed.

"My sister's husband got me on with the city, picking up garbage."

Zach grabbed for anything that might keep the conversation going. "You know a lot about sports."

"Got that from my daddy. He just knew 'bout the Negro Leagues, though."

"She's pretty, isn't she?" Zach went out on a limb. "Rosalee, I mean."

The boy looked at his feet and did a funny, somehow familiar thing with his mouth. "Yeah."

"Smart, too. I'm thinking she'd be impressed by someone who excelled in the material from class."

"Not me then." Disappointment sounded clearly in his voice.

Perhaps the very same whim that had led Zach to set down his history book and turn the afternoon's lesson to sports now told him to dispense with formalities such as registration. "You know, I might be able to help."

"Don't see how."

"I could lend you a book or two. Work with you—"

"Like I said, my job."

"Whenever you could come, just like today. It could be right after work, or on your day off. If class is already over, I could spend some time with you."

The boy's eyes darted in the direction of the big oak. "Rosalee." He said the word as gently as if he held a flower in his hands. "You know that Rosalee pretty well?"

"I think I've got an idea what's important to her."

"Okay, I reckon. Yeah, let's try."

"Good. My name's Zach."

"I'm Charles."

The boy drew himself up to his full height, such that Zach saw only the emerald green of C.J.'s eyes, the ones he wanted to drown in. He looked away, chastising himself for being just another stupid white person who thought all Negroes looked alike and, most of all, for being unable to stop thinking about her.

❊   ❊   ❊

The bell had rung signaling the lunch hour. The kids who lived too far away to go home were outside with their sack lunches or gathered around tables in various classrooms, some talking, others devouring books from the Freedom School library. Since it was a Wednesday, Grandma Willie was in the kitchen, directing a couple of the women teachers in setting out the food she'd brought for teachers and staff. As usual, she was dressed as if for church, a pretty but worn dress covering her ample frame, her hair neatly braided and wrapped around her head.

Lunch on Grandma Willie's days included the stand-bys: a large pan of cornbread and bowls of coleslaw and collards. Sometimes, ladies from her church would offer up chickens for her to fry. Grandma Willie always added one of her trademarks. Today it was her cornbread salad. She said it was nothing more than bell peppers, onions, and tomatoes from her garden mixed with cheese, mayonnaise, and leftover cornbread, but Zach suspected a secret ingredient.

As he pulled one book, then another from the library shelves, considering it then putting it back, he thought about the woman who'd opened her home to him for the summer, insisting he call her Grandma Willie. With her brown crepe-paper face and hands, she must be closer to the age of his great-grandparents. She was wearing her favorite church dress today. He would have said it was blue. She had taught him it was called cerulean, like the sky on the most perfect of summer days, with a hint of green from the earth reflected back to heaven. *Sara Leanne*, she pronounced it, as if it were a beautiful girl's name.

"Looking for something?"

Zach turned to see Elizabeth Nadler, from Winnetka, Illinois. He thought of her as the kind of girl C.J. would say was perfect for him. Like a good many of the volunteers, Elizabeth was Jewish. And, of course, she was a college student. Those were the things C.J. would emphasize. If that was all that mattered to him, he could long ago have chosen Sarah back at law school.

He admitted that Elizabeth was also pretty, smart, and fun to be around. But she had nothing over C.J. in any of those departments. C.J. was beautiful inside and out. Her common-sense pragmatism and people skills were enviable. And fun? There was no other way Zach would rather spend time than simply being with her.

He thought about Elizabeth's commitment to the cause, how they'd already spent a lot of time together talking, including walking to and from their host family's homes, just two doors down the street from each other. But, he asked himself, if talking about the cause was so important, why hadn't he fallen for Flo? He loved Flo like a sister.

No, C.J. was the one for him. She would come around, learn to take more risks and stand up for herself. He could help her with that. Didn't the freedom song "This Little Light of Mine"—*shows what the power of love can do*—say it all?

Having Elizabeth as a friend for the summer was perfect. He knew there was a boyfriend back in Winnetka, and she knew there was someone waiting for him.

"Yeah." He smiled at her. "I'm looking for a book to take home, so I can work with Grandma Willie on her reading."

"Zach! You should call her *Mrs.* Morgan, like we all do our hosts," Elizabeth reprimanded.

"I've tried. She sat me down with a plate of cake and glass of milk the same way she always does when I need setting straight. 'Oh, honey,' she said. 'No one's called me Miz Morgan since I was fifteen. That was on my wedding day. And it seems like I've been a grandmomma near about my whole life. So, if you and I are gonna be living together, I reckon you got to call me Grandma Willie.' "

"Is she a beginning reader?"

"I don't think she can read a word."

He'd told Elizabeth about the morning he found Grandma Willie raking garbage off the front lawn. "What's it say?" she'd asked, handing over a piece of paper from her apron pocket.

He'd stared at the words, unbelieving, trying to decide whether to lie. It was one thing, as one day followed another without a trace of the missing men, to allow his fear for himself to edge toward the corners of his mind. But the danger he was bringing Grandma Willie was something else entirely.

"I can take it," she'd said.

Finally, he'd read, "More trash to go with what's staying with you." Stuffing the note in his pocket, he'd rushed to add, "I'll find another place right away."

"No." She'd planted her hands firmly on her hips and wagged her head. "I'll be needing you to stay right where you're at, so's you can teach me to read. I reckon I done found me a reason to learn, if folks gonna be leaving me notes." She'd laughed heartily at her joke, but he'd seen the sadness in her smile.

"Elizabeth," Zach said now. "Grandma Willie asked me to be sure to pick something with real pretty pictures."

She scanned the children's books, then held out *The Snowy Day* by Ezra Jack Keats. "How about this one? The illustrations are gorgeous, and the story is lovely. It's about a boy who wakes up to discover that it snowed during the night. I think you'll have fun reading it together."

"That clinches it then." Elizabeth's French class was a favorite at the school. Her kids could be heard through the walls in the other classrooms, squealing with laughter and shouting, "Liberté, liberté, liberté," when they knew the answer or had a question, the way kids in other classes shouted, "Freedom, freedom, freedom," rather than raising their hands. "What crazy things went on in French class today?"

She told him about the *Where is it?* game, with her naming parts of the body and asking kids to point and say, *Ici. Où est votre tête? Où est votre jambe? Où sont vos cheveux? Où sont vos yeux?* "They're really quite good at it. They're so thrilled to be learning a foreign language, they just eat it up. So, I went faster and faster and faster until I had everyone, including me, confused. We were laughing so hard we were crying."

"Y'all come and get it while it's hot," yelled Grandma Willie from the kitchen.

"Où est votre estomac?" Elizabeth said.

"Ici," said Zach, patting his belly and laughing.

❈   ❈   ❈

Grandma Willie's tiny, immaculate house was three blocks from the Meridian Baptist Seminary building, a brief distance that could seem unending in the heat, especially with a police car trailing Zach and Elizabeth as they walked to school, one man or another leaning out the window to leer and call them nigger lovers and Communist bastards. The volunteers went everywhere they could on foot, if only to avoid the danger of having blacks and whites riding in the same car. When the distance to their destination was too great, and especially at night, they rode in cars whose inside lights had been disconnected so they wouldn't come on when the door was opened. This was just one of the survival rules drilled into them all in Oxford. *Don't stand in front of a lighted window at night, making yourself a target. Sign in and out at the COFO office.* And the biggest taboo of all: *No dating between blacks and whites.*

Zach liked the few steps he had to travel alone between Grandma Willie's house and the house where Elizabeth stayed. When he was early for meeting her, he would visit Grandma Willie's garden. Standing there in the morning, among the well-tended rows of vegetables, he came as close as he ever did to praying.

Tonight, he was being dropped off after a mass meeting at First Union Baptist Church. Again, there had been little to report on the disappearance of Chaney, Schwerner, and Goodman, still being laughed off by local whites as a hoax. Again, volunteers and Negro citizens had sung together. The prayerful yearning of "Oh Freedom" rising to the rafters still rang in his ears. *And before I'll be a slave, I'll be buried in my grave . . .*

As the CORE staffer's car traveled from the church to Grandma Willie's house, it passed black and white neighborhoods, intermingled as if in a game of fifty-two-card pickup, where black and red cards were thrown up in the air and scattered randomly. On the way to the church, they'd seen the fog machine beginning its rounds in the waning light. Indeed, the clouds that surged from the truck were a beautiful sight, making Zach wish he could be wrapped up in their softness. But the smell soon changed things. The sickly sweet smell of poison. And in each neighborhood, the children, Negro and white alike, chased the fog.

It was late when he let himself into Grandma Willie's house. She was waiting up for him, as if he were her own child.

"Would you like to read?" he asked.

She smiled and pulled *The Snowy Day* from behind her back.

He followed her to the very back of the house, turning off lights as they went. In her sewing room, by the dim light of a table lamp, they pulled two chairs close together. Grandma Willie had made terrific progress since he borrowed the book from the school library. Her favorite part to read was about the small Negro character Peter walking in the snow. "Crunch, crunch, crunch," she liked to say, sometimes forgetting to stop at three crunches. And she would lean her body left and right as little Peter pointed his toes this way or that.

Suddenly, they heard tires crunch the gravel of her driveway. They held their breath and heard glass shatter in the front room. The sound of laughter was followed by the squeal of tires as a car peeled away. Heart pounding, Zach crept to the front of the house, picking up his baseball bat on the way. In the moonlight, he saw the rock that had smashed the glass. Nearby was a bound stack of leaflets, resembling for all the world newspapers dropped off for a boy's morning delivery route. They stared together at the crude writing, admonishing the Communist civil rights workers against mongrelization. He did not read these words to Grandma Willie.

"Don't," she said evenly, stopping him from going outside to look around. "There's boards in the lean-to if you wouldn't mind putting some up. But first I'm gonna fix us a little something, just like always."

As Zach bent to rake bits of glass onto a dustpan, he heard her hobbling about the kitchen. She soon called him to the table and set a plate before him with a huge hunk of yellow cake topped with pineapple and brown glaze. Her upside-down cake was every bit as good as the one Sissy and Emily had served that night before C.J.'s first visit back to Poplar Springs. But he toyed with it absently.

Before he met Grandma Willie, C.J. was the strongest woman he knew. Yet he couldn't imagine her family bringing a volunteer into their home. He recalled a book one of the organizers had given him in Ohio and shook his head. Dr. Woodson's words—"When you control a man's thinking . . . he will find his 'proper place' and will stay in it."—rang so true that he seemed to have written *The Mis-Education of the Negro* about C.J.'s family.

"Do you know a town called Poplar Springs?" Zach asked.

"Had somebody up at our church once who moved from over that way."

"Do you think the same kinds of things go on over there?" He spread his hands toward the front room, with the window with the gaping hole.

"Honey, I've heard things in Meridian ain't that bad compared to lots of other places." He felt his skin crawl and squirmed in his chair, having read the reports of violence in places like the Delta. "You know somebody from Poplar Springs?"

He stuffed a big forkful of cake into his mouth and chewed, remembering C.J. next to him at the piano that long-ago summer night, her beautiful face flush with pride as she learned to play a song. "Chopsticks," he'd told her it was called, not "Heart and Soul." Even then, he must have known he was falling in love, with someone he dared not rush.

"I think I'm only beginning to know her. She lives in Chicago now. But I just can't picture her doing what you're doing—"

"You got to stop that," Grandma Willie said sharply. "Ain't no two mules pull a wagon exactly the same. This friend of yours—she young? She got a family?"

"Yes, ma'am."

"Her family own their own house like I do? Or do they live on a white man's land?"

"I—don't know. Her dad and uncle built the house they live in now, but she never said if the house is paid for."

"Her family working for white folks who can take their jobs from 'em for no good reason? Or, they be lucky like me, with my husband's pension from the railroad?"

"Yes, ma'am. No, ma'am."

"Well, child, I ain't got nothing nobody can take from me but my own life. If somebody wants that, I reckon they can have it, 'cause I just about done used it up anyways. Now finish up so's you got the strength it'll take to put up them boards."

CHAPTER 18

Thursday, July 16
From Meridian to Winnetka

Mrs. Gray's rooster clock clucked twice. It was the time of day C.J. dreaded almost as much as the night. Her mind became particularly hard to control while preparing a meal she'd made dozens of times before.

She took out the tiny date book she always carried now and stared at the calendar with the neat ticks, each marking one less day until Zach came safely back to Chicago. Trembling at the memory of him saying he had to fight for a world where they could be whatever they wanted to be to each other, she counted twenty-five Xs and prayed he would not disappear like those three boys.

Their names and faces were seared in her memory. James Chaney was a Negro from the very town where Metairie lived. Michael Schwerner and Andrew Goodman were white boys from New York. In their FBI photos, they each looked so sad that she wondered if they'd somehow known what was going to happen. Her heart had come to an absolute stop, she was certain of it, when Mr. Cronkite looked out at America from behind his *CBS Evening News* desk and said: "Three young civil rights workers disappeared in Mississippi on Sunday night near the central Mississippi town of Philadelphia, about eighty miles northeast of Jackson." But that was Monday, June 22. She'd gathered her wits about her enough to realize that Zach would still be in Ohio, getting trained for the Mississippi Summer

Project. Then, because he would follow the three from Ohio to Missis-sippi and take up the work they'd begun, she had renewed her praying for him in earnest.

The smell of garlic and sizzle of the rump roast browning in the pot called to her. She turned the meat and went back to chopping carrots just as a key clicked in the back door.

C.J. waited for Mrs. Gray to poke her head into the kitchen. Lately, she'd been showing up at home at odd times, when C.J. would have expected her to be at the jewelry store. She would putter around for a while, then appear wherever C.J. happened to be working and begin talking her ear off. Her face would resemble her son's when he came home from school wanting an audience. Ever since Johnny's friend Richard Simms had the boy from the South Side stay at his house, Johnny seemed to regard C.J. as his, to offer proof his family was doing better on the score of getting to know a Negro.

In the first of these chats, Mrs. Gray had talked excitedly about her new friend, Nancy Simms. Mrs. Gray had gotten a copy of the *Winnetka Talk*, then invited Richard's mother to meet for coffee. As she learned, Mrs. Simms sold real estate and was making, in Mrs. Simms's own words, "a nuisance of herself." She'd been asked to sign a petition objecting to Negroes coming on the beach in suburban Highland Park, some ten miles north of Winnetka. Of course she'd said no, adding that she wouldn't any more think of doing that than she would have signed a similar petition about keeping Jews out, Jews just like her own lifelong friend Rachel Nadler.

Mrs. Simms had also talked about a proposed referendum in Novem-ber, putting the question of open occupancy before Illinois voters. Op-ponents of open occupancy labeled it "forced housing" and defended the right of homeowners to sell or rent to whomever they pleased. Proponents argued that open occupancy protected the rights of everyone, no matter their color or religion.

"The Negro couple Mrs. Simms sold to in that part of Evanston said Negroes prefer to be together, not scattered all alone among the whites," Mrs. Gray had told C.J., right before asking, "What do *you* think? I mean, how do Negroes feel about this?"

"Well, I reckon everyone wants to live in the nicest place possible," she'd managed to reply.

God bless Mrs. Gray for asking, she had thought that day. God help her to understand why their relationship didn't allow her to truly answer. *I'm not every Negro*, she couldn't say. *I wish it was me you wanted to know.*

Since that first chat, things had only gotten worse. Each conversation gave C.J. something new to worry about, but none more so than the one about Wednesdays in Mississippi.

"This summer, women from northern cities are visiting the freedom schools and community centers," Mrs. Gray had said. "The thinking is that the women going down can report on conditions in Mississippi and bring attention to civil rights once they're home again. Nancy has already been accepted. She gave me an application. I'd like to see your Mississippi, so I could know you better. And, of course, your Zach is there registering voters—"

"Miz Gray, you don't need to go to Mississippi. I'm right *here*," C.J. had wailed. She'd lowered her voice to add, "What I mean is, I'll tell you *anything* you want to know. Just promise me you won't go—too."

"There, there, dear. I brought you something." Mrs. Gray had rummaged in her purse and held out a folded piece of paper. "It's a newsletter by Joey Nadler, whose sister is teaching at the Meridian Freedom School. That's where your sister lives, isn't it?"

Now, as C.J. turned the roast again, Mrs. Gray finally made her way to the kitchen. She scurried in. But then, as if she'd forgotten why she came, she stopped at the window to prune a dead leaf from the philodendron.

C.J. went to the sink to clean the potatoes, not sure why she felt fear well up inside her like a sob.

Mrs. Gray reached out to touch her arm. "The Wednesdays in Mississippi folks accepted my application," she said. "I'll be going with Nancy's group, to Meridian."

In her hand, the bristles of the vegetable scrubber began tearing away the skin.

"We leave on Tuesday."

We, that awful word Zach had used at dinner in this house not two months ago, signaling that there was no turning back for him.

Mrs. Gray and her projects.

She dropped the scrubber in the sink with a clatter and stared at Mrs. Gray. As their eyes met, Mrs. Gray nodded, letting C.J. know she understood her fear and appreciated it. "I'll be okay, C.J. Now, I need your help getting ready over these next four days. And, of course, I'm counting on you to look out for the children and Mr. Gray until I get back."

"Yes'm, I'll do that," she said sadly.

That night, alone in her room, C.J. reached for her comb in the drawer of the nightstand. Her hand brushed the newsletter Mrs. Gray had given her. She'd skimmed it, stuffed it the drawer, and forgotten about it. Now, with Mrs. Gray going to Mississippi, too, she wanted to read it again, for clues about what might await her there.

Across the top, *From Meridian to Winnetka* in a patchwork of letters cut from a magazine. Beneath that, a typed note from a boy named Joey Nadler. Twelve years old. C.J. pictured Charlie, at the Poplar Springs bus station when she left for Chicago, his twelve-year-old face growing smaller until the bus pulled out of sight.

Charlie was seventeen now. On her last trip home, he'd stood tall enough to look her square in the eye when she reminded him about keeping up his grades so he could go to college. She picked up the most recent photograph of her family—Charlie with her parents, Metairie, George, and the grandbabies Anna and George Jr. She traced Charlie's face before setting the picture back on her nightstand, knowing she would always hold the boy, framed by the window of a bus, in her heart.

Beneath this Joey Nadler's note saying how proud he was of his sister, Elizabeth, was a letter from her. *The kids are full of questions*, she wrote. *They wanted to know why I came. The answer is complicated and simple at the same time. I don't think any two of the volunteers are motivated by exactly the same thing. I told them the story of The Wizard of Oz and how I loved to watch it with my little brother. How the wizard was really just a man behind a curtain making everybody afraid. How each of them has the power within—like Dorothy with the ruby slippers—to get home; have a heart, a brain, courage. That I came because I wanted them to know they have the ruby slippers.*

Zach had said it was because of C.J. that he had to go. For the first time, she wondered if he was like Mrs. Gray, wanting to get to know a Negro. Was that what she was to him? If that was it, there wasn't a place under God's great heaven where things could work out between them. If that was it, she reckoned he and Mrs. Gray might just as well have stayed put in Chicago.

These kids are eager to learn whatever we have, Miss Nadler's letter went on. *Can you believe I'm teaching French?*

No, C.J. could not. She'd certainly never heard of a Mississippi school for Negroes teaching a foreign language. What use would it be for maids and cotton pickers? She crinkled her brow, trying to conjure up an image of a classroom of eager Negro students. All she could see was the dull, resigned eyes of her old classmates.

We read a lot to the little ones, most days during lunch and before and after school. My favorite little boy's favorite book is The Snowy Day. *The hero is named Peter, just like this precious Mississippi Negro child. The high school kids are reading Richard Wright's* Black Boy. *Finally, with the books folks have sent us from all over the country, these kids are seeing themselves in books.*

C.J. found that hard to believe, too, as she did the idea of the volunteers being allowed into Negro churches in Meridian to talk about registering to vote. Brother James would surely have a heart attack. She was equally flabbergasted by what Miss Nadler wrote about staying with a Negro family in Meridian and that some two hundred kids had signed up to attend the Meridian Freedom School. But what shook her to her very core was the idea that the students were confronted with questions like these: *What do white people have that you want? That you don't want? What do black people have that you want to keep? Get rid of?*

Like in Elizabeth Nadler's funny story, C.J. knew she had the power to go home someday. But to have love, go to college, be brave enough to act—those were for someone else. She turned off the bedside lamp. "Oh, Zach," she murmured as she fell asleep.

❖   ❖   ❖

C.J. arrived in Hyde Park on Saturday afternoon feeling guilty. She'd offered to stay and help Mrs. Gray prepare for her trip, but Mrs. Gray had insisted she take her day off. Now, standing before the mailboxes in the lobby of the brownstone, she shivered in the mid-summer heat. Would she worry about Zach every minute he was gone? She placed her palm against the metal and tried to see through the tiny window. She had no right to hope for a letter from him. He hadn't even written to Flo.

Finally, she turned the key and pulled out a stack of envelopes. Rapidly, she shuffled. One for Mae, two for Sissy, one for Emily. There, one addressed to her with Metairie's return address. She was about to open it when the next one stopped her cold. It was addressed to Flo, in Zach's familiar hand. The return address said *2505 ½ 5th Street, Meridian, Mississippi*. Good Lord! Was Zach in James Chaney's hometown? She ran upstairs, hoping Flo would be there. She opened the apartment door to find her relaxing on the couch.

"Hey." Flo smiled up at her, but the smile changed to a frown when she saw C.J.'s face. "What on earth is it?"

C.J. dropped her satchel and went to sit next to her. She threw the rest of the mail on the coffee table and held out Zach's letter, speaking only with her eyes.

Flo opened the envelope like the precious thing it was, their first and perhaps their only connection to Zach until he came back to Chicago. "Dear Flo," she read.

"Oh, no, Flo!" C.J. said, stopping her. "That's meant for you. Just read it and tell me he's okay."

Flo scanned and spoke in bursts. "Evenings and weekends, he's doing some canvassing of voters, like he hoped. But his main job is at the Meridian Freedom School. He teaches Negro History, American History and Government, and English Expression, and leads a sports club after classes let out." She looked back at the letter. "His greatest fear came as he crossed the Mississippi state line under the cover of darkness. He and the others pleaded with the God of their choice that their out-of-state license plates would not be noticed." Flo looked at her, then at the letter, then back at her.

"Tell me," C.J. said finally.

"I think you should hear this part, just the way he wrote it. He says, 'Don't worry too much, Flo. I *will* come back, to be with C.J.'"

C.J. inhaled sharply. Flo reached out to pat her hand, then read more out loud.

"You know, I wrote her a letter, too. But I don't know if I'll mail it. What I wrote—well, I'll speak of that when we see each other. For now, I'm working and learning. Remembering you saying there's lots of Alabamas in Alabama."

It was almost too much to take in. C.J. told Flo about Mrs. Gray's upcoming trip to Meridian. "Now I got to worry about the both of them."

"But Miz Gray can check on Zach, like she said this Wednesdays in Mississippi trip is all about," Flo countered.

"I suppose." C.J.'s gaze fell on the mail she'd thrown on the coffee table. Metairie's letter lay on top of the scattered pile. Aimlessly, she opened it.

She read without really taking in the words, until these: *Now Charlie's talking about dropping out of school. Momma and Daddy are beside theirselves.*

"That boy is crazy as a bedbug if he thinks I'm gonna stand for him quitting school," she muttered. "Not after I worked to put the dream within his reach."

So George says to them, send Charlie to us for the summer. He'll see can he get him on with the city, collecting garbage. I'm awful proud of my man that he's got such influence with the boss. Charlie's earning more than he ever did helping out Daddy at the Wilsons'. It's good, him seeing a man earning a right decent living for his family. And Charlie being here with no way to get back to Poplar Springs but the bus keeps him away from that trouble-making William.

But now I got me one more to clean up after. And me being extra busy here, I can't get to Poplar Springs that often to check on Momma and Daddy. I surely hate that, what with Daddy seeming so tired all the time. When you thinking on coming home? I sure do wish you was here to help.

C.J. had noticed her daddy being slower when she was last home. She should have asked him about it. Thank goodness for Metairie, the one in the Evans family most likely to think of herself. Lord knew their momma's letters, always filled with good news and hugs and kisses, never would have let on how bad things had gotten.

All her fretting about Zach. All her work over the past years, the money she'd been saving. What use was any of that if she couldn't help her family in the way they needed it? "Flo, I've got to go to Mississippi."

"To see Zach?"

"Good heavens, no. My family needs me." Hurriedly, she explained. "I promised Miz Gray I'd take care of the children and Mr. Gray while she's gone. But I aim to be on a bus the day she returns. I got to head straight back to Evanston right now, so's I can talk this out with Miz Gray." She hugged Flo, grabbed her satchel, and walked out the door.

Back in Evanston, C.J. found Mrs. Gray in the kitchen having tea.

"Goodness!" Mrs. Gray said as one hand went to her heart. "What are you doing back, C.J.?"

"I wanted to talk, ma'am."

"You sit then, dear." Mrs. Gray hopped up to fill another tea ball and take down a second cup and saucer.

She watched Mrs. Gray pour, then accepted the cup and laced her fingers around it, feeling the steam.

For the first time, Mrs. Gray looked into C.J.'s face. "What *is* it, dear? Oh, my—is it Zach? Have you heard from him?"

C.J. flushed. "Not me, ma'am. I don't reckon I will . . . But Flo, he wrote to her. And, Miz Gray, Zach is in Meridian."

"In Meridian? Registering voters?"

"No'm, he's teaching up at the freedom school with that girl, Elizabeth Nadler. You got to see him, please. Make sure he's okay."

"You see, C.J.? It must be meant for me to go to Meridian." Mrs. Gray looked rather pleased with herself.

C.J. hesitated. "Miz Gray, I did get news from my sister Metairie. You may not remember, but she's got a husband and two small children to care for. And now my brother Charlie's moved in on account of him being too much for my momma and daddy to handle right now. Metairie says Daddy's been a mite peaked lately, and Charlie's talking about dropping out of school."

Mrs. Gray's face filled with compassion as she listened to the rest.

"Now I'll stay put right here 'til you get back, but I got to be on that bus come Friday."

"Well, of course, dear." Mrs. Gray set her tea ball on her saucer. "We can spare you for a trip home."

"Not a visit ... exactly ... ma'am." It was dawning on C.J. that she hadn't thought this through.

"To stay?" Mrs. Gray looked alarmed.

When C.J., suddenly busy trying to figure out exactly what she was asking for, said nothing, Mrs. Gray traced the platinum rim of the Huntington teacup. "So much has changed," she said.

C.J. assumed she was thinking how Mrs. Kennedy had selected this pattern and now her husband was dead. Maybe thinking, too, how she brought C.J. into the dining room and now she might be leaving. She watched her go most of the way around the cup, then back up and go the other direction.

"I don't know how bad things are. I'll have to go back and forth between Poplar Springs and Meridian, doing what it takes to make sure everyone is okay. All I know is my family needs me."

"Then go help them." Mrs. Gray spoke sharply. "We'll hold your job for you, as long as you need."

C.J. stiffened. "I couldn't ask you to do that. It could be weeks."

"C.J." Mrs. Gray's voice had suddenly gone soft. "Why did you leave? At Thanksgiving dinner, when Johnny asked about the Klan, you didn't deny it."

C.J. rested her elbows on the table and her chin on her hands. Her right hand took hold of her left index finger, like a small child might wrap its chubby hand around one of its mother's fingers. She closed her eyes while she wrestled with her thoughts. She decided it was better for Mrs. Gray to know, what with her going down to Mississippi in a few days.

"It wasn't safe for me." C.J. measured out the words carefully.

"Did something happen, like with Flo?"

C.J. shook her head. As she got up to fill their cups, a low, hollow laugh escaped. That was the funny thing. Nothing had happened like with Flo.

But she had lived for so long with the fear that it would, she was angry and not even sure at whom. She sat back down, heavily, feeling too tired to hold up her body and her past. "It was a man by the name of Corrigan," she blurted.

And out poured the things she'd almost managed to forget. The men at the meetings. The threat to her family if she breathed a word of what she'd heard. Mrs. Corrigan, so jealous she gave off hatred like an injured skunk. At some point, Mrs. Gray reached out to hold her hand. Each time C.J. looked, expecting judgment, she saw the eyes of a mother hearing that her child had suffered.

When C.J. was finally quiet, Mrs. Gray asked, "What will you do—if you go back for good?"

"I'll clean houses like before."

"This man's?"

"If he asks, I reckon so."

"C.J., Zach wouldn't want—I don't—I know I've made mistakes, pushed you when you weren't ready. But I've come to feel almost like a mother to you, and that's what mothers do. I want you to listen."

Mrs. Gray told C.J. that she was young, smart, and beautiful; reminded her how well she was doing with her piano lessons. She admitted there were problems in Chicago, too. But she thought C.J. had a better chance right here. "And you and Zach need more time, to figure out what you mean to each other. You can't just pack up and go back to Mississippi for good, knowing he'll be back here making his life. Promise me you'll keep an open mind."

She watched Mrs. Gray's watermelon hair bouncing around her face like tiny springs and seethed. *You ought to be the one promising, not to go messing in things you don't understand.* But C.J. felt her concern and caring like a cooling salve. And she promised.

CHAPTER 19

Sunday, July 19
Summer School

On the third Sunday afternoon in July, Joan Barnes sprawled on her living room floor with the comic strips. Aromas from dinner lingered in the air. Steak, always the best cut her mom could find at the A&P. Baked potatoes and green beans, generously buttered. Warm, flaky biscuits that held fat, juicy strawberries and gobs of whipped cream. Sounds of her family revolving around the living room mingled comfortably. Her mom playing Henry Mancini at the piano, her dad rustling the rest of the newspaper and making little squeaking sounds when he shifted in his leather easy chair, and her little brother Andy popping in and out to announce his latest Lego creation.

Yet her mood aligned with the weather. The steady beat of rain on the roof, like one long run-on sentence that had begun this morning, was punctuated by lightning slicing the sky. She counted—*one Mississippi, two Mississippi*—until the thunder caught up. The storm cloud was close at hand. She scoffed at whoever made the decision to include *Charlie Brown* in the funny papers. Half the time it was really rather depressing. There wasn't one character among the cast who wasn't a pathetic ball player. And today, as usual, Charlie and his team made poor choices and offered lame excuses, sending them down in defeat once again.

But despite keeping her indoors with nothing to do, the rain wasn't the problem. Nearly as common in August as in July, it had only threatened to ruin one birthday party in the last five years. A tradition, with her entire class invited for swimming and cake. That one time they'd been almost ready to get out of the pool anyway and head to her house. This year, it might as well rain all day because the Poplar Springs city pool was closed indefinitely.

City officials had announced their decision to close, rather than desegregate, on Friday. They blamed President Johnson for signing the Civil Rights Act into law, making segregation in public places illegal. What, she wondered, was wrong with *their* pool? And why now? She was turning twelve, busy figuring out how to convince her mom to get her a two-piece like those in *Seventeen*. Look how they'd ruined her tradition!

As if in sympathy, Joan's mom made one of her rare mistakes while playing, sounding like she'd mistaken a black key for a white one or vice versa. Joan heard the paper making more noise than usual and looked up to see her dad watching her. "Still feeling sad, honey?" he asked.

"It's not fair is all!"

"Well, you're not going to sit around and mope all summer." He frowned. She waited for him to add, *Life really isn't fair, Joani.*

"It *isn't* fair," he said instead. She thought she saw a twinkle in his eye. "The Neshoba County Fair will be here in a few weeks."

"Yeah." She wondered if Carol would invite her to the Whitehead cabin again this summer.

He laid the paper across his lap, then crossed his legs and settled back into his chair. "Did I tell you my best friend Ed, from medical school, called yesterday?"

"No." She was having trouble keeping up. "How is he?"

"Just fine. And he sends his love. Wanted to let me know about some folks coming to Meridian soon." One moccasin-clad foot began to keep time to the music. "They're with the Medical Committee for Human Rights, running free clinics around Mississippi this summer. Ed wondered if I could help out at the Meridian clinic, at a school there."

"Won't the school be closed?"

He shook his head. "This is a summer school, for Negro children. The teachers are college students from around the country."

"Don't those kids have real teachers, at *their* school?"

"Well, yes. This is special, just for this summer. Some of these kids' families can't afford to see a doctor. And the college students are away from their regular doctors. The clinics give shots and check-ups and take care of anyone who might get—have an accident."

"Why do they need you?"

"Doctors need what are called privileges in order to care for patients in hospitals and write prescriptions." He crossed his legs in the opposite direction. "These doctors don't have privileges in Mississippi, since they're from other states. I can help them with that."

"That's nice, Daddy." She returned her attention to the comics.

"I was thinking—" He cleared his throat. "That you might come with me."

"Dad! The most Negroes I've ever been near was that day in your *secret* waiting room." She looked at him accusingly.

He raised an eyebrow and continued. "Now hear me out. You'll be in seventh grade this fall, able to start working on the Girl Scout Marian Award. I'm sure your troop leader has mentioned the community service project."

Joan nodded helplessly, feeling things getting worse by the minute.

"I'll be so proud when it's your turn to have the Bishop present your award at St. Stephen's."

She scowled, hating it when her dad tried to trick her.

"Remember when he came last year?" His eyes seemed to light up with the memory. "He praised Maggie Williams for her project and what she learned. Thanked her for letting her light shine to the world."

"Sure, but there are lots of projects I can do right here. Collecting food or used clothes, raising money—"

"Maybe so, but I could use your help. And it will be good for us to spend time together."

"Mom needs me. To help with Andy."

"Moon River" suddenly ended, and Joan's mom looked up. "Now I can manage fine, honey," she said.

Joan's dad smiled. "That settles it. We'll give this a try, on Wednesday."

"But—how am I going to come up with a project at a summer school for *Negroes*? I mean, do you remember Big Daddy talking about the coloreds being dim-witted and shiftless?"

"We don't talk like that in our family," he said, his voice rising. "We respect our elders, but Big Daddy has different ideas. I've been thinking lately about what's right." He lowered his voice to normal again and smiled. "There might even be a chance for you to spend time with Carol at Big Daddy's house in Meridian. You'd like that, wouldn't you? But remember what I just said."

He turned his attention back to the newspaper. Joan scowled even harder as she stared at poor Charlie Brown.

❊   ❊   ❊

Joan's dad normally closed his office on Wednesday afternoons. He'd asked his nurses to reschedule any morning appointments for another day and to stay in the office to call him in case an emergency came up; if one did, he and Joan could be back in Poplar Springs in forty-five minutes. That left the entire day free for Meridian. She had finally been consoled with the promise of spending a couple of hours with Carol at Big Daddy's house.

Now, she and her dad stepped from the car at the base of the Meridian Baptist Seminary. The yard was surrounded by a chain-link fence, leaving no way for them to get through, even if they chose to scale the hill. From where they stood, the steepness of the incline made the three-story building seem massive. This Negro summer school was certainly bigger than St. Stephen's Academy.

"This can't be the right place, Daddy," she whispered.

"We must be on the back side, honey. We just need to walk around." He carried his black bag in one hand and put his other arm around her shoulder.

She stuck to him the way she had on her first day of first grade. They made their way past the playground, scattered with kids about her age, and up the front steps where teenagers gathered—girls in dresses, boys in T-shirts or short-sleeved button-up shirts and pants. She gawked, even as her white skin betrayed her by flushing red. The prettier, skinnier girls reminded her of C.J. She wondered for an instant what C.J. would look like now after five years. None of the boys was familiar in any way.

"Good morning. Excuse us, please," her dad repeated as they moved through the throng and inside. Some smiled or nodded.

Some kid must have run inside when he saw them arrive, because a white man immediately strode down the hall toward them and introduced himself as the principal. "We've set up an exam area near the kitchen," he said. "That way, you have running water."

He ushered them into a room and introduced a short, trim man probably around her dad's age. Dr. Marty Levinson was losing his hair. His shiny red crown said he'd tangled with the Mississippi sun and lost.

"Any friend of Ed's," said Dr. Levinson, revealing perfect white teeth when he smiled.

She watched as he showed her dad the records they kept of immunizations and treatments and the supplies they had to work with. Tongue depressors, cotton, applicators, and more, all sent from outside Mississippi by the Medical Committee for Human Rights, were labeled and neatly arranged on the shelves along one wall. He said some of the teachers had helped set up the makeshift exam tables. Jacob, a carpenter, had built the room divider that surrounded one of the exam stations.

Her dad nodded his approval, but she thought it all had the look and feel of his waiting room for Negroes—like everything in it was a hand-me-down. She suddenly thought to wonder about the care he gave Negroes and whites. Could it be as different as his waiting rooms?

"Here, Joani," he said, handing her a large pitcher. "Could you go to the kitchen, wash this out, and fill it up with water?"

She sighed, thinking that being here was going to feel like forever if this was the way she'd be spending her time. Back in the exam room, the morning sun slanting through the windows was already raising the temperature.

Her dad poured water into a kettle and turned on the hot plate. As she parked herself in a shaded corner with a cross-breeze, the first patient arrived. Dr. Levinson suggested her dad do the honors.

"My throat's hurting me pretty bad, sir," said the teenage Negro who Dr. Levinson introduced as Evelyne. "I didn't want to miss nothing today at the school. So, my momma said go on."

How odd, Joan thought, wanting to be in school in the summer. She couldn't wait to spend time with Carol, see Big Daddy's house for the first time, have some fun.

"Would it be okay if I take a look?" Her dad was using his make-you-feel-better voice. His touch appeared gentle as he felt the glands on the sides of Evelyne's neck. He finished his exam, showed her how to gargle with warm salt water, and sent her back to class.

After a while, a young white woman came in. Joan hadn't expected to see any white patients. Good, she thought, this would make it easy to compare.

"Hi, Patsy," said Dr. Levinson. "This is Doc Barnes and his daughter, Joan. Patsy teaches literature. She's from Boston."

After that, Patsy and Dr. Levinson spoke in hushed tones until he said, "Since you'll probably need a prescription, I'm going to ask Doc Barnes to do the pelvic exam."

Joan didn't know what that was, but her dad asked Patsy to come with him to the exam table behind the big screen. He took a lot more time with Patsy than he had with Evelyne. Joan wondered whether that was because Patsy was white or because she had a more serious problem. Patsy came out holding a piece of paper Joan recognized from her dad's prescription pad. "Try to get that filled right away," he urged.

Her dad and Dr. Levinson talked a while about the Medical Committee for Human Rights. Dr. Levinson explained that the volunteer doctors were coming in for two weeks at a time. Someone else would take his place next week. "We're grateful for your support, Doc Barnes. Not just writing prescriptions and getting hospital care, but being a liaison for our operations."

They were interrupted by a boy, probably about Joan's age, who came in with his arm in a cast and sling, holding a black pocket comb and tissue paper. The cast ran from his knuckles up under the sleeve of his T-shirt. Joan immediately noticed his smile, at once disarming and sad.

"How's that arm, Ben?" Dr. Levinson asked.

"It's itching me something fierce."

"I hope you're not using that comb to scratch it. You break the skin, that could cause an infection."

"No, sir. This is my kazoo."

"Let me take a look, then maybe you'll play for us." Dr. Levinson took Ben's temperature and checked his skin the best he could, then sprinkled baby powder inside the cast. "That should help some."

There came that smile again. "Listen at this. We're gonna add this to our jazz band." A bit awkwardly, Ben positioned the tissue paper and raised the comb to his lips. His humming produced a marvelous sound. Everyone clapped. Ben asked Dr. Levinson to sign his cast, then sauntered outside.

Joan was intrigued. Maybe Ben was going to practice with the jazz band. "I'll be back in a bit, Dad," she said.

She followed Ben, staying far enough behind so as not to be noticed. When he suddenly darted out of sight, she found herself alone in a library. Her mom and dad had bookshelves in every room of the house but the bathroom, yet the names on the spines of these books were almost all unfamiliar. James Baldwin, W.E.B. Du Bois, Gwendolyn Brooks, Countee Cullen, Lorraine Hansberry, Langston Hughes, Zora Neale Hurston, Martin Luther King Jr., Richard Wright. She did recognize Booker T. Washington, the name etched onto the Negro high school in Poplar Springs. The situation was little better in the children's section. Here and there was a familiar book with animal characters, and she found one of her favorites, *Harold and the Purple Crayon*. But the only other books with faces like hers in the pictures were about children in other countries. Reading would be no fun at all, she thought, if you couldn't imagine yourself into the story.

"You must be Doc Barnes's girl."

Joan jumped at the sound of the voice and, guiltily, returned a book to the shelf. She looked up into the blue eyes and dimples of a man she thought could be a movie star he was so handsome.

"My name is Zach," he said. "My next class is about to start down the hall. Would you like to join us?"

She thought she would be happy to go almost anywhere with this man. Before she realized what she was doing, she was inside a classroom, being introduced as she stared into the faces of about ten Negro teenagers seated around a large table. One of the girls pulled out a chair next to her and made a welcoming gesture with her hand, inviting Joan to sit by her. Gratefully, she sank into the chair. She sat wide-eyed and mute throughout Zach's English Expression class.

"Let's use what we learned yesterday in Negro History for our discussion," he said. He had the students take turns recalling the accomplishments of Negro scientists.

The awe in their voices told Joan they were as surprised by what they were saying as she was to be hearing it. Lewis Latimer was a draftsman for Alexander Graham Bell and Thomas Edison. Dr. George Washington Carver developed more than a hundred products from the peanut, including an oil proven to help in treating infantile paralysis. He produced almost as many things from the sweet potato. *I've eaten that!* Joan almost said out loud when she heard tapioca mentioned. Lloyd Albert Quarterman and J. Ernest Wilkins Jr. worked on the Manhattan Project that developed the first atomic bomb during World War II.

Joan was even more surprised by the students, not dim-witted at all. She wondered how Zach had been lucky enough to get every single smart Negro from the entire school in his class.

Neither could she imagine behaving with her teachers at St. Stephen's in quite the same way as these kids were. She'd been sent to the principal's office once for asking a question that seemed far less inappropriate than those these kids dared to ask Zach. She nearly fell out of her chair the first time someone shouted out, "Freedom, freedom, freedom." She figured out eventually that that was their way of showing they had a question or an answer to offer.

"Freedom, freedom, freedom!" said the girl who had invited Joan to sit.

"Yes, Rosalee," Zach said.

"I know we always got to come back to your questions on the board there." Rosalee smiled.

Joan snuck a peek at the board. *What do white people have that you want? That you don't want? What do black people have that you want to keep? Get rid of?*

"So," Rosalee continued, "I'm gonna bring that up now while we're talking 'bout the Manhattan Project that led to the bombs being dropped on Japan. I *want* more Negroes to get good educations and discover and invent stuff. But I *don't* want them to use that to do bad things."

When the bell rang, Zach's class exited the classroom amidst commotion outside. Joan followed him, hoping for more attention. As he craned his neck, she peered around him to see a group of well-dressed white ladies in the hall, surrounding what she guessed was one of the teachers.

"Elizabeth, dear," gushed a lady whose watermelon curls danced from beneath her hat. She took the younger woman's hand in both of hers. "I'm Donna Gray. I'm just thrilled to meet you. Your mother and Mrs. Simms have told me so much about you."

The lady talked like Joan's parents and many of the teachers here at the summer school. She was clearly not from Mississippi. As several others in the group began talking, Joan realized they must be Yankees, too.

She heard Zach inhale sharply, then murmur what almost sounded like "C.J." Then he began excusing his way through the crowd, leaving Joan behind. "Mrs. Gray, wow! What are you doing here?"

"Oh, Zach, thank goodness." She embraced him, then frowned, drawing back to examine him as though he had been in an accident and she expected to find cuts and bruises. Seeming satisfied, her face relaxed.

"I had no idea you were part of this Wednesdays in Mississippi group. But"—he smiled at Mrs. Gray and Elizabeth—"I see you've met my other favorite lady from Chicago's North Shore."

Mrs. Gray reached out to squeeze Elizabeth's hand. "My friend Nancy Simms and Elizabeth's mother are dear friends. We've been to the COFO office and the community center and are on our way to a luncheon with some local Negro ladies at St. Paul Methodist Church. We'll be back to sit in on some afternoon classes."

Why were these ladies here? Why were the teachers from outside Mississippi? Why was her dad here? What was this place that he called "a special summer school for Negroes?" Was he telling her everything he knew? Joan couldn't put her finger on it, but she was sure there was more to it. It gave her an eerie feeling. She shuddered just as her dad arrived to take her to Big Daddy's.

As they rode, she studied her dad. Seeing him look so tired made her realize that, in some strange way, she'd actually begun to enjoy herself this morning. She'd been frightened at first, but the fear had rather quickly given way to worry over what she should be doing while everyone else moved about with a purpose. She'd felt at once conspicuous and invisible, both probably for the same reason: she was the only one of her in the school. It was when she'd let the feeling invisible take over that things had begun to get better.

"So, honey, remember your manners with Mr. Whitehead," her dad said suddenly. His voice was no longer the make-you-feel-better one. It sounded squeezed.

"Of course, Daddy."

"You know your mom and I have taught you that not saying something is a kind of lying, but . . ."

He suddenly became focused on studying the street signs. They passed a golf course and a sign for the Northwood Country Club. She watched his hands, one crossing over the other on the steering wheel as they rounded a corner. Hands that had rested firmly but gently on her shoulder or brushed away her tears.

"But you just need to know that some won't approve of my working at the school. Do you understand?"

She did not, but she nodded because she knew that's what he wanted.

Her dad turned into a circular driveway and stopped before the red brick steps that led to the French doors flanked by white columns. She got out, but moved backwards, trying to take in the entire house, its white exterior set off by carefully manicured hedges. *My word!* And here Big Daddy's rather small, simple cabin on the Neshoba County Fairgrounds had made her wonder if he was a little poor.

The doorbell was promptly answered by a Negro woman in a starched black dress with a spotless white apron. C.J. had never worn a uniform. Neither had Annabel. "Mr. Whitehead and Miz Carol are in the solarium," she said. "I'll show you there."

"Joani, I've got to hurry back to work. I'll pick you up at three-thirty." Her dad leaned down to hug her, taking a moment to rest his cheek against hers. Then he nodded to the woman and left.

The maid ushered Joan toward the back of the house and into a room nestled among loblolly pines and magnolia trees. A table was set with linen napkins tucked into napkin rings and what seemed like far too many dishes and pieces of silverware for three people. The room was comfortably cool, yet sunbeams danced through the floor-to-ceiling windows and across the parquet floor, right up to a wicker sofa where Big Daddy held court, challenging Carol to a game of checkers.

"Well, if it isn't our Joey!" he hooted. Then, "You can serve now, Trudy."

Carol jumped up and ran to give her a hug. Joan hugged back, then held Carol at arms' length. "How'd you get your hair so straight?" she asked.

"Orange juice can curlers."

"You're kidding, right?"

"Nope." Carol laughed. "You hungry?"

Big Daddy waited at the table, holding out chairs for them. Joan nodded, and they all settled themselves while the maid brought in a platter of boiled shrimp, another with corn-on-the-cob, a pitcher of sweet tea, and dishes with butter and cocktail sauce. Joan watched Big Daddy, not wanting to make a mistake. He peeled a shrimp and presented it to her with a flourish.

"You got your big birthday party all planned, Joan?"

Carol's question wiped the grin right off her face. "I—we haven't figured out an activity yet. You know we can't have it at the pool this year."

"Why not?"

"Poplar Springs closed the pool. Didn't you hear?"

"No! I've been spending lots of time in Meridian with Big Daddy."

Big Daddy grunted. "That's right. Don't you know but some trouble-making coloreds tried to get up in there, thinking that Civil Rights Act is going to change things in Mississippi. Dim-witted, the lot of 'em."

"Big Daddy, you should have heard how smart the Negroes at the school sounded this morning!" The words were out of Joan's mouth before she could stop them.

It seemed like a piece of shrimp got caught in his throat. "Negroes at what school?"

"Don't you know?" she echoed him, trying to lighten things up, even as her dad's warning rang in her head. "The special summer school for Negroes."

"You mean that Freedom School?"

"Yeah, maybe. My dad is doing some doctoring there. Helping people who can't afford it." She stuck her chin out a bit, proud of her dad for that, but worried by the look on Big Daddy's face when he said, "Is he, now?" Joan looked helplessly at Carol.

"Can we be excused, please?" Carol asked. "I want us to have time to listen to my new records."

Big Daddy's face relaxed. "Sure, y'all run on then. Have some fun before the doc gets back."

Carol led Joan up a winding staircase and down the hall to her bedroom. She hurried to the record player and held up a stack of forty-fives. "Every number one Beatles hit on *Billboard*, from 'I Want to Hold Your Hand' to 'Love Me Do.'" They listened to them all, over and over, trying out the newest dances.

"And . . ." Carol leaned down, rummaged through a box, and came up holding an album. "'The Rolling Stones.' Guess what my favorite is." She handed over the cover but ran her finger down the titles on side two, stopping at 'Carol.'"

"You're so lucky," Joan said.

"Yeah, Big Daddy buys me most anything I ask for."

Joan hoped her dad wouldn't be mad she hadn't kept her mouth shut. "Show me how you use the orange juice can rollers," she said.

All too soon, the doorbell chimed. When the maid called them, Joan and Carol straightened up the room and ran to the solarium. They stopped short just outside, to listen.

"My great-granddaughter cares about your daughter. Hell, I like you, Doc." Joan reached for Carol's hand. "Now this thing with them boys, that ain't no disappearance."

"What's he talking about?" Joan whispered.

Carol shrugged.

"It certainly ain't the Klan, or murder. It's a hoax is all. And don't nobody much care about a nigger school. If those Yankee teachers want to waste their time on dimwits, that's up to them. But I'm telling you, stay away from the adults and that voter registration business."

"I appreciate your speaking to me, sir. Now, Joan and I should be leaving." Her dad reached out to shake Big Daddy's hand as she and Carol scooted into the room.

"Thank you so much for having me, Carol and Big Daddy." Joan smiled, trying again to ease the tension.

"Anytime, Joey!" The old man winked.

The ride home was quiet at first. Joan noticed her dad's hunched shoulders and worried she'd let him down. Finally, wanting to talk, needing to talk, she did. "Daddy, this morning, Patsy got more time with you than Evelyne did. And Patsy got to go behind the screen."

"Well, Patsy—" He cleared his throat. "Had to be examined with her clothes off."

"Still, it seems like you maybe took better care of her."

"Honey, when I became a doctor, I made a promise called the Hippocratic Oath. It starts like this: *I solemnly pledge to consecrate my life to the service of humanity.*"

"Consecrate like at Communion? When Father Frank makes the bread into the body of Jesus?"

"In a way, but consecrate also means to dedicate to a divine purpose.

And here's the really important line. *I will not permit considerations of religion, nationality, race, party politics or social standing to intervene between my duty and my patient.*"

"Huh?"

"It means whether a person is Negro or white, I've promised to give them the best treatment I know how."

She thought for a while, again picturing her dad's separate waiting rooms. "What about the other stuff? Does it matter if the Negroes don't get Little Golden Books, magazines, or comfortable chairs and have to go in the back door?"

Her dad looked at her so long she worried he'd drive right off the road. Then, looking straight ahead again, he said, "Life is a series of steps in getting somewhere. If you don't take the first step, the rest don't matter. Maybe someday the other can be changed."

For some reason, Joan heard the tone in Big Daddy's voice when he said, *I'm telling you, stay away from the adults.* She wanted to talk about something happier. "I followed that boy Ben this morning, after Dr. Levinson looked at his arm. I wanted to see if he'd make more music. He got away from me, though."

She thought her dad's shoulders fell a foot and he sighed with the weight of the world. "That's James Chaney's little brother," he said. "James and two white men from New York are missing. Nobody knows for sure what happened to them."

"Oh. I could see something in his face. Like he had a light inside, but he'd lost something, too."

Her dad shot her a quick look. "Dr. Levinson told me everyone fears the worst."

"What's that mean, Daddy?"

"They may have been killed, Joani. That boy may have lost his big brother." He reached out to hold her hand.

"But Big Daddy said it was nothing."

"Yes, he did."

Once again, Joan felt invisible and conspicuous, remembered being cool in the solarium despite the rays of sunshine. "I'm sorry. I shouldn't have told Big Daddy about us being at the school. But sometimes . . . I just say what I think."

"Now, I'm proud of you for that, Joani." He patted her hand.

"I'm proud of you, too, Daddy."

CHAPTER 20

Wednesday, July 22
Promises

When the last of his Negro History students had filed from the classroom, Zach turned to Mrs. Gray, still seated at the table. She was more dressed up than he'd ever seen her. And her sunny, open face made her seem almost as young as the students. But her vibrant red hair and solicitous manner were exactly as he remembered.

She beamed at him. "Zach, dear, thank you for letting me sit in on your class. You're so good with them. And they're bright as new pennies, every single one. The thought of them so happily giving up their summer to go to school is amazing. I struggle to picture Jenny and Johnny doing that."

"I'm glad to see you, Mrs. Gray. It means a lot to all of us."

"Elizabeth said ours are the first friendly white faces she's seen in Mississippi, other than the doctors', of course." Her smile drooped slightly as she added, "I've been afraid to stop smiling."

"How was the luncheon at the church?"

"Truthfully, it was quite uncomfortable. Our Negro hostesses and all of us with WIMS were very friendly. But some of the local ladies weren't talking, whether because they were uninformed or afraid, I can't know. I had a dickens of a time with the lady I was seated next to. I put all kinds of questions to her. Had she been to the Freedom School or met any volunteers? What would she like folks in other parts of the country to know about Mississippi? She answered each question with 'I ain't in *nothing*,' until I was forced to stop asking. Another told me the Negro community was none too pleased by the COFO workers being in Meridian. I was particularly shocked by the elderly lady who told me she's been registered to vote for some fifty years and anybody who wants to vote already does."

Zach sighed.

"My friend Nancy had a little better luck. She sat between a teacher and a lady hosting one of the volunteers. The teacher was articulate and candid. She said it's not so much the violence that keeps Negroes from trying to register as it is their knowing about those who've lost their jobs because of it. The lady who hosts a summer volunteer is a maid. Her employer was worried about losing *his* job if anyone found out he knew and didn't stop her. He made her promise to say he knew nothing about it."

"The fear is like a multi-headed monster," Zach said.

She looked at him sheepishly then. "You know, I'm suddenly more able to put myself in C.J.'s shoes, how uncomfortable she must have felt—at Thanksgiving, and when I asked her to join the family for meals."

"C.J." Zach realized he was tapping out "Heart and Soul" on the table and clasped his hands together. "I understand her a little more each day."

"That's good, very good." Mrs. Gray stopped, seeming to gather her thoughts. "She and I have talked more lately, I mean on a more personal level. I think there's so much you and I don't understand about her. The pull of her family, for one thing. Her brother's become a bit much for their parents to handle. And, apparently, her father might be ill. Anyway, as soon as I get home, I'll be putting her on a bus to Poplar Springs."

Zach bolted upright.

"And Zach, dear." She stressed the word *dear*. "I'm worried she'll decide to stay in Mississippi for good, even go back to working for that awful Klansman. I asked her to promise to give herself time to find out what you two mean to each other."

"Thank you for that," he said simply.

She nodded. Then, looking like a child turning to a parent for answers, she implored him with her eyes. "I see it, Zach. I know you do, too. Mississippi, Chicago, the world—we're all one. There's so much to be done."

They were both briefly silent. He felt tired deep in his bones. Overwhelmed by what there was to do just at the school, even with willing participants. Fearful, for himself, Grandma Willie, the missing three. Curious as to whether Mrs. Gray shared the gratitude he'd expressed to C.J. for pulling him into the struggle.

"What will you do, after the summer project ends?" she asked.

"I don't know," he answered honestly. "But, yes, I see it, too."

Nancy Simms popped her head into the classroom then to let her know the group was leaving. Zach hugged Mrs. Gray as tightly as she had embraced him when they first saw each other that morning. Another in the long, short, saturated *days missing*. He counted thirty-two now.

❀　❀　❀

S till in his classroom after most everyone had left the building on Thursday evening, Zach listened to the whisk-whisk of his broom and the scratch-scratch of Charles's pencil. The small pile of dirt gathering beneath the broom looked suddenly like broken glass, reminding him of Grandma Willie and what happened at her house. She was partially right about Meridian. Even as the fate of the missing three haunted the Summer Project workers, the steady stream of reporters and FBI shielded them from what might have been: the freedom school teacher arrested in Hattiesburg, the summer volunteer shot at as he drove through Jackson, the bomb set off outside the Mileston Freedom Center. Still, he'd lain awake most of last night, worried that something terrible was about to happen. He'd kept his baseball bat by his bed and leapt up at the slightest sound.

The silence of things *not* happening in Meridian made Zach realize both his sweeping and Charles's writing had stopped. He turned to see Charles staring at him.

"You say something?"

"Yeah. You got a girl?"

"There's one I care a great deal about." In about forty-eight hours, she would be less than a hundred miles from here. But she might just as well be back in Chicago. He could no more go to her parents' house to see her than he could fly to the moon.

"She know how you feel?"

She had refused to see or speak to him before he left. "I'm not sure."

"Well, what you waiting on?"

Zach was angry at her. But if she suddenly stood before him, asking please come back, live for me as I live for my family, he knew he would. "It's complicated."

"But—"

He held up his hand. "We talking about me or you? Have you let Rosalee know how you feel?"

"I'm thinking on it." Charles twirled his pencil like a baton. "She's been talking to me real nice since I've come to some classes."

"I've seen her take notice myself. So, what are *you* waiting for?"

"I reckon she's always gonna be way smarter than me. And her family's better off. Her father's the head janitor up at the high school. My daddy's a farm hand, and my momma and sisters clean houses." He went to the window and hoisted himself onto the sill. "You ever know it to work out, between people so different?"

"Well, first of all, book smarts aren't the only kind. But you've come along so fast. I can picture you going to college, doing important work, having a family, being someone others look up to. Others like Rosalee."

Charles was leaning toward him as if pulled by the force of the possibility. "And second of all?" The boy put a hand to his mouth to cover his broad grin but couldn't hide the sparkle in his eyes.

Zach had tried to get C.J. to take a class, go after something for herself. "Forget differences," he said a little too sharply, trying to shake off thoughts of her, his stubborn belief that they really weren't different at all. "What makes a relationship is being able to say anything to each other."

"You think I should tell Rosalee?"

"I think you should aim for the best, in love and life."

"I think you should tell her, too."

"Who?"

"The one you think is the best."

Together they rearranged the chairs. "Thanks," Zach said, meaning it in more ways than one. "I'll see you tomorrow."

"I—could you help me with one more thing before I go?"

Zach checked his watch and nodded. Charles pulled out the book he'd loaned him a few days earlier. *The Mis-Education of the Negro*, by Dr. Carter G. Woodson. Admittedly, it was a ridiculous response, but he hadn't known what else to do when Charles looked at him with his searching emerald eyes. "Why you think some folks want educating and some don't?" the boy had asked. "I got someone I got to talk with about it." Zach had been helpless as to how to explain he didn't think it was about wanting at all.

"I been staying up late nights, studying this."

"Yeah?" Zach bent to straighten a chair.

"I started with what you're always telling us Dr. Woodson talked about. You know, 'bout making a person feel like they belong at the back door?"

Zach nodded, recalling the passage from the book. *When you control a man's thinking you do not have to worry about his actions . . .*

"While I was hunting for them words, I got to reading."

Charles wasn't a strong reader, and Dr. Woodson's book was scholarly. The boy must have worked hard.

"I found this." Charles pointed to a passage Zach had underlined. "I can't figure some parts, but I got me a thought on what it all means to say." Zach listened, hope teetering like a baby considering its second step. "Now if you could just help me learn to read this right."

They put their heads together and worked until Charles felt confident. Zach touched him on the shoulder. "You've done amazing work with this book—and with the time you've been able to be here at the school. Is there any way you could be here fulltime?"

Charles pursed his lips. "Well," he said finally. "That's what this is about, me needing to convince my sister and brother-in-law. They're set against it."

"Can I help somehow? Maybe talk with them?"

"Oh, no, thank you kindly. They wouldn't cotton to that. But—my other sister is coming on Tuesday. She's the one in the family who fixes things. She'll help me. She just has to."

Zach was in the process of standing, but he sat back down in his chair, hard. He put a name on it then, the sense of familiarity he'd felt since the first day he and Charles talked. It was C.J. This boy's eyes held the same intensity hers had when she begged him not to say he was going to Mississippi for her. And her brother was named Charlie. His heart raced as he considered that *this* might be C.J.'s Charlie. But for now at least, he couldn't bring himself to complicate things by asking.

❊   ❊   ❊

C.J. and her daddy waited at the bus stop up the hill from the Evanses' house. They'd left early and walked slowly, but Daddy was bent over with his hands on his knees, working to catch his breath. When the bus arrived, they climbed onboard and deposited their fares.

She caught herself about to steer her father into the first available seat but instead kept on down the aisle. *So much has changed*, Mrs. Gray had reminded her, right before she hugged her goodbye at the Chicago bus station. Right before she made her promise again to keep an open mind about a relationship with Zach. Well, the white faces sitting up front on this Poplar Springs city bus said not even the Civil Rights Act amounted to a hill of beans. Her daddy was sick—how sick, nobody knew—and still he had to move to the back of the bus.

They passed all the old familiar sights on their way to Doc Barnes's office on the outskirts of downtown Poplar Springs. C.J. hadn't even considered going to the Negro doctor. He'd seen the family through several emergencies, including Charlie's broken arm and Daddy's bout with pneumonia, and worked his fee out in trade. But it had taken less than twenty-four hours back home for instinct to tell her Daddy needed more than what the kind old man could offer. After sitting next to her daddy yesterday as he tried not to cough during services at Hope Baptist, hearing her momma admit at supper that his cough had been hanging on for months, and getting angry when he lit up a cigarette and sent himself into a coughing fit, she'd made him promise to see Doc Barnes.

Thankfully, the bus deposited them right in front of the two-story brown brick office. They followed the sidewalk around the building and entered through the red door. "Thank y'all for getting Daddy in," C.J. leaned across the desk to whisper. There'd been no appointment available when she called first thing this morning, but she'd pressed the receptionist to ask Doc Barnes if he could see them while she was in town. Now, she and her father were shown straight into an exam room.

The door opened before too long. "C.J., it's good to see you again." Doc Barnes held out his hand to her daddy. "Mr. Evans, I'm pleased to meet you, although I'm sorry to hear from your daughter that you're not feeling well."

"Thank you kindly. She's always said good things about y'all." Daddy smiled, but the talking had started him coughing.

Doc Barnes took his medical history, then proceeded to examine him, getting a blood pressure reading and listening with his stethoscope. Even C.J. could tell from across the room that her daddy's breathing didn't seem right. She kicked herself again for not asking questions the last time she was home. Reassured by her momma's letters, she'd let her worry slip into the background and gone on with her life in Chicago. She hung her head at her selfishness.

"C.J.," Doc Barnes said. "Would you and your father be able to go on to the hospital from here?"

Her hand flew to her chest. "Does Daddy have to stay in the hospital?"

"No, I'd just like to get an X-ray taken while you're here. I can call over there and get everything set up for you."

"Yessir, then." She worked to keep the alarm from sounding in her voice.

"Now, when might we know the results?" her daddy asked. C.J. could see the worry on his face.

"That will take several days. I'll call when I hear from the radiologist."

Once again, she would be in one place when she needed to be in another. "My sister Metairie is expecting me in Meridian tomorrow. Could you call me there?" She gave Doc Barnes the number, thanked him again for fitting them in, and helped her father outside to wait for the bus.

The next afternoon, Metairie kept up a running guided tour of Meridian as she drove from the bus station toward her house. But with George Jr. squirming in her arms and little Anna standing on the floor in the back, trying to see over the front seat and jabbering away in her ear, C.J. wasn't really paying attention.

"See that building there? That's the old Baptist Seminary." Metairie was reaching across the front seat to poke her in the arm.

C.J. looked up to see kids on the playground. They were dressed as if for school in the middle of summer. She tensed so noticeably that the baby looked up at her curiously.

"They call it a Freedom School," Metairie went on. "College students are running it. Troublemakers coming in here from all over, with this civil rights group called the Council of Federated Organizations. You heard of it?"

"I reckon." She had her eyes peeled, searching for Zach, but couldn't figure why Metairie would know or care about the Freedom School.

"Charlie is up in that awful place this very minute. Excuse me, *Charles*, as he now insists on being addressed."

"What?" C.J. nearly shouted. "Charlie in school? But your letter said George was getting him on with the city."

"I know. It's just part-time, after work. But don't that beat all, him finally wanting to go to school and picking this one? They call it a Freedom School. But we gonna be slaves again, I just know it, if you can't talk some sense into that boy."

C.J. could scarcely believe what she was hearing. Her temples began to throb as Metairie pulled up in front of her house. All the houses on this street were small and close together, but their paint looked fresh and the yards were tended to. They got the kids and her suitcase inside.

"Y'all c'mon in here," Metairie said. "I ain't found the time to get your room made up."

Anna had a firm grip on C.J.'s skirt, and George Jr. had fallen asleep. C.J. glanced left and right as she followed Metairie through the living room. A floral rug, worn but still presentable, graced the hardwood floor. Voile curtains danced at the windows. A sofa and chair, both plain but seemingly new, faced a television on the opposite wall.

The kitchen was uncluttered, but a few dirty dishes were stacked in the sink and a half-eaten bowl of pablum sat on the highchair tray. The room opposite Metairie's and George's held a crib and things that looked like Charlie's. The room across the hall from the bathroom looked like a little girl's. It was tidy, up until the moment Anna released her hold on C.J. and began dragging toys out and depositing them everywhere.

"This is a fine house, girl," C.J. said. "Y'all are passing Momma and Daddy by in that regard."

Metairie smiled. "My man is very responsible. He saved his money for a down payment all the time we was courting. But we got a mighty big mortgage to pay." She sighed heavily.

Still holding the baby, C.J. watched as Metairie began changing the sheets on the bed, making up a pallet for Anna on the floor, and complaining about Charlie. "You'd think he'd be grateful, being able to stay with us and save money from the good job George got him. But he wants more, he says."

C.J. was still reeling from the twin shocks of Charlie being in the Freedom School and so close to Zach. "What you mean?"

"Here I am, thinking he's going to help out around here, pull his weight. But every single day after work, he's up at that school doing heaven knows what. And Wednesdays when he's off, he's up in there for the entire day."

"Well," C.J. ventured. "Isn't the reason he's with y'all in the first place because he wanted to drop out of school?"

For a moment, she'd had the ridiculous thought that Charlie might somehow be safer because Zach was there. But Metairie's withering look brought her back to reality.

"Listen at you, Miz Yankee know-it-all. We got his mind off all that and onto a good job, with George setting him an example. I got a fence

I intended on him whitewashing and a long list of chores. Ain't none of them getting the time of day."

With the bed made, Metairie stomped off toward the kitchen. C.J. gently laid George Jr. in his crib. "What can I do to help with supper?" she asked when she found Metairie yanking things from the refrigerator.

"It ain't supper that needs your attention, C.J. The well being of my family is at stake. Charlie's going along with not wearing his work uniform to the school anymore, but everything else I say is falling on deaf ears. If George's boss finds out about Charlie being at the Freedom School—" She slapped a hand to her chest, inhaled, and slowly exhaled. "He could take away both their jobs. And the bank could cancel our mortgage. We wouldn't just not be able to help Momma and Daddy with the stress of having Charlie for a son, we'd be moving back into their house!"

"We should talk about Momma and Daddy." She hated to make things worse, but Metairie needed to know, especially since Doc Barnes could be calling with news on the X-ray.

Metairie listened, chopping vegetables with a newfound vengeance. "Daddy so bad you got to take him to a white doctor? Lord, that settles it!" she said. "We can't send Charlie back to them right now. You got to tell him he can't be going to that school no more."

The front door opened, and in walked Charlie. Anna bounded down the hall screaming, "Uncle Cha-cha!" He grabbed her hand and began leading them through the steps of the dance. She gazed up at him like a woman in love.

C.J. couldn't help smiling, but Charlie could read the look in her eyes. He patted his niece's head and held out his arms to C.J.

"Hey, Charles," Metairie said stiffly as he kissed her cheek.

"Y'all started without me, I see," he said. C.J. was struck by the calm determination in his voice. "Okay if I say a few things, then?"

His sisters nodded.

"C.J., Metairie and George say we got to put this to you. I'm asking to go to the Freedom School fulltime. Not that I ain't grateful for the job George got me. It *was* more than I could've asked for. Y'all know I never did see much point in schooling. But this summer changed things, on account of a special teacher and someone else special I wanted to get to know. You got to meet the both of 'em, C.J."

"Oh, baby boy, I can't be going up to that school. You can't ask me to do that." She wrung her hands.

"You scared? C.J., I ain't never known you to be afraid."

"'Course she's scared," Metairie said with a snort. "Same as George and me are and you *should* be. I hear things, you know. Them Chaney kids, the little one and the sisters, are up there. You got Yankees coming and going. The police bother the ones at the COFO office. It's just a matter of time 'til they be coming into that school, too."

"Can't you just make do with going after work and on Wednesdays?" C.J. said. The pain she saw in his eyes then seemed greater than what she was feeling.

"What we're arguing about—well, it ain't about not dropping out of school no more. I'm gonna finish high school for sure. And, C.J., you been planning on me going to college, but that was *your* dream."

She opened her mouth, but he held up his hand to stop her. "I've been learning at that school this summer. One thing is why some folks got the dream and some don't. If you could come tomorrow, you could see for yourself. We're having an assembly to talk about our dreams. You could hear about *my* dream."

With everything in her, she wanted to avoid that. But his look had become that of a twelve-year-old boy. "Just tomorrow," she said weakly.

"And you got to promise whatever C.J. says goes," Metairie chimed in.

"Fair enough," Charlie said.

CHAPTER 21

Wednesday, July 29
I Have a Dream

The sun rode low in the sky, casting long shadows as C.J. and Charlie set out on foot for the Freedom School. She jumped at each and every one, seeing a hooded Klansman here, a dishonest policeman there, or—worse, still—Zach. At the school, she saw the students milling around outside, in the yard and on the steps, looking like so many giants. But, no, they weren't actually taller than kids she'd gone to Booker T. with. It was the way these kids stood, proud and erect. She searched their eyes for dullness and resignation but saw only the bright lights of hope and enthusiasm.

Right away, a girl approached them. Hair worn longer than most and a dress that suggested Meridian's equivalent of The Mademoiselle distinguished her from the others even before C.J. saw the look of adoration on Charlie's face.

"Hey, Charles," the girl said, touching his arm. "You ready for the assembly?"

"I sure am." He shuffled his feet, took the girl's hand, then reached for C.J.'s. "C.J., *this* is Rosalee." He spoke very earnestly. "She's . . . my girl."

Searching their eyes—Rosalee's, then Charlie's—C.J. was certain the two of them were in love and right together. A sob, bittersweet and tinged with envy, caught in her throat. "Now, I surely can see why you'd be wanting to get to know this lovely girl, baby b—Charles. Rosalee, I hope we'll get to know each other."

"Charles and I hoped you would come today," Rosalee said. "If I can answer any questions or show you around, just ask." She smiled at Charlie and moved away to talk with some of the other girls.

C.J. hadn't found a way to tell Charlie about Zach last night. Now, as she followed her brother into the school, she tried to put a name on how she was feeling. The closest thing she could compare to was the day she'd walked into the Powell home in Skokie, exhausted from a day on one bus after another, an inexperienced Negro girl at the mercy of white strangers, about to get a glimpse into her future.

Charlie's first class was French. He introduced her to Elizabeth Nadler. It was strange seeing Elizabeth after reading her letter, almost as if she'd been spying. It was stranger still being in a class taught by a white teacher. But C.J. laughed with delight when she realized the class was singing "Old MacDonald." By the third stanza, she had figured out where to insert the name of the animal and begun singing along, though quietly for fear of getting it wrong.

She and Charlie moved on to a class called "Freedom and the Negro in America." The teacher, a pale, wiry man from San Francisco named Jacob, seemed delighted by her presence. He said the class had been talking about the problems of the Negro in Mississippi and it would be good for them to hear about the problems of the Negro in the North. "Would you be willing to say a few words?"

She waved her hands in resistance, but Charlie pressed. "Please, C.J." She sighed and nodded at Jacob.

"Excellent," he said. "Let's start with a song, to help us think about what we mean when we say we want freedom." He led them in "Freedom Is a Constant Struggle."

C.J. didn't know the words. But the melody sprang naturally from her soul, familiar, as so many of the freedom songs would be, from years of singing in church. Though the children's voices wrapped around the words and lifted them up, she felt herself sinking into the loneliness she often felt when arguing with Flo and Zach about freedom. *The Montgomery bus boycott led to the Supreme Court outlawing the city's segregation laws*, he'd said that first time in Harry's Deli. *In effect, they declared segregation on city buses illegal everywhere.*

Zach saw freedom as an ever-expanding circle, like a balloon that could be blown up bigger and bigger without bursting. C.J. saw freedom as the size of a human heart, never bigger or smaller. *They said that about schools a long time ago, and Greyhound buses and the like*, she'd said. *I guess what they say doesn't mean much in Mississippi.*

Jacob gestured then to let C.J. know the floor was hers. She told the students that she was a live-in domestic and, on weekends, shared an apartment near the University of Chicago with five other girls.

"That sounds like fun!" said a couple of kids in unison.

"Well, sure. Spending time with friends is fun. There's a part of Chicago called the South Side where we like to go. It's near about as big as Meridian, I reckon, and the stores and restaurants are all owned by Negroes." The kids gasped. "But six days a week, I'm living and working in a white family's home, feeling like the only Negro on earth."

"You get paid any more than a maid in Mississippi?" one girl asked.

"Yes, and the stores will take our money same as white folks'. But I don't make enough to ever buy a house like the ones I've worked in. And no white homeowner would sell to me in such a neighborhood, even if I could afford to buy."

"Why'd you move on up there?" asked another student.

"I'm making money so I can come home and help my family toward a better life." She thought of Buddy Corrigan but held her ground on admitting the whole truth.

"We got plenty of problems, mind you," she continued. She talked of the amusement park for whites only, where Negro men were hired to egg on the crowd until someone dunked them. And the Freedom Day school boycott less than a year ago, when Chicago Negroes protested, to little avail, the overcrowding and underfunding of their schools.

Even as she was busy thinking of negatives about the North, she couldn't help remembering being in Wooded Park with Zach. He'd bemoaned the slowness of change. She'd told him he was wrong, that everything had changed because she was up a tree with him.

She shook her head sadly as she spoke of her friend Flo, the dreamer who longed for *a better Alabama, where I can vote and make decent money, where crow is forever out of season.* "Even Flo admits she's longing for something that may never be." She looked around the room. "What I always say is, folks got to stop asking for freedom and know we get that from inside."

❁   ❁   ❁

Joan turned the handle of the mimeograph machine in the tiny office next to the kitchen. She'd cut the stencil herself, student compositions titled "I Have a Dream," selected by the teachers to be read during the third-period all-school assembly. She'd checked and double-checked the stencil and was certain there was not a single mistake. It was painstaking work, typing without making a mistake. You couldn't fix it with correcting fluid like you could regular paper. You simply had to start all over again. But she liked the feel of the crank turning in her hand, the sight of all those copies, edges aligned, waiting to be handed out in the auditorium—the responsibility.

Today was her second time accompanying her dad to the Freedom School. He'd felt so good about helping out here that he'd decided to close his office all day every Wednesday for the rest of the summer. She'd protested more loudly this time than the first, complaining she didn't know what to do with herself while she was there. It made her mad when he suggested she have a little patience and an idea would come to her. Amazingly, he'd been right.

They'd arrived this morning to find Elizabeth in a tizzy because she hadn't finished cutting the stencil and had to teach her classes. Her long hair, dark like Joan's, was held back in a ponytail, but damp tendrils framed her face.

"I can do it," Joan had said proudly. "My Girl Scout troop has helped put together lots of bulletins for St. Stephen's. I'm actually the best at it, if I do say so myself."

Elizabeth had gushed with gratitude as she handed Joan the stack of compositions still to be typed.

"Why are they all called 'I Have a Dream?' "

"Martin Luther King's speech."

Elizabeth's answer suggested that that explained everything. But Joan had stared blankly. What could the man she'd heard described as a trouble-making—she edited out the n-word in her thoughts—preacher have to do with this?

"There should be a copy around somewhere," Elizabeth said.

Joan studied her as she searched the office, wondering if Elizabeth was Zach's girlfriend or just a friend. If she got closer to Elizabeth, maybe she could get closer to Zach.

"Dr. King gave this brilliant speech last summer at the March on Washington for Jobs and Freedom. Zach and some of the others were actually there to see him." Joan couldn't decide whether the admiration in Elizabeth's voice was for Dr. King or Zach, but she'd ask Zach about this march if she ever got the chance. "Some say this speech helped get the Civil Rights Act passed."

"Yes, of course," Joan mumbled, remembering her ruined birthday party.

"Here you go." Elizabeth held out several stapled pages. "Now I've got to run to class. Thanks again!"

Joan cranked out the last copy of the students' compositions, sighing with relief that the stencil hadn't torn. Job completed, with twenty minutes to spare before the assembly! She sat down again at the typewriter, wondering what to do until then, and noticed the copy of Dr. King's speech. She picked it up and began to read.

The language seemed a little high and mighty, not what she would have expected from a Negro preacher. She paused on the line about the Negro still not being free, wondering why Negroes kept talking like slavery was still around. She'd heard them singing about it here: *And before I'll be a slave, I'll be buried in my grave . . .*

This man must like to talk, Joan thought as she plodded through the first half of his speech. She was surprised to hear him mention whites who were at the march, then recalled Elizabeth saying Zach had been there.

She squirmed in her chair as she read about "Whites Only" signs stealing dignity from Negro children, thinking of the time she'd talked Carol into trying the water from the colored fountain in Highland Park and the separate water fountains all over Poplar Springs—in the A&P, the courthouse, and the library. She wondered who decided Negroes in Mississippi couldn't vote.

Finally, he got around to his dream, which he said came from the American dream. Her dad talked about the American dream. *In America, everyone can make their life better by working hard*, he always said.

Martin Luther King's dream went on and on. There, another mention of Mississippi. And another. He mentioned other states, mostly all in the South, but none as often as Mississippi. Why?

Even more often than Mississippi, Dr. King mentioned freedom, right down to the very last words of his speech. Joan was shaking her head when one of the older Negro boys appeared in the doorway.

"Hey. You're Joan, right?" he said. "I'm Charles. Elizabeth sent me to get the copies."

He took a step into the room, revealing a woman behind him. At first, Joan thought she was seeing double. Charles and this woman stood shoulder to shoulder, had the same slender build. She felt off balance as she looked up into the woman's face, not quite to her eyes. The woman was smiling, so she dared to look higher. Green eyes just like Charles's.

"Oh, and let me introduce y'all. Joan, this here's my sister C.J. C.J., Joan is Doc Barnes's daughter. He's running the free clinic here at the school."

The years since C.J. said goodbye seemed to whirl away like leaves in an autumn wind. Joan stared, wanting only to be called "little friend" again.

"Joan and I go way back," C.J. said.

Joan thought C.J.'s eyes twinkled. This was definitely her face. But she wasn't as skinny as she used to be. And she'd gotten even prettier.

"Well, what do you know?" Charles looked at his watch. "I've got to get on stage. Joan, could you sit with C.J. at the assembly?"

Joan nodded, and he left. C.J. had her head tilted now, as if studying her. Just the way Joan remembered, C.J.'s face was at once open and secretive, not giving too much of anything away. For some reason, she also remembered C.J. saying something about being strong, with a mind of her own. She still did not know what that meant.

"Well," C.J. said finally. "I don't know where to go, and I got to get a good seat to watch my brother. Can you show me?"

She was still standing outside the room. Joan looked at her feet, then at C.J.'s, then at the line that separated linoleum from the wood of the hallway. She suddenly saw the seam in her driveway, the "magic line" she was not supposed to cross back when she was three. She would have to step over the line today, though, wouldn't she?

"This way," she said.

＊　＊　＊

C.J. sat anxiously beside Joan Barnes, waiting for the assembly to begin. Her pocketbook rested in her lap while she tried to keep her head down and scan the crowd for Zach at the same time. Why hadn't it occurred to her last night to ask Charlie about his teachers? It wasn't until he began taking her around to his classes that she'd begun to worry she would walk into a room and find herself facing Zach in front of other people. Now Zach was somewhere in this auditorium, among the teachers and well over a hundred students.

The chatter among the audience faded to murmurs as one of the teachers walked onto the stage, where those selected to read portions of their compositions were seated. When Jacob clapped his hands and shouted, "Freedom, freedom, freedom," everyone fell silent.

"I guess everyone knows we've been listening to Martin Luther King's 'I Have a Dream' speech in some of the classes. More than two hundred thousand people heard Dr. King give this speech in Washington last August. Thousands more watched on TV. The speech was historic because it showed that Negroes have dreams and aren't afraid to tell the world what those dreams are. The teachers asked you all to share your dreams. The younger kids drew fantastic pictures. You can see them taped to the wall all along the hallway. The older kids wrote essays. Now, six of them are going to share what they wrote with the whole school." Jacob gestured toward the center of the stage.

C.J. shifted and stretched. There were Charlie, Rosalee, and four kids she did not know.

A girl stood first. "I'm Lynette," she said shyly before turning her attention to her paper and reading hesitantly. "This summer we've been learning that we're smarter than we thought. Not just us kids, but all kinds of Negroes. There have been Negro scientists like Dr. George Washington Carver for many years now. One day, if lots of our dreams come true, there could even be a Negro president. But my favorite to learn about was poets like Langston Hughes, Countee Cullen, and Gwendolyn Brooks. They made me dream I could be a poet, too. I dreamed so hard that I wrote my very first poem. It's called 'I Didn't Know.' I also dreamed I could read my poem in front of a big crowd like Martin Luther King did. So, here goes."

Lynette dropped the hand with the paper to her side and looked around the room as she recited from memory. Her voice was suddenly strong. "I didn't know my people, how smart we are, what we have done, what we can do. I didn't know my rights, how much like everyone else's they are, what responsibility they bring, what that means I must do. I didn't know my skin, how to love it, what to feel about it, what to do in it. But in the Freedom School, I learned to dream, and now I think I know."

A tall, broad-shouldered boy, looking very serious, was the next to step forward. "I'm Jackson. My daddy was a soldier. He fought next to white men, but when he came home he got treated same as before. I have a dream that I can be a soldier. Like my daddy, but different because I'll be fighting for a country where my rights are the same as white soldiers." He looked down then and shuffled his feet. "I used to dream there was people interested in what I think and schools where asking questions don't get you in trouble." When he looked up again, an impish grin had taken over his face. "Now I already got one dream come true!"

"Hi, I'm Theo," said the third student, a cheerful-looking, bright-eyed boy. "I love to eat." He laughed nervously but seemed to relax when the kids laughed with him. "I dream about never being hungry because I can go in any.restaurant I see, right through the front door, and sit down to eat."

C.J. glanced at Joan, whose attention was firmly fixed on Theo. Did it surprise her to hear that Theo would like to be able to eat where she ate? She wondered that and so much more.

Joan sat with the same ladylike posture C.J. remembered from the last time she'd seen her. On that summer night five years ago, Joan had been fresh from her bath and wearing her baby-doll pajamas. C.J. was still reeling then from the disappointment of being ordered to serve lemonade to her friends. She couldn't quite forgive the child, yet she couldn't fully blame her either. She'd told her as gently as she could that she was leaving for Chicago. Joan had worried they'd never see each other again. And, now, here they were sitting side by side once more. The magic girls, just like C.J. had said. And, just as on that night, she could only wonder what they would each do.

"You see," Theo continued. "All I really want is freedom. Jacob told us having a dream isn't about pie in the sky. But I think maybe freedom is like a pie, a pie so big that white folks could share it and still have enough not to feel hungry themselves."

"My name's Annie," said the girl who followed Theo. She was thin and angular, almost as hard-edged as her words. Her hands gripped the sides of her paper as she read, never looking up. "I had a dream about Negroes and whites together, being friends and whatnot, anywhere in America. And nobody saying nothing stupid. Like look over yonder at that white man and nigger gal. Let's kill the both of them."

C.J. began to tremble, hearing Zach as clearly as if he suddenly stood behind her and spoke into her ear. *I'm going to fight for a world where we can be whatever we want to be to each other.*

The next to speak was Charlie's beautiful girl. "I'm Rosalee," she said. "My daddy got very sick once and had to go to the hospital. They put him down in the basement. Do you know what all is in the basement? There's cockroaches and rats that scurry about, even with the lights on. There's the boiler that heats the water and the pipes that carry it upstairs to the nice rooms where the white people go to be sick. I have a dream of freedom for anybody who has to get sick to be able to go to the nice part of the hospital."

Sweet Jesus, don't let my daddy have to be down in the basement with the rats, C.J. prayed.

And then Rosalee broke out in glorious song. Line by line, one student at a time joined her in "Come and Go with Me to That Land," singing of the day when there would be no Jim Crow or burning churches, until their powerful young voices, creating a crescendo of conviction, concluded with, "There'll be freedom in that land where I'm bound."

At last, it was Charlie's turn. He waited patiently for the voices to subside. Standing tall and proud, he said, "My name is Charles. I came to Meridian because my brother-in-law got me work on a garbage truck. That was plenty good enough for me. I never did see much point in schooling."

C.J. thought about how hard the entire family had pushed Charlie about school. Would she have to be satisfied—if he couldn't see his way clear to share the dream she had for him—with the high school diploma that would thrill their momma?

"I came to this school the first time because I saw a beautiful girl sitting out in the yard under the oak tree. It's one crazy school for sure." He shook his head. "The teachers say the main thing we're learning isn't reading or arithmetic or any of that. It's how to question."

C.J. shook her head, too. Where was Charlie going to need that in a world such as this?

"I came back because a teacher kept asking me to. This special teacher is named Zach."

C.J. gripped the strap of her pocketbook.

"So, I started thinking on questions. And one came to me. Wonder how come some folks want educating and some don't? Zach loaned me this here book called *The Mis-Education of the Negro,* by a man name of Dr. Woodson." Charlie held it high, then opened it and began to read.

"*If we had a few thinkers we could expect great achievements on tomorrow.*" His voice was deep and strong. "*Some Negro with unusual insight would write an epic of bondage and freedom which would take its place with those of Homer and Virgil."*

C.J. was so proud of the way he was reading. Slowly and carefully, but with feeling.

"Some Negro with es—es-the-tic appreciation would construct from collected fragments of Negro music a grand opera that would move humanity to repentance. Some Negro of phil-o-soph-ic pen-e-tra-tion would find a solace for the modern world in the soul of the Negro, and then—"

Charlie closed the book. C.J. held her breath along with everyone else.

"Men would be men because they are men."

He grinned at his sniffling audience. "Any of y'all wants help making out parts of what I read, y'all see me later."

C.J.'s laughter mingled with that of the crowd, appreciating Charlie's joke and his right to call himself Charles.

"So, what's that got to do with a dream?" He searched the audience until he found her. "I'm set on going to college. Because I learned any man's hope is in education. Even ours. And what I reckon is important is that going to college has become *my* dream."

Her eyes brimmed with tears. She assumed the assembly was done and hurriedly dug in her purse for a handkerchief. The six kids on the stage shouted out in unison, "What do *you* dream, Jacob?"

He looked startled, seemed to take a long moment to think. "I guess I'm like all of you. I have one dream that's already come true—having bright, enthusiastic students who have good questions and dare to ask them. But I have a dream that I'm not a white man, at least not where that means you have to yessir me, or you automatically respect or hate me. I dream that everyone, Negro and white, will see me as an individual."

C.J. sat back in her chair and frowned. Here was a white man talking about feeling like she did about Mrs. Gray and Zach wanting to get to know a Negro, not her. She suddenly remembered Zach in the girls' Hyde Park apartment—getting testy when they'd all expected him to know what she should do about Mrs. Gray's Thanksgiving invitation, just because he was the white person in the room—and softened.

The audience stood, applauding, then began to disperse. The hand on her arm then could only have been Zach's. She did not even need to turn to know.

His hair was longer, his shoulders broader. His eyes were . . . always so gentle. Those eyes, they pulled at her now, almost fiercely, as if he'd been dying of thirst and found water.

She felt a force, like a powerful magnet or the wind off Lake Michigan, connecting them physically, trying to move them closer and closer until there was nothing between them, not even air. He led her down the hall, into a small room. Held a chair for her, then sat so close his knees touched hers. She tried in vain to separate their knees or make her eyes look away.

Casting about desperately for something to say, she blurted, "Did you know Charles was my brother?"

"It seems silly now, but no."

"Same last name?"

He shook his head, a grin tugging at his lips. "Well, since he didn't register, I never did learn his last name."

"You really had no idea? Most folks say Charlie's the spitting image of me." She was teasing him now and beginning to enjoy it. How had she ever wished she could avoid him?

❊   ❊   ❊

When C.J. walked away with Zach, Joan was left alone with her awkwardness. She'd smiled up at him, and he hadn't even noticed her. C.J. had left without a word. The students had scattered to the winds for lunch. Not sure where to go or what to do next, Joan wandered into the kitchen.

The woman there was the oldest person she'd ever seen, even older than Big Daddy, judging by the lines in her face. If the Barneses' ancient maid Annabelle had ten wrinkles, this woman surely had a hundred. Yet, surrounded by oversized pots and pans, she reminded Joan of Shirley in the cafeteria at St. Stephen's. Shirley made the best sweet rolls under the sun.

The smells in the kitchen told Joan this woman must be a mighty fine cook, too.

"Hey." The woman had spotted her. She was about to turn away, but the voice was friendly. "You must be Doc Barnes's daughter, hmm?" The woman had a great big smile, appearing to wink at her when the sunlight glanced off her gold tooth.

"Yes, ma'am. My name's Joan."

"Well, then, Joan. Folks call me Grandma Willie. Would you mind helping me out? The teachers will be in here ready to fix themselves plates shortly. I got no one to help me today, 'cause they all in a meeting with the principal."

"What can I do?" Joan went to the sink to wash her hands.

"The coleslaw is waiting in the ice box, and the collard greens are just ready to be dipped out of the pot. I got to keep my eye on the chicken so's I can turn it. But I need to put together my special sweet rolls, and that's where you come in."

Joan's mom made the kind out of the can. But Negroes must just know how to make them better. She could hardly believe her luck. She was quite possibly about to discover Shirley's secret.

Grandma Willie pulled a huge bowl from the oven. "Here's the dough. We got to punch it down and roll it out. You want to have at it?"

Joan hesitated, hating to disturb the puffy, sweet-smelling mound.

"Make a fist and give it a good smack."

She did as she was told, then grinned. "That was fun!"

Grandma Willie smiled and guided her in rolling out the dough on a floured board and brushing it with melted butter. "You do seem a far sight happier now that you're busy," she said casually.

Before Joan knew it, she was telling Grandma Willie about C.J. How they hadn't seen each other in five years and the awful way she'd treated her back then. How C.J. probably didn't even remember it, much less that she used to call Joan her little friend, seeing as how she'd gone off to talk with Zach without so much as a goodbye. How Joan needed to talk to her, tell her she was sorry even if she didn't remember it.

"Listen up, child," Grandma Willie said. "This here's my secret about sweet rolls."

Joan's eyes opened wide, and she bounced slightly on the balls of her feet.

"Most recipes you'll ever see call for cinnamon in the filling. Just cinnamon, no other spice. I add a little allspice and nutmeg and—most important of all—a dash of love."

They spread the filling, rolled the rectangle into a jellyroll, and sliced it. They mixed the brown sugar, butter, corn syrup, and nuts and spread that in the bottom of a huge baking pan.

"I think you're right to talk to this C.J., baby," Grandma Willie said. "It ain't never gonna hurt to say you done wrong and you're sorry. Just like it ain't never gonna hurt to add a dash of love."

"Grandma Willie? Is this your regular job, cooking and all? I mean like in a school cafeteria. You're awful good at it, but you're kind of old to still be working." Joan clamped her hand over her mouth then, embarrassed by having said "old."

"I'm old indeed. Near about as old as Jesus." Grandma Willie laughed at her joke. "But this ain't a job like getting paid. It's what some folks call a labor of love. Kind of like the teachers. They're not getting paid either. Everybody's just doing what they do 'cause it needs doing and it's right."

Together they placed each roll in the pan, covered the pan, and set it in the oven. "We'll just let that rise, then bake them rolls while the teachers are eating. They gonna be delicious!" This time Grandma Willie winked for real.

Joan helped get the rest of the food set out just at the teachers began to file in. She fixed herself a plate to take into the tiny office next door. She had some thinking to do. Before she left, she said she'd be back to help clean up, and she thanked Grandma Willie for her secrets.

The office had a U.S. map on one wall. She stared at it as she ate, imagining all the places the teachers were from. And then it came to her. She would organize a lunch for the lunch ladies at the Freedom School. It would be a secret. She'd ask each teacher to make a food known in their part of the country. And, since they weren't getting paid either, she'd find a way to help pay for the ingredients. Joan smiled then, knowing she'd found her service project for the Marian Award and, thus, found her place at the Freedom School.

❊ ❊ ❊

In the small room, behind a closed door, Zach fought against himself. He wanted desperately to take C.J. in his arms and kiss her, a kiss that would make it clear that he loved her. The dangers that suffused this summer made it seem all the more important that she know this.

She hadn't shrunk from his hand on her arm as he led her here or moved away when their knees touched, and that was encouraging. Yet the Summer Project's unequivocal rule against interracial dating stopped him now. Were he a Negro and she white, he could be killed. His being white and her Negro would sound echoes of white men able to have a Negro woman whenever they wanted. Coming to Mississippi had forced him to see that it was all more complicated than he'd thought back in Chicago.

"Really?" she asked again, the gleam in her eye getting stronger. "You couldn't tell Charlie was my brother the minute you laid eyes on him?"

She was teasing him mercilessly now. He blushed furiously.

"You've always spoken of your brother as Charlie. And, of course, there's Charlie Parker. I guess, for the longest time, it just didn't occur to me your high school-age brother could be in Meridian. But I always sensed something when I was around him, especially when I looked at his eyes. And when Mrs. Gray told me you were coming home and Charles told me his other sister was coming, well . . . He said his other sister could fix it so he could attend fulltime, that she was the one in the family who fixes things."

Zach watched a shadow of pain cross C.J.'s face. "Coming to this school is complicated," she said.

"C.J.," he interrupted, wondering whether she meant complicated for her or Charles. "You don't seem as angry as the last time we saw each other. Are you?" He let hope sound in his voice.

"Truth be told, I'm too confused to be angry right now." She sighed. "Charlie and Metairie got me between a rock and a hard place, with the both of them expecting me to support their position."

"I have to admit I really don't know what the conflict is about. I asked if it would help if I talked to the family."

She gave him the same look Charles had, as if he were a child who had said something innocently funny. "I got to thank you for what you've done with Charlie. College has always been *my* dream for him. But I reckon a person's dream's got to come from inside them. No one else wishing and hoping it is gonna make it happen. What Charlie said today—well, it's thanks to you he's got the dream."

"He's very bright and a wonderful boy. I told him, and I truly believe this, that I see big things in his future."

"Of course, if I only think about Charlie going to college, this would be easy. He should do anything that keeps the dream alive. But our family's involved." She went on to tell him how George, based on the strength of his relationship with his boss, had gotten Charlie the job picking up garbage. How frightened her sister and brother-in-law were. Neither one thought the boss knew about Charlie coming here, but they were mighty worried what would happen if Charlie quit and the boss found out why. They'd wracked their brains to figure out what to say and come up empty-handed. "I wouldn't be surprised if Metairie got so scared she wouldn't let Charlie stay with them anymore."

"You know," Zach said, "police cars swarm around the COFO office, and the cops walk right in there without any warning. But for some reason they don't really bother us here. There shouldn't be much chance of George's boss finding out Charlie is coming here."

"Zach, you got to see how you saying there shouldn't be much chance of it won't amount to anything with Metairie."

"If your sister kicks Charles out, well, we can deal with that if it happens." He looked at her hard then. "Charles is almost a man. Lots of folks are taking chances, and your brother is willing to be one of them."

He felt her stiffen. All this time, their knees had been touching. He knew he needed to back off for now. "So, did you get my letter?"

"Letter? Flo . . ." She shook her head. "No, when did you send it?"

".Mailed it maybe a week ago."

"We must've just crossed paths. What did it say?"

"The murders, what it's been like here. But—" He suddenly felt shy. "I also wanted you to know why I came. I think I've been trying to get to know you through the place where you grew up."

Her emerald eyes searched his face. She seemed bemused. "And did you?"

"I think . . . I've gotten to know you as much as I can without your help. And not as much as I want to."

"Oh, Zach." Under the force of his gaze, she suddenly reached out. Took his hand, held it in hers. "When do you leave here?"

"Classes end three weeks from Friday."

"When you're safely out of Mississippi, then I can forgive you. For now, I declare the rift to be healed."

CHAPTER 22

Thursday, July 30
Playing by Ear

"What did you say to George's boss?" Metairie screeched. "And tell me, dear Lord, you did *not* mention that school!"

Seated next to Charlie, facing Metairie and George across their kitchen table, C.J. shrugged off the thought that her sister's words sounded strangely familiar. She'd blessed the children for the distraction they provided during supper, but now they'd both been put to bed. If Metairie had been livid last night when she realized C.J. was siding with Charlie, tonight she was beside herself with anxiety.

C.J. tried to stay focused on the argument at hand but was worried about Doc Barnes not having called with news of her daddy's condition. She hated not knowing. Suddenly, she recalled her momma saying, *Tell me your daddy knows about this*, the day Charlie went swimming in the Wilsons' lake.

"No, sister." Charlie spoke deliberately. "I thanked the boss kindly for the opportunity to work for him and said I had another commitment I needed to tend to. I offered to work out the week so as not to leave him in a pinch."

"You tell him," Metairie commanded, turning to George. "Tell *Charles* what your boss said."

"Metairie, calm down—" C.J. tried.

"I won't be told what to do in *my* house," Metairie snapped.

George squirmed uncomfortably, and his normally good posture seemed to have betrayed him, making him appear shorter than usual, even sitting down. "The boss man said, 'Nigger workers are a dime a dozen. But your brother-in-law was a good one, like you.' "

Metairie waved her hand in the air, signaling George to come on and spit out the rest of it.

" 'It puts me out having to find a replacement. I got to think twice if you come asking for any more favors.' That's all he said."

"I'm really sorry, George. I surely didn't mean to cause you a problem at work."

"And yet, that's exactly what you've done. We got to have you out of this house right away, the both of you, before anyone thinks we're supporting that school," Metairie said.

C.J. had thought Momma was overreacting, too. But she'd felt her momma's fear and come around to her way of thinking: *know your place; stay safe*. Metairie had said what a big mortgage they had. And George's boss was a white man. She was right to look out for her family. As C.J. reached out to touch her hand, the phone rang.

George hurried to answer it. "C.J.? Yessir, just one minute please."

"I'm calling about your father," Doc Barnes said to her hello.

She listened, struggling to hear between the lines of what he was saying. "What should we do, Doc Barnes? Just tell me. I'll see to it."

The faces across the room reflected her growing alarm.

"Thank you kindly, sir." She hung up and returned to the table.

"Is Daddy bad sick?" Metairie asked.

"Doc Barnes called it chronic bronchitis. Says it can be managed for many years. But Daddy's got to see him regularly and take medicine."

"Is Daddy gonna be able to work?" Charlie asked. "I could get a job after school, or . . ."

"Absolutely not," C.J. said. "You got to focus on your schooling. Daddy can rebuild his strength and get back to work. He's got to stop smoking is all."

The four of them exchanged knowing looks as C.J. pictured her father rolling a cigarette each evening on the porch to the tune of one of his favorite albums on the phonograph. Then she and Metairie went round and round while George and Charlie tried to stay out of their way.

"Well, y'all can stay here a few more days," Metairie said, relenting slightly.

"Ah, Metairie. Where can I go? And this ain't fair to C.J.," Charlie said.

"Fair to C.J.? How I see it, this is her fault!"

"Charlie, Metairie, y'all stop." C.J.'s voice had become stern. "I'll speak to Momma and Daddy in the morning. And I'll get me and Charlie out of your house by Monday. Now, I'm going on to bed. So, I'll say my goodnights."

She tiptoed into the bedroom she shared with Anna and quietly got undressed. But once in bed, she sat upright, knees hugged to her chest, her mind working. She was caught again. Getting herself and Charlie out of Metairie's house meant one of two things. She would either have to take him with her to Meridian, putting more stress on her parents and ending his time at the Freedom School, or ask Zach for help.

She twisted the hem of her nightgown, trying to figure a way out. Her momma's final words, when C.J. had protested that Charlie made a simple mistake, came back to her now. *There's no such thing as mistakes with white folks, especially for boys. They don't get no second chances.*

She thought of grownup Charlie. He had the dream now, of going to college. She'd said it herself earlier, he had to focus on his schooling. Charlie might never get a second chance. She knew what she had to do.

The next morning, she got up early. She had breakfast made for everyone and asked Charlie to bring his plate outside to the porch to eat.

"Today after work, I want you to come straight here. We'll go to the school together. I'm gonna go on up there this morning, though, to get things started."

"Who you gonna talk to?"

"Zach."

Charlie raised an eyebrow. "But you don't even know him. I wanted to introduce you after the assembly, but I went off with Rosalee and it slipped my mind."

"Yes..." She clasped her hands and looked down at them, then back up at Charlie. "Yes I do."

"How can you?"

"Zach tell y'all he's from Chicago?"

Charlie nodded.

"We met there. That's all you need to know for now." Reflexively, she checked that all his buttons were done and searched his face for caked-on egg. "You best take that plate inside and get on to work."

She did the dishes, dressed carefully, and told Metairie she was going out. During the walk to the Freedom School, she felt less frightened than she had two days earlier, yet equally apprehensive.

She asked a few people where she might find Zach and was directed to a room where the teachers worked on their lesson plans and reading the students' work. His smile when he saw her was like so many times before, like the sun around which his twin dimple moons revolved.

"Can we talk? Do you have time?"

"Always," he said. "Let's go outside."

❊   ❊   ❊

"C'mon, you can do it," called a small voice. C.J. followed the sound to a huge tree in the yard. A young girl perched on a branch of the live oak, her bare feet dangling, and encouraged a small boy up the tree, just as she had once coached Zach up into the arms of the ancient burr oak in Jackson Park. *You can feel Mississippi up here*, she'd said to him, quite certain that was as close as he would ever come.

"I still wish I had a camera," he said, telling her he was remembering, too.

"You still think nothing's changed since Babe Ruth?"

"You still think everything's changed?"

"I reckon the truth lies somewhere in between." She sighed. "Charlie has the dream of going to college. It's *his* now. I can't ever thank you enough for that."

He shook his head.

"I thought long and hard on it. But I had to tell Metairie I support him coming up here fulltime 'til summer school lets out."

"And?"

"And Metairie kicked us out. She wants us out by Monday." She went on to tell Zach about her father being sick, that she would have to get back to Poplar Springs soon anyway, to make sure he was following Doc Barnes's orders, and might have to stay there a while. "Can you help, like you said? Can you find Charlie a place to stay?"

"I'll get right on it," he said. "We'll figure this out." He scratched his head, as if he'd already gone to work on the problem. "But—" He cast a long, hard look her way. "Mrs. Gray said she asked you to promise something."

C.J. blushed furiously. "Zach—"

"If you go to Poplar Springs right away, and stay there a while, when will you do what you promised?"

"I—while I'm there, I reckon."

"I don't think so. I think we need time together." He frowned, then brightened, as if he'd had an idea. "I've got to go out for a bit. But let me introduce you to a couple of people. Stay for lunch and the children's jazz band. We'll talk more when I get back."

He led her to one of the other teachers. "C.J., this is—"

She and Elizabeth both laughed. "We've met," Elizabeth said.

"Charlie brought me to Elizabeth's French class."

"Good—"

"Want to join me for lunch, C.J.? I'm going to listen to the jazz band while I eat."

Zach threw up his hands. "I see I'm not needed at all." He winked at C.J. and was gone.

She followed Elizabeth to the kitchen and took a plate of food that was every bit as good as her own momma's. They carried their plates into the auditorium where little Ben Chaney, his arm in a cast and sling, seemed to be in charge of a bunch of kids using a washboard, spoons, washtub bass, and comb and tissue paper. The sound they produced made C.J. smile with absolute delight.

"Don't they make terrific music together?" Elizabeth asked, clapping along.

They concluded with a freedom song, "We Shall Not Be Moved." Ben got everyone started on pitch and called out the words for each verse. C.J. watched the boy, marveling at his spirit in the wake of his big brother's disappearance.

Suddenly, he said, "What words can y'all make up for this song? Call it, Tommy."

"Having fun together!"

And the kids were off, singing, "We are having fun together . . ."

"We will all be friends forever," sang a girl.

"We are making our own music," Ben called out. The children laughed and sang.

Elizabeth invited C.J. to attend her next class, but she asked if she could use the piano instead. She seated herself, hoping to recapture the children's song. Automatically, her hands moved into position for "Minuet in G," a song she knew so well. As if by magic, they were in the right place for the first few notes of "We Shall Not Be Moved."

After hearing the children sing so many verses, she had the melody planted firmly in her head. If they can make music, so can I, she challenged herself. She worked at it, losing herself in the quest. When she had it figured out, she played it again and again, wanting to burn it into her memory.

She felt someone watching her and looked up to see Zach. She was embarrassed, but his smile seemed encouraging. "Don't stop," he said.

"That's all I can figure. Miz Gray can play songs without music, but I don't know all of how she does it."

"May I?" He nodded at the piano bench, and she scooted over.

"I know Mrs. Gray has taught you some chords. Can you play a C chord?"

C.J. played C-E-G.

"Good. How about a G chord?"

C.J. played G-B-D.

"Now, most of the songs we sing around here use a few common chords. Some are a bit trickier. Here's a D7."

They worked for a while, with Zach calling out the names of chords and C.J. playing them. Finally, he said, "Now, you play the melody, and I'll play the chords."

When they'd finished, she was grinning from ear to ear. "You figured out the mystery of how Miz Gray can play anything under the sun without a single note written down on paper! You got to teach me, please."

"All right, then." He rolled up his sleeves. "I'll play the melody and call the chords."

With all the persistence and enthusiasm with which they attacked "Chopsticks" the first time they sat side by side before a piano, Zach and C.J. worked until she had mastered hands together.

"It's like little Ben sang," she said, smiling at Zach. "We are making our own music."

He leaned toward her then. She jumped up from the bench.

She heard Charlie saying, "Wow! I didn't know you could play," and turned toward him.

"Oh, my! I clean forgot about you—"

"It's okay, C.J. When you weren't at Metairie's, I just came on here. Did you talk to Zach?"

"She did." Zach was beaming. "Charles, the lady I stay with has invited you to stay at her house until school lets out."

"You kidding me? Grandma Willie?"

"Grandma Willie indeed. And"—Zach's eyes met C.J.'s—"the lady Elizabeth stays with says C.J. is welcome to stay with her."

"Now, Zach, I told you I got to get on home to help my parents."

"You also promised Mrs. Gray."

As Charlie watched the two of them, his face went through a rainbow of expressions. Then he and Zach spoke to each other as if she were no longer there.

"'I think you should aim for the best, in love and life.' That's what you said when we talked about Rosalee and me."

Zach's face looked suddenly hard-edged, controlled. "I also said it's complicated."

"Well, that don't nearly sum it up. And you—" He turned to C.J. "You said, 'That's all you need to know for now.'"

"Charlie, I—"

"If this don't beat all. I worship the ground the two of you walk on. And I never could've imagined this. Before this summer, I never knew a white man worth getting to know. Zach, you changed that for me. I reckon you two need to figure out what is. C.J., maybe you need to stay in Meridian a little bit longer."

C.J. looked at Charlie and Zach, two of the three men who meant the most to her in the world. "I'll think on it this weekend," she said, knowing she had to decide which family she came from—the fear, handed down by her momma and daddy, that was driving Metairie so hard right now, or the hope Charlie had been learning.

❊　❊　❊

On Saturday afternoon, Joan's dad delivered her to Big Daddy's for a sleepover with Carol. Once again, the doorbell was promptly answered by the maid.

"Have a good time, honey," her dad said, handing over her small suitcase. "I'll see you at Mass in the morning."

"Miz Carol is in the solarium. This way, please, Miz Joan."

She followed the black dress through the foyer, with its winding staircase and lush plants in large brass urns. The polished dark oak banister sparkled in the sunlight. It was a gorgeous day. On the drive from Poplar Springs to Meridian, she had stared dejectedly at the wide-open sky, populated with the cottony clouds of Mississippi summer. From the air-conditioned car, fields, stands of trees, houses, and barns seemed to squiggle from beneath a gauzy curtain of blazing heat and oppressive humidity. She'd hoped it would rain all day today, the day she would have celebrated her twelfth birthday at the Poplar Springs pool with all her friends from St. Stephens. She was grateful to Carol for having the sleepover. Yet she couldn't shake the feeling that it was like a consolation prize.

At the doorway to the solarium, the maid stepped back to let Joan enter. The room was festooned with balloons, crepe paper streamers, and a large banner proclaiming HAPPY BIRTHDAY, JOAN! As she took in the decorations, the room erupted in noise. She looked around to see Carol, surrounded by what seemed to be most of their St. Stephens classmates, all yelling, "Surprise!"

"I thought—" She held up the suitcase still in her hand. "How did you do all this?"

Carol was grinning broadly. She came to take Joan's suitcase and lead her to the wicker sofa. "I had help from Big Daddy and your parents."

One kid after another came forward, pulling a wrapped present from behind the sofa where Big Daddy had sprawled the last time Joan was here. She admired and appreciated each gift until only Carol was left holding a package. It was a large shallow box, the kind that usually held clothes at Christmas. The flocked wrapping paper was soft pink laced with white flowers.

Carol set the package on the coffee table. "I'll give you mine after we have cake," she promised, just as the maid wheeled in a three-tiered creation, more like a wedding cake than a birthday cake. Gumdrop-colored roses, their petals artfully curved and shimmering with sugar, ringed each tier.

Joan peered at the roses and decided they were, indeed, somehow made of gumdrops. "It's beautiful!"

"You cut the first slice, Joan," Carol ordered, reaching up to tug the large red bow that held her ponytail a little tighter.

Joan served herself and handed the knife to the maid. "It's delicious, Carol," she said, though she was too busy smiling at the sight of her friends to eat more than a few bites.

When everyone had put down their plates, Carol retrieved her gift. Though Joan hated to disturb the beautiful package, she finally tore into it and peeled back tissue paper. She was startled, then confused, almost angry, as she pulled out a beach towel, cover-up, and flip-flops. She stared open-mouthed at Carol, afraid to speak.

"There's more," Carol said, looking like she would burst with pride.

Deciding Carol couldn't have meant to be mean, Joan peeled back another layer of tissue paper and inhaled sharply at the sight of the exact two-piece yellow bathing suit she'd admired in *Seventeen*. "My mom . . ."

"Said this would be fine." Carol grinned. "Guess where we're all going?" She turned to the other guests and squealed, "To a pool party, courtesy of Big Daddy!"

Joan shook her head. "Where? How? I figured every pool in Mississippi would be closed this summer."

"Not at Big Daddy's club," Carol said.

The maid showed everyone where to change into their suits, then lined them up in the foyer while she went to get Big Daddy. He appeared, dressed in khakis and a white shirt and wearing a wide-brimmed hat, then motioned them through the front door and onto the circular driveway, where he realigned them in twos. Not a car was in sight.

"Y'all stay together and follow me," he commanded, then proceeded to march them past the golf course that backed up against his property and the signs for Northwood Country Club and right up to the most amazing pool. As he settled himself in a chaise lounge, a Negro man appeared and moved an umbrella over to shade him. He took Big Daddy's drink order and scurried away to retrieve it.

No pool had ever looked so inviting. Suddenly, it was a glorious day. Joan held her head up and her shoulders back as she traveled the concrete skirt of the pool, past the bank of chaise lounges and the lifeguard stand, to the diving board. With forced deliberateness, she removed her new cover-up, stepped out of her flip-flops, and climbed the ladder. Her dive was perfect.

She came up looking for Carol and found her close by. The kids were soon involved in a game of Marco Polo. They played by the rule that everyone but the Marco could get out of the pool as long as they kept one body part in the water. This resulted in a lot of jumping in and out of the pool.

Laughter resounded amid the shrieks of "Marco" and "Polo." By the time everyone had taken a turn as Marco, Joan was worn out. She spread her new beach towel on a chaise next to Carol's and basked in the sun.

Carol soon plopped down beside her. "Having a good time?" she asked.

"Are you kidding? When you said pool party, I just figured you meant the public pool at Highland Park. I mean, I don't even know. Maybe that got closed, too." She shaded her eyes with one hand and gazed at her sunlit friend. "This is the absolute best thing anybody ever did for me in my life. I don't see how I could possibly be any happier. Thank you so much." She closed her eyes again and felt the sun baking her.

"The whole situation was just wrong. Your pool party's a tradition. Big Daddy agreed."

"Uh-huh."

"He said he had half a mind to take us to Highland Park, just to show his support. Meridian's got an understanding with its coloreds—keeping the pool open and them out. That Civil Rights Act won't change things here."

"So, why didn't he?"

"He said, 'Joey's birthday's got to be special. It'll be more special at the club.' "

She loved how Big Daddy called her Joey, and she was touched that he wanted to make her birthday special. So, why was she suddenly thinking about the Freedom School? *Don't nobody much care about a nigger school,* he'd said. She'd heard a couple of teachers talking about testing the Civil Rights Act, going round to different white restaurants to see if they'd give a table to Negroes.

Down the aisle, Big Daddy still reclined in his chaise. The Negro man was suddenly at his side, replacing his drink with a fresh one.

A song began to float through Joan's head. It was called "I'm Gonna Sit at the Welcome Table." She shook her head, as if to rid herself of a pesky mosquito, and silently sang "Happy Birthday" to herself. But the freedom song was back. *I'm gonna tell God how you treat me one of these days.*

She jumped up. "Let's go back in, Carol. I'm getting too hot."

❀   ❀   ❀

The Mt. Olive Baptist Church sanctuary was packed as another of Mississippi's ubiquitous ninety-five, ninety-five days—where the humidity equals the temperature—was drawing to a close. The mix of volunteers, students, and those who had come to discuss the Freedom Democratic Party shifted and rearranged themselves on the hard pews. The concert was about to begin.

"I'm glad the meeting is over," said Jacob. He and Zach were seated in the front row.

Zach smiled at the kids clustered around Elizabeth and Gwendolyn across the aisle. But he was angry at C.J. for refusing to attend "one of *those* meetings." She would fear for this minister—so unlike her Brother James—who was allowing his church to host such a meeting, and be unnerved by the Meridian sheriff standing steely-eyed in the back. But Zach almost didn't notice that kind of thing anymore. He sometimes thought he would give almost anything just to sit next to her, doing something normal like listening to music, forgetting the way things were.

She'd taken the entire weekend to decide whether to stay in Meridian or go immediately back to Poplar Springs, refusing to see him, saying she must decide alone. Yesterday morning, she'd shown up at the Freedom School with her suitcase and said, mysteriously, "I chose hope."

Everyone applauded as the folk singer, Pete Seeger, stepped front and center, just like the preacher did on Sundays. Seeger secured the strap on his guitar and began with an instrumental. His first few songs were old ones, about America. He seemed to move around the world then, singing of different types of people. Zach found his voice reassuring, often in stark contrast to his lyrics, which spoke the unvarnished truth. He relaxed as the folk singer led them in a sing-along.

"It's nice to have the night off," Zach said to Jacob, "to not have to be the one leading the group."

Soon, the room erupted with "If I Had a Hammer." Then Mr. Seeger soothed them with "The Water Is Wide." And then he switched to banjo and thrilled the kids with "Abiyoyo," the story of music bringing down a wicked giant—a story, Pete said, that was based on a South African lullaby and folk story. The banjo or was it the story? seemed to animate Seeger, causing him to dance and hop and skip and jump around.

The crowd joined Seeger fully from the moment he concentrated on what Pete called "our songs." Zach let his mind wander, imagining the final song tonight. It would surely be "We Shall Overcome," for this song was always sung last at any gathering. Each person in this church, whether black or white, old or young, would sing as one. Each person would cross his arms and take the hands of the person to his left and to his right. If only C.J. were here. Then one of the hands he held would be hers—he yearned for the fading memory of her touch as she took his hand after the assembly at the Freedom School—and he would wish for the folk singer to invent new lyrics, making the song never end.

Another song ended. Seeger was silent, looking down for what seemed a long time. The crowd rustled in their pews. Then he stood tall. The deliberate squaring of his shoulders caused Zach to focus on the color of his shirt, a blue as temperate as the man. *Sara Leanne*, Zach could almost hear Grandma Willie saying, as if speaking of a beautiful girl.

The bodies have been found, Pete told them, buried in an earthen dam.

Love and death. Mickey's wife, Rita, and the wives James and Andy would never know. God help him, but he wanted to love and live, to be with C.J.

Zach thought he had never felt such silence. Dreamlike. No one shouted for revenge against the Klan. Rather, the air seemed to swell as if in a collective breath of determination to continue the fight.

But dreams can be dangerous, as Annie had said at the assembly. *Negroes and whites together . . . nobody saying nothing stupid. Like look over yonder at that white man and nigger gal. Let's kill the both of them.*

Zach felt a sob welling up within him. He felt ashamed to admit that it was less for the three dead men and more for his dream. Whether or not he and C.J. could be together had nothing to do with what he'd been working for this summer. It was up to her. Her decision, just as she'd decided whether to stay in Meridian or return to Poplar Springs. Just as she'd said back in Chicago at the piano—*There are some things I can do for you. But they have to be mine to decide.*—when he couldn't, or wouldn't, understand. Just as she'd said after the assembly: *A person's dream's got to come from inside them. No one else wishing and hoping it is gonna make it happen.*

Days missing had climbed to forty-five and stopped, like a broken clock, like the lives of James Chaney, Mickey Schwerner, and Andy Goodman. And Zach would have to learn a new way of telling time.

"We must sing 'We Shall Overcome' now," said Pete. "The three boys would not have wanted us to weep now, but to sing and understand this song."

Seeger began alone, his gentle voice resounding through the church. Reflexively, Zach crossed his arms and reached for the hands of those beside him. The church rustled with the sound of arms crossing and reaching for hands, even across the aisles.

Voice layered upon voice, verse upon verse. Zach, too, sang the verse renouncing fear. And yet he was afraid. Tomorrow he would again be a teacher. How would he break the news to those who had not already heard? How would he comfort students when his heart was broken? He stared at the inscription on Pete Seeger's banjo: *This machine surrounds hate and forces it to surrender.*

※　※　※

"C'mon, Dad," Joan urged, slightly ahead of him as they made their way across the yard toward the Freedom School on Wednesday morning.

"You're in a hurry." He smiled at her.

"I have things to do—for the teachers." She needed to enlist their support and start organizing the thank-you lunch for the lunch ladies. And she was determined to keep it a secret.

"Any ideas yet for your Girl Scout Marian Award project?" he asked.

"I'm working on that, too. Can you trust me?"

He looked at her sideways. "Okay, Joani. I think you understand the requirements. Let Mom or me know if we can help."

Inside, she hugged her dad goodbye and went in search of teachers. "Anybody seen Zach or Elizabeth?" she asked the ones who were directing some of the younger children as they decorated a large banner with the words Freedom Is A Struggle.

"I'm sure they're working with our delegates, planning for the convention," Gwendolyn said.

Now Joan remembered. The Meridian Freedom School was hosting this weekend's statewide Freedom School Convention. Charles, Rosalee, and Jackson had been chosen to represent Meridian. A hundred out-of-town delegates would be arriving Friday evening.

The principal seemed to be everywhere at once, his look measured and watchful. When Joan passed teachers and students cleaning and organizing chairs and tables, she asked again about Zach and Elizabeth. "That way," someone said, pointing toward the little room where the teachers prepared their lessons.

Eavesdropping outside the closed door, Joan heard Zach talking about the big question the students would tackle this weekend—*When we elect people to government office, what do we want them to do?* Frustrated by everyone being too busy to talk to her, she moved on.

Alone in the small office near the kitchen, she paced. All this civil rights stuff kept getting in the way of her plans. But, passing the mimeograph machine for perhaps the tenth time, she suddenly realized she could make up a flyer and put it in the teachers' mailboxes. She sat down and scratched out details by hand before typing the stencil. The date would be two weeks from today. Each teacher was responsible for bringing a dish that was typical of their part of the country. Each teacher would be given three dollars from her fund, to help pay for groceries. She'd started the fund with birthday money from her grandmothers and was raising more from babysitting and a lemonade stand.

As she clicked the typewriter keys, she heard faint singing, unusual because it was a solitary voice. She stopped typing and crept to the doorway. So heartbreaking was the sound that she thought the singer must have lost all hope. She peered around the corner, into the kitchen, and was shocked to see normally jovial Grandma Willie in tears. Joan stood for a moment, not knowing what to do. When she turned to go, Grandma Willie looked up and quickly dabbed her face with her apron.

"I'm sorry," Joan said. "I didn't mean to disturb you."

"Well, child. I reckon I ought to be ashamed of myself, crying like this."

"But what's wrong?"

"Ain't you heard?" Grandma Willie looked like the possibility was beyond belief. "Well, maybe not, if you ain't been in a class. And that white rag of a newspaper won't be out 'til evening. They—found the missing boys' bodies yesterday."

Joan's hand went to her mouth. "You mean Ben's big brother?"

"Yes, James. And Mickey and Andy, too."

Tears sprang to Joan's eyes. She hadn't known one of the boys had the same name as her own little brother. "Did you know them?"

"Not Andy, no. But Mickey's the one talked me into letting a volunteer stay with me this summer. That's how I come to know Zach. Mickey was a fine young man all the tough boys looked up to. And I watched that sweetheart James grow up."

"Then it's okay to cry, right?"

"The teachers and preachers are all saying them boys wouldn't want our tears. They'd want us to keep our minds stayed on the freedom fight. I just don't know, me being so old, if I'll live long enough to see it."

As Grandma Willie talked, she had laid down her knife, leaving heads of cabbage still to be chopped for coleslaw.

"Can I help you finish fixing everything?"

"No, honey, but thank you. You run on, find someone else to listen to. Someone talking right."

"Yes, ma'am." As Joan walked away, she heard Grandma Willie pick up where she'd left off with "This May Be the Last Time."

". . . that we walk together. It may be the last time, I don't know."

Joan knew only that nothing had ever sounded sadder.

Down the hall, students were gathering for Zach's English Expression class. She wandered into the classroom, pulled a chair into a corner, and sat down.

"I didn't know these three," Zach said. "Mickey and Andy left Ohio just as most of my group was arriving for training. And Andy was only in Mississippi for about twenty-four hours. But many of you met Mickey, and many of you have known James your whole lives. I was hoping, well, that you could tell me about them."

His voice had risen, as if he questioned whether anyone would take his suggestion. But the room seemed to erupt in memories.

"Mickey was a big guy," said one boy. "Tough, not afraid of nothing. He went up in the jails and bars to talk to the boys like my brother, the ones always getting in trouble. Said the way for them to have respect was to fight for something important."

"Yeah," said a girl. "Them boys helped get this school set up on account of Mickey telling them it was important. And my brother, he'd come home laughing about Mickey playing games with the little ones."

"Grandma Willie said she let Zach stay with her because Mickey asked her to," Joan blurted.

She reddened as everyone looked at her and stopped talking. But Zach gave her a kind smile. Then he asked, "What did Mickey's eyes look like?"

"Nice, real nice," Rosalee said. "Not like white eyes we ever knew before."

The memories of James Chaney were somehow less specific and more intense. "He worshipped the ground Mickey walked on. Didn't say much, but everybody listened if he did talk."

"That sweet baby Ben just about says it all, don't it?" Lynette asked. "Him up here at the school, putting his twelve-year-old feet in those big shoes, carrying on the fight for his big brother."

The room buzzed for a while with kids sharing how they'd heard. It seemed to Joan there'd been a lot of Negroes knocking on each others' doors last night, spreading the word. Still, some kids had come here today, unknowing, just like she had.

"I wasn't surprised," Jackson said. "Soon as I heard they was missing, I knew they'd been murdered. But, Lord, to hear about all the bodies found, most with no name put to 'em, while the FBI and sailors and all were searching rivers looking for these three. That just sent my mind to spinning."

This truly threw Joan. What had Big Daddy said? *It's a hoax is all.* Why did he say that? *It certainly ain't the Klan, or murder.* What did *he* know? She'd seen how smart Jackson was. She couldn't dismiss what he said, the way Big Daddy could. A sense of disquietude, like what she felt at her pool party, came over her.

As class drew to a close, Zach suggested they end it by singing "We Shall Overcome." *Everybody in his place.* Joan heard Big Daddy's voice from years ago, even as two students in the back row moved toward her, their arms crossed, each reaching out a hand.

She remembered being little and holding C.J.'s hand while crossing a busy street. She'd never touched a black boy, though. Dreamlike, she suddenly imagined another classroom, all white kids except for one Negro. The Negro looked around, but no one extended a hand. The mean boy who had taunted her in King's Drugs was there. The Negro kid accidentally bumped into him, causing him to shout, "Somebody blow me off. That nigger just touched me!"

Joan looked around. Jackson's and Rosalee's hands were still extended toward her. She reached out and took them, completing the circle.

CHAPTER 23

Wednesday, August 12
On the Midway

It was Wednesday. Like every other Wednesday night in Meridian, most folks were in church. C.J. and Zach were not. Despite the growing push for the volunteers to be out enrolling people in the Mississippi Freedom Democratic Party, he had taken this night off and begged her to skip church with the Reid family. As she walked the two doors down from their house to Grandma Willie's, wearing jeans as he'd asked, she wondered why.

The sun had dipped below the horizon, and the sky was awash with the glow of twilight. She was about to knock on Grandma Willie's back door when a whistling caused her to nearly jump out of her skin.

"C'mon, you can do it." She followed the sound of Zach's voice and found him perched on a tree branch, his bare feet dangling. The branch could be no more than five feet off the ground, but it was the thought that counted.

She laughed. "Where are your shoes?"

He leaned forward slightly, revealing his sneakers. He'd tied his shoelaces together and hung his shoes around his neck.

Her heart seemed to beat out the words "Mississippi, up here, come feel" as she scrambled into the tree and onto the branch above his. With a deliberateness and reverence that seemed to stop time, he took off her shoes, knotted the laces together, and handed them up to her, brushing the hem of her blue sleeveless blouse.

On this mid-August night, the old tree was dense with leaves. Its tangle of greenery sheltered them, making her feel less afraid, despite the intensity of Zach's gaze.

"Blue's your color, I think," he said.

"I thought you said it was pink."

"I was wrong. It's every color." He looked suddenly sad. "Pete Seeger's shirt was blue. Once he broke the news, I just kept looking at his shirt and thinking of you and the color. It's Grandma Willie's favorite—cerulean, but she pronounces it *Sara Leanne*, like the name of a beautiful girl. Of course, that's why I thought of you."

She flushed. "We haven't really talked about it, what with you all tied up with the convention. You know, I went to James Chaney's service because I couldn't figure out how to say no to Miz Reid. Staying with them is a bit like living with white folks in Chicago. They have expectations. I reckon Mr. and Miz Reid thought I'd be like Elizabeth, unafraid and dedicated to the cause. So, they just announced the time we'd be leaving." She sighed. "Them being that way, it was a problem getting out of going to church tonight. I had to say Charlie needed me."

"I'm sorry you had to lie. I'll try to make it up to you," he said mysteriously. "But how'd you feel at the service?"

"'Course I first heard they'd found the bodies from Elizabeth that night when she came home from the concert. That hit me hard, being certain they're dead, and because that's what I've been terrified would happen to you."

He reached up, rested a hand on her knee. She looked at him, drinking him in, then went on.

"I never knew how you could risk putting your family through what James Chaney's family is going through. Hearing about Emmett Till was one thing. Seeing the misery of death up close, in the eyes of the Chaney family, is another. But it got me thinking. Maybe it's all bigger than choosing between family and something else."

Neither spoke for a while. Zach seemed to be waiting for her to go on, but she wasn't ready, was still figuring it out.

"Y'all talk about the convention afterwards?" she asked. "Elizabeth came home exhausted. Proud of the kids and the work they did drawing up a platform. She really liked that they included French in the education plank. But she seemed—I don't know, ashamed about them feeling the need to say in the housing plank that every home ought to include a complete bathroom and kitchen sink."

"I think it breaks her heart sometimes, the realities," he said. "The kids were nothing but uplifted, though. Talking about meeting Mrs. Hamer and folks from the Mississippi Freedom Democratic Party. In class, when Jackson talked about it, he looked just like at the 'I Have a Dream' assembly. He said, 'They asked *us* what did we think was important to say at the National Democratic Convention when the bus carries them up there to Atlantic City.'" Zach laughed. "I swear, his eyes opened as big and round as the wheels of a bus."

"It is about the dream, isn't it, Zach? I remember you asking me in Chicago what I'd like to do for me. This week has been kind of like with the Grays back then, with me not knowing what to do with my time. Waiting to see you every now and then. Calling my parents every day. Reading to the little ones at the school and practicing on that piano. I reckon I didn't even understand the question back then."

They sat quietly until the light had nearly faded. Then he put on his shoes and jumped to the ground.

"There's more," he said, motioning her to follow. He walked over to the back wall of Grandma Willie's house and squatted in the grass. "Come see!"

He'd spread out a blanket. There was a basket, and he began to pull things from it. Two Cokes and something wrapped in paper. He popped the tops and handed her a bottle, then undid the wrapping to reveal two sandwiches. Though the bread was plain store-bought white bread and the tuna salad wasn't fancy, C.J. thought her sandwich was every bit as delicious as the one she'd had at Harry's Deli that first day with Zach and Flo. As they ate, they leaned back against the wall of the house and stretched out their legs on the blanket. There was no house behind Grandma Willie's, and the mature pines and blooming bottlebrush that ringed the yard provided a thick screen that made the spot on the blanket feel as if it were an enclosed room.

"I don't believe it!" C.J. said when Zach pulled out two pieces of cake. "That's babka, isn't it? You?"

"Well, I called my mother to get the recipe, and Grandma Willie helped a bit with the baking."

She took a bite and declared the babka just like Harry's.

"Stay here," he said. "I'll be back in ninety seconds."

He hurried inside. Suddenly, soft music came through the window. The sound was faint, but it was Charlie Parker in all his glory. Charlie Parker as she'd heard him through the window of her parents' house. Charlie Parker as she'd never heard him before.

When Zach returned, he sat closer to her. He looked up at the stars, pointing occasionally. He breathed in deeply. "There's a smell to the air here, an openness to the sky that's Mississippi to me in all its goodness."

"Yes," she said, sighing contentedly.

Zach reached into the basket again and pulled out a small wrapped package. He held it out to her.

"What is it?" she said, not moving a muscle.

He smiled. "You'll have to open it to find out."

Unable to imagine what could be inside, she fumbled with the bow and paper. She lifted the lid of the box to reveal something silver. It was a tiny, perfect piano on a chain. "What—why?" she managed to say.

He seemed suddenly shy. "It's a charm. A symbol, really. I don't know what it will be, C.J. But I know that you're going to find your dream, too. The one that comes from inside you. The one nobody can wish or hope for you."

"Zach, I—"

"Shush now." He took her hand in his and held it until the Charlie Parker album was done.

"I have to go," she said. "I told Miz Reid I wouldn't be late with—what I had to do with Charlie."

"I know."

"I don't want to, though." She brushed away a tear. "It seems like you're saying goodbye, like that's what tonight has been about."

"Oh, no, C.J." His voice broke, and she watched him fight to control it. "I'm making memories for us to cherish, no matter what we decide. But you have to know how I hope this will go. I'd lay down my life for you. If I believed you loved me, or could come to love me, I would wait for all eternity. In *my* dream, we're together forever, married, with children. But how it is between me and you, that's a bit like how it is between you and Charles. You had to let him find his dream. I've got to do that for you."

She squeezed his hand hard, then got to her knees and sat back on her heels in order to look him directly in the eye. "Thank you for tonight. I'm sorry I can't say more right now. But please remember that a week ago last Monday, I chose hope."

She looked back just once. Then she walked to the Reid house, her hands clasped as if in prayer, clutching the tiny piano. Tears gathered in her eyes, like so many people come to pay their respects to James Chaney and his family at the church. She stepped gingerly, knowing she would always hold her feet in the highest regard, because they had been touched by Zach.

Later, as she was getting ready for bed, Elizabeth watched her closely. "I don't get it," she finally said.

"What?"

"Zach told me you two knew each other in Chicago. And he's so very fond of and committed to your brother. But—"

C.J. blinked.

"What *are* you to each other?"

"We're fr—"

"No." Elizabeth waved away her words. "There's a look in his eyes when he speaks of you, when he asked me to ask Mrs. Reid if you could stay here."

Now C.J. shook her head.

"I mean, you must have lived with this your whole life. They had to tell us in Ohio, though, drill it into us. No interracial dating."

"I understand," C.J. said, feeling anger boil up within her.

"I hope so. It frightens me, for both of you."

※　　※　　※

As Joan rode north toward Philadelphia, Mississippi, she chatted up a storm with Carol's Aunt Betty, working hard not to think about two of the many things she'd read lately in the *Poplar Springs Herald*. This was the very highway that Ben Chaney's brother had driven with the men from New York before they all got killed. And the best she could figure, their bodies had been found not too far from the Neshoba County fairgrounds. She was also struggling to forget the two lies that led to her riding with Aunt Betty rather than her dad.

The first lie, to Carol, had been fairly easy. *Oh, I really want to come. But I don't think my dad can make it this year.* She hadn't even been sure her dad would allow her to go. But she had to try. Carol was her best friend, the truest and best after that wonderful birthday party she'd thrown. And being at the Freedom School, the only white girl in a school full of Negroes, did wear on her. In the fall, she'd go back to her own school and forget all about it. But that brought her right back to Carol and needing to keep her friendship.

The second lie, to her dad, had been much worse. Delivered with a sympathetic hug—*Carol's invitation was just for me this year, Daddy. And it's a sleepover. I hope you don't mind*—it made her feel a bit like Judas betraying Jesus with a kiss. She tried to tell herself she was doing it for her dad, to spare him having to sit through Big Daddy's jokes about Yankees. But she knew better. Her dad was less likely to stay silent this year, and she just couldn't risk a conflict between him and Big Daddy. It might be silly, but she still fancied Big Daddy as her very own grandparent.

When the conversation with Aunt Betty, who conveniently was coming to the fair later than the rest of Carol's family and had offered to bring Joan, petered out, Joan closed her eyes, summoning the smell of ribs slow-cooking outside the Whiteheads' cabin. Instead, she breathed in Christmas a thousand times over and envied Carol. The Whiteheads had roots as deep as the pine forest the car was passing through, roots that made Carol and Big Daddy strong, confident in their thinking. Nothing like what Joan was feeling lately.

Suddenly, just like always, they were there. A sticker on Aunt Betty's car allowed them to pass the area where she and her dad always parked and drive right on to Happy Hollow.

"Hey, y'all, it's Joey and Aunt Betty!" Big Daddy yelled from the porch as the car pulled to a stop in front of the cabin.

Carol ran to the car and grabbed Joan's suitcase. "I'll set this inside. I want to get right to the Midway."

Joan watched Big Daddy handing out instructions and money to the kids. Today, his shaggy white hair was topped by a straw hat, and the clasp on his western bolo was a small Confederate flag, its blue cross studded with diamonds.

"Y'all go on ahead," he said. "I'll be along directly."

Joan and Carol took off in a herd of Whitehead cousins but were soon left behind while Joan turned her head this way and that, taking it all in. They walked through Founder's Square and past the Pavilion where they were to meet Big Daddy for the speeches. As they snaked through the opening between cabins to the north and east, the Midway suddenly sprawled before them. A glittering oasis of fun, sandwiched between street after street of cabins on the left and the racetrack on the right.

Joan looked past the Ferris wheel and taller rides and marched straight to the carousel, remembering the one Big Daddy had taken her and Carol to in Highland Park in Meridian. She and Carol picked out animals across from each other. This carousel was far less beautiful, but Joan laughed and waved as she took in the ever-changing three-hundred-sixty-degree view.

She followed Carol from one ride to another, checking her watch in between each one. "We've got to go soon," she warned, in a voice solemn with responsibility. "Big Daddy wants us there in time to hear the governor. I've never been here for the speeches. Big Daddy says they're important."

"Let's get some refreshments, then."

They stood in line to buy fried pickles and fresh-squeezed lemonade from Lindsey's. Strains of "Dixie" led them toward the pavilion. Joan started to sing along, but a low-flying prop plane drowned her out.

"Look!" Carol pointed as confetti blanketed the air in white.

People grabbed at the falling paper.

"I got one!" Joan said.

"They giving something away?"

"No, it's just some paper called *The Klan-Ledger*. Special Neshoba County Fair Edition."

Joan scrambled into the bleachers. Sandwiched between Carol and Big Daddy, she felt sweat beading on her forehead. She folded the flyer into a fan, then stood with the crowd to cheer the Honorable Paul B. Johnson. He was soon talking about civil rights and integration. She didn't know what she'd expected, but this proved she'd been right to lie. Things would go much more smoothly without the chance for her dad and Big Daddy to disagree.

"Y'all pay attention now," Big Daddy ordered.

"Integration is like prohibition," the governor said. "If people don't want it, a whole army can't enforce it."

"Amen on both accounts," Big Daddy said.

"Segregation is the only way to peace and harmony between the races."

Joan nodded, fanning. Big Daddy was the one who'd made her see the sense in everyone knowing their place in life. She liked to think of it as destiny, in the way that Big Daddy had once said she and Joey Heatherton would be big one day. Destiny and family—being part of what Carol had. She scanned the crowd, only now realizing there wasn't a single Negro face among them and brushed aside the thought. She smiled up at Big Daddy. He patted her knee.

Governor Johnson carried on, saying something about bad parents letting their kids invade Mississippi this summer. College kids who were trying to stir up trouble among the coloreds. Joan suddenly felt a little queasy but attributed it to the heat, the rides, and the sour pickles and lemonade. But "invaders" seemed to ring a bell. She thought one of the articles in the *Poplar Springs Herald* had referred to the college kids like Zach and Elizabeth as invaders.

"Some of them came up missing a while back," Carol whispered as Governor Johnson went on to wish good riddance to the reporters who had tried to misrepresent the law-abiding folks of Neshoba County. *Murdered*, Jackson had said. *It's a hoax is all*, Big Daddy had said. *It certainly ain't the Klan, or murder.* "There are 803 missing people in New York, and someone needs to get there and find *them*," said the governor.

As the crowd roared with laughter, Joan uncrinkled her fan and studied the *Klan-Ledger*. She couldn't help noting that the *Freedom Star* put out by the newspaper club at the Freedom School was a lot more professional looking. She'd been doing their mimeographing and was going to have a tiny story in this week's edition, finally letting the secret out and announcing next Wednesday's lunch for the lunch ladies. She and the girl who did the layout of the stories—Jaleesa—had started talking a bit, too.

Her eyes fell on phrases—*Communist agitators, Bolshevik demons*—and an article about how the Communist revolutionaries were trying to destroy Christian civilization. Communists in Mississippi? *Impossible*, she thought, as Governor Johnson urged them on with their reunions and fun.

When the speeches were done, Big Daddy ordered the kids back to the cabin to fix themselves plates before they took off on their own again. There were no set mealtimes, but the kitchen stood constantly ready to dispense food.

That day and into the night, Joan and Carol examined the arts and crafts, canned goods, and produce entered in competition in the Exhibit Hall. They rode their favorite rides all over again. And they listened to music, then trailed the band who led a little parade down the Hollow. Carol explained that this kind of thing was done in New Orleans.

Finally, it was time to try to sleep. Big Daddy marshaled the children, organizing them into the many bunk beds on the somewhat shaky second floor of the cabin. There was no privacy, and the wait for the single bathroom could be long. Joan brushed her teeth with a cousin named Miranda. An older girl, with perfectly straight blond hair and nails painted hot pink. From Meridian, she thought Carol had said. As they left the bathroom, Miranda gripped Joan's arm, stopping her.

"I heard your daddy doctors niggers," Miranda hissed.

"Excuse me?"

"Yeah, up at that Freedom School. We don't take kindly to traitors, coming in and messing with our way of life. Your daddy a Yankee, too, like those teachers?"

"My dad's a *doctor*, helping sick people."

"Well, I heard your daddy talk, when he's been here with you before. He talks like a damn Yankee."

Through tear-filled eyes, Joan looked up to see Big Daddy, looming just outside the door. He had a grip on Miranda's arm, which had caused her to let go of Joan's. His voice was low but as firm as his grip.

"Mandy, honey. Joey's a guest in our home. We're showing her our way. And being rude to guests isn't our way, now is it?"

"No, sir. Sorry, Joan." Miranda sulked off to her bunk.

But Joan couldn't stop crying. She suddenly pictured more Mirandas, as others found out about her dad working at the school. She'd told him she was proud of him, though. And she was. It was so confusing. "I'd like to call my dad, please, Big Daddy," she said between sniffles. "I want to go home."

"Now, honey, that wouldn't be a good idea, your dad out driving around at night all alone."

Joan went cold, remembering a note they'd found on the windshield one day when they were leaving the school. Her dad had stuffed it in his pocket without letting her see it and driven all the way back to Poplar Springs in silence. "Yessir," she said.

"You'd best get some sleep now. This is all things grownups should be taking care of, not for little girls to worry about." He patted her head and motioned her on her way.

She blinked back her tears and summoned a half-smile for Big Daddy. But she lay awake long into the night. She'd been having such a good time, until that awful girl made her feel like she didn't belong. But she guessed she didn't. And not just because she was Catholic or had Yankee parents, but because she was confused among people who were absolutely certain. She knew things they didn't. She knew smart Negroes, nice Negroes, Negroes who wanted the same kinds of things she wanted, like going to college when they grew up.

As if those kids stood suddenly outside Big Daddy's cabin in single-minded chorus, she could almost hear "I Want My Freedom." Of the many freedom songs that seemed to be sung at the school at the drop of a hat, this was her favorite. Its tune was the same as "You Are My Sunshine," which her dad had taught her and all the neighborhood kids to perform in rounds in a backyard talent show one summer vacation. Yet all this summer, she had wondered why everybody was always talking about freedom.

In the bunk across from hers, Carol was asleep, breathing with her mouth open. Moonlight dove through the window, illuminating the slats of the bunk above Joan's, the one where Miranda also seemed to be asleep. Joan suddenly missed her dad like an ache, wished she hadn't lied, wished she hadn't felt she needed to. Tonight, she thought freedom meant being yourself without having to lie or pretend. She clung to the memory of singing with her dad, even as she wondered how free she was.

CHAPTER 24

Wednesday, August 19
Summer's End

Even the weather seemed to align in support of Joan's non-southern thank-you lunch for the lunch ladies and host families. Rain, almost a certainty at some moment on any given Mississippi summer day, was absent. The fog might have come all the way from Jacob's hometown of San Francisco, along with his contribution, a seafood stew called cioppino.

The offerings of the twenty-one Meridian Freedom School volunteers overflowed the small kitchen. Foods that didn't have to be refrigerated or kept hot spilled into the tiny office where Joan worked at her report for the Girl Scout Marian Award, hoping to finish it today before she left.

Jaleesa had taught her the five W's and one H of journalism. Joan began with the "why," explaining that getting to know one of the lunch ladies, Grandma Willie, had sparked the project. She clipped her article from the *Freedom Star* to cover the "who, what, when, and where." But she needed to fill in the part about how getting to know Jaleesa had caused the project to expand. Jaleesa's family was hosting Max, one of the volunteers. When he asked Jaleesa for ideas about how he might thank her parents, she'd come to Joan. And so, today, both lunch ladies and host families were being celebrated.

Joan moved on to describing everything that went into pulling off the lunch. She'd raised money to buy groceries and gotten permission from the principal to use the school auditorium. Ben Chaney's jazz band had agreed to perform while the guests ate. Students she'd sat with when Zach invited her to his class offered to set up tables and chairs.

Teachers started popping into the office, asking if it was time to take in the food. Joan put aside her report to help. She recalled a movie in science class of a flower blooming in just a few minutes. The transfer and arrangement of the food seemed just as miraculous. The sight of it all together was shocking. She'd suggested each volunteer put a small sign by their dish, identifying what it was and what part of the country it was from. She looked for names—Zach's, Elizabeth's, and Max's—and read *babka*; *cholent, a meat, potato, bean, and barley stew*; and *pork loin roast with sauerkraut, onions, and apples*. New England was represented by clam chowder and Boston baked beans with salt pork, bacon, and molasses. New Yorkers had brought Waldorf salad and New York cheesecake. There was Minnesota wild rice and Texas chili and sheet cake.

Promptly at noon, the building began to buzz with guests being greeted by their respective volunteers. It reminded Joan of parents being met and shown around by their children on the last day of Girl Scout Camp. She wondered how many of the volunteers had gotten help in their host family's kitchen the way Zach said he had. She pictured him and Grandma Willie working side by side and hoped it had been that way for everyone, getting to know each other and sharing their cultures.

C.J. waved from across the room but stayed with the Reid family. Grandma Willie came right up to Joan. "Child, if this don't look amazing. It's gonna be something trying it all."

A teacher named Gwendolyn began to cry as she surveyed the array of foods from across America. "Wow, I guess we're really going back to all these places in two days." Grandma Willie gave her a hug.

While everyone ate, the principal made a short speech. "They say the way to a man's heart is through his stomach. You folks who've fed and sheltered us this summer are the heart and soul of Freedom Summer. We hope our favorite foods from other parts of the country find their way to your hearts and convey even a fraction of our gratitude."

Joan roamed the room like a proud parent. When the last guest was gone and everything had been cleaned up, she returned to the office and the next question on the report: *Was the project successful?* As she typed a description of the chatter, oohs and aahs over the food, and hugs, she began to fume. If it had gone so well, why hadn't she even been mentioned? Her mood didn't help at all as she came to the last, and most important, part: *What did this project teach you about others and about yourself?*

She clicked away at the keys, producing an entire paragraph. But when she read it back, there wasn't one thing in it she hadn't already known before she started the project. She ripped the paper from the typewriter and slid low in her chair, giving her paragraph an accusing eye.

"Not going so well?" asked a man's voice.

She looked up to see the principal standing in the doorway. Embarrassed, she quickly sat up straight and worked her face into a more friendly arrangement. "It's my report on the lunch project."

"Ah, yes." He nodded thoughtfully. "It's a good thing you've done, Joan. We might have overlooked the chance to thank these folks if it weren't for your project."

"Really?"

"Oh, yes. And we can never thank them enough. For risking their jobs and lives to let white folks stay in their homes. For bringing food to feed us when they barely had enough to feed themselves. Sometimes a little thank you has to go a long way."

She nodded, recalling his words—*a good thing* you've *done. And we can never thank* them *enough.* She rolled the words around in her mind, like marbles in her hand, trying to see them in a different light.

The principal studied her face, perhaps sensing she needed more. "I was at the church a couple weeks back when Pete Seeger performed a song called 'One Man's Hands.' Forgive my singing, but—" He launched into a story with crazy math. First one man, then two tried to tear down a prison. Then two plus two plus fifty added up to a million. He stopped, looking embarrassed. "Do you know what the song is trying to say?"

She shook her head.

"We're all part of the whole. What we do, we'll do together, no one of us really more important than the next person."

His voice was really pretty bad. Still, she wanted to remember the song because of how he'd explained it. "Will you sing it one more time, please?"

As he sang, she scribbled down the words. "I think I've got it, thank you."

He smiled, and as he turned to leave, her hands were already poised over the typewriter. She typed furiously, trying to keep up with her thoughts. Then she pulled the paper out and read.

Summer is not for school. That's what I always thought. It's for taking things easy, having fun, and resting up for next fall. Negroes aren't smart, either, and they're not like us—that's what I'd heard. When you do something nice for someone, they ought to say thank you. That's good manners like my parents always taught me.

And then my dad brought me to the Freedom School. When I came up with my project, I thought I was doing something amazing that I'd get thanked for. In a way, I guess I was really doing this project for me. When I didn't get a big thank you, I felt bad.

But then a very nice man at the school explained it to me. He said my project really needed doing and nobody else might have been able to do it. He said what matters isn't getting credit. What matters is picking up the slack to help get the whole thing done. And I learned that being part of something big feels good. I think I want to do it again.

She closed with the words of the freedom song the principal had sung in his very off-key voice. She put all the pages of her report together with a paper clip, then checked the clock. Her dad would be ready to leave soon, and many of the students might have already gone home. She rushed to the room where the newspaper club met, where Jaleesa was often the last to leave as she worked on layout of the coming edition of the *Freedom Star*.

"Hi," Joan said, feeling suddenly awkward when she found Jaleesa alone. "I—this is my last day coming here, and there's something I wanted to tell you."

Jaleesa's face seemed open, but she didn't say anything.

"The principal told me today's lunch was important. So, I wanted you to know that. Your newspaper helped make it a good lunch. And your idea to include the families who let the teachers stay with them this summer was good. So, thanks!" Joan held out her hand.

When Jaleesa shook it, they both smiled. Joan started to go but then turned back. "Oh, and thanks for teaching me something about journalism."

After supper that evening, Joan's mom left her and her dad to clean up the kitchen as she rushed off to a garden club meeting. "We're so proud of you, honey," she said. "Your report is wonderfully written, so well organized. I'm sorry we'll have to wait to talk more."

As Joan cleared the table while her dad put away leftovers, her impatience grew. She filled the dishpan with hot sudsy water, then turned toward him. "Couldn't you and I talk about it?"

He hesitated, but finally agreed. "You've grown up so much in just a month. Remember feeling sorry for yourself about your party? And saying *it's not fair*?"

She scrubbed furiously at food stuck on one of the plates. It had been almost a week since the Neshoba County Fair. She needed to tell him the truth, and she figured she might as well get it behind her. "I kind of lied about Carol's invitation. They would have been glad for you to come, too. But I didn't want you and Big Daddy to disagree."

"I see." Her dad reached for the rinsed plate and a dishtowel.

"I was probably right, too, especially with what happened with Carol's cousin Miranda. She said she heard you doctored—you know. I stood up for you, but she was so mean. I got to thinking what if kids at school this fall talk like that, and I started crying. I wanted to call you to come get me, but Big Daddy said it wasn't safe."

"Did you mention the lie in confession on Saturday?"

She nodded.

"Then let's talk about the other. It can be really hard to stand up for something when everyone else seems to disagree."

"That note on the car . . . tell me nobody's going to hurt you."

"I can't promise you. Now that we're done at the school, though, I think it'll be okay. But—" Their eyes met over another rinsed plate. They each held on to it for a moment. "Your mom and I think it's best that you not hand in your report to the Girl Scouts."

"What are you talking about?"

"We don't want to make things harder for you. Your troop leader is a good person. But your mom has heard her talk at the beauty parlor against civil rights. We should have realized this before, but she's not likely to make waves with a project connected with the Freedom School."

"I can't believe this," Joan said. "I didn't want to go there. Y'all made me. Now you're telling me my project's no good 'cause I did it there?"

"I know it's not fair," her dad surprised her by saying. "We'll help you any way we can with another project."

But his taking away her argument only made her madder. What Miranda did was hurtful and confusing enough. This was worse because she'd worked hard for something, deserved to get her Marian Award, and couldn't because of somebody's stupid attitudes about civil rights.

Her dad threw the dishtowel over one shoulder and reached out to hug her. "Change is a strange thing, honey. It comes in fits and starts. I always thought I gave the same care to all my patients, regardless of the door they came through. But this summer has made me wonder if taking away a little of a man's pride isn't somehow bad for his health."

"You thinking of making your Negro waiting room nicer, Dad?"

"Something like that. But not right now. I think you and I both took an important first step this summer. Now we have to keep an eye out for our next one."

"Isn't that like lying?"

"I guess it is." He sighed deeply. "But it's also like hoping."

Joan felt her anger cooling but her confusion deepening. She began to sing "You Are My Sunshine." Her dad joined her. Soon, she was laughing at his off-key singing, so much like the principal's, and silently rooting for hope.

❖   ❖   ❖

On the last day of classes, Zach said well over a hundred goodbyes. He could not recall a time when he'd felt so much for people he was leaving, or wanted—needed—to say so many goodbyes. Through them all, C.J. waited.

Now, they stood facing each other in the tiny room where they'd sat together, knees touching, after the "I Have a Dream" assembly. Her suitcase sat ominously in the corner, a shaft of strong Mississippi sunlight striking it from the small, high window. "I have to get to Metairie's soon," she said. "George is driving me to the bus station."

The light glinted off the tiny piano charm that hung on a chain around her neck. Zach reached out to touch it. "I hope this helps," he said. "I'll call you. I'm not sure when, because I don't want to intrude. But at least to check on how your dad is doing."

Her eyes, the ones he wanted to drown in, walked his face as if memorizing it. Then she held out her hand for a handshake. He took it, and she wrapped her left hand around their two clasped hands. He reached out his left hand to touch her shoulder, but, unable to resist, pulled her toward him and kissed her with all the passion he had so long denied.

He felt her body melt against his, and she returned his kiss. All too quickly, she pulled away and clutched the piano charm, meeting his eyes once more. "I won't take this off until I make a decision," she promised. And then she was gone, leaving him to wonder why, now that he was leaving Mississippi, he felt like a soldier going off to battle.

Soon after, Zach, Elizabeth, Jacob, and Max boarded the bus to Atlantic City. Zach appreciated the volunteers who stayed to close up the Meridian Baptist Seminary, but he couldn't understand the ones who left immediately for home. He thought everyone who'd taught classes, registered voters, and sung freedom songs in Mississippi this summer and lived to tell about it should be with the Mississippi Freedom Democratic Party. After all, the entire summer project had been about securing the right to vote for Mississippi Negroes. Watching the sixty-two MFDP delegates unseat the Mississippi Democratic Party would be the crowning glory of this summer's work.

Once in Atlantic City on Saturday night, Zach and the others made their way to an area bar. Over beers, they watched TV and talked.

The Credentials Committee hearings, with Mrs. Fannie Lou Hamer taking center stage, had been moved to the Convention Hall ballroom, with sufficient space to allow news coverage. "Just wait 'til folks hear her," Jacob said.

"It feels like a shoo-in," Max said. "Freedom Democrats have followed party rules to the letter. Open precinct meetings, properly publicized. Electing both Negro and white delegates. All they should have to do is present their case and claim their right to be the officially recognized Democratic Party of Mississippi."

"It feels good having right on our side," Elizabeth agreed.

But live network coverage was abruptly preempted when President Johnson called a press conference. "That'll hurt," Zach said, "not being able to hear Mrs. Hamer talk about being jailed and beaten, shot at, and fired from her job, all for trying to register to vote."

They ordered another pitcher and food and talked on. Later that night, the compelling images Mrs. Hamer had painted—of two Negro prisoners forced to beat her with a blackjack, the first working until he dropped from exhaustion and the second taking over—led the networks to run her speech on the news.

"I swear that hit me just as hard as when Mrs. Hamer told it to us in Ohio," Elizabeth said, wiping away a tear.

"All of this is on account of we want to register, to become first-class citizens," Mrs. Hamer said in closing. "And if the Freedom Democratic Party is not seated now, I question America. Is this America, the land of the free and the home of the brave, where we have to sleep with our telephones off the hooks because our lives be threatened daily, because we want to live as decent human beings, in America?"

Another group of civil rights supporters stopped by their table and shared the news that a "compromise" had already been proposed and rejected. It had suggested that the all-white party keep their voting privileges by swearing an oath of loyalty, and the MFDP be seated as "honored guests."

Throughout the weekend, more supporters arrived from around the country. Late Monday night, they began a round-the-clock vigil on the boardwalk outside Convention Hall. This felt to Zach more like what he'd expected to be doing when he signed up for the summer project: Visibly, publicly demonstrating for change in the American political system. Carrying signs bearing giant sketches of James Chaney, Mickey Schwerner, and Andy Goodman, and hand-painted slogans such as *Seat the Freedom Delegates*, *Help Produce Democracy*, and *One Man, One Vote*. Walking in circles or back and forth before newspaper and television reporters and curious onlookers, while singing the freedom songs that had buoyed them all summer.

In shifts, the vigil keepers adjourned to nearby churches where they lay in sleeping bags on rock-hard pews. Zach and Elizabeth traded off with Jacob and Max. On one of these sleep-scarce occasions, he and Elizabeth talked back and forth until someone finally shushed them, then moved outside.

"What are you going to do now that this summer's over?" she asked.

"I haven't decided. I'm expected back at law school, but I might go to Mississippi."

"You'd go back? To Meridian?"

"Jackson, more likely. The Lawyers' Committee for Civil Rights needs volunteers, law student grunts."

"And C.J.?"

He met her firm gaze. "What do you mean?"

"It didn't take long, once she showed up in Meridian, to figure out she was the one back in Chicago. She tried to convince me you were just friends. I told her I was worried for both of you, for your safety. She certainly knows better, having lived in Mississippi almost her whole life. It was you I thought might do something stupid."

"Well, you don't have to worry now," he snapped, his eyes locked on hers.

When she finally looked away, he sighed. "What are you going to do?"

She shrugged. "That should be such an easy question. My boyfriend and I were talking marriage before I left. And he officially proposed in his latest letter. We'll see."

When their rest shift was over, not having rested at all, Zach and Elizabeth returned to the boardwalk. They joined a conga line on the beach, singing "Wade in the Water." Hope fueled their dancing and singing.

On Tuesday afternoon, the MFDP met in Union Baptist Church to vote on a new compromise in which the all-white party would still be seated if they signed a loyalty oath. In addition, MFDP delegation chairman Aaron Henry and white delegate Rev. Edwin King would be seated as delegates at large, each getting one vote, and 1968 convention rules would prohibit segregation. Mr. Henry and Rev. King spoke to the vigil keepers at a rally that night. Mrs. Hamer led them all in freedom songs. The mood was somber as deliberation began.

Throughout discrimination and death, the movement had believed the system would work, but the MFDP had played by the rules and lost. In the end, the sixty-two members of the MFDP delegation determined that they'd come too far to settle for anything less than unseating the Mississippi Democratic Party and voted to reject the compromise. In the closing hours of the convention, they returned to their supporters on the boardwalk, linked hands and sang "We Shall Overcome."

Elizabeth broke down in tears. Zach put his arm around her to comfort her. But his words were anything but soothing. "It's going to be hard going home," he whispered. "We've been living in a cocoon this summer, with our idealism. But we're going to crash right back into the lives we left behind."

"Until the fall," he'd signed the letter he left on the piano in Chicago when C.J. refused to see him. His plan had seemed beyond question then. He would come home to her and declare his love. Then they would move forward together. But she, just like those involved in this convention, was back in the real world, and change would not come easy for her either. He fought with everything in him not to rush to a bus bound for Mississippi and insist that she come away with him.

On the last Friday of August, a week to the day from when he'd said goodbye to C.J., Zach waved farewell to his friends and boarded another bus. He was headed home, to New York, where his parents and Anne would embrace him—a sweaty, smelly mess—because he was alive, perhaps never even understanding why he had had to go. As C.J. said, a person's dream had to come from inside them. No amount of wishing and hoping by someone else would make it happen. The MFDP had to go home to Mississippi, face themselves in the mirror each day, and move forward. C.J. had to find her own dream. And there was so much still to overcome. Zach would find his own next steps. But he'd keep the promise of their kiss.

CHAPTER 25

Wednesday, September 23
More Lessons

The rocker C.J.'s daddy had carved so long ago slapped steadily at the porch floor. C.J. cradled a pile of purple hull peas, likely the last of this season, and a pan. Another pan sat on the floor. She was shelling almost as fast as her feet were pushing. Ripping open the hulls. Dumping peas in one pan. Throwing hulls in the other with a thwack. Her thumbs were stained purple, her thumbnails tender.

"You going somewheres in that chair?" Momma asked.

"Huh?"

"You're rocking awful hard. You'd do better to fetch the keys and use that car you bought us."

Momma nodded in the direction of the 1961 Buick sedan parked in the yard. It sparkled in the September sun, as if feeling Charlie's love. He'd already washed it twice. And that good-for-nothing friend of his, William, had proven good for one thing after all. He'd taught Charlie to drive a while ago. Charlie had taught C.J. and helped her get her license. Since then, she'd been getting to know Poplar Springs all over again, from behind the wheel of a car. She'd registered Charlie at Booker T. and now drove herself back and forth each day for work at Mrs. Harwell's. She rested easier knowing she could get Daddy to Doc Barnes or the hospital without relying on the bus.

"Soon as that boy of ours gets home from school, he'll be bending your ear, wanting you to hand over the keys," her momma went on.

C.J. massaged her sore thumbs and chafed at the need to go—somewhere. Do—something. More likely than Charlie having time to go for a drive was him coming home from school with homework harder than the night before. She could help reasonably well with world history and English. Even biology—thanks to all her daddy taught her through the years, while they walked the Wilson farm. But more and more with each passing day, algebra was stretching the limits of what she'd learned in business math.

She pictured last night's homework—linear equations—and heard Charlie read, "Five-x plus seven-x equals seventy-two."

"What'd you get?"

"X equals six?"

"Did you check it?"

"Yeah."

"Okay, here goes." She reached for a paper and pencil. "Five times six is thirty. Seven times six is . . . yes, forty-two. Thirty plus forty-two is seventy-two. Looks right to me."

They'd continued that way until the last problem. "Solve eleven plus three-x minus seven equals six-x plus five minus three-x," Charlie read.

"Good Lord!"

Again, C.J.'s pencil scratched at the paper. Through the screen door came the sounds of the autumn night—Momma softly singing, someone's cat mewing, katydids chirping. She struggled through her solution and gave Charlie a perplexed look. "Every which way I try, I keep coming up with four equals five!"

"Me, too."

"I figured there was always an answer in math. I reckon it's time we took Miz Johnson up on her offer."

Miss Johnson—Claudia—was the counselor C.J. and Charlie had been shuttled off to after C.J. demanded to see the principal during registration. Sitting in the office of Miss Etheridge, as old as Booker T. itself, and hearing her say she didn't see college in Charlie's future, C.J. had decided she needn't kowtow any longer. It was one thing being told back when she was in school that her future was cleaning white folks' houses and another entirely for Miss Etheridge to discourage Charlie.

C.J. remembered Claudia and Metairie playing together at recess at the Mill Road School. Since then, Claudia had graduated from Tougaloo College in Jackson. "I hear y'all been making some trouble," she'd said, with her hands on her hips and a stern look on her face.

"Claudia," C.J. had said too firmly, having failed to realize that she was teasing. "We got us the first Evans to graduate college standing right here. We just need you to tell us how we're gonna make it happen."

"Well, determination, that's half the battle."

The three of them had mapped out a plan. Charlie would need to take the most difficult courses Booker T. had to offer. C.J. would study along with him and review his homework. If he needed help she couldn't give, they would come straight to Claudia.

C.J. flicked a hull into the pan at her feet with a resounding thump.

"Goodness!" Momma said. "Anyways, I can hear Charlie now, saying 'C.J.?'" She made her voice go low. "'Momma ain't seen her grandbabies in the longest time.' His face would be frowning, all concerned like. 'How 'bout I carry her over to Metairie's this weekend?'"

"And once you got ready to come on home, you'd have to call over to Rosalee's house to see could Charlie spare the time."

Momma threw back her head and laughed deep in her throat. C.J. managed a weak smile, thinking of the strain that was still there between her and Metairie.

As if she'd forgotten that Charlie was at all involved, Metairie seemed to be carrying a grudge against C.J. alone. Making remarks, whenever they got together, about how George had been assigned to a less favorable shift or hadn't gotten an expected raise, and making no bones about blaming her for not getting Charlie out of the freedom school and out of Meridian.

"It's the heat, though, Momma. I was just trying to keep a breeze on myself. I surely don't recollect this kind of heat in September. It's ninety degrees today if it's a one."

"It is mighty hot for September, but I can't complain. First off, praise Jesus that Miz Harwell needs you fulltime. It's a blessing you're back, helping our boy and your daddy." Momma traded her half-empty pan for C.J.'s full one. "I'll just take them peas inside and let you keep at it. Your fingers are a far sight faster than my old ones."

She turned, then stopped. Leaned down and kissed C.J.'s head. "And me, honey, helping me. Lord knows how we got on without you all this time."

Alone on the porch with her responsibility, C.J. felt tears dampen her hands and recalled being in the Harwells' downstairs bathroom on her first day back there, almost a month ago. Staring at the yellow ring around the drain, she'd imagined water dripping, ever so slowly, the entire time she'd been away, creating the stain no one had bothered with.

She'd looked at that stain for well over a week before finding time to tackle it. While she scrubbed, she listened to Mrs. Harwell struggling at the piano. Mozart, from a book of nineteen of his sonatas. The book was always out, like a stain Mrs. Harwell had to get rid of.

That day, C.J. was still puzzling over more than she'd managed to figure out. It was clear Mr. Harwell no longer lived here, but not whether he was dead or alive. The lawn seemed freshly mowed since yesterday, so maybe he still looked after the house. She'd expected Lacey and Franklin Jr. to be grown and gone, but neither one had called or come by. Why did Mrs. Harwell have C.J. doing her baking for the church, while she spent her days moving between the piano and her bedroom?

"C.J.!"

She'd hurried in to find Mrs. Harwell leaning so close to the sheet music her eyelashes nearly brushed the page.

"You said you'd had some lessons. Can you tell me what this note is? I just can't make it out."

"Wonder why it's so small?"

"It's a grace note."

C.J. counted her way up the staff, twice to make sure. "I think it's the D two octaves above middle C."

Mrs. Harwell gave it a try. "That's it." She resumed her playing.

C.J. shrugged and returned to the bathroom, suddenly determined not to stop scrubbing until she could make the sink look the way it had when she used to tend to it. Somehow that would make it okay, being back here without her friends. Without Zach. Something splashed her hand then, making her look up at the bathroom mirror. Tears. She'd watched them fall until there were no more. Until there was only the set of her jaw and the hollowness in her eyes. She had seen—no, heard—this before. The sound that was not quite right when Mrs. Harwell played. C.J. named it desperation.

The rest of that afternoon, she thought about desperation. Why did Mrs. Harwell feel it? How could she find out? As she served supper, C.J. decided the only way to know was to ask. While she cleaned up the kitchen, she recalled her Chicago employers, the roundabout ways in which she'd gained their confidence. Mrs. Upton had been the hardest. But then C.J.'s common sense saved one of her dinner parties. What did Mrs. Harwell need help saving?

Before she left that evening, C.J. went to Mrs. Harwell's room. The curtains on the big picture window were open, revealing the well-tended lawn against the dusky sky. Mrs. Harwell reclined on the chaise.

"Doc Barnes keeps this up so nicely," she said, as if continuing a conversation she and C.J. had been having for a while. "It's a pleasure to sit here."

"Yes'm, it's very nice." C.J. allowed herself a moment to admire the view, all the while wondering how the very man Mrs. Harwell once asked her to spy on had come to be doing the lawn. She looked back toward the chaise. "May I talk with you?"

Mrs. Harwell's eyes darted back and forth, giving the impression of a rabbit caught by a dog. But she nodded and pointed to the small chair at the dressing table.

C.J. played with the car keys in her hand. "While I was away, I worked for three very different families. I found things went best when I understood how I could help them the most . . . I'd really like to know how to help you the most."

With only the small bedside lamp on, the room was rapidly growing dark. But she thought Mrs. Harwell wiped at tears.

"It's called multiple sclerosis."

C.J. waited, needing to know more, not wanting to hear. Mrs. Harwell went on to explain there was no cure, no way to know how fast her condition would worsen. For now, she had deteriorating vision, fatigue, and unsteadiness when she walked.

"Some people, though, lose sensation in their fingers. And their muscles grow very weak. I have to play them all—" She choked back a sob. "Before it's too late."

"Them all?"

"The music in the piano bench—Mother's."

"Yes'm. I appreciate you telling me. If there's any way I can help . . ." She waited until there was only darkness and the faint yellow circle cast by the lamp.

"Goodnight, C.J."

The next day, C.J. had been dusting the living room while Mrs. Harwell sat on the sofa.

"There's something I'm wanting to know," she'd begun. "When you were away—well, how did you come to take piano lessons?"

"It was the last lady I worked for. When she found out I wanted to learn some piano, she said she'd teach me. She had a piano near about as beautiful as yours."

C.J. waited while one hand moved back and forth in Mrs. Harwell's lap, as if in time to music only she could hear.

"That piano bench is full of music. And I'm working through it every day, bit by bit. I'm just thinking someone else working through it, too, might be a good idea. Could you play something for me?"

"On your piano? No, ma'am." C.J. wagged her head.

"It's okay," Mrs. Harwell urged.

"But I don't have any of the music anymore."

"Is there a piece you've memorized?"

"Just this minuet by Bach we were working on."

"Would you play that for me, please?" Mrs. Harwell waved both hands toward the piano.

C.J. walked on legs of rubber, as if she were about to touch the face of God. She sank slowly onto the bench and traced the keys, seeing them as made of gold rather than ivory. Finally, she played.

But after only a few measures, her fingers stumbled. She looked at Mrs. Harwell, embarrassed. "I don't—I can't—"

"You have a nice touch, C.J., just as I hoped. I'd really like for you to give it another try. I'm sure you can do it."

She noted those words as the kindest Mrs. Harwell had ever uttered in her presence. They made her want to continue. *If you can see it, you can play it*, Mrs. Gray had said so often. C.J. imagined fine ladies and gentlemen dipping to the music, just as Mrs. Gray taught her. Measure by measure, the minuet came back to her.

"Your first teacher has done a fine job. Would you let me teach you, too?"

And so began hours at the piano, where Mrs. Harwell sometimes felt strong enough to sit beside C.J. on the bench but other times asked to be propped up on pillows on the sofa, sometimes jabbed at the sheet music with her pencil but other times patiently coaxed a lift of the wrist or curve of the fingers that totally changed the sound C.J. produced. Days that started with preparing breakfast, making up the bed, doing a little cleaning and ended with fixing supper and settling Mrs. Harwell for the night. Days otherwise filled with scales and theory and practice, sometimes broken by C.J. rushing to grab something from the oven before it burned or drive Mrs. Harwell to the church to deliver a cake. Days truly unlike any she'd ever gotten paid for.

As she shook her head in amazement over the new Mrs. Harwell, the phone rang into the quiet of the Evanses' porch. She kept right on shelling. It seemed she thought of Zach with every breath, wondering what was taking him so long to call and imagining where he was, all the while unable to answer the question of what she wanted the two of them to be to each other. But day had followed day without him calling.

"Daughter?" her momma said as she came back outside and sat down. "There's a man on the phone asking after you."

C.J. gathered the unshelled peas in her apron and hurried inside. "Hello?" she said a little breathlessly.

"It's good to hear your voice."

Zach's voice seemed to conjure up a vision of him, almost as if he were in the room. She reached out, and in so doing, let go of the apron, scattering purple hull peas across the kitchen floor.

"How's your father?"

She told him that Daddy was recovering from his latest bout. She was taking walks with him on the Wilson farm, helping him build up his strength again. The whole family was trying to keep him from his cigarettes.

Zach waited. She fired questions into the silence. "You must be back in school now. Or is that next week? How's Flo and them?"

"I haven't seen them yet. It was good to see my folks and Anne, though."

She stared at the mess on the floor, beginning to sense something different in his voice—resoluteness. He must be losing patience with her. She knew what he wanted to hear. Across the miles his achingly blue eyes reached out to her, trying to lock on and pull her back. She squeezed her eyes shut against the memory. But it was as if she had looked at a light, then looked away. The blue became a thousand brightly colored stars flashing in the darkness.

Tell him you love him! a voice screamed from inside her head. *But he'll want to know what that means,* the voice argued. Could they simply talk? Could she have more time to let his voice wash over her, fill up her soul?

"You'll never guess what Miz Harwell and I are doing."

"Eating lunch together?" he said. They both laughed.

"Almost as miraculous. She's teaching me piano."

"You keep coming back to that somehow, don't you?" he said.

She fingered the charm on the chain around her neck. "Maybe it's my lucky charm. Oh—and you got to hear how well Charlie is applying himself in school."

"What about you, C.J.?" Zach asked, in an echo of another conversation.

"It's not easy being back here, I'll admit. Things were so different in Chicago. I'm—"

Tell him! Tell him you love him, but that's all you know. "Zach, I—"

The screen door banged, and in walked Daddy, holding his tobacco pouch.

"Daddy, no!" she said. Then, "Excuse me just a moment." She put her hand over the phone while she begged him not to smoke.

When he left the kitchen, she came back to the phone, apologizing. "Doc Barnes says the worst thing Daddy can do is smoke. We try everything we can think of, but it's a hard habit to break." She closed her eyes for a moment, searching for strength. "Zach," she said again, but the moment was gone.

"It's okay, C.J. I know how hard this is for you." She could hear him take a deep breath and let it out slowly. "That's why I've made some decisions."

She could feel what he had yet to say bearing down on her like a freight train, but could no more stop it than she could snap her fingers and have the peas fly back up into her apron. She traced a black mark on the worn counter top. The mark was small, really. But in her momma's otherwise spotless kitchen, it seemed huge.

"I'm not in Chicago, by the way."

"What? Where are you?"

"Jackson."

"Why?" Her voice took on a slight edge.

He sighed. "The simple answer is I've decided to take time off from law school and work for the Lawyers' Committee for Civil Rights. There's still so much legal work, even with most of the summer volunteers having left Mississippi. And we're working towards voting rights legislation."

Had he expected her to say no? Maybe her answer really didn't matter that much to him. Yet she could still feel his lips on hers when he kissed her goodbye at the school.

"But the truth is we each need time apart. First, before anything else can happen, even if you decide to go back to Chicago. And—" She heard his voice break and realized this was hard for him, too. "I almost took a bus straight to Poplar Springs after things went so badly in Atlantic City. I wanted to bring you away with me."

"I feel my dream like a forgotten word, right on the tip of my tongue, Zach. But I just can't say it yet."

"Maybe the charm I gave you will help somehow . . ."

"Maybe it will." She swatted at tears and tried to gather the peas into a pile with her feet. But the phone cord kept stopping her from reaching them.

"There's one more thing. Know this, C.J. I *love* you. *You* are my bashert, my soul mate. *You* are the one who makes me feel the spark."

"Will you call me again?" It was all she could think to say.

"Of course."

Before he hung up, he gave her his number and told her he would always be there if she needed him.

She sank to the floor under the weight of her emotions. Then, one by one, she began to pick up the purple hull peas.

CHAPTER 26

— Six Years Later —

September 1970
The Magic Girls

The air in Poplar Springs was cooling off slowly on this mid-September evening, as Joan rocked with C.J. on her porch. The house at their backs was bigger and nicer than the Evanses' house, but the porch was the same in every detail, right down to the castor bean plants that grew along the railing and the rockers Lewis had made C.J. and Quincy as a wedding present. Through the open windows, they could hear Quincy riffing on his guitar.

"Be sure to call Zach at this number, soon as you get to Chicago," C.J. said, handing Joan a folded piece of paper. "You're gonna feel like you're too busy, settling in at the university. But he can help you get your bearings."

Joan thought about orientation four days from now and shivered with excitement and nervousness. "You've talked to Zach lately?" she asked. It had been a year since Lewis's funeral, which both Zach and the Barnes family attended. "Y'all must be better friends than I thought."

C.J.'s emerald eyes took on a faraway look. "We've been very good friends ever since we met in Chicago," she said, "although we hit a rough patch last year."

"Because your dad died?"

"Not just because of that, no." She sighed deeply. "Let me tell you a story."

Joan snuggled into her chair, carried back to the days when she sat at C.J.'s feet while she ironed.

"I'll start with the part you already know. You remember how Quincy and I got together?"

Joan nodded. She'd been at the wedding reception at Hope Baptist, where the story was told numerous times. When Mrs. Harwell died, she bequeathed her piano to C.J., who decided she was meant to make good use of such a beautiful gift and found a new teacher so she could continue her lessons. Head Start had opened education centers around Mississippi the year before. Deciding not to look for more work as a maid, she became a music teacher at the Poplar Springs center. They had no instruments, though, not even a tambourine. She remembered the washtub bass and comb-and-tissue kazoo the children's jazz band used at the Freedom School, but wanted more for these kids who were now her responsibility. She wanted a piano for them, and Mrs. Harwell had also left her some money. So, she'd gone shopping. That's where she met Quincy, a musician who'd performed in Chicago a while, then come home. He worked in the music store, selling and repairing instruments, doing a little teaching.

"I reckon you didn't know Zach stayed on in Mississippi after the Freedom School ended," C.J. said.

"No, we didn't really talk at the service."

"The summer of sixty-four changed so many people's lives. If Zach had never volunteered, or was sent somewhere other than Meridian . . . if Momma and Daddy hadn't sent Charlie to Metairie's . . . if Daddy hadn't gotten sick. Well, who knows what might have been?"

"Wow!" Joan said. "You and Zach? How'd that happen?"

"We had special feelings for each other," C.J. confessed. "Zach told me it was my decision—what we would be to each other. He went to work as a volunteer with the Lawyers' Committee for Civil Rights in Jackson for a year, then back to Chicago to finish law school. He was waiting for me to decide whether to go back, too.

"While Zach was in law school, Elizabeth got in touch with him, wanting to talk with someone who'd been in Mississippi. She'd married, and her husband couldn't relate to what she'd gone through. I·could hear in Zach's letters and phone calls how the friendship that began in Meridian between him and Elizabeth was deepening, just like the friendship between Quincy and me was. I encouraged him to move on, though I hadn't fully made up my own mind. He said no, folks wait for each other to finish school and the like all the time. And"—her voice broke slightly—"he'd promised to wait for me for all eternity, just as long as there was a chance. Then Daddy got worse, and I stayed on here. Elizabeth got divorced. Momma needed me so. I reckon the hope died when Daddy did."

Joan swiped at tears.

"But it's a good story, honey. Even though life moved forward too fast for Zach and me to ever go back, we both found love again."

"Why are you telling me this?" Joan asked.

"Well, 'cause we're the magic girls, and you're going to Chicago where things are different than what you've grown up with, yet so much the same. I want you to know what a fine, smart man Zach is. That he can be there for you, same as he's been there for me."

They rocked in silence for a while before Joan said, "Last year *was* a big year. For me, it started on July 20. I was visiting my friend Carol in Meridian the day they desegregated the Highland Park pool. Her great-grandfather—Big Daddy they called him—was *not* pleased. 'Everybody in his place' is what he always said. Still, it seemed to me like a time when all things were possible, because a United States astronaut walked on the moon that day. Now, I wonder what Meridian's black folks were feeling, if stepping into that pool for the first time seemed like a bigger accomplishment than stepping onto the moon."

She reached to pluck a leaf from the castor bean plants. "After being at the Freedom School a few times, I thought about not being friends with Carol anymore because of Big Daddy. He just kept digging in his heels, saying things that didn't fit with what I was seeing. But then he'd be so nice to me. And I think he looked out for my dad, even though he despised the idea of him doctoring at the school. It was so confusing."

She stared at the leaf, turning it over and over. "That fall, the work was finished on my dad's integrated waiting room. He'd been thinking about it since 1964, but what finally pushed him to do it was your dad being in a wheelchair and having trouble getting around the building and into the Negro waiting room. So, who do you think gets hurt and is one of the first white patients through those integrated doors?"

"Big Daddy, I reckon."

"Close." Joan laughed. "It was Carol, brought in by Big Daddy when they were in a car accident right in front of Dad's office. He didn't have a scratch, but she was cut up and broke her leg rather badly. While they waited for the ambulance to take her to the hospital, Dad's black nurse stopped the bleeding and got her comfortable. The paramedics were putting Carol in the ambulance when Big Daddy turned to me, with such a strange look on his face that he almost didn't seem like himself, and said this: 'Everybody in his place, I've always said. Today, your daddy had everybody in their place, and I'm grateful for it.'"

Joan talked of her senior year and the forced desegregation of Poplar Springs High the past January. "Carol was in a full-leg cast, with pins in her bones, and her recuperation took quite a while. Big Daddy insisted she stay at PSH, not leave for the new private high school like her parents wanted and so many of our friends did. That way, I could be there to help her. We talked a lot then. She told me all kinds of things. Like how Meridian kept a lid on violence during the summer of 1964."

"After the murders, of course," C.J. said. "We watched violence continue in other parts of Mississippi. But you're right. Meridian seemed like a grease fire someone snuffed out by putting the lid on a skillet."

"Yeah, Carol said it was a delicate balance, harassing volunteers at the COFO office and going and coming between where they stayed and everywhere else, but leaving the school alone. Mostly the Klan just thought like Big Daddy—*what's the harm in a school for dimwits?* Oh—" She cast a quick look C.J.'s way. "I'm sorry."

C.J. nodded for her to continue.

"But they knew better than to draw any more attention. And so the word simply went out that nothing else was to happen. Imagine that, the power of that!" She shook her head. "I don't know if it's a good thing or a bad thing. I just feel like I have to leave, see what it's like somewhere else."

C.J. looked at her earnestly. "I hope you're not going off thinking everything will be so much better up north."

Joan smiled, remembering how as a little girl she'd been amazed by the way C.J. understood things she hadn't even explained. "I confess I first thought about moving away when my parents wouldn't let me submit my thank-you lunch project to the Girl Scouts."

"I can tell you, a whole lot of change is needed everywhere. Just ask Zach."

Joan nodded, but she was thinking about the day she ordered C.J. to serve lemonade, when she'd let her desire to fit in turn her around from what she knew to be right. She'd been disrespectful. But maybe worse, she hadn't stood up for C.J. when Cindy asked if she was one of those *uppity niggers*.

"I came here to say goodbye, but also because there's something I need you to understand. No, that's not it. Maybe you can help me understand." She recalled the boy in King's Drugs, saying neither niggers nor Catholics belonged. "It's about a word . . . Do you remember the headline in the paper a while after they found the bodies of those Freedom Summer volunteers?"

C.J. raised an eyebrow.

"I'm just gonna say it." Joan scrunched up her eyes until she saw the large black letters on the white paper: *"The Nigger was Found on Top," Says Dozer Operator.* She opened her eyes and repeated it, saw C.J.'s eyes flash.

"Folks talked about that headline at my church. A girl I went to high school with knows the man that wrote it. She lives in Meridian now and works up at the paper, cleaning. My friend asked the man did he know how bad that headline hurt, for the boys to be dead and then James Chaney to be called that. The man looked at her all patient-like and said, 'Well, Bessie, *that's* what the dozer operator said. 'Course y'all know *I* would never say such a thing. We were just quoting that dozer operator.' My friend knew she could lose her job over it, but she said, 'Sir, all due respect, some part of you must know them quotes don't make it okay.' "

"How'd it make *you* feel, C.J.?" Joan hung her head. "I don't know if you remember. But one of my friends called you that a long time ago. And I—well, I just let her 'cause I was mostly thinking about myself. When you left right after that day, I thought it was because of me."

"I didn't take kindly to the treatment," C.J. admitted. "But I think you and me both have been a mite too hard on you 'bout it."

"It was important to me, being your little friend. I was wrong to act that way."

"It was the way things were. I was hurt because I expected more of you. But you were just a child, caught up in something bigger than you."

"Anyway"—Joan met C.J.'s eyes—"I was wrong, and I'm sorry."

After a moment, C.J. smiled, though her eyes still looked sad.

"You reckon y'all are always gonna be called—that terrible name?"

"Maybe so, honey. But maybe we won't always have to *feel* like niggers."

Joan rested her bare forearms on the rocker's arms, expecting to have to swat at a mosquito now and then but finally relaxing into the chair. She saw seven-year-old Cindy and Sally Ann and teenaged C.J. "Do the fog machines come way out here?" she asked.

"No. I put in castor bean plants just like Momma did." C.J. swept her arm the length of the porch rail.

Joan could almost hear the old truck clanking down her street. Suddenly, she was with Cindy and Sally Ann again, laughing as they chased the cloud, fading in and out of view whenever a slight breeze took the fog in unexpected directions. A choice—one of her bad ones.

C.J. pushed the rocker into motion with her feet. Joan copied her, enjoying the sound of the runners slapping the boards of the porch floor. It made her feel peaceful. "I asked you when you left me to go to Chicago if we'd ever see each other again. Do you remember what you said?"

C.J. smiled, then stood and came over to Joan's chair. Just as she had back then, she hugged her tightly. "Now, that's probably not up to you or me. But we're the magic girls, aren't we? Me, being born like a magic trick, and you with your magic line on the driveway. Who knows what we might do someday?"

Joan thought about that for a moment. What she'd learned that summer was that freedom meant choices. As C.J. straightened and Quincy came out onto the porch and wrapped his arms around her waist, Joan knew she was ready. Chicago was only the next step. She was ready to move her magic line.

Acknowledgments

Writing *The Fog Machine* has been a journey of discovery—capturing history, lest we forget or never even know it, and exploring what enables and disables change in human beings. I am indebted to my guides. Pearlie Mae Clark and Bill Ready Sr. painted a picture of the time and place in which I grew up. Heather Tobis Booth and Reverend Ed King filled in details and steered my early research. Gail Falk provided historical documents, helped strategize, and reviewed as I dove deep into the history of the Mississippi Summer Project in Meridian in 1964. I also thank Chicago Sinai Congregation, Harriet Hausman, Rabbi Robert J. Marx, Chuck Mervis, and Rabbi Paul Saiger for my enlightenment about Judaism.

Faye Inge and Vickie Malone were first to recognize *The Fog Machine*'s academic potential. Jackie Roberts was first to champion *The Fog Machine* for book clubs. Shea Peeples was first to welcome *The Fog Machine* into her library (Wescott Library in Eagan, MN) to be read by young adults. Seattle's Mercer Island Library hosted my first adult book group exchange. Members of Meridian, Mississippi's first graduating class under federally mandated desegregation (Meridian/Harris High School class of 1970) were first to participate in a community read.

My brother Tim chased down leads and helped in any way I asked. My children Dani and Timothy missed too many dinners with me during critical points in the schedule. Barbara Chintz, Dr. Bill Scaggs, Barbara Ellis, and Micki Dickoff dropped into my life at just the right moments to move this novel forward. Special friends Vicky Goplin and Sheri Speckan read multiple versions of the manuscript, celebrated accomplishments and consoled me during discouraging times, and enriched the story by hours of discussion. And through it all, my husband Gary Dion read, brainstormed, encouraged, and picked up the slack so I could write.

Chapter Notes

Historical authenticity has been a guiding principle in the writing of this novel. Being historically authentic means to me that events portrayed either actually happened—in that time and place, in that way—or could have happened. Or, that no one who actually lived the events in the book would likely take significant issue with such a presentation.

For example, there was no "free clinic" at the Meridian Freedom School. However, the Medical Committee for Human Rights staffed a clinic in Jackson for Freedom Summer volunteers from all over Mississippi. And the Meridian Freedom School is an authentic choice for where to set the clinic, especially for having Doc Barnes volunteer, because the Klan did not watch the Meridian Freedom School as they did other locations such as the COFO office or Freedom Center.

The following notes address deviations for the sake of the story, cite sources, and offer further information or more specific acknowledgments.

CHAPTER ONE

- Page 8: Barbie® Doll debuted at the American International Toy Fair in New York on March 9, 1959.

CHAPTER TWO

- Page 16: John L. Bissant (1914 – 2006) played for the New Orleans Black Pelicans in 1938. The Negro Leagues used the same balls as the major leagues. However, balls were kept in play as long as possible, and keeping a ball as a memento was uncommon.

CHAPTER THREE

- Page 27: "Prettiest Train" (New words and arrangement by Benny Will Richardson. Collected and adapted by Alan Lomax.) Global Jukebox Publishing (BMI). Courtesy of The Association for Cultural Equity. Musicologist, writer, and producer Alan Lomax (1915 – 2002) recorded Benny Will Richardson, a prisoner at Mississippi's Parchman Farm in 1947, singing "Prettiest Train." The song can be streamed at http://goo.gl/lSYEBJ. To learn about the work of Alan Lomax, visit http://www.culturalequity.org. For full lyrics and background on the prison farm system, refer to "Crime and Prison Songs: 'Prettiest Train' " posted by Anthony Vaver on March 30, 2011 at http://www.earlyamericancrime.com/songs/prettiest-train.

CHAPTER FOUR

- Page 34: The Quickie Automatic Sponge Mop was invented in 1950 by Peter Vosbikian Sr. who patented the self-wringing action.
- Page 40: For more of the "Klan Kreed," from the *Kloran* of the White Knights of the Ku Klux Klan, Realm of Mississippi, refer to http://archive.org/stream/Kloran/kloranwhiteknights_djvu.txt.

CHAPTER FIVE

- Page 59: Clennon King (1920 – 2000) was the second African American to attempt to enroll at the University of Mississippi. His June 4, 1958 attempt resulted in arrest and commitment to the Mississippi State Mental Hospital at Whitfield.

CHAPTER SEVEN

- Page 82: First marketed in Philadelphia, PA, in 1942, Sunbeam® White Bread was a popular brand on every table in the South in the 1950s. The Miss Sunbeam® image was created by children's book illustrator Ellen Segner.

CHAPTER EIGHT

- Page 97: The Dentzel Carousel and Carousel House at Highland Park in Meridian, MS, were designated as National Landmarks in 1977. Gustav Dentzel manufactured the carousel in 1896 for the 1904 St. Louis Exposition. Meridian acquired the carousel in 1909. The carousel house is the sole surviving original carousel house built from a Dentzel blueprint.

CHAPTER NINE

- Page 127: As a teenager, Claudette Colvin became a plaintiff in Browder v. Gayle, the 1956 Supreme Court case which declared Montgomery's bus segregation laws in violation of the Fourteenth Amendment. For more information on Claudette Colvin, read her August 28, 2013 article in *Essence* magazine at: http://www.essence.com/2013/08/28/unsung-hero-civil-rights-claudette-colvin and a Congress of Racial Equality historical article at: http://www.core-online.org/History/colvin.htm.

CHAPTER TEN

- Page 138: C.J.'s remembrance is adapted from this, by Chicago historian, educator, and activist Timuel Black, quoted on the Palm Tavern website at: http://palmtavern.bizland.com/palmtavern/id16.html. "Oh, 47th Street was where it all happened. 47th Street, you'd stand on the corner of 47th Street and South Park and if you stayed there, that was what they said, if you stayed there long enough almost anybody you knew in Chicago would come past there sometime during the day."

CHAPTER FOURTEEN

- Page 201: Read the entire prayer in the *Union Prayer Book*, 1940, page 336.
- Page 202: The sermon on destiny at fictional Mevakshei Tzedek is drawn from a 1982 sermon by Rabbi Howard Berman: "The Faith of Classical Reform Judaism" in which Rabbi Berman spoke of the principles of Classical Reform and quoted Dr. Emil G. Hirsch (1851 – 1923), rabbi of Chicago Sinai Congregation for forty-two years.

CHAPTER FIFTEEN

- Page 217: The hammer, bell, and song are key elements of the song "If I Had a Hammer (The Hammer Song)" written by Pete Seeger and Lee Hays and made popular by Peter, Paul, and Mary.
- Page 217: Chicago Area Friends of SNCC was founded in January 1963 and ended around 1968. Unlike many other "Friends of SNCC" groups, who primarily supported SNCC's work in the South, CAFSNCC was also very active in local Chicago civil rights struggles.
- Page 222: Mrs. Gray refers to "A Raisin in the Sun" (1959) by Lorraine Hansberry.

CHAPTER SIXTEEN

- Page 237: The story at the reflecting pool was shared with me by Rabbi Robert J. Marx, founder of the Jewish Council on Urban Affairs who marched with Dr. Martin Luther King and worked tirelessly for housing equality on Chicago's North Shore.
- Page 245: Award-winning journalist and documentarian Rich Samuels produced "Civil Rights on the North Shore: Bringing the Movement Home," after discovering a 1964 WNBQ documentary which included the exchange between Chicago's South Side and Winnetka. Profiled in the documentary are Oscar Johnson and Jim McNulty. As a seventh-grade Raymond School student, Johnson spent a week in April 1964 living with McNulty's family in Winnetka and attending Sacred Heart School.
- Page 251: For a link to an image of this brochure, refer to the Civil Rights Movement Veterans website at: http://www.crmvet.org/docs/msfsdocs.htm#msfs_recruit.

CHAPTER SEVENTEEN

- Page 259: The civil rights movement was already active when Freedom Summer volunteers Mickey and Rita Schwerner arrived in Meridian in January 1964. There was an NAACP chapter with an active youth group, working with Medgar Evers in 1963. As well, CORE (Congress of Racial Equality) was organizing in the Meridian area and around the state.
- Page 259: The Meridian Baptist Seminary building which housed the Meridian Freedom School was a three-

story brick building built in 1920. MBS was the first Mississippi school to issue high school diplomas to African Americans.

- Page 266: Published in 1962, *The Snowy Day* by Ezra Jack Keats featured the first African American protagonist in a full-color picture book.
- Page 269: Dr. Carter G. Woodson (1875 – 1950), known as the "Father of Black History," was the second African American to earn a PhD at Harvard University. Negro History Week, which he proposed and launched in 1926, became Black History Month in 1976. *The Mis-Education of the Negro*, first published in 1933, is the best known of his more than 30 books.

CHAPTER NINETEEN

- Page 285: COFO volunteer Mark Levy served as coordinator of the Meridian Freedom School. His (and Donna Garde's, an art teacher's) photos, which can be viewed at https://picasaweb.google.com/QCCRMVETS/MeridianMissFreedomSummer1964PixByMarkLevyAndDonnaGarde and are housed in the Mark Levy Collection at the Civil Rights Movement Archive of Queens College, took me back to 1964—to orientation in Oxford, OH; Meridian in July and August; and the Democratic National Convention in Atlantic City, NJ.

CHAPTER TWENTY

- Pages 297-298: With appreciation to the National Park Service; Mary McLeod Bethune Council House National Historic Site; DCWaMMB; National Archives for Black Women's History, I have based my character Mrs. Gray's dialogue on documents from the National Council of Negro Women, Inc. Records, Series 19 and a verbatim transcript of an audiotape of the debriefing session of the WIMS Washington/Maryland Team that traveled from July 21-23, 1964. Arriving in Meridian, MS, July 22, the team visited the COFO Office, Community Center, and Freedom School and attended a luncheon with local black women at St. Paul Methodist Church.

CHAPTER TWENTY-ONE

- Page 315: Fictional Meridian Freedom School students Theo's, Annie's, and Rosalee's and teacher Jacob's "I Have a Dream" speeches are drawn from writings of actual 1964 Meridian Freedom School students and one of their teachers, shared with me by another teacher, Gail Falk.

CHAPTER TWENTY-TWO

- Page 336: Brother James, C.J.'s pastor at Hope Baptist in Poplar Springs, fed her drive to stay safe with his waiting-on-heaven ministerial posture. But there was a range of support for the movement among black ministers in Mississippi during the period of this story. Two Meridian ministers serve to illustrate those openly supportive of civil rights. Reverend Richard S. Porter Sr., pastor of First Union Baptist Church, helped gain agreement to use the Baptist Seminary as a freedom school and supported COFO staff in recruiting homes for volunteers to stay in. Reverend Clinton O. Inge Sr., pastor of New Hope Baptist Church, championed equal educational opportunity. He drove daughter Faye and the other four students who comprise the Meridian Five to all-white Meridian High which they desegregated in 1965.
- Page 338: Pete Seeger's speech is drawn from an article in the *Pittsburgh Post-Gazette*, dateline August 10, 1964, Meridian, Mississippi. "Rights Worker's Reaction to Murders in Miss.," is an excerpt from a letter by Freedom Summer volunteer Gail Falk, to her parents.
- Page 339: Two factors contributed to the Freedom School Convention being held at the Meridian Freedom School: the connection to Schwerner, Chaney, and Goodman and the space and facilities available. The Meridian Freedom School was referred to by many as the "palace" of the freedom schools.
- Page 339: For the full platform of the Mississippi Freedom School Convention—held August 7-9, 1964, in Meridian, Mississippi—refer to the Civil Rights Movement Veterans website at http://www.crmvet.org/docs/fs_plat.htm.
- Page 341: Remembrances of Schwerner, Chaney, and Goodman by fictional Meridian Freedom School students are inspired by an article in the *Pittsburgh Post-Gazette*, dateline August 10, 1964, Meridian, Mississippi. "Rights Worker's Reaction to Murders in Miss.," is an excerpt from a letter by Freedom Summer volunteer Gail Falk, to her parents.

CHAPTER TWENTY-THREE

- •Page 350: For more about Mississippi Governor Paul B. Johnson's speech at the 1964 Neshoba County Fair, see *Three Lives for Mississippi*, by William Bradford Huie, and *We Are Not Afraid: The Story of Goodman, Schwerner, and Chaney and the Civil Rights Campaign for Mississippi*, by Seth Cagin and Philip Dray.
- Page 351: Students at various freedom schools produced newspapers during Freedom Summer. The newspaper published by students at the Meridian Freedom School was called the *Freedom Star*.
- Page 351: The phrases "Communist agitators" and "Bolshevik Demons" appear in *The Klan-Ledger: Special Neshoba County Fair Edition*, which can be found in the M365 Ben-Ami (Rabbi David Z.) Papers, Box 1, Folder 6, Civil Rights in Mississippi Digital Archives housed by the University of Southern Mississippi Libraries. A digital reproduction of the 2-page document can be viewed at http://digilib.usm.edu/cdm/ref/collection/manu/id/314.

CHAPTER TWENTY-FOUR

- Page 361: Text and audio of Mrs. Fannie Lou Hamer's testimony before the Credentials Committee at the Democratic National Convention in Atlantic City, NJ, on August 22, 1964 can be found at http://americanradioworks.publicradio.org/features/sayitplain/flhamer.html.

CHAPTER TWENTY-SIX

- Page 379: An article with the headline "A BULLDOZER SEAT VIEW OF FINDING OF 'RIGHTERS' BODIES: 'First Thing We Saw Was A Foot,' Dam Digger Says, 'The Nigger Was Lying Kind of On Top of White Men' " appeared in the *Meridian Star* on Sunday, September 20, 1964.

❊   ❊   ❊

In addition, freedom songs are an essential element of the "Freedom Summer" section. During the writing of this portion of the novel, I consulted *Sing for Freedom: The Story of the Civil Rights Movement Through Its Songs*, compiled and edited by Guy and Candie Carawan, 2007 edition, on a near daily basis, taking inspiration and searching for songs that suited the mood of a scene.

Because a song's mood was paramount in my choosing it, I have not always adhered strictly to conventions for when and where certain freedom songs were sung. For example, Grandma Willie sings "This May Be the Last Time" while working in the Freedom School kitchen, even though this song, as a freedom song, was only sung in SNCC staff meetings.

The following freedom songs are referenced:

CHAPTER SEVENTEEN

- Page 260: "We Shall Not Be Moved" is an adaptation of a traditional song.
- Page 260: "Ain't Gonna Let Nobody Turn Me Round" is an adaptation of a traditional song by participants in the Albany Movement.
- Page 260: "We'll Never Turn Back" is an adaptation of a traditional song with new words and music by Bertha Gober (SNCC).
- Page 265: "This Little Light of Mine" is a traditional song. Harry Dixon Loes composed the original children's song in 1920.
- Page 267: "Oh Freedom" is an adaptation of a traditional song by SNCC members. The original is believed to date back to the newly-post-Civil War era.

CHAPTER TWENTY-ONE

- Page 309: "Freedom Is a Constant Struggle" was written by Robert Slavit.
- Page 317: "Come and Go with Me to That Land" is an adaptation of a traditional song.

CHAPTER TWENTY-TWO

- Page 335: "I'm Gonna Sit at the Welcome Table" is an adaptation of a traditional song by SNCC members.
- Page 337: "We Shall Overcome" is a musical and lyrical adaptation by Zilphia Horton, Frank Hamilton, Guy Carawan, and Pete Seeger of the old African American hymn "I'll Overcome Someday." First used as a protest song in 1945 by striking tobacco workers in Charleston, SC, "We Shall Overcome" became the unofficial anthem of the American civil rights movement.
- Page 340: "This May Be the Last Time" is a traditional spiritual with words by Citizenship Schools.

CHAPTER TWENTY-THREE

- Page 353: The words for "I Want My Freedom," sung to the tune of "You Are My Sunshine," are by the Reverend Mrs. Elvira Bailey.

CHAPTER TWENTY-FOUR

- Page 356: Words for "One Man's Hands" are by Alex Comfort, music by Pete Seeger.
- Page 363: "Wade in the Water" is a traditional spiritual.